On the rare occasion Finn had allowed the memory of Georgie to flow unfettered through his mind, she either sat at the bar, exuding confidence and vibrancy and dazzling him with flirty banter and smoldering smiles, or lay sprawled across his bed as morning dawned, looking flushed and tousled and sleepily sexy.

Now, with the bombshell she'd just dropped, he couldn't think at all.

His mind had gone blank. His pulse was thundering and a cold sweat had broken out all over his skin. His vision was blurred. The room seemed to be spinning.

"What?" he said roughly, his voice sounding as if it came from far, far away while the disorientation intensified.

"You, well, *we* have a son," she said. "Josh. He's six months old."

Lucy King

THE SECRETS SHE MUST TELL

HARLEQUIN®
PRESENTS®

Recycling programs
for this product may
not exist in your area.

ISBN-13: 978-1-335-40328-5

The Secrets She Must Tell

Harlequin Enterprises ULC
22 Adelaide St. West, 40th Floor
Toronto, Ontario M5H 4E3, Canada
www.Harlequin.com

Printed in U.S.A.

Lucy King spent her adolescence lost in the glamorous and exciting world of Harlequin when she really ought to have been paying attention to her teachers. But as she couldn't live in a dream world forever, she eventually acquired a degree in languages and an eclectic collection of jobs. After a decade in southwest Spain, Lucy now lives with her young family in Wiltshire, England. When not writing or trying to think up new and innovative things to do with mince, she spends her time reading, failing to finish cryptic crosswords and dreaming of the golden beaches of Andalucia.

Books by Lucy King

Harlequin Presents

Passion in Paradise
A Scandal Made in London

Other books by Lucy King

The Couple Behind the Headlines
One More Sleepless Night
The Reunion Lie
One Night with Her Ex
The Best Man for the Job
The Party Starts at Midnight

Visit the Author Profile page
at Harlequin.com for more titles.

PROLOGUE

SHE COULDN'T TAKE her eyes off him.

Sitting on the crimson velvet banquette that curved around a table upon which sat a bottle of bubbles chilling in a bucket, Georgie Wallace took a sip of champagne and felt it fizz down her throat to join the unfamiliar buzzing in her stomach.

Her pulse thudded in time to the beat of the sultry music drifting over from the dance floor. The blood pounding through her veins was thick and hot. This pull, this dizzying breathlessness, this inability to concentrate on the conversation going on around her had never happened to her before.

But then, she'd never seen anyone quite like *him* before either.

She'd noticed him the moment he'd entered the room what felt like an eternity ago but could only have been a matter of seconds. One minute she'd been laughing at something one of her friends had said, the next the air had started vibrating with a strange sort of electric tension that had sizzled straight through her, igniting her nerve-endings and robbing her of all coherent thought. Her gaze had located the source of it with the precision of a heat-seeking missile, and the impact of seeing him had dealt a blow to her senses from which she'd yet to recover.

Now he was striding across the floor away from her, dominating the space as if he owned it, all towering height, confident authority and purposeful intent. Anyone in his way instinctively stepped out of it. No one appeared inclined to inform him of the club's no-jeans policy.

'Magnificent,' Georgie murmured to herself, watching transfixed as he slid onto a stool at the far end of the busy bar and summoned the bartender with nothing more than a barely perceptible lift of his head.

That was what he was.

In command.

Compelling.

And clearly in need of a drink, if the way he knocked back the one that appeared in front of him was anything to go by.

'Huh?' said Carla, her oldest and best friend, who was sitting beside her and who she could see out of the corner of her eye was bopping to the music while plucking the bottle from the bucket to refill her glass.

'The guy at the bar,' Georgie said, unable to wrench her gaze away.

'Which one?'

Wasn't it obvious? 'Far left. Dark hair in need of a cut, checked shirt.'

'Big and broad with his sleeves pushed up?'

'That's him.'

Carla replaced the bottle in the bucket and sat back. 'A bit dishevelled for my liking,' she said after a moment's consideration. 'Nice back, though. Good shoulders.'

'Very.' With muscles clearly visible beneath the cotton that stretched across them, they were possibly the finest set of shoulders Georgie had ever seen.

'Did you get a look at his face?'

'Not properly.' Just a tantalising glimpse of a strong masculine jaw and straight nose as he'd stridden past her.

'It would be helpful if he shifted round a bit more.'

'True,' Georgie said with an assessing tilt of her head. 'But even if he did, he'd still be too far away to make out the details.'

'Shame.'

It was indeed, because just imagine if his

face matched up to the promise of his body. He'd be breathtakingly gorgeous and that was something she wouldn't mind taking a good, long look at.

But, intriguingly, what was equally as arresting as his physique on the move was his stillness and his containment as he sat alone at the bar. Now furnished with another drink, which he was taking more slowly than the last, he seemed to be utterly lost in thought, an island of immobility in a sea of activity, his bleak sobriety a sharp contrast to the hedonistic atmosphere of the club, and oddly desolate.

Who was he?

What was he doing here?

And would he like some company?

At *that* distantly familiar thought, Georgie inwardly stilled, her heart skipping a beat before racing.

Oooh, how *interesting*.

Once upon a time, as an out-of-control teenager desperate for parental attention and discipline, she hadn't thought twice about approaching good-looking men in bars for a spot of light flirting or dirty dancing, and she'd been extremely good at it.

But ever since she'd come to the distressing realisation at the age of sixteen that if she wanted boundaries she'd have to set them for herself, she'd given up that sort of reckless, impulsive behaviour and had knuckled down to the serious business of adulting. With a love of rules that had been missing from her upbringing, she'd pursued a career in law—much to the horror of her hippie parents—and had slowly built the structure she craved into her life.

She'd had dates, of course, relationships even, but they were casual affairs with guys at college or, later, with men she generally met at friends' dinner parties, men she already faintly knew instead of random strangers picked up in bars.

And, while she'd liked and respected and fancied all of them, none had made her heart race particularly fast. Her last relationship—six months with a perfectly nice but ultimately unexciting banker—had fizzled out over a year ago and she'd neither lamented its demise nor been on the lookout for another.

For the last twelve months, in fact, she'd become so engrossed in the job she loved, so determined to get the promotion she'd been after, that she hadn't given the opposite sex a moment's consideration. She hadn't wanted the distraction. She hadn't needed the hassle.

Tonight, however, with her promotion in

the bag and her foot easing off the accelerator a fraction, it appeared she wouldn't mind some of both.

'Good *song*,' Carla said in response to a shift in the music as she bopped about on the seat a bit more energetically. 'Want to dance?'

Not particularly.

In fact, Georgie wanted something quite different. Because, while hitting the dance floor with her friends and forgetting all about the brooding hunk at the bar would be by far the safest, most sensible option, she didn't *want* to forget about him. And for once she didn't *want* to be sensible. She wanted to meet him. Talk to him. Flirt with him. She wanted to give in to the scorching heat and the dizzying lust rushing through her and see where they took her.

She couldn't remember the last time she'd experienced such an intense and immediate attraction, or felt so alive. She hadn't realised how much she'd missed the heady thrill of sexual excitement, how long she'd been treading water. Besides, it was her birthday. If she couldn't let her hair down tonight of all nights, when could she?

'Maybe later,' she said, her stomach tightening and her pulse racing at the thought of what could happen if she went for it.

Beside her, Carla stilled, her eyes wide. 'Oh? But you usually love dancing.'

'I think I might go over and see if I can't cheer him up instead.'

There was a moment of stunned silence, and then an incredulous, 'Seriously?'

'Why not?'

'Because he does *not* look like the sort of suave, sophisticated professional you usually go for these days. He looks...untamed.'

'I know.' And that was the attraction.

'Are you certain?'

'Yup.' Ish. Her chatting up skills were a bit rusty, and not only might he not be in the mood for company, he might also be spoken for. But what was the worst that could happen? If she crashed and burned, she could always give a nonchalant shrug and leave. If, on the other hand, she didn't, and the attraction she was experiencing turned out to be mutual...well...the outcome could be explosive.

'I thought you'd given up doing that sort of thing.'

'It's only conversation,' she said while thinking, Well, maybe. To start with, at least.

'Sure it is,' said Carla with a wry grin that Georgie couldn't help returning as she put down her glass and got to her feet, her stomach churning with nervous excitement.

'Wish me luck.'

'Good luck. Not that you ever needed it. One thing, though…'

'What?'

'Just in case it *isn't* only conversation and you leave before we're back from the dance floor, message me his name and a photo, and call me in the morning.'

Oblivious to the energy and buzz surrounding him, Finn Calvert stared unseeingly into his drink, his usually ordered thoughts a jumble, his legendary focus blitzed.

Twelve months. Eighteen at most. That was how long his father had left.

Details of the phone call he'd received an hour ago, which had ripped him apart and shattered his world, ricocheted around his head.

Four weeks ago, unbeknownst to him, his father had gone to his doctor complaining of a prolonged cough and shortness of breath. Subsequent tests had revealed lung cancer. Metastasised. Incurable.

Devastating.

Ever since his mother's death when he was young his father had been his only family. He'd been the one who'd brought him up and who'd fished him out of the trouble he'd got into as an angry teenager. When, at eighteen, Finn had announced he wanted to buy the bar where he'd been working and which was up for sale, his father had been his initial investor. Over the years he'd subsequently proved a solid sounding board and his staunchest supporter, and the bond they shared was deep and unassailable.

Now he was dying, and there wasn't a thing he—Finn—with all his wealth and influence, success and power, could do about it.

His jaw clenched and his fingers tightened around the glass as he fought back a hot surge of emotion, a tangle of helplessness, injustice and rage. Why had his father waited so long before seeing his GP? Why hadn't ever he said anything about not feeling well?

And how had *he* not noticed that anything had been wrong? His father could be guarded at times and had practically invented the stiff upper lip, but that was no excuse. Nor was the acquisition of a hugely grand yet derelict Parisian hotel, the renovation of which had become so complex that Finn had barely had a moment's thought for anything else. He should have made time. He should have visited his father more often. Then he might have seen that something wasn't right.

But he hadn't and now it was too late, and

the guilt and the regret were crucifying him in a way that, contrary to his hopes, alcohol was doing nothing to dull. All he wanted from the whisky he was drinking was oblivion. Just for tonight. There'd be time for stoicism and practicality in the morning. But the whisky might as well have been water because the pain was as excoriating as it had been an hour ago and his chest still felt as if it were caught in an ever-tightening vice.

By coming here he'd chosen the wrong place, he thought, downing the remainder of his drink and feeling the burn momentarily scythe through the turmoil. It was convenient, certainly, but it was too loud, too damn full of fun and laughter. He ought to leave and go in search of a darker, quieter, harder bar, one where he could sit on his own in the shadows and the alcohol would flow without question.

And he ought to leave now.

'Hi.'

The soft voice came from his right, puncturing the fog swirling around in his head and freezing him mid-move. The sexy, feminine timbre of it hit him low in the gut and wound through him from there, heating the blood suddenly rushing through his veins and reigniting sensation everywhere.

Automatically, Finn lifted his head and

turned it in her direction. She was standing a foot from him, enveloping him with an intoxicating combination of heat and scent, confidence and vibrancy. His gaze locked onto hers, and in that instant the overall impression he had of dark, tousled hair, dazzling smile and a short black sequinned dress was pulverised by a punch of lust so strong it nearly knocked him off his stool.

Lost in the soft brown depths of her eyes and unable to look away, he felt his pulse slow right down. The noise and activity of the club faded. His surroundings disappeared. His head emptied of everything but a strange sense of recognition.

Which was absurd, he told himself, getting a grip and blinking to snap the connection. His foundations had been rocked. His defences were weak. Recognition? No way. They didn't know each other.

But they could.

They could get to know each other *very* well.

Because the intense attraction that had hit him like the blow of a hammer was not one-sided, he realised as he let his gaze drift over her in a leisurely assessment. She felt it too. Quite apart from the fact that she'd been the one to approach him, he could see it in the dilation of her pupils and the rapid rise and fall of her chest. In the flush on her cheeks and the accelerated flutter of the pulse at the base of her neck. He could hear it in the hitch of her breath and feel it in the way she was now very slightly leaning towards him.

And it occurred to him then that perhaps there were other ways to achieve the mindlessness he craved. Perhaps a night of hot sex and dizzying pleasure would succeed where alcohol had failed. Just the thought of it was pushing aside his father's devastating diagnosis and his own reaction to it. Imagine the reality. If he switched his focus and put his mind to it he wouldn't even have to imagine.

'Hello,' he said, giving her a slow smile that had felled many a woman over the years and was clearly no less effective tonight, if the sparkle that appeared in her eyes was anything to go by.

'Would you mind if I joined you?'

'I can't think of anything I'd like more.'

CHAPTER ONE

Fifteen months later

STILL NO NEWS.

Oblivious to the faint thud of music coming from the club below, Finn tossed his phone onto his desk and stalked to the window, frustration boiling through him as he stared out through the Georgian sash window into the dark London night.

It had been two months since he'd found the adoption certificate amongst the papers left behind by the man he'd always considered to be his father, and he was no closer to discovering the truth surrounding his birth now than he had been the moment he'd figured out what he was holding and his life, already shattered by grief, had blown fully apart. The only people who could shed any light on anything were no longer around to ask, and the investigation agency he'd hired—

allegedly one of the best in the country—had hit a dead end with every lead.

The paralysis was driving him demented. All he wanted was answers. All he needed was clarity. He'd thought the sorrow and emptiness that had consumed him in the days following his father's—no, *Jim's*—death and the realisation that he was now all alone in the world had been harrowing, but at least there'd been a feeling of closure. At least there'd been a logical, if agonising, process to get through.

Now there was nothing but chaos. Where order and certainty had once ruled Finn's world, confusion and doubt now reigned. He no longer knew what to believe; facts he'd never once had cause to examine now tormented him day and night. Who was he? Where did he come from?

The questions that spun around his head and left scorching trails of betrayal in their wake were many and relentless. Why had he been adopted? Where and who was his real family? Had he been abandoned? How had he ended up where he had?

And, most crushingly, why had he never been told the truth? There'd been eleven thousand opportunities to explain the circumstances surrounding his adoption, give or take a day or two, and eleven thousand opportunities missed. Why keep it a secret? His father, the man he'd so admired and looked up to, who'd circled the wagons when his mother had died and to whom he'd turned for advice and support back in the early days of his business, had become a stranger overnight.

As a result Finn had no idea how much of his thirty-one years on the planet had been genuine and how much hadn't. In the absence of fact, his previously staid imagination ran riot. In the darkest moments, when he couldn't sleep and prowled around his penthouse apartment unable to stop the constant churning of his mind, he found himself revisiting the circumstances of his mother's death. He'd only been ten when she'd stepped out into a road and been hit by a bus. The driver had sworn she'd seen him coming, had even looked him straight in the eye, but why would she have done it deliberately, a pale-faced, tight-jawed Jim had immediately countered, when she'd had no reason to take her own life and everything to live for?

The coroner had ruled her death an accident and Jim had always unflinchingly maintained this verdict, but in the cool, calm quiet of the early hours of the past couple of weeks the doubts had crept into Finn's head and taken root. Jim had lied to him about his birth, had lied to him his entire life, and now he couldn't help thinking, what if he'd been lying about that too? What if his mother's death *hadn't* been an accident? What if every time she looked at him, her *adopted* son, she was reminded of what she'd never been able to create for herself? What if that had finally become too much to bear? What if she'd deliberately stepped in front of that bus because of him, because in some way he'd failed her, because he'd behaved too badly or somehow hadn't been a good enough son?

If he'd been able to think logically, rationally, he might have seen this extrapolation for the unlikelihood it was, but logic and reason were long gone. His identity, his history, his entire belief system had been decimated and he didn't know what to think or who to trust any more. He couldn't even trust himself. He'd been taken for a fool and deceived his whole life, yet had never suspected a thing. The instincts he'd always considered rock solid and uncannily reliable were clearly worthless, and as a result his ruthlessly efficient decision-making ability had vanished. His concentration was shot and his attention to detail was history. His usually long fuse was now microscopically short, and he was snapping and snarling at anyone who had the misfortune to cross his path.

He neither recognised nor liked the man he'd become, a man who no longer knew his place in a world he'd always dominated, but there didn't seem to be a damn thing he could do about it. The armour he'd taken for granted had been brutally stripped away and he was all at sea, unanchored and rudderless, and it was hell.

'Boss?'

Shaking free of his tumultuous thoughts, Finn turned from the window to see the club's doorman standing in the doorway.

'Yes?' he all but growled.

Bob, built like a tank and in possession of an attitude to match, didn't even flinch. 'There's someone looking for you.'

'Who?'

'No idea. But she's outside, asking if anyone knows you.'

'She?'

'Brunette. Mid-to-late twenties, I'd say. Slim. Could be stunning if she tried. Not really dressed for partying. She's saying she met you in the bar the October before last. She sounds like a fruitcake if you ask me, but I thought you should know in case she turns out to be a crazy stalker or something.'

Finn's brows snapped together. 'CCTV?'

'Sure.'

The doorman pulled a device from the inside of his jacket and hit a couple of buttons. 'There she is,' he said, pointing at a figure on the screen.

Finn took the device, examined the live feed and froze, his entire body clenching with recognition and an unwelcome punch of heat.

Georgie.

Once met, never entirely forgotten, much to his irritation.

If he chose to, he could recall the night they'd spent together as clearly as if it had been yesterday. The heated looks they'd exchanged at the bar, the heavily laden conversation, the bizarrely intense connection... The chemistry between them had been incredible. The sex had been hot and wild, the best he'd ever had. Over and over again that night she'd given him the oblivion he'd craved, and for a brief mad moment as dawn had broken he'd been tempted to ask for her number before remembering that they'd agreed to one uncomplicated night only, and, in his case, why that was. He'd had enough on his plate with Jim's illness. He'd been in no way looking for anything more. But that hadn't stopped her invading his dreams and giving him uncomfortably sleepless nights for weeks afterwards.

'What does she want?' he asked, ignoring the heat and handing the device back with an odd sort of reluctance.

'She won't say. Just keeps flashing around this photo of you on her phone.'

The same photo she'd taken outside his club, *just in case*, she'd said with a foxy smile that had thumped him square in the chest? Had to be. She wouldn't have found one anywhere else. Despite owning a company whose portfolio boasted seven-star hotels, top-end bars and clubs, and restaurants with six-month waiting lists, he rarely appeared in the media. He didn't need to; the firm that dealt with his PR was outstanding.

'What would you like me to do?'

Good question, thought Finn, shoving his hands in his pockets as he searched for the answer that not so long ago would have come to him instantly. If Georgie had come looking for him before his entire life had been turned upside down he'd have wondered if perhaps she'd been having as much trouble forgetting him as he had her, and whether she might be up for a repeat performance.

But now he didn't know what to think and because he didn't, because his behaviour was currently so unpredictable, he ought to have her sent on her way and put her out of his mind. Besides, he didn't need to know why she was here. They were done months ago and the last thing he wanted was potentially even more chaos and complication.

And yet for some unfathomable reason, despite his better judgement, he *wanted* to know why she was looking for him, now, after all this time. It intrigued him, shifted his focus and gave him a welcome respite from the turmoil. Frankly, her reason for showing up here couldn't be any more destructive than anything else that had happened to him over the last couple of months, could it? 'Send her up.'

With a heavy heart, Georgie locked her phone and stuck it back in her bag, weariness and despondency washing over her in a great, drowning wave. Coming to the club where she and Finn had met all those months ago had been a long shot, but she hadn't known where else to try.

She'd spent two days trying to track him down with nothing to go on except his first name and a photo. Unsurprisingly, the internet had yielded nothing. The records held by the hotel in which they'd spent the night were data protected, and her enquiries here had met with blank stares and stony silence.

Which meant she was all out of options and back at square one, she thought, anxiety churning around in her gut as the hopelessness of her situation hit her all over again. She had no job, little money and home was, for the moment, a tiny, damp bedsit in a crime-ridden part of London. Because of what had happened, she was unemployable. Her prospects were nil. Her confidence had hit rock bottom and her judgement was unreliable. How she was going to manage going forward she had no idea.

Digging deep to stave off the relentless despair, Georgie turned to leave, only to freeze when she heard a brusque, 'Stop.'

She swung round, her heart banging against her ribs, to see the man with the muscles and the unpromising attitude, he of the stony silence and blank stare, bearing down on her.

'Don't worry, I'm going,' she said, lifting her hands and backing off as he came to a halt in front of her.

'Wait.'

She blinked. 'What?'

'The man you're looking for,' he said curtly. 'He's upstairs.'

At the unexpected information, Georgie's

stomach gave a great lurch and her pulse leapt. 'Really?' she said, glancing up and seeing nothing but dark windows and an absence of movement.

'Follow me.'

He turned smartly on his heel and, for a moment, she dithered. Was it true? Could she really have found him at last? On the other hand, how likely was it that Finn was indeed up there? Why would he be? What if Muscles was part of some dastardly trafficking scheme or something and taking her to a place from which she wouldn't return?

No.

Ridiculous. That was what she was being. Utterly ridiculous. She was in no danger. She needed to banish the wreck she was these days, beat back the paranoia and channel the fearless Georgie of the October fifteen months ago, who hadn't hesitated to go for what she wanted and watch out anyone who got in her way. The old her was in there somewhere. She had to be.

Gritting her teeth, Georgie determinedly shook off the frightening darkness that was gathering at the edges of her mind in an all too familiar way and the memory of the confusing, terrifying thoughts that had consumed her for much of the last six months, and set off in the doorman's wake. She stepped through the door and into the club, and was immediately hit by a wall of noise, a burst of heat, and a deluge of memories that had her momentarily stopping in her tracks with their vividness.

There was the bar where she'd walked up to Finn and asked if she could join him, she thought, recalling the desire that had swept through her when she'd looked at him and realised he was as breathtakingly gorgeous as she'd hoped. Where he'd given her that devastatingly wicked smile and she'd known in that instant that they'd be leaving together. Where they'd sat close and flirted, their gazes locked, their bodies communicating on an entirely different level, their off-the-charts chemistry sizzling and soaring until they hadn't been able to take any more.

When she'd breathed into his ear that she wanted to leave—with him—he'd taken her hand and led her out of the club with flatteringly indecent speed. He'd pulled her into a dark doorway and kissed her until her knees went weak and her stomach dissolved into a puddle of lust. He'd then taken her back to his hotel room where they'd spent hours burning up the sheets of his bed before parting in the morning with no promises and no regrets.

It had been everything she'd been hoping for. It had been perfect.

And then, a while later, not so perfect.

With a sigh, Georgie let go of the memories, and resumed her progress across the room, aware of the curious glances she was attracting, which were hardly surprising, since her appearance gave a whole new meaning to the phrase 'dressing down'. She hadn't dressed up for this meeting. She hadn't dressed up for anything in a long time. Would her zest for life, her energy, her libido, ever come back? Would *she* ever wholly come back? Who knew?

As she followed the doorman up the stairs at the back of the club her heart began to thump, not with excitement, as it had the last time she'd been here, but with nerves. How was this going to go? She didn't have a clue. On one level she was sure that seeking Finn out was the right—the only—thing to do. Yet, on another, she didn't know him, she didn't know how he was going to react, and therefore the outcome was scarily unpredictable.

At the top of two flights of stairs Muscles rapped on a door and opened it. He stood to one side and gestured for her to go in. Georgie took a deep breath in through her nose that she let out slowly through her mouth, and, on legs that felt like jelly, stepped forwards.

And there he was. Standing at the window in the shadows with his back to her, the same broad, muscled back she'd raked her nails down while gasping his name and writhing with pleasure.

The door closed behind her. Finn turned and her breath left her lungs. She'd forgotten just how attractive he was. How breathtaking the impact of his indigo gaze on her could be. The intensity of his focus sent an unexpected bolt of heat shooting through her that for the briefest of moments sliced through the icy numbness she'd lived with for what felt like for ever and made her wish she had the energy to care about the whole make-up-hair-clothes thing.

As the seconds stretched and the silence throbbed she dragged her gaze from his and ran it over the rest of him. He looked harder than she remembered, as if life had knocked him about a bit. Less forgiving too, which perhaps didn't bode well for this meeting. Possibly even a bit wary about why she was turning up out of the blue like this. None the less compelling, though. None the less in command as he stood there utterly still, utterly in control, his feet apart and his hands in his pockets. And if he seemed bigger and broader than she remembered...well, maybe that was because she'd shrunk.

She lifted her eyes back up to his and she thought she saw a flicker of heat, of shock, in the depths of his. But it disappeared before she could work out if she was right, and whatever he'd been thinking was now hidden behind a mask of neutrality. She couldn't gauge how he felt about her being here. Or if he felt anything at all, for that matter. Not that he had any reason to. What they'd had had been a mutually agreed one-night stand, nothing more. She'd hardly expected the same laid-back, full-on seduction she'd been on the receiving end of when she'd initially approached him all those months ago. She wasn't expecting anything. Hoping for, yes, but expecting, no.

'Hello,' she said hoarsely, her heart pounding and her mouth dry. 'So you probably don't remember me, but—'

'I remember you.'

'Good,' she said with a shaky attempt at a smile. That made things slightly easier. At least she didn't have to first explain how they knew each other. 'How have you been?'

A shadow flitted across his expression. 'Fine. You?'

Not quite so fine, actually, although there was no way she was telling him how not fine she'd been. She had far too much to lose. 'Couldn't be better.'

'I'm delighted to hear it.'

'I can't believe I found you.'

'How hard have you been trying?'

'Very. I didn't have much to go on. Just your first name and the photo I took when we left here that night.'

He gave the briefest of nods. 'Just in case.'

'It seemed sensible.'

'You kept it.'

'As a memento.' Which, in hindsight, was deeply ironic when she'd ended up with a memento of a totally different kind. 'Anyway, I remembered that you looked comfortable at the bar. You didn't pay the bill. I wondered if you had a tab and, if you did, whether you might be a regular. Now I know differently.' She glanced around the softly lit space that contained a mahogany desk, a couple of chairs and sage green walls lined with books. 'Do you manage the club downstairs?'

'I own it.'

Right. That made sense. He'd said he worked in hospitality and he hadn't struck her as the type to take orders. 'No wonder no one threw you out for wearing jeans.'

His dark brows snapped together in a deep frown. 'What?'

'Nothing.'

'As fascinating as this trip down memory lane is, Georgie, I'm busy. So get to the point. What are you doing here? What do you want?'

He was right. The time for dithering was over. Finn had a right to know and she badly needed any support he might be prepared to offer. She stuck her hands into the back pockets of her jeans to hide the trembling and took a deep breath. 'Well, the thing is, you…we… well, basically, Finn, our one-night stand left me pregnant and as a result you have a son.'

CHAPTER TWO

WHEN FINN HAD instructed Bob to send Georgie up he hadn't given much thought to what he was expecting with regards to her appearance. On the rare occasion he'd allowed the memory of her to flow unfettered through his mind, she either sat at the bar, exuding confidence and vibrancy and dazzling him with flirty banter and smouldering smiles, or lay sprawled across his bed as morning dawned, looking flushed and tousled and sleepily sexy.

He barely recognised the on-edge, wary version standing in front of him. Her dark hair was scraped back from a face that was ghostly pale. Her eyes were dull and her cheeks hollow. Her clothes were hanging off her. Above the neckline of her white T-shirt, her collarbones stuck out, and her jeans hung loose on her hips despite her belt being tightly buckled. It was as if someone had switched off her light, and once he'd got over his shock he'd found himself wondering what had happened to her.

Now, with the bombshell she'd just dropped, he couldn't think at all. His mind had gone blank. His pulse was thundering and a cold sweat had broken out all over his skin. His vision was blurred. The room seemed to be spinning.

'What?' he said roughly, his voice sounding as if it came from far, far away while the disorientation intensified.

'You, well, *we*, have a son,' she said. 'Josh. He's six months old.'

A son.

Josh.

Six months old.

The words flew through the air, bulldozing a path through the chaos and hitting his brain like bullets, where they pulverised the fog and cleared the way for indisputable logic and instinctive denial.

A baby?

His baby?

It was impossible.

Or at the very least improbable.

'We can't,' he said thickly, grappling for some kind of hold on this.

'We can. We do.'

'You said you were on the pill.'

'I was.'

'So what happened?'

'I don't know,' she said with a slight frown. 'I might have been sick. Or on antibiotics. I don't remember.'

Disbelief barrelled through him. 'You don't remember?'

'No.'

How could she be so cool, so calm? Could she possibly have done it deliberately? At the thought his blood chilled and his gut churned. 'How convenient.'

Her eyes narrowed. 'What are you suggesting?'

'What do you think?'

Her chin came up. 'Believe me, I did *not* plan it. I did not plan *any* of it.'

'What makes you think he's mine?'

'You're the only person I slept with at the time. The last person I slept with actually.'

'Do you expect me to believe that simply because you say so?'

'Well, yes. But it doesn't matter. I have photos,' she said, twisting slightly to rummage around in her bag before extracting her phone and fiddling with it for a moment. 'Here.' She walked over to him and held out the device. 'Take a look. Swipe left. There are lots.'

For a moment Finn stared at the phone

as if it were a live grenade. His heart hammered against his ribs. He went hot, then cold. He wanted to look. He didn't want to look. He didn't know what he wanted, but it didn't seem to matter because, with a hand that wasn't entirely steady, he was reaching for the phone anyway and lowering his gaze, and one glance at the screen was enough to detonate what remained of an already shattered life. Because the baby in the photo, with his shock of thick, dark hair, laughing blue eyes, and rosy, chubby cheeks was the spitting image of him at a similar age.

The blow of recognition winded him so hard he couldn't breathe. The floor tipped beneath his feet and his knees nearly gave way. But somehow he remained upright and somehow he managed to blindly swipe through the pictures that followed, the overwhelming sense of familiarity intensifying with every passing second.

The truth of the child's parentage was undeniable.

Which meant that he was a father.

A violent rush of emotion rocked though him then, tangling up with the issues surrounding his own parentage and his feelings about Jim and Alice, which he couldn't even *begin* to unravel. And quite suddenly, out of the hot, bubbling chaos roared a protective instinct he didn't know he had and a clamouring primitive need to claim what was his above all else.

He could forget for now that Georgie had kept the existence of this child from him. He could ignore the myriad questions bombarding his head, adding to the confusion and turmoil. There'd be time for explanations and answers and analysis later. Right now he wanted—no, *needed*—to see his son.

'Where is he?' he said, handing her phone back and knowing the images on it would remain imprinted on his memory for ever.

'With a friend.'

'Take me to him.'

She stared at him for a moment, her eyebrows shooting up. 'Now?'

'I've missed all six months of my son's life,' he said, his jaw tightening and his tone chilly as he thought briefly of how much she'd denied him even if he didn't yet understand it. 'I don't intend to miss a moment longer. So yes, Georgie. Now.'

In an ideal world, Georgie would have chosen to introduce Finn to his son on neutral territory, such as a park or a café, or, really, anywhere other than the dingy bedsit she now called home. However, she hadn't thought it wise to suggest they wait until morning. Once he'd recovered from the shock, Finn's stunned disbelief had very obviously turned to simmering anger, and why would she want to provoke that?

Sitting in the passenger seat of the top-of-the-range car that he was driving through the dark streets of the city and feeling the tension still radiating off him in great waves, Georgie could understand his animosity and resentment. From his point of view, she'd deliberately kept her pregnancy and his son from him. She'd denied him key moments in Josh's life. He didn't know that she hadn't even realised she'd been pregnant until she'd given birth. He didn't know that, subsequently caught in the terrifying grip of post-partum psychosis, she hadn't had the capacity to track him down. Nor did he know that as soon as she'd recovered enough to be able to make a choice about what to do next, she'd gone about rectifying that.

Nevertheless, despite Finn's stony silence and tightly leashed displeasure, she was glad she'd managed to find him, and unbelievably relieved that he appeared to want to be involved. His reaction to her blurted revelation could have gone either way. They barely knew each other. When they'd originally met it had been all about the sex. Neither had been looking for an in-depth character analysis of the other and, while she had felt an odd sense of connection, conversation had been sparse. So, upon hearing about Josh, Finn could easily have simply handed her phone back, told her he wasn't interested and thrown her out. But he hadn't, and for that she was inordinately grateful.

She was also more than a little nervous, she had to admit as she laced her fingers tightly in her lap while her stomach began to churn. At the moment he looked to be too busy absorbing the shock of fatherhood to question why it had taken her so long to contact him, but there'd come a point when he'd ask. And when he did, what would she say? He didn't seem the sort to be satisfied with a vague 'it's been a busy time' kind of explanation, yet she'd never told anyone the full extent of what she'd been through, not even Carla.

So should she tell him? As Josh's father, he deserved to know the whole unvarnished story, and as part of her recovery it had been recommended she share it. But if she did, what would he think? What would he do? There were so many possible outcomes to this thing she'd set in motion, she thought, her stomach knotting as she stared out into the damp night. Some she could only hope for, some she dreaded, some remained unknown.

But one thing *was* certain.

While she couldn't avoid telling Finn the truth for ever, she could at least put it off until he actually asked. Maybe even beyond that. She didn't have to share it all *now*. And so, until the moment of reckoning came, until she had no option but to confess all and hope for the best, she was saying nothing.

If Finn had been asked to describe the route he'd just driven or name the neighbourhood in which he now found himself he'd have drawn a blank. The moment he'd registered the fact that he was on his way to meet his son, everything had become a blur, a great maelstrom of emotions and thoughts that he could barely absorb, let alone process. He'd had to shut down in order to be able to concentrate on driving and that was how he'd remained during the entire half-hour journey.

Now, however, as he stood in a room that was smaller than his en-suite bathroom yet apparently incorporated a bedroom, kitchen and living area, his brain was waking up and his senses were returning. He could hear the sink tap dripping rhythmically. The musty smell of damp invaded his nostrils. Behind him, the door opened and then closed behind the friend he distantly recalled being introduced to as Carla Blake, who'd been minding Josh while Georgie pitched up on his doorstep and exploded a world already off kilter.

Yet his focus was all on the cot in the corner and the child lying within it.

As he slowly walked towards it, his pulse pounded and his mouth went dry. He gripped the top rail, his knuckles white, and looked down. At the sight of the baby, lying on his back with his chubby arms out and his tiny hands curled into loose fists, his breath caught and his chest clenched.

'Do you want to pick him up?' he heard Georgie say quietly in the gloomy darkness that was illuminated by one bare lightbulb.

No. Yes. More than anything. 'I don't want to disturb him,' he said gruffly, mesmerised by the gentle rise and fall of the blanket that covered the little body.

'You won't. He takes a while to settle but once he's out, he's out. Just make sure you support his head.'

He reached down and lifted the bundle of warm baby and bedclothes to him, his throat tight. Josh snuffled and then settled against his chest, and he felt the warmth of his son's body seep into every inch of him, filling him with an emotion he didn't recognise and couldn't begin to describe.

He was so tiny, so vulnerable. And only six months old. The same age as Finn had been when he'd been adopted. Who could give up something so precious? And why would someone want to? Had he been too difficult? Too demanding? Had his biological mother needed help in the same way it seemed Georgie did, if her descent from glorious, kick-ass girl-about-town to nervous, ghostly wreck was anything to go by? Had his own mother not had it?

Yet more unanswerable questions.

But this wasn't about him right now. This was about the baby he was holding. Already, there was nothing he wouldn't do for this child, he thought with a burning conviction he could hardly comprehend. Nothing. Never mind that he had no experience of babies. Never mind that he hadn't ever wanted responsibility of this kind before. He had it now and, whatever the circumstances, he would never abandon Josh. He would never give up responsibility for him. His son would never have cause to wonder who he was or where he came from. His son, his flesh and blood and, as far as he knew the only relative he had left in the world, would have everything that was in his power to give. And be. Because Finn may or may not have been good enough for either his biological or adoptive parents, but he'd do his damnedest to be the best for his son.

Here was his chance to right past wrongs. To try and move on from the still raw sense of betrayal and rejection he felt. To plan and to build and to focus on something greater. He was no longer alone. He now had a purpose beyond work and an escape from the chaos. And as he bent to settle the baby back in the cot, missing his sweet smell and soft weight already, he realised that, for the first time in months, the way forward was crystal clear. On this, at least, he knew exactly what to do.

Pushing aside messy, incomprehensible emotion and replacing it with easier to understand practicality, Finn straightened and turned to face Georgie, who was leaning against the one kitchen unit that the bedsit contained, looking oddly flushed and on edge.

'Here's what's going to happen,' he said, watching as her chin came up and her eyes narrowed slightly at his tone.

'Oh, yes?'

'Josh is coming home with me.'

She blinked. 'What?'

'This place isn't fit for habitation.'

'I know.'

'It's a health hazard.'

'I know.'

'He's not staying here.'

'Well, he's going nowhere without me,' she countered, and for the briefest of moments Finn toyed with the idea of telling her that he could easily take Josh without her. That he had the power and resources to remove her from the picture altogether, especially in view of her straitened circumstances, and could do so with a click of his fingers.

But he knew what it was like to grow up without a maternal figure and the gaping hole that had left in his life. The man he'd considered his father had done his best, but Finn had no doubt that much of the trouble he'd got into as a teenager had been an outlet for the delayed rage and injustice he'd felt at his mother's loss.

And then there was the situation he was currently in. He'd been denied the truth about his parentage and as a result now seethed with resentment and frustration. He wouldn't wish the torment he'd experienced as a boy and was now experiencing all over again on anyone, least of all his own child. Therefore, while Georgie was an added complication, she was a necessary one.

'Alright,' he said. 'You come too. Get what you need for tonight and I'll have the rest of your things moved to my place in the morning.'

'For how long?'

'Until we figure out what happens next.'

'We?'

At the question in her voice, Finn inwardly tensed. He'd never been part of a 'we' before. He'd never had to be, never wanted to be, had no clue how to be. But so much of his life had become uncharted territory recently, what was one patch more? 'We,' he confirmed with a brief nod before stalking over to the cupboard and reaching up to pull down a bag that had been stashed on top of it. 'Start packing. You have five minutes.'

Since her bedsit was minuscule and the possessions she had with her meagre, Georgie took only four minutes, and one of those she spent arguing with herself.

The old her would have protested loudly at being ordered around in such an autocratic fashion. She'd have demanded to know who Finn thought he was and what century he was living in before telling him where to go and shoving him out the door. But, while part of her wished she had the energy to conjure up that version of herself, the other part of her, the current Georgie, the one that was exhausted and desperate, whose judgement was skewed and who couldn't trust herself, was too grateful to put up any kind of a fight. To have someone else make the decisions and take responsibility was such a relief. Finn's authority and decisiveness imbued her with the confidence that if something should happen to her, her son would be safe. After months of not being able to make choices, she'd finally made the right one. She and Josh badly needed rescuing, and Finn being the one to do it was absolutely fine with her.

Besides, he clearly wasn't planning to leave without them and the last thing she wanted was a stand-off leading to more time spent in this place. The flat was small enough without Finn in it. With him in it, it felt even more claustrophobic. There was just so much of him too close. His size and proximity and sheer presence made her aware of him and the narrow bed in a way she hadn't expected and definitely wasn't comfortable with. When he'd lifted Josh out of the cot, and held his son's tiny body against his big, broad chest, her stomach had clenched and her entire body had flushed.

Now, as she moved around the space, around *him*, gathering the things she and Josh needed, she could feel his cool, assessing eyes on her, and his scrutiny caused her skin to prickle and a strange heat to seep through her. Not that it mattered how Finn made her feel. Even if he *had* been interested in her in the way he once had been, which clearly and thankfully he was not, she was far too fragile for that sort of thing these days, so it was just as well her libido had gone AWOL. And, besides, she had other, far more important things to focus on now.

Zipping up the bag, Georgie handed it to Finn and went to pick up their son. From above there came an ominous thud followed by a loud crash that made her jump. And as she locked the front door of the bedsit and followed Finn down the dimly lit stairs she thought that whatever his reaction when he eventually learned the truth, however precarious her position in all this, the future had to better than the past.

What a night.

A couple of hours ago all Finn had had to worry about was the frustrating lack of results the investigation into his adoption had generated. Now he had a son being tucked up in one of his spare rooms by an unexpected house guest, and he was pacing up and down in front of the wall-to-wall windows of his sitting room wondering what more the universe could possibly hurl at him. Battered didn't come close to describing how he felt about everything that had happened this evening. He'd been on the receiving end of one punch to the gut after another, and, quite frankly, how he was still standing he had no idea.

And that wasn't all he couldn't fathom. There was also the conundrum that was Georgie. What had happened to her? he wondered as he strode to the drinks cabinet and poured himself a large Scotch. When they'd originally met she'd been vivacious and sassy and intoxicating, out celebrating her twenty-fifth birthday with friends. She'd told him she worked as a lawyer specialising in defamation, that she'd just been promoted and had her eye on a partnership. She'd been living in Kensal Rise, and he specifically recalled her telling him, out there on the street in between hot, drugging kisses, that if they wanted privacy the flat she shared with three others was not the place to go.

Clearly she'd fallen on hard times, but

how, and why? She'd had a baby, yes, but that wouldn't have felled the Georgie he'd met fifteen months ago. That girl would have taken a baby in her stride and carried on conquering the world.

And, on the subject of timings, why was he only finding out about his son now? Why had she taken so long to contact him? Why the secrecy? He couldn't stand secrets. Ignorance put a man at a disadvantage. It robbed him of control and rendered him powerless and weak, and he should know because he was living it.

Well, he'd had enough of being kept in the dark, he thought, knocking back half his drink and resuming his pacing. The issues surrounding his adoption aside, he had a multitude of questions to ask Georgie about Josh, and the minute she reappeared he was getting an answer to every single one of them, whether she liked it or not.

CHAPTER THREE

OBLIVIOUS TO THE drama going on around him and having remained asleep throughout, Josh handled the move to Finn's place with ease. Georgie, on the other hand, was having slightly more trouble adjusting.

She'd been too relieved to see the back of the bedsit to give much thought to where Finn might be taking them, but even if she had, the seven-star hotel where they'd spent that wild night together would not have crossed her mind. Yet here they were, in the penthouse, no less, which boasted a stunning sitting room, a state-of-the-art kitchen, a library and a terrace. The upper level comprised of three en-suite bedrooms—two of which were interconnecting—and a separate wing that had been presumably designed for staff. The chandeliers were crystal and the linen on her bed felt as though it had a thousand thread count. The walls throughout were painted a soft white, and neutral rugs covered glossy dark oak floorboards.

The whole apartment smelled divine and the sense of peace and tranquillity was like a balm to her soul. She couldn't imagine a greater contrast to either the bedsit or the mother-and-baby unit of the psychiatric ward where she'd spent close on five months, and once again a wave of gratitude and relief washed over her, along with a hefty dose of curiosity. Who exactly was he, her knight in shining armour who owned a nightclub, drove a Lamborghini and lived in a seven-star penthouse?

Leaving the door to Josh's room ajar in case he needed her, Georgie went down the stairs, crossed the hall and stopped in the doorway to the sitting room. Finn was pacing up and down in front of the window, a near-empty glass in his hand and a deep frown creasing his forehead. When he saw her, he came to an abrupt halt. His jaw was set, his eyes were dark and intense, and something in his expression, in the way he was looking at her, sent a shiver down her spine.

'Is everything all right?' he said.

'Everything is very all right,' she replied, ignoring the shiver and mustering up her second smile of the day, which had to be a record. 'I just wanted to say thank you for everything you've done.'

'You're welcome.'

'You have no idea how grateful I am for your support.'

'Josh is my son.'

And what was she? An inconvenience? Undoubtedly. Finn didn't even want her here, she knew, remembering how he'd grudgingly told her she could come too when she'd swiftly disabused him of the idea that he'd be taking Josh without her.

'I didn't realise you actually lived here,' she said, dragging her gaze from his to sweep it around the room upon whose threshold she was hovering. 'When we met you said you were renovating. I assumed your stay was temporary.'

'I was, and in that room it was temporary.'

'But why live in a hotel?'

'Why not? I own it.'

Her gaze snapped back to his and her jaw dropped. 'You *own* it?'

'Yes.'

'As well as the club where we met?'

He gave a brief nod. 'Among other things.'

'Who *are* you?' she said, thinking that in hindsight it was a question she should have asked him last October. She still didn't even know his last name. She'd had to leave that space on Josh's birth certificate blank.

He muttered something that sounded remarkably like 'Good question', which made no sense all, but then added something that did. 'Finn Calvert,' he said. 'Look me up some time. Right now, though, we need to talk. Or rather, you do.'

As his gaze drilled into her Georgie went still, her pulse beginning to thud alarmingly fast. 'Oh, well, I really just came to say thank you and goodnight. It's been quite a day.'

'You're telling me.'

'I'm exhausted.'

'Too bad.'

'Any chance we could talk tomorrow?'

'No.'

She stuck her hands into the back pockets of her jeans and shifted her weight from one foot to the other. 'Because, ah, you know, I think I hear Josh crying.'

'No, you don't,' he said, the brusqueness of his tone reflecting the flint in his expression. 'Carry on prevaricating, Georgie, and I'll have a team of investigators looking into you so fast it'll make your head spin.'

Her eyes widened. 'Are you serious?'

'One phone call. That's all it will take. I have them on speed dial.'

Why would Finn have investigators on speed dial? was her instant thought in response to that, but it was a question for later. Because clearly the moment she'd been dreading had come. Would he really get her checked out? Or was he bluffing? Either way, it didn't really matter. She couldn't take the risk that he would do precisely as he threatened. She needed to control the narrative. She needed to provide context and detail to the cold, clinical facts. It was important that Finn understood exactly what she'd been through and sympathised. She needed him on her side. It wasn't going to be easy. In fact, it was probably going to be hell, but it had to be done.

'All right,' she said with a nod as her stomach began to churn.

'Sit down.'

On legs that felt as weak as water Georgie walked over to the sofa Finn indicated and perched on the edge of it, because to sink back into the soft cushions would result in an inadvisable degree of relaxation. She waited until he'd folded himself into one of the armchairs on the other side of the coffee table, then took a deep breath. She opened her mouth, then closed it and gave a helpless shrug. 'I'm not quite sure where to start.'

'How about by telling me why I am *only now* finding out I have a six-month-old son?'

She inwardly flinched at his tone, but it was as good a place to start as any, so she pulled herself together and mentally spooled back to the beginning. 'As I told you earlier this evening,' she said, deciding to start with the marginally easier bit, 'you're a hard man to track down.'

'You've had fifteen months.'

'Not quite.'

His brows snapped together. 'What do you mean?'

'I didn't know I was pregnant until I went into hospital with severe stomach cramps back in July and had Josh four hours later.'

The silence that suddenly fell vibrated between them, laden with astonishment and disbelief. The tick of the clock on the mantelpiece, marking the passing of the seconds that felt like minutes, was deafening.

'You didn't know you were pregnant?' he echoed eventually, the intensity of his gaze pinning her to the spot and making her squirm.

'No.'

'How is that even possible?'

'That's a question I've asked myself many times.'

'And?'

'I apparently had what's called a cryptic pregnancy,' she said, rubbing her damp palms down her denim-clad thighs. 'I carried on taking the pill, so I didn't miss a period. I didn't have morning sickness or any other signs. Because I was so busy at work I was exhausted anyway. Maybe I ate a bit more and gained a couple of pounds, but I put it down to stress-related comfort eating and cut back.' She paused to give him time to at least partly absorb what she'd said, then added, 'I realise how this must sound.'

'You can't have any idea how this sounds,' he said darkly. 'Implausible doesn't come anywhere near it.'

She couldn't blame him for his scepticism. If she'd been in his shoes she'd have dismissed the idea as ridiculous too. 'It's rare but it happens. To one in about two thousand five hundred women. I had an anterior placenta. If I ever felt any movements, I put them down to tummy rumbles. I really had no idea. When my waters broke and I started having contractions right in the middle of A&E, no one was more surprised than me.'

And wasn't that an understatement? Stunned and terrified was a more accurate description of the feelings that had stormed through her. She'd never felt physical pain like it. She'd thought she was dying. And then, when realisation had dawned, the awful, horrible confusion. How could she be pregnant? How could she not have known that she was? She wasn't stupid. She wasn't uneducated. Yet in those bewildering, petrifying moments she'd felt both.

'And subsequently?' he said bluntly, yanking her out of the chaos and confusion of the delivery room and back to the present. 'Josh is six months old.'

'The whole thing came as a massive shock to me,' she said, remembering with a chill how quickly and devastatingly her smooth, well-ordered life had been blown apart. 'I was totally unprepared. I hadn't been to any antenatal classes. I'd read no books and looked nothing up. I had no baby things and absolutely no idea what I was doing. I was thrown in at the deep end and expected to swim. It's been a busy time and insanely tough.'

His dark gaze held hers, not allowing her to look away, not letting her off the hook for one second. 'Still, Georgie. Six months.'

'I know.'

'Well?'

This was it. Her moment of reckoning. 'Could I possibly have a drink? I'm not pre-

varicating,' she added in response to the sharp
arch of his eyebrow. 'Truly. I could just do
with a bit of fortification.'

'That bad?'

Worse. 'Maybe.'

'What would you like?'

'Whatever you're having.'

'Scotch.'

'That'll do. Neat. No ice.'

With a brief nod, Finn got to his feet and
strode over to the bar to fix her drink and
refill his while Georgie tried to marshal her
thoughts, her mouth dry and her heart pounding. How much should she tell him? What
could she leave out? Was there anything she
could do to make this easier? Unlikely.

'Thank you,' she said, accepting the glass
he held out and taking a long, slow sip of the
whisky. 'Delicious. Peaty.'

The look he gave her was forbidding, his
patience clearly stretched. 'Georgie.'

Right. OK. She lowered her glass and
braced herself for the guilt and shame and anguish that still crucified her even though she
knew that none of it had been her fault. 'So,
as I said,' she said, her voice shaking a little
despite her efforts to control it, 'Josh's arrival
was unexpected. It was also extremely trau-
matic. Not from a medical point of view—in

those terms it was very easy apparently—but from a mental one. I'd left home that morning expecting to be given some strong prescription painkillers. I'd envisaged being back in time to finish the report I'd been working on. Instead, ten hours after being admitted, I went home with a tiny newborn baby.'

She looked at him, willing him to at least try to understand, however big an ask that was. 'The shock was cataclysmic. I can't begin to describe the weight of responsibility. Or the terror. I was all on my own and I had no clue what to do. I didn't know how to feed him or soothe him or anything. For forty-eight hours neither of us slept, which meant that nor did my flatmates, who were quick to point out I was now in contravention of the tenancy agreement and threatened to call the landlord.'

She glanced down at the glass she was turning in her hands, the amber liquid swirling continuously. 'I phoned my parents but they didn't answer, which I more or less expected, since we hadn't spoken for a while, so I rang Carla, the friend of mine you met earlier. She came over and scooped us up and took us back to her house. And that was great for a couple of days. I scoured the internet and read books and did a crash course in babies. And I got a bit better at changing Josh's nappies and feeding him and generally looking after him. But as the shock wore off, reality kicked in.' She looked up at Finn, who was sitting impossibly still, his eyes dark and his expression unreadable, although she guessed he wasn't missing a thing. 'Did I ever mention my five-year plan?' she asked with a slight tilt of her head.

'You mentioned having one.'

'Well, that went out the window. And so did all the structure and routine I'd created for myself and have always depended on. My life fell completely apart, and for the first time in years I had no idea where I was heading.' She shook her head, the memories swirling. 'It was all so overwhelming. I went into a sort of spin and it happened really quickly and really intensely. I wasn't sleeping much anyway, but suddenly I wasn't sleeping at all. My appetite all but disappeared. And then I started doing things that were really out of character. Like talking really fast one minute then not uttering a word for hours. I developed panic attacks and became convinced that Carla's neighbour was following me. I even called the police one night,' she said, biting her lip and remembering how scary it had been to realise on some level that what she was doing wasn't normal, wasn't right, but not knowing why she was doing it and not being able to do anything about it. 'Anyway, eventually I was admitted to the psychiatric ward of my local hospital, where I was diagnosed with post-partum psychosis.'

'Which is what?'

'Like postnatal depression but worse.' Far, *far* worse. 'I stayed there for a week and then a bed came up in a mother-and-baby unit a hundred miles away. Josh and I left there ten days ago,' she said, glossing over five intervening months, since Finn did not need to know how bad it had got before the medication had kicked in and the therapy had started to take effect. In any case she doubted she could even begin to explain how terrifying the delusions and the hallucinations and the disorientation had been, or how distressing she'd found it knowing that she wasn't well. The feelings she'd had for Josh, or, rather, the lack of them, were far too upsetting to put into words, and Finn would never understand her gut-churning dread that the long, dark tunnel she'd been in had no end. He'd never fully understand any of it. No one could.

'And that's why it's taken so long for me to contact you,' she said, determinedly not letting those agonising memories descend but instead focusing on the man who was now looking at her a little as though he'd been slapped round the head with a wet fish. 'I wasn't in a position to do so. As soon as I was, I did. And that's it. Now you know everything.'

Everything? *Everything*?

He knew *nothing*.

Watching dazedly as Georgie finished her drink, set the glass down on the coffee table and sat back against the cushions, Finn could barely recall his own *name*. He was reeling too hard, too stunned and shattered to be able to make head or tail of anything. Whatever explanation he could possibly have envisaged, none would have come anywhere near the one she'd just given him.

That she was telling the truth was without doubt. He might have had suspicions initially—who wouldn't?—but not for long. No one would make up such a story, and no one could fake the emotion that had emanated from her, despite her attempts to contain it. When she'd been talking about what she'd been through, her voice had cracked and her eyes had become twin pools of pain. Her hands had trembled and her anguish had been palpable, and her obvious distress had cut right through him.

On one level he could identify with some of what had initially happened to her. He knew what it was like to have your life turned upside down and your plans destroyed. He'd experienced the sort of catastrophic shock that imploded your world, and the subsequent feeling of being utterly at sea. In that respect their recent histories were not unalike.

As for the rest, however, he couldn't *begin* to imagine what she'd been through. He thought he'd been having a rough time, but compared with her past six months, his had been a breeze. Giving birth like that must have been terrifying. Finding herself wholly and solely responsible for a tiny, helpless human being that came with no instruction manual must have been petrifying.

And then afterwards… God, he didn't even know what post-partum psychosis was. But it sounded horrendous, like hell on earth. Georgie hadn't gone into detail about her stay in hospital but what she *had* revealed had been harrowing to listen to, let alone to actually live through, so how had she got through it? *Had* she got through it? Well, clearly she'd recovered at least to *some* extent because she and Josh were here, not that it was any thanks to him.

He should have been there, he thought, a white-hot streak of regret and guilt suddenly burning through the defences he hadn't had time to shore up. He should have known. Never mind that he couldn't have. Never mind that her recent experience was no one's fault, not even his. And never mind that even if he *had* been around he probably wouldn't have known her well enough to recognise the out-of-character behaviour or any of the other signs that indicated she was ill.

What mattered was that he hadn't been there for his father, and he hadn't been there for Georgie and Josh either. History had apparently repeated itself and that ended right now because, while he hadn't been able to help his father or the Georgie of then, he *could* help her now. In whatever way she needed, whenever she needed it. He wouldn't let her, *them*, down.

'How are you doing now?' he asked gruffly, aware suddenly that she was looking at him with the expectation of some sort of response.

'Better. Much better.'

'And Josh?'

She released a long, slow breath and the

troubled expression that flitted across her face made his chest tighten with renewed regret that things hadn't been different for her.

'I'd like to be able to say that I've totally bonded with him and everything's great,' she said carefully. 'But the truth is that, while I *am* getting there, it's a work in progress. For a long time I couldn't look after him properly. I couldn't even look after myself. He was cared for by hospital staff so we didn't get a chance to create that connection that everyone talks about and I missed many milestones.' She shifted on the sofa and frowned for a moment as if something had suddenly occurred to her. 'But maybe subconsciously I knew that there'd be a time when I was OK because I took photos and kept a diary. I did everything that was recommended. And I think it's working. Now I find him fascinating. I can't imagine not having him around, and when I think… Well… I'd rather not think about any of it actually.'

As she tailed off Finn could see the undeserved guilt and shame in her eyes, which deepened his regret, but he could also recall the fire in her expression when she'd stood there in her flat and told him that Josh was going nowhere without her. Perhaps the bond between them was stronger than she was able to recognise right now.

And, seeing as how he was now thinking about where she and their son had been living… 'How on earth did you end up in the bedsit?' he asked, seeking some sort of refuge from the emotions battering him by switching to practicalities.

Georgie blinked at the sudden change in subject and visibly shuddered. 'It was all I could afford.'

'What happened to your job?'

'A couple of weeks after I was admitted to hospital I got an email from my company saying that as a result of restructuring my position no longer existed.'

He frowned. 'A coincidence?'

'I doubt it. But I was in no state to object. The pay-off was pathetic.'

Bastards. 'What about your parents?'

She gave a wry smile. 'Even if we were on speaking terms, a hippie commune is the very last place I would choose to raise a child. Believe me, I have first-hand experience and it wasn't all that great.'

'Friends?'

'It's all been too much for many of them and I was too far away. And I couldn't ask any more of Carla. She'd already done so much...' She paused for a second, swallowing hard as a quick frown creased her brow, seemingly lost in thought, but a second later she'd rallied. 'Besides, she has her own life to lead. Her job is insane.'

'Remind me to thank her some time,' he muttered, not wanting to even think about how alone Georgie had been, how desperate she must have felt.

'She's going to be intrigued by this latest turn of events. If she wasn't going away for work tomorrow I have no doubt she'd be banging on the door first thing.'

'She's welcome any time.'

For a moment she didn't say anything, just looked at him, her eyes shimmering with gratitude that he did not deserve when his help had come so late. 'You have no idea how glad I am to have found you.'

His pulse thudded heavily and something shifted in his chest. 'Likewise.'

'You may not think that when Josh is screaming the place down.'

'The walls are soundproofed.'

'That's a relief.' She gave him a faint smile. 'So. Is there anything else you'd like to know?'

Probably. No doubt there were questions he hadn't even thought of. But in all honesty he couldn't take any more tonight. He was utterly drained. God only knew how she had the strength to smile after everything she'd just told him. But then, compared with what had come before, he supposed relaying an account of it would have been a walk in the park. Her courage was staggering. Her resilience was a thing of awe. He'd thought that he was pretty tough, but he had nothing on her. He had nothing at all. 'We'll talk more in the morning.'

CHAPTER FOUR

WHILE GEORGIE GOT ready for bed she reflected that, as she'd suspected, it hadn't been easy telling Finn her story. In fact, reliving events even on the most superficial level had been horrible and exhausting. But it had also been cathartic. The weight and severity of what she'd been through had been overwhelming and now that she'd shared some of it she felt slightly lighter, as if a socking great rock was beginning to lift from her shoulders.

It had helped that Finn was such a good listener. He'd offered no opinion and no judgement. He'd just sat there letting her talk. Of course, it was entirely probable that there'd simply been too much to take in for him to be able to respond with anything more than the most basic of questions, but nevertheless she was grateful for his restraint. And his involvement. It was such a relief to know that she was no longer in this alone, but who exactly was she in it with?

Remembering his suggestion to look him up, Georgie fished her phone out of her bag, then climbed under the gorgeously soft covers of the enormous bed. She tapped his name—complete with surname—into a search engine and spent the next fifteen minutes clicking on links and reading articles.

But, instead of cementing the feeling of safety and security that had been burgeoning inside her, what she discovered blew it wide apart. Because, while she'd already guessed that Finn was successful—what with owning a hotel and a club, driving a top-of-the-range car and living in a penthouse—never in her wildest nightmares would she have imagined that he was one of the richest men in the world.

Yet he was.

His company owned hotels and bars and clubs and restaurants and he was worth billions. He'd worked his way up from virtually nothing to become a top player in his industry. His power was immense and his influence was wide-reaching, and it was suddenly terrifying because now she couldn't help thinking that what if, once he'd had time to absorb the truth about where she'd been and what she'd been doing for the last six months and reflect on it, he considered her unfit to be a mother to his son? What if he tried to take Josh away from her in earnest? She wouldn't stand a chance. If it came to a custody battle, a judge would take one look at her with her recent mental health record and another at Finn with his billions and that would be that. Case closed. She was sure of it.

She'd gone into so much detail, she thought, a wave of nausea rolling up from her stomach to her throat. About her behaviour. About her conflicted feelings towards Josh. She hadn't told him the worst of what had happened, but it had been enough. More than enough.

Her vision blurred and a cold sweat broke out all over her skin at the thought of how much she'd revealed, how vulnerable she'd made herself. What had seemed such a relief a mere half an hour ago now felt like the biggest mistake of her life. What did he think about it all? What could he be plotting? How could she possibly sleep, not knowing what he intended to do next? Morning was too far away. She needed clarification now.

Throwing back the covers, Georgie leapt out of bed and crossed the hall. When she reached his room she didn't think to knock; all she could focus on was protecting Josh and herself and fighting her corner. She opened the door and strode in. Finn was standing next to the bed, wearing a look of surprise on his face and nothing but a towel wrapped around his hips.

'I have one more thing to say,' she said hoarsely, barely able to hear her own voice above the thundering of her heart, 'and it can't wait until morning.'

'What is it?'

'I am not perfect. I am still in recovery. But I can do this. And I am capable. I am not a risk to either myself or Josh and I never will be. I will not let you take my son away from me. I will *never* let you take him away from me.' She stopped, breathing hard, the force of the emotion swirling through her nearly knocking her off her feet.

'What are you talking about?' he said with a frown. 'I have no intention of taking him away from you.'

'You did earlier,' she fired back. 'In the bedsit.'

'Yet here you are.'

His dark, steady gaze was locked on hers and something in it, together with the very valid point he'd just made, calmed some of the wildness whipping about inside her. 'How can I believe you?'

'You have my word.'

'I don't know you well enough yet to know if that means anything.'

'Then you'll just have to trust me.'

'How can I?'

'My mother died when I was ten,' he said, a shadow flitting across his face. 'I know what it's like to grow up without one. It is not something I'd ever wish to inflict on my own son. Josh will always know both his parents.'

His words sank in and she swallowed hard. 'Do you really mean that?'

'I do,' he said with a brief nod.

'OK, then,' she said, letting out a breath as the tension and steam inside her eased. 'Good. Thank you.'

'Was there anything else?'

'Ah, no. Sorry to barge in like that. I didn't realise you were…' What? What had he been doing? Her gaze, which had been fixed firmly to his, broke away to travel over the rest of him. His hair was damp. The exposed skin of his broad, muscled chest gleamed in the soft golden light of the room. He'd clearly just come out of the shower, and, now that she wasn't all fired up with needing to say her piece, it hit her with the force of a freight train that she was standing in his bedroom and he was practically naked.

'… In the middle of something,' she finished lamely, feeling her cheeks burn as she dragged her eyes back up.

'Obviously not.'

'Sorry.'

'Next time, knock.'

There wouldn't be a next time. 'Right. Yes.' She cleared her throat. 'Of course. Sorry. Again.'

His dark blue gaze glittered. 'Goodnight, Georgie.'

'Goodnight.'

When Georgie woke up the following morning, it was with great reluctance. Not only was she so warm and cosy she didn't want to leave the cocoon she'd fashioned out of the duvet, but she was also still utterly wiped out.

It had taken her a long while to fall asleep. She hadn't been able to stop thinking about everything that had happened the evening before, starting with the moment Finn's bouncer had told her to stop and wait. She could scarcely believe any of what had subsequently unfolded was real, yet here she was, safe and warm and no longer wretched and desperate and on her own.

And then there were the dreams she'd had once she *had* managed to drift off, dreams that seemed to involve her and Finn and what might have happened if, instead of fleeing his room, she'd walked up to him and rid him of his towel. Details of what followed were hazy and the whole idea of it was absurd, of course, but nevertheless, why she should be going there, even subconsciously, was a bit baffling.

As was the fact that light was streaming in through the blinds, which, seeing as how it was January, meant that it must be late.

Too late.

And too quiet.

And then mid-yawn, mid-stretch, it suddenly struck Georgie that she'd woken of her own accord and she froze, panic coursing through her. Why hadn't Josh woken her as usual?

Something was wrong.

Icy cold and shaking, she threw back the duvet and leapt out of bed. She raced to his cot in the room next door, only to find it empty.

Where was he? Who had taken him? What had Finn done?

Terror gripped every inch of her. Her knees gave way and she had to cling to the rail of the cot to stop crumpling to the floor. Her heart was thundering and she felt as if she'd been cleaved in two. She couldn't have lost her son, having only just found him. Fate couldn't be that cruel. But where had he gone? What was she going to do?

And then a burst of sound pierced the fog of alarm and desperation, rooting her to the spot and pricking her ears.

A gurgle. A stream of giggles. A low masculine voice.

Slowly coming out of her daze, Georgie felt reason return and the terror subside. Josh was OK. Everything was all right.

Still trembling, her pulse still racing, she followed the sounds to the glossy kitchen, where she found Josh sitting in a brand-new pristine high chair, with Finn beside him, feeding him. Upon the black granite worktop that looked as if it had never met so much as a chopping board sat plastic bottles and tubs of milk powder, bibs and muslins, tiny plates and cutlery, all the paraphernalia an infant required and lots more besides.

Stunned into immobility, she watched Finn expertly spoon food into Josh's waiting mouth, with hardly any of it splattering onto the tray or the floor, and to her shame she felt a surge of resentment. Where had all this stuff come from? How did Finn know in less than twenty-four hours what it had taken her months to figure out? She'd found feeding her son unbelievably fraught. She'd been riddled with anxiety and uncertainty, convinced she was somehow going to poison him by getting the proportions wrong. She still was on occasion. Yet Finn made it look so easy. Unfair didn't *begin* to describe the situation.

'Good morning,' he said, shooting her a dark glance which he then raked over her, his jaw tightening minutely. 'Did you sleep well?'

Ish… 'Yes,' she replied, ignoring his obvious, if unfathomable, objection to her pyjamas. 'Did you?'

He muttered something non-committal and turned his attention back to Josh. 'Help yourself to some breakfast.'

She looked in the direction in which he'd nodded, and at the sight of the array of pastries and fruit enticingly arranged on a great silver platter her mouth watered and her stomach rumbled. God, it had been a long time since she'd come across anything so appetising. She filled a plate and then took a seat opposite him.

'How long has Josh been up?' she asked, pouring herself some coffee and taking a fortifying sip.

'A couple of hours.'

She frowned. 'I didn't hear him.'

'You were dead to the world.'

'But you weren't.'

'No. I was doing some research.'

No need to ask into what.

'And some thinking.'

'Oh?' she said, picking up a *pain au chocolat*. 'About what?'

'What happens next.'

'Which is?' She took a bite and nearly groaned with pleasure.

'Firstly,' he said, his gaze dipping to her mouth for a second and darkening, 'I've hired a nanny.'

Georgie nearly choked on a flake of pastry. A nanny? Why would he do that? Didn't he trust her? Didn't he think she could cope? Just because she'd had a lie-in this morning didn't mean she couldn't. And what else had he unilaterally arranged? Lawyers? Psychiatrists? What? Her heart was beating too fast. Her breathing was too shallow. She had to calm down.

'I said I could do this,' she told him, her mouth dry and the *pain au chocolat* turning to lead in her stomach.

'I don't doubt it,' he replied, all steady calm and cool self-assurance.

'Are you sure about that?'

'Yes. However, you've been ill. You need rest.'

'I need to be with Josh. We need to strengthen our bond.'

'I suspect your bond is stronger than you realise.'

At that, hot anger flared into life inside her. How dared he be so patronising? What did he know about anything? One night of research and he was an expert? She didn't think so.

'Another stranger in his life will be confusing,' she said, ignoring the tiny stab of guilt she felt when he visibly flinched. 'I don't want a nanny looking after my son. I don't need that kind of help.'

'Well, perhaps I do,' he countered with a bluntness that whipped the wind from her sails.

This wasn't just about her any more, she realised with a shock. She had to consider the situation from his point of view too. His life had irrevocably changed overnight. This was new territory for him. She had to give him a break. And maybe, on occasion, she *did* need the kind of help a nanny would provide.

'When does she start?'

'The day after tomorrow.'

'Full-time?'

'Days only.'

'OK, fine,' she said, a bit grudgingly nevertheless. 'But you should have discussed it with me first.'

He gave her a long look and then gave a brief nod. 'My mistake.'

'From what I read last night, you don't make mistakes.'

'This isn't business.'

'No.' Although quite what it was she had no idea. 'And secondly?'

'Secondly, I'm taking some time off work.'

Oh? At the thought of him being around to witness her struggles and her ineptitude, her skin prickled. But, seeing as how she'd requested his support and he'd supplied it, she could hardly protest. 'I read you were a workaholic.'

'That was before I became a father,' he said, glancing at Josh, who was banging a spoon on the tray of his high chair, his expression softening a fraction. 'I intend to get to know my son. Everything he is and everything he does. Nothing is more important.'

He meant it too, Georgie thought, her resentment morphing into wistfulness as she watched Finn watching his son with an intensity and interest she'd never had from either of her parents. It was silly and slightly shameful to be jealous of a six-month-old, but there it was.

'You'll need to show me what to do,' he added, sliding his gaze back to her, the lingering warmth in his eyes easing some of the numbness that filled so much of her.

'*You're* asking *me* for advice?' she said with a quick glance at the extensive baby kit he'd somehow masterfully amassed.

'You have a head start on me.'

'Not much of one.'

'Yes, well, I know nothing. Before last night I'd never been this close to a baby, let alone had to take care of one.'

Slightly taken aback by his frank admission, because in her experience rare was the man who confessed he needed help, although she supposed that, unlike many men of her acquaintance, Finn had nothing to prove, she asked, 'So where did all this come from?'

'My COO's off on maternity leave. I called her and she sent me a list of essentials. And that's it.'

It was strangely reassuring to know that she wasn't the only one at sea. 'Well, I'll *try*.'

'OK, then,' he said, flashing her a sudden smile that lit up his whole face and momentarily dazzled her. 'Let's do this.'

An hour later, Finn found himself in Josh's room, grappling with the concept of a wriggly, giggly child, a nappy that needed changing and not enough hands.

How could such a simple thing be so difficult? Georgie had told him what to do before heading off for a bath and it hadn't seemed that complicated, yet he'd been at it for ten minutes now with no success. His company tax returns were easier to get a handle on than this.

Nevertheless, there was absolutely nothing he'd rather be doing. One of the many reasons it was taking so long and proving so tricky was because he kept being distracted by his son. He'd only just managed to lay him flat when he'd found himself transfixed by the curve of his right eyebrow for a good thirty seconds, by which point Josh had kicked several crucial pieces of equipment to the floor and they'd had to start all over again.

At least Georgie had left him to it and wasn't around to witness his rare incompetence and his even rarer sentimental fascination with another human being. With any luck she had no idea either of how her brief but disturbing foray into his bedroom last night had affected him. In she'd barged, all stunningly fired up one moment and then staring at him as if she wanted to gobble him up the next. He'd caught a flash of hunger in her eyes and heard the breathlessness of her voice, and a reciprocal burst of hot, dizzying desire had shot through him. After she'd left he'd had to take another shower, a cold one, and he had the feeling that he'd be taking many more if his response to how she'd looked walking into the kitchen this morning, all warm and flushed and tousled, was anything to go by.

Finally achieving the impossible and sticking the nappy tabs in the right places and then somehow managing to guide two wriggling legs back into a pair of tiny trousers, Finn lifted Josh off the table. As he did so their eyes met and held, and as they stared at each other, stock still and fascinated, he felt something deep inside him twist. The physical similarities he and his son shared were startling. He hadn't resembled either Alice or Jim at all. And suddenly he wondered, did he look like either or both of his biological parents? Did he have his father's nose? His mother's eyes? A grandparent's mouth? Would he recognise them if he ever had the chance to meet them? Would they have the same connection he felt with Josh?

Would he *ever* find the answers he sought?

'How did you get on?' said Georgie, coming into what was now the nursery and snapping him out of his impossibly frustrating thoughts.

'It's harder than it looks.'

'You'll get the hang of it. If I can, anyone can.'

Hmm. 'Did you want something?'

'The rest of my things have just arrived. I was wondering if you'd like to see the photos of Josh that I took while we were in hospital.'

'I would.'

She took a couple of steps towards him until she was closer—too close—and shifted her glance from him to Josh. 'He looks so like you,' she said, her voice filled with warmth and softness.

He took a step back, his pulse skipping a beat. 'Yes.'

'Maybe we could compare pictures. Of both of you as newborns.'

Impossible. There weren't any of him at that age. When going through his father's attic he'd found a few photos of himself at six months old, and endless photos of himself older than Josh was now, but none younger, which he'd wondered about until he'd found the certificate of his adoption and it all made sense. 'Another time.'

'All right.'

'I'd like you to talk me through Josh's

routine,' he said, carrying his son out of the nursery, which was far too small and claustrophobic with Georgie in it too, down the stairs and into the sitting room.

'To be honest, he doesn't really have one.'

'Do you want him to?'

'More than anything. What do you think?'

'I'm as big a fan of structure as you are.'

'Be still my beating heart.'

And, as his gave a great thud in response to the smile she flashed at him, Finn set Josh gently on the mat on the floor and thought that the least said about that particular organ, beating, thudding, lurching or doing anything else for that matter, the better.

The following morning, Georgie stepped through the front door of the apartment and dropped her bag on the console table. The therapy session she'd just had had been a mixed bag, as indeed had the last twenty-four hours.

On the one hand, as she'd told the therapist, she was now glad Finn had made her tell him some of what had happened to her. If she did inevitably have the odd day when things got a bit much, and her anxieties descended, it would come as no surprise to anyone, which in turn would ease some of the stress of it.

Furthermore, she'd discovered that a problem shared was literally a problem halved. Not that Josh was a problem, of course, but undoubtedly, on a practical level at least, parenting with Finn was a whole lot easier than doing it on her own. She hadn't realised how much she'd relied on the support of other people when she and Josh had been in hospital or how stressful she'd found having to be constantly on the alert without it.

And, although it was early days and she couldn't be certain the novelty might not wear off, Finn certainly seemed to be reliable. Last night he'd told her he'd take the night shift, since a grizzly Josh had a tooth coming through, and this morning at dawn she'd gone through to the nursery to find him sprawled in a chair with their son, arms out, draped across his chest, both fast asleep. One big hand had lain splayed on Josh's back, protective, warm and secure, and the sight had melted her heart.

However, warring with the feelings of relief, gratitude and warmth were the resentment and jealousy that she'd experienced over breakfast yesterday and which hadn't entirely ebbed. To her shame, despite Finn's generosity and support, she'd been relieved to see his initial uncertainty and clumsiness when left on his own to deal with the messier side of parenting. Not that it had lasted for long. His natural competence had soon risen to the challenge, and watching him interact with Josh subsequently, his ease and instant adoration highlighting her own failings, was like a twist of the knife in her chest, every single time.

Such as now, she thought, coming to an abrupt halt in the doorway to the sitting room, her breath catching in her throat. Finn and Josh were lying on their fronts on the floor, nose to nose. Josh was grabbing at Finn's mouth, giggling and squealing while Finn, resting his chin on his hands, was patiently letting him, simply staring back at him in awe.

She ought to be glad that he'd taken to fatherhood so well, she knew, taking in the scene and feeling an ache throb deep within her. She ought to be relieved that he seemed to be taking his responsibilities so seriously. She shouldn't be jealous of a connection that was instant and deep. She shouldn't feel bitter about the fact that it was a connection she'd been denied. She should be glad that Finn looked to be taking an approach to parenthood that was so different to her own experience.

She was all that, and she wished she could shake off the negativity and focus on the positives, but she couldn't and she lived in fear that at any moment the ugly emotions swirling around inside her would rise up and make her say or do something she might regret.

'How did it go?' he asked, glancing up at her, his eyebrows raised.

'All good.'

'Come and join us.'

She gathered her hair up and gave it a quick twist, then with a small smile shook her head. 'Maybe later.'

CHAPTER FIVE

THE ARRIVAL OF the nanny went some way to easing the volatility of Georgie's emotions. Mrs Gardiner was a sensible woman of sixty with decades of experience and spot-on instincts, whom Josh adored. Discreet, non-interfering and non-judgemental, she knew exactly when to step in with a subtle suggestion and when to back off and leave Georgie to it.

As the days passed and they settled into a rhythm, Georgie's strength and well-being improved. Her belief in herself and her confidence grew, and gradually her insecurities and doubts lessened. The more she saw how Finn's continuing interest and involvement benefited their son, the less she saw him as a threat, and her resentment and jealousy started to fade.

Unfortunately, with this progress came a growing awareness of Finn not just as a father but as a man, a man with whom she'd once burned up the sheets. The excruciating moment she'd barged into his bedroom was becoming harder to forget. The dreams she'd had immediately afterwards were getting worse and more lurid in their detail, and now, alarmingly, during the day too the image of him standing there in just a towel, wet and semi-naked, kept popping into her head, sending her temperature soaring and stealing her breath.

That he was gorgeous went without saying, and it was true that she'd developed something of an obsession with his strong and capable hands that had once been so hot and skilful on her body but were now so infinitely careful and gentle when handling Josh. But it was more than his many physical attractions that tugged at something deep inside her. It was his endless patience, the wholehearted attention he paid Josh and his rock-solid dependability. His self-confidence and reassuring air of authority. For a girl who'd had none of that growing up, these traits of his were incredibly appealing.

As a whole, Finn was heady stuff and she found it all very confusing. She'd become increasingly tongue-tied around him and went bright red whenever she did manage to hold any sort of conversation with him, and it was a mortifying state of affairs because she'd never been the bashful sort.

It was therefore a good thing that in the evenings, once Josh had gone to sleep, Finn disappeared to catch up on work. At least she was spared agonising small talk over supper while trying to sort out how she felt about everything and trying not to remember the things they'd once done together, even if they probably did need to get to know one another better on a level other than the carnal.

However, things would settle down soon enough, she reminded herself for the hundredth time as she navigated the pushchair into the café where she'd arranged to meet Carla for an impromptu weekday lunch a week later. It was a period of adjustment, that was all.

And once they had adjusted she and Finn would discuss how to move forwards. Even though he'd already told her that he'd take care of both her and Josh financially, which was one less thing to have to worry about, at some point in the not-too-distant future she'd have to dip her toe back into the world of work and see if anyone would employ her. She'd loved her job. She couldn't imagine not ever working again. Mrs Gardiner had said she would stay as long as she was needed, so maybe she'd even go with them when Georgie and Josh eventually moved out of the penthouse and set up home somewhere conveniently near by.

Spying Carla sitting at a table in the corner that had plenty of space for a pushchair beside it and feeling a grin spread across her face, Georgie made her way over.

'Hi!' she said, giving Carla, who stood up, a quick kiss on the cheek.

'Wow, you look better,' said her friend with a smile.

'I feel better,' Georgie replied, taking off her coat and sitting down. In honour of the outing she'd styled her hair for the first time in months and slapped on some make-up. This morning she'd looked at herself in the mirror and noticed with delight that the colour had returned to her cheeks and her eyes had regained the sparkle she'd missed so much. 'Practically back to normal.'

'Hotel penthouse life is clearly suiting you.'

'It is. I don't have to lift a finger, so I'm getting plenty of rest. Finn has food sent up and it's so delicious I've put on a stone.'

'You needed to.'

Georgie grinned. 'I know.'

'Any regrets?'

Only that she turned into an awkward teen with a crush whenever Finn was around. 'None at all.'

'I'm glad.'

'So am I.'

'And how's my gorgeous little boy?'

'Thriving.'

'Can I have a cuddle?'

'Of course.' Reaching down, Georgie unstrapped Josh, eased him out of the pushchair and handed him over. 'How was your trip?' she asked, watching as her son tried to grab Carla's necklace and feeling her heart squeeze when he giggled.

'Good,' said Carla, taking his chubby little hand and wiggling it instead. 'Exhausting. The usual obstacles to overcome but nothing I couldn't handle. Far more interestingly, how's your hot baby-daddy flatmate?'

Eeew. 'Please don't ever refer to him like that again.'

Carla grinned. 'Is he as gorgeous as you remember?'

Every bit of it. And much more so now she'd caught glimpses of the man beneath the very attractive surface. 'Yup,' she said, automatically thinking about him in a towel and inevitably, irritatingly, feeling herself blush.

'Aha!' said Carla, who was extremely perceptive and knew her way too well. 'Intriguing. I sense a story. Once we've ordered, you need to tell me absolutely *everything*.'

Where the hell were they?

Listening to Georgie's voicemail recording click in for the dozenth time, Finn hung up and tossed his phone onto the buttoned ottoman that had once remained uncluttered but now served as a general dumping ground for things that hadn't existed in his life pre-Georgie and Josh.

He'd arrived home half an hour ago after a lengthy meeting, expecting to be greeted by the noise and activity that over the last two weeks he'd become used to, and that unexpectedly he'd begun to welcome, in fact, since it provided a distraction to the continued lack of progress the investigation agency was making in locating his real parents.

Instead, he'd been met with silence. Georgie hadn't left a note and she wasn't answering her phone, and it was Mrs Gardiner's day off. He had no idea where anyone was, and he didn't like it. He didn't like it one little bit, not least because it had just occurred to him that Georgie could waltz out of here taking Josh with her at any point. In fact, he thought as his pulse skipped a beat and he suddenly went icy cold, she could well have already done so.

When they'd first moved in she'd badly needed his support. She'd been in no fit state to take control and only too happy to let him dictate what was going to happen. Now, however, she was stronger, fitter. He'd watched the transformation happen—the hollows in her cheeks slowly filling out, a healthy pink replacing the grey tinge to her skin. He'd witnessed with a strange sort of pride her increased confidence and the growing ease with which she interacted with their son.

In response to the way she'd blossomed, he'd experienced an annoying and frustrating surge in attraction, which he had no hope of assuaging, since not only was she still incredibly vulnerable, but it was also blindingly obvious that she had absolutely no desire to explore the possibility that the chemistry that had once consumed them still existed. She could barely even look at him and when she did she clearly found it uncomfortable, which was why he absented himself every evening. He claimed he had to work, but he didn't because, despite being in total control of his company for the last thirteen years or so, he'd recently discovered that he had no problem with delegation.

Instead he spent the time in the basement of the hotel, either whipping up a storm in the gym or ploughing up and down the pool to ease the need and frustration pummelling through him. How could she not share the attraction he felt so strongly? he found himself wondering. Exactly how fragile was she still? And then, why the hell couldn't he seem to stop thinking about his son in relation to his father?

The longer he spent with Josh, the greater the connection that built and the deeper the fascination that grew, the more he regretted the fact that the two had never had the chance to meet. Would his father's illness have been easier for them both to handle if they'd known about Josh? Would it have brought happiness? Would it have bought them both more time? It was a regret that was irrational and made no sense. His so-called father deserved no sympathy and no forgiveness. Yet that didn't stop the insidious wistfulness creeping into his head and taking root.

Frustratingly, no amount of exercise seemed to clear his head or calm his body, and Georgie's unexplained absence this afternoon was making things worse. Although he could work out from the fact that nothing seemed to have been taken that she probably *hadn't* gone for good, as she got even better there'd be less keeping her here, and that was a concern.

He wasn't losing Josh, he thought with a touch of grim desperation as he stalked into the kitchen to make himself some coffee. Not now. Not ever. He was loving the time they were spending together getting to know each other. He found him utterly intriguing and was continually staggered by the depth of the bond he shared with this tiny person, for whom he would willingly die.

Yet how could he stop Georgie from walking out and taking Josh with her? With what she'd been through he had some leverage but using it did *not* appeal. The legal route would take months. Realistically, there was nothing he could do.

Unless…

He froze suddenly, his pulse racing and his head spinning.

There was one way. A bit dramatic possibly, but, without doubt, binding.

Commitment had never held any interest for him before. He'd witnessed Jim's grief when Alice had died, all the more potent for his restraint, as well as the lingering sadness that had tinged his life for the remaining twenty years he'd had of it. Finn had no desire to experience any of that for himself, regardless of the examples of happiness set by the one or two of his friends who had married. To date he'd never met anyone who'd threatened the status quo and right now, with the frustration and confusion he felt over his identity, he was not in any position to enter into a relationship with anyone.

Apart from his son.

During the two months following Jim's death, he'd found himself dwelling increasingly on the idea of love and what it meant, and finding it tainted because surely lying and betrayal formed no part of it. But Josh had made him reconsider. The strength of his feelings for this tiny person, *his* tiny person, blew him away. He was *not* losing him and he was *not* having Josh growing up not knowing him. So if hitching himself to Georgie was the price he had to pay to secure Josh then that was what he'd do and to hell with the X-rated dreams it might give him and the additional discomfort it would no doubt cause her.

His swift but absolutely right decision had nothing whatsoever to do with a subconscious desire to create the family that deep down he might possibly crave. Or the fact that he'd got used to having them around and couldn't stomach the thought of the silence and emptiness their absence would bring. And of course he wasn't worried about abandonment and rejection and being left all alone again. What he'd come up with was a purely practical solution to an unthinkable possibility and a means to eliminating a very great risk, and he'd implement it just as soon as she turned up.

Which, *finally*, he thought darkly as he heard the sound of the front door opening and closing and abandoned the coffee to stride towards it, was now.

'Where have you been?' he said curtly, relief, a shot of unwanted desire and something else undefinable making him sound short.

Having parked the pushchair just inside the door, Georgie glanced up at him, her eyebrows raised no doubt in response to his tone. 'Out,' she said, turning her attention to Josh, unbuckling him and lifting him free.

'Where?'

'We had lunch with Carla.'

'I called.'

'My phone ran out of battery.'

'It's late.'

'We were chatting. I lost track of time.'

'You should have left a note.'

As she fitted Josh to her hip, she turned to him, her eyes narrowing minutely and her chin jutting up. 'Are you implying I'm some-how accountable to you, Finn?'

No. Yes. Dammit. 'No.'

'So why are you so cross?'

'You weren't here when I got home. That's never happened before. I was worried.'

She froze, tension suddenly pouring off her as the colour bled from her face. 'Josh is fine,' she said, her voice tight. 'Truly. Look.'

What? No. She couldn't believe that he'd think she'd hurt him, could she? Hell, just how bad had things got? 'That wasn't what I meant at all.'

'Really?'

'No,' he said with a decisive shake of his head.

'Then what did you mean?'

There was no way he could explain the emotions that had ripped through him when it had occurred to him that she and Josh might have gone for good. He wasn't entirely sure he fully understood them himself. Perhaps it would be best to get to the point. 'I have a proposal.'

Her gaze turned quizzical, wary. 'What kind of a proposal?'

'A way forward that will suit us all. Per-manently.'

She frowned. 'By "proposal" you don't mean marriage, do you?'

'No.'

'Phew. Thank goodness for that.'

'I wouldn't go thanking goodness just yet.'

'Why not?'

'Because instead, you and I are going to enter into a civil partnership.'

If Georgie hadn't been holding on quite so tightly to Josh she might well have dropped him in shock. A civil partnership? Was Finn being serious? He couldn't be. And yet he didn't look as if he was joking. His jaw was set and he wasn't smiling. His gaze was fixed on hers with an intensity that was both unnerving and oddly exciting. He clearly meant every word.

'What on earth makes you think *that's* a good idea?' she asked, ignoring the little leap of her pulse and concentrating on the fact that a civil partnership may not technically be marriage but it was just as much of a commitment and equally unnecessary.

'It will provide security for Josh.'

Not 'would' but 'will', she noticed. So this wasn't a hypothetical proposal. Finn had given it quite a bit of thought already and evidently considered it a fait accompli. Too bad for him that she didn't. 'He already has security without it,' she pointed out. 'We've added your name to his birth certificate and he now carries your surname instead of mine. Plus financially you've set him up for life.'

'That's not enough.'

Of course it was enough. It was more than enough. So what was going on? What more security could Josh have or need? Unless it wasn't only Josh Finn was thinking of. 'Is this in some way about you?' she asked, since there was absolutely no chance it was about her.

Something flickered in the depths of his eyes, something that suggested she'd hit the nail on the head. 'Why would it be about me?'

Hmm. 'You do know that I have no intention of ever preventing Josh from seeing you or vice versa, don't you? Even if I wanted to, which I don't, I don't see how it would be possible.'

'I have no doubt you mean that at the moment.'

Ouch. 'Don't you trust me?'

'It's early days.'

'I'm well aware of that,' she said coolly, still stinging at the realisation he didn't see her progress in the same light as she did.

'Then you'll understand why a formal arrangement is necessary.'

'I can understand why you think it might be, but I don't agree.'

'It will benefit you, too.'

Oh? 'In what way?' she asked, transferring Josh to the other hip.

'Commit to me and you'll have the stability you admitted you need. You'll never want for anything again.'

Well, materially that might be true, yet he'd promised her that already. And what about him? What advantages would it have for him? Was he somehow hoping for a friends-with-benefits sort of thing? He'd better not be. 'What would you get from it?'

'Peace of mind.'

'Anything else?'

'No.'

Right. So not sex. Obviously. Stupid of her. Why would she even have thought it when he showed absolutely no interest in her like that? Damn those scorchingly hot dreams she'd been having about him.

'What would happen if either of us met someone else?' she asked, thinking that, while she couldn't imagine ever doing so herself, Finn was gorgeous and a billionaire and presumably had women flinging themselves at him left, right and centre. She'd seen zero evidence of it to date, but that could well change once things settled down.

'We'll cross that bridge if and when we come to it,' he said, which wasn't exactly a denial. 'Think about it, Georgie. What do you have to lose?'

The hint of arrogance and condescension in Finn's voice annoyed her even more than the tiny irrational stab of jealousy she felt at the thought of him with another woman, but actually none of this was about her, was it? This was about Josh. Too much of his short life had been taken up with her illness and she owed it to him to make amends. Goodness knew she hadn't been the best of mothers. In fact, she must have been among the worst.

Surely he'd be better off with two parents together. Didn't the statistics suggest precisely that? The inconvenient and all-consuming attraction she felt for Finn would fade to a manageable level eventually. It already had done a bit. Look at the way the shock of his suggestion had rid her of her ridiculous embarrassment around him.

And they were hardly strangers any more. She'd even go so far as to say that they had a weird kind of connection that had nothing to do with Josh, an odd sense of recognition that made her think 'oh, that's right, it's you', which she'd felt the night they'd met, and which hit her with increasing regularity now.

And really, how bad would such a situation be for her? she thought, on one hand barely able to believe that she was even considering Finn's preposterous suggestion yet on the other totally seeing the sense of it. They got on well enough. And he was right. She *would* have the stable family unit she'd always yearned for, along with the security that Finn could provide.

If they were joined in partnership he wouldn't be able to just get up and leave, would he? Should she have a relapse he wouldn't abandon Josh, and therefore he wouldn't abandon *her*. They'd be safe. He'd told her she'd always have his support, which she believed, and she wasn't going to get anything like it anywhere else. She wasn't exactly an attractive prospect and it wasn't as if there was anyone else waiting in the wings.

Ultimately, despite his arrogance and condescension, Finn had a point. She really did have nothing to lose. In fact, she had everything to gain, and so, to ensure the best future for Josh in particular, it really was a no-brainer.

'All right,' she said with a brief nod. 'If it's a civil partnership you want, it's a civil partnership you shall have.'

CHAPTER SIX

THE CEREMONY TOOK place in a register office a stone's throw from Finn's hotel a week later, the usual lengthy bureaucracy associated with such an event magically disappearing the moment he produced an enormous cheque, which only went to demonstrate yet again that once he wanted something he didn't stop until he got it.

The arrangements hadn't been complicated in any case. Georgie had only wanted Carla there, and, apart from their son, Finn had no relations. His mother had been hit by a bus when he was ten, he'd told her, his father had died of terminal cancer around three months ago, and he had no siblings. He was as alone in this world as she was, and when she'd discovered this she'd had the fanciful notion that by hitching her wagon to his she might be rescuing him as much as he'd rescued her.

Faintly unsettled by that thought and unwilling to acknowledge what the accompanying squeeze of her heart might mean, Georgie had joked that it was going to be a small ceremony, and indeed it was. She wore a knee-length ivory dress and matching coat. Finn had on a dark suit that fitted as if made for him, which it probably was, and a snowy white shirt open at the collar that drew attention to the firmness of his jaw and strong planes of his face.

She didn't know quite why they'd dressed up. There was nothing remotely weddingy or romantic about either the venue or the occasion. But that didn't douse the flicker of warmth that uncurled deep within her when they stood together with a thankfully beautifully behaved Josh in Finn's arms while Mrs Gardiner, who'd doubled up as the second witness, took the photo she'd insisted on taking after they'd all signed the register. Nor did it stop her noticing how smoulderingly hot her new… What? Not husband… So partner…? How smoulderingly hot he looked and how delicious he smelled close up.

Not that any of that mattered, any more than the weird idea that the ceremony was somehow special did. She'd get over that nonsense. Nothing had changed. And, while the way Finn made her physically feel was going to continue to be hard to ignore, it wasn't impossible. She was made of stern stuff. If she could get through the insanely tough initial stages of post-partum psychosis, she could handle this inconvenient attraction, however insistent. It wasn't as if there was any other option when how she felt was so clearly one-sided. She was hardly going to throw herself at him and suggest a repeat of that wild night they'd spent together. Heaven forbid. His likely rejection would be mortifying.

However, for the sake of their son, she and Finn could be perfectly civil and mature about all of this, and she, at least, intended to start with the lunch they were about to embark upon to mark the occasion. Carla had gone straight back to work after the ceremony and Mrs Gardiner had taken Josh back to the apartment for his customary nap, which left her and Finn in one of the many restaurants in his company's portfolio, together and on their own for the first time in weeks.

'What shall we toast to?' she asked, once they'd sat down at their table and a bottle of champagne had been delivered and poured.

Finn arched one dark eyebrow. 'Is there any need to toast anything?'

'I think so... Ooh, I know. How about to no longer being alone?'

He didn't say anything, merely carried on looking at her steadily, his gaze unwavering and unfathomable, and for one horrible moment she thought she'd got it all wrong. But just as she was beginning to feel a bit of a fool sitting there with her hand outstretched, he touched his glass to hers and gave her the faintest of smiles before lifting the glass to his lips and tipping half of its contents down his throat.

'So why didn't you want any of your friends to be a witness?' she said, taking a sip of her own drink and for some reason feeling ridiculously pleased that she hadn't got it wrong after all. 'Come to think of it, do you *have* any friends?' She hadn't heard any mention of any.

'Of course I do,' he said, setting his glass down and twirling the stem between his fingers and thumb. 'One of them's on honeymoon, and it didn't seem worth bothering any of the others for something that was merely a formality.'

Oh. Right. Well. That told her. Just as well she hadn't been harbouring any ideas of their civil partnership being anything other than purely practical.

'Do they know about me and Josh?' she asked, slightly distracted by the mesmerising movement of his fingers, as so often happened whenever she looked at his hands.

'If they do it'll have been via the press.'

So he wasn't exactly shouting the news of their union from the rooftops. Which was fine. There was absolutely no reason why he should, she told herself, lifting her gaze and getting a grip. 'Will I ever meet any of them?'

'I imagine so.'

'I look forward to it,' she said, realising with some surprise that it was true. She wanted to know more about this man and, weirdly, not just because he was the father of her child.

'Why didn't you want your parents there today?'

With a jolt she refocused and, as usual whenever she thought of her parents, a tight knot of anger and resentment and God only knew what else formed in her stomach. 'There wouldn't have been any point,' she said, hearing the faint note of bitterness in her voice and inwardly cringing. 'They wouldn't have come even if we had been on speaking terms. Marriage and civil partnerships are far too conventional for their way of life.'

'You mentioned they live in a commune.'

'That's right. They do.'

'Where?'

'I have no idea. They travel around. They always have.'

'Even when you were young?'

'Even then.'

'What was it like?'

'Great in some ways, awful in others,' she said with a casual shrug designed to hide the strange combination of pain and happiness that accompanied memories of her childhood. 'When I was very young, not having to go to school was fantastic. I had no set bedtimes and I could eat what I liked, although, since we only really had lentils and vegetables, I guess that wasn't such a luxury. The first time I had a grilled tuna steak I thought I'd died and gone to heaven. It's still my favourite thing to eat. Anyway, there were no boundaries and zero discipline. In hindsight, I must have been totally feral. We all were, really.'

'All?'

'Wherever we lived and however many families we lived with, there were always *lots* of children.'

'It sounds idyllic.'

'I know,' she said, considering it from the point of view of growing up with only one parent and no siblings. 'But it wasn't.' Not for her, and definitely not for Carla. 'Not for a teenager, at least.'

'Why not?'

She frowned for a moment. 'I think sub-consciously I really needed those boundaries to prove that I mattered. That my parents did actually care about me. And because I didn't have any, I went looking for them.'

'How?'

'I became a classic attention-seeking teen. I used to dress up and hang out in bars and order drinks while underage and flirt with all sorts of inappropriate people, desperate for someone to come and haul me home and ground me after some stern words.'

'And did they?'

'Nope,' she said with a sigh of the deep disappointment that annoyingly she still couldn't seem to shake even now, a decade later. 'Never. Once I got caught shoplifting and was delivered home by the owner of the shop with a warning and the only thing my parents were cross about was that the face cream I'd nicked wasn't organic. Eventually I figured that the only person who was going to look out for me was me and so I decided to take control of my own life. I managed to blag my way into a sixth-form college and then got into university. As if that wasn't conventional enough, I became a lawyer, at which point my parents pretty much disowned me. We haven't been properly in touch much since.'

'Do you miss them?'

She stared at him, for a moment completely taken aback. What an odd question. She'd never thought about it like that. She'd always been too stuck in a rut of simmering resentment and disappointment to allow herself to grieve for the loss of what could have been.

'I think I miss the *idea* of them,' she said after a few moments of consideration. 'I envy families. I never really had a proper one. The commune was no substitute. I was angry with my parents for a long time. Maybe I still am a bit. They let me down in every way possible. They failed at everything. No child deserves to feel unloved and unwanted. They should have been responsible. They should have been *better*. It's kind of in the job description.'

A job description that was hers now, she thought, making a silent promise to be the best parent she could for Josh. She might not have got off to a good start on the motherhood front but she would now do everything in her power to prevent her son *ever* feeling the way she had. Josh would never have to question whether he mattered. Whether he was truly loved. He'd never feel he had to find support elsewhere. He would never have to seek the attention he craved by hitting bars and clubs and engaging in unsuitable flirting.

'Do they know you've been ill?'

She shook her head. 'I didn't see the point of telling them. They wouldn't have been any help. They'd have just boiled up some hemp and sung a song or something. They've had the luxury of never being properly ill. At least, as far as I'm aware.'

'Have you told them about Josh?'

'I emailed my mother and got a reply warning me about the dangers of disposable nappies.'

'Their loss.'

And so it was, she realised as those two simple words sliced through the complex emotions she felt about her upbringing and pulverised the resentment and the pain. Finn was right. Her parents would never know her or him and they would never know their grandson, and that *was* their loss.

It wasn't her fault that they'd been so undeserving of the role. However much she might have wondered over the years what she'd done wrong or what she could have done differently, the answer to that was nothing. The responsibility for her well-being had been entirely theirs.

Well, she was done with them and with

looking back. She had to look forward. Her family was Josh now. Maybe even Finn too, who was perceptive and clever, who'd just shone a spotlight on the knotted mess of emotion she'd lived with for years and unravelled it in an instant and who was not a man to be underestimated. In any department.

Feeling strangely lightheaded while at the same time all warm and fuzzy, Georgie sat back and watched as he drained his glass, her gaze snagging on the strong column of his throat and the tantalising wedge of flesh that his open-necked shirt revealed.

'So what was growing up like for you?' she asked with a touch of huskiness that she cleared with a tiny cough. 'It must have been tough not having a mother around.'

As he lowered his glass she saw a shadow pass over his face and a flash of bleakness in the depths of his eyes. 'It wasn't the easiest of times.'

'Before that?'

'I don't really remember.'

'How did your father cope?'

'As well as could be expected.'

'Do you want to talk about it?'

'I'd rather not.'

Fair enough. She was more than happy to back off. The afternoon was far too sunny for such sombre conversation and there was no need to push a topic that was clearly off limits. She and Finn had plenty of time to talk about histories and dreams. Years, in fact, she thought, the reality of what she'd agreed to hitting her suddenly and making her head swim for a moment. 'Will you tell me about your business, then?'

'Which bit of it?'

'Well, how did it come about?' she asked, thinking that, honestly, getting him to open up was like trying to get blood from a stone.

'When I was eighteen and had left school I started working behind the bar of a club in the centre of the city.'

'I bet you were good at it.' With his darkly devastating looks and brooding charisma she had no doubt that people—well, women mainly—would have been tripping over themselves to be served by him.

'I was,' he said with the glimmer of a smile, the tension she could see gripping his shoulders easing a little. 'I was very good at it. And more importantly I got a massive kick out of it.'

'You didn't want to go to university?'

'I had a place at Oxford to read Maths but I gave it up.'

'That was brave.' University for her had been a lifeline and she'd loved it.

'It was the arrogance of youth.'

'Which in your case was justified.'

'So it turned out. Six months later the club had become a go-to destination and hit all the A-lists. Soon after that the manager, who also owned it, fell ill. He had to take some time off and I stepped in. I started doing the books, figured out where savings could be made and margins improved, and wound up increasing the profits by fifty per cent. When it eventually came up for sale I bought it. I worked bloody hard and I expanded and diversified and things went from there.'

Admiration and awe surged through her. 'And you did it all on your own.'

'With the support of my father,' he said, his mouth twisting slightly as his smile faded. 'He lent me the money to buy the club in the first place, and gave me endless advice. He was an accountant and very shrewd.'

'You must miss him.'

He didn't answer, just looked so tortured for a moment that it tugged on her heartstrings. 'Was it quick?'

'It took around a year,' he said, his voice oddly flat. 'I received his diagnosis the night you and I met.'

She gave a slow nod of understanding. 'That was why you looked so sad.'

'Did I?'

'Well, desolate really.'

'I was drowning my sorrows.'

'And then I rocked up and intruded. Sorry about that.'

'Don't be,' he said. 'You were the perfect distraction.'

Her breath caught and a hot shiver ran through her. 'You were the perfect birthday present,' she said huskily. 'It was a good night.'

'It was better than good.'

His dark, glittering gaze remained locked onto hers and scorchingly vivid memories suddenly poured into her head. The air surrounding her thickened. The hustle and bustle of the restaurant faded. Up until this point she hadn't realised how much of a chaperone, a shield, Josh had been. Without him, she felt wild and carefree and she suddenly wanted to stand up and lean over and kiss the man sitting opposite her looking at her so intently. Her mouth was dry and her heart was pounding, and deep inside she ached. She wanted to grab his hand and take him home and have him seduce the hell out of her all over again.

But none of that would happen. It couldn't,

even if the heat and desire *had* been mutual, which it clearly wasn't. What with the risk of pregnancy and the chance that it might induce another psychotic episode, she was never having sex again. It was vaguely ironic that her libido had returned when it was of least use but she had to ignore it. Starting now, she thought, shifting to alleviate the ache only to accidentally knock his knee with hers and jolt as though electrocuted.

'Sorry,' she muttered, blushing fiercely while mentally throwing her hands up in despair.

'No problem,' Finn replied, unlike her, completely unmoved by the moment, if the inscrutability of his expression was anything to go by. 'We should order.'

Despite appearances, Finn was anything but unmoved by his brand-new civil partner. Theoretically, the ceremony should have changed nothing. The whole event had been a legal and bureaucratic process designed to bind Josh to him permanently, and that was it. He hadn't given Georgie a ring or planned a honeymoon and the lunch they'd had afterwards had hardly been a celebration.

However, for some baffling reason things *had* changed. A week in and there now seemed to be an inexplicable intimacy about living with her that somehow hadn't existed before. At night he'd started imagining her in bed and what he might do to her should he find himself ever in it with her. In the mornings, when he heard the sound of the shower running, he now envisaged her in it, wet and naked.

He seemed attuned to her every movement. Her scent lingered even when she wasn't around. When home, she'd taken to wandering around the apartment in tiny shorts and T-shirts that drew his gaze to her long legs and spectacularly returning curves. When going out she did at least put on proper clothes, none of which were either particularly tight or revealing, but that didn't provide much relief. He knew what lay underneath regardless, and to his immense irritation he couldn't stop thinking about it.

And then there were the little things that he'd noticed and now couldn't un-notice, such as her habit of nibbling the end of the pen that she used when writing in her diary. The extraordinarily expressive delight with which she savoured the food she ate. The way she gathered her hair up and then with a sort of flick of her fingers twisted it once before letting it go.

He couldn't stop thinking about *any* of it and he existed in an agonising, limbo-like state of wanting to back her up against a wall and slake his desire yet not being able to do one damn thing about it, of yearning to escape her mind-scrambling orbit but needing to be as close to his son as possible. At least she had no idea of the battle raging inside him. She couldn't. If she did she'd never prance around the place so scantily clad. She wasn't that foolish.

Nevertheless, everything else about the situation was driving him demented, and despite his best efforts to contain it his mood of recent days had not gone unnoticed. From time to time he'd caught her looking at him, her eyes on him searing his skin and burning through him, as if deliberating whether to question him about it.

She was doing it now, sitting out here on the terrace that overlooked London, staring at him from over the rim of the mug she drank coffee out of every morning, which had 'world's sexiest lawyer' emblazoned across it, as if he needed a reminder.

'If you have something to say, just say it,' he snapped, unable to stand the scrutiny and the suspense any longer.

'All right,' she said, putting her mug down.

'I've been thinking. What would you say to spending your evenings up here with me instead of disappearing off to wherever it is you go?'

What? No. No way. He barely trusted himself with her in the presence of their son and Mrs Gardiner in broad daylight. He and Georgie in the evening alone with soft lighting and an even softer sofa was *not* happening. 'Work needs me,' he said, which was a big, fat lie, since the team to which he'd delegated everything was doing just fine.

'It would be good to spend some time together without Josh.'

'Why?'

'There are things we should discuss.'

'Like what?'

'How we move forward.'

'Josh is having a nap. We can discuss that now.'

'He's due to wake up any moment and I'd like to know more about you without distractions.'

That wasn't happening either. Talking about himself wasn't something he was particularly fond of doing at the best of times. Right now it was the last thing he wanted to do. And she *was* the distraction. 'You know everything there is to know.' Everything that was relevant, anyway.

'OK, fine,' she said with an exasperated huff. 'You know what? Forget it. I do think we need to talk about the future, but really, I'd just like the company. It's lonely up here on my own every evening. It's quiet.' She gave a careless shrug. 'I dare say I'll survive, though.'

Well, now, how was he to respond to that? Just when he thought he'd successfully shut her down, along came guilt to hit him in the gut like a ton of bricks. He had no excuse really, and to persist with pretending he did would simply be cruel. He wasn't having her feeling lonely because he had an issue with self-control. He'd just have to cope. Because hadn't he vowed to provide her with what she needed whenever she needed it?

'All right,' he muttered, nevertheless slightly wishing that he had less of a problem with breaking promises. 'I'll make some adjustments.'

'Thank you,' she said with a smile so dazzling that it blinded him to the realisation that she'd got up and was walking over to him.

By the time he did register what she was doing it was too late. Before he could brace himself, she'd come to a stop right in front of him and bent down, her scent and her warmth scrambling his senses. The world skidded to a halt and every inch of him froze. Then she reached out and touched her hand lightly to his head, threading her fingers through his hair, and for one heart-stopping, delirious moment he actually thought that she was going to lean in and kiss him.

'What are you doing?' he said hoarsely, his mouth dry and his body aching unbearably.

'You have a piece of toast in your hair.'

She removed her hand and stepped back and he didn't know whether to be gutted or relieved, what to think or what to do, although breathing would be a good start. Followed by getting the hell out of here before he completely gave in to temptation and turned some of his wilder imaginings into reality.

'Where are you going?' she called as he leapt to his feet and stalked back into the apartment as if he had the hounds of hell at his heels.

'Meeting.'

CHAPTER SEVEN

EYEING FINN WARILY as he paced up and down his sitting room one evening several days later, Georgie frowned. Up until a few days ago she'd thought that everything was going really rather well. He seemed pleased with their civil partnership and, although it was a struggle, she was just about keeping a lid on the attraction that she felt for him. She'd had a slight blip when she'd discovered that he'd added tuna steak to the menu of dishes that continued to be sent up, and gone all breathless and gooey inside at the realisation he'd remembered what she'd told him at that lunch, but she'd recovered well enough. It hadn't meant anything. She needed building up, he'd told her when she'd thanked him. She needed the protein. That was all.

Lately, however, Finn had become weirdly distracted, frequently grumpy and anything but friendly. Physically he was around as much as ever, more so now he spent the evenings with her, but spiritually and emotionally he seemed to be on a whole other planet. He volunteered little in the way of conversation and his answers to her questions were monosyllabic.

The tension that now radiated off him had to come from somewhere and she didn't think it was caused by Josh, since being with him was the only time Finn didn't seem stressed. So maybe it was her, she'd begun to think. Maybe he was more annoyed by her habit of leaving the milk out than she'd realised. Maybe she was doing something else wrong. It wouldn't exactly be a first.

Whatever it was, though, Josh was picking up on it now and she'd had enough.

Closing the journal she filled in nightly, and setting both it and the pen she used on the ottoman, Georgie tracked his restless movements for a moment and then pulled her shoulders back and went for it. 'OK, Finn, what's wrong?'

'Why would anything be wrong?' he said, shooting her a glare, which did rather prove her point.

'You're wearing a permanent scowl these days and you've taken to prowling around the apartment like a caged animal.'

He stopped mid-pace and with what looked like a Herculean effort cleared his expression and shot her a tight smile. 'Everything's fine.'

'Hmm,' she said with a sceptical frown. 'Is it work?'

'No.'

'Is it me and Josh?'

'Why would it be you?'

'I'm very aware that this has all been a huge upheaval for you. The noise and the mess, I mean. It would be completely understandable if you were finding it hard. Your life has changed immeasurably.'

'That's nothing new.'

Her eyebrows lifted. 'Sorry?'

'Nothing,' he said curtly. 'Everything's fine.'

'Are you sure?'

'Yes.'

'Anything you want to talk about?'

'No.'

In the face of such intransigence Georgie gave up. She could try till she was blue in the face and she wouldn't get anywhere. 'OK,' she said. 'It's your call. I rather feel that if you carry on like this sooner or later you're going to burst a blood vessel, but have it your own way.'

'Have it *my* way?' he said with a bark of humourless laughter. 'You have no idea.'

'Then tell me.'

She shifted to make herself more comfortable, just in case he did want to talk, and suddenly something inside him seemed to snap.

'All right,' he said, his eyes blazing and his hands curling into fists. 'You're right. There is something.'

'What?'

'Do you think, for once, you could put on a bloody dressing gown?'

And with that he turned on his heel and strode out, leaving Georgie staring after him, reeling and agape.

What on earth...?

What was wrong with what she was wearing? There was nothing immodest about the baggy T-shirt or the board shorts that she had on, yet what he'd just said and the way he'd glowered at her while saying it implied that not only did he consider it to be the skimpiest outfit he'd ever seen but also that it bothered him.

However, why would it? He wasn't affected by her. Unless he was, of course, and that tension he was obviously feeling could actually be some kind of sexual frustration because, contrary to what she'd assumed, he *was* still attracted to her.

But no. He couldn't be. She'd seen no evidence of it. There'd been no long, heated looks, no off-the-charts chemistry and no sizzling subtext to their conversations. If that was the case, surely there'd have been signs...

But maybe there had been, she thought suddenly, her heart quickening as the clouds in her head parted to reveal possibilities that had hitherto been hidden. What if some of the looks Finn had given her over the last few weeks, some of his expressions that she hadn't been able to decipher and some of the strange things he'd done, were in fact cases in point?

Take, for example, the way his gaze dropped to her lips pretty much every time they ate together. She'd always vaguely assumed he'd been staring at a stray crumb or perhaps a bit of parsley stuck between her teeth. But what if instead he'd been bombarded with thoughts of kissing her the way she always thought about kissing him whenever she caught herself looking at his mouth? And what about his habit of taking a step back whenever she approached? Could he be doing that because he found her proximity somehow disturbing?

He appeared to have such a tight grip on his control, but maybe the absence of a reaction hid a very different kind of response. What if when she'd barged in on him that night and found him naked save for a towel he hadn't been as unmoved as he appeared? What if when her knee had brushed against his the day they'd had lunch, he'd been as affected as her? And what if his disappearance every night was less about catching up with work and more about avoiding her?

Or was she seeing signs where there were none?

It was entirely possible, but, if she was right and these were signs that she'd missed, then she was not only an idiot but she was also not as back to her old self as she'd imagined because that Georgie would never have missed anything.

But that wasn't important right now. Assuming she hadn't got things completely wrong, Finn appeared to want her and she might as well admit that she wanted him. She'd tried to ignore it and treat him like a flatmate, as if she were back in her old flat in Kensal Rise that she'd shared with three others, two of whom had been men she'd had no interest in, but that hadn't exactly worked. Despite her best intentions, she hadn't been able to entirely stop fantasising about him naked, about what they might get up to if she should happen to find herself in his vicinity naked too.

So what was going to happen next?

They clearly couldn't carry on like this. Things would eventually come to a head and erupt. And what was she going to do when they did? Well, she was never having sex again obviously, but, assuming Finn was amenable, there was no reason they couldn't do other things. From what she remembered he'd been spectacularly good at those other things and he hadn't exactly complained about her skills either.

Did she have the courage to tell him what she now quite desperately wanted, she wondered, her heart beginning to pound with excitement as her stomach churned nervously. Once upon a time she wouldn't have hesitated, but now… On the other hand, while she *had* been scarred by what had happened to her, it didn't have to define her going forward, did it?

So how hard would it be to go to Finn and tell him what she wanted? All it would take was guts, and heaven knew she had plenty of those. If she tried her hardest and he still sent her away, if she'd read too much into

things and got completely the wrong end of
the stick, then so be it. After everything she'd
been through she could handle a spot of mor-
tification. She could handle anything.

Cursing himself for what he'd revealed, and
deeply regretting his momentary loss of control, Finn stormed into his room and slammed
the door. If only Georgie had backed off and
left him to stew. Instead she'd pushed and
prodded and told him to have it his way,
which was an absolute joke since his way involved her being horizontal in his bed, sighing and gasping beneath his hands and mouth,
a scenario that wasn't going to happen. As
if that wasn't enough she'd then leaned back
and lifted her legs to tuck them under her, a
movement that made the fabric of her tiny T-
shirt tighten enticingly against her breasts,
and he'd lost it, any hope he might have had
of making it out of there with his pride in-
tact history.

His movements jerky, Finn yanked his T-
shirt over his head and tossed it on the bed,
only to spin round at the sound of his bedroom door opening. Georgie stood there, silhouetted in the space, and as a bolt of desire
shot through him, nearly taking out his knees,
he swore beneath his breath.

He should have known she wouldn't let his parting shot go. He should have known she'd follow him. That perhaps he subconsciously *had* known and had wanted her to do so, so that they might continue where they'd left off that first night she'd barged into his room, wasn't something he wanted to contemplate ever. Because if that *did* turn out to be the case it would mean his attempts to get a grip on his unpredictable behaviour had utterly failed.

'What is it with you and knocking?' he said, practically at the end of his tether with his inability to control the futile attraction he felt for her.

'Sorry.'

She stepped forward into the light, into his territory, and he saw that she didn't look sorry. She didn't look sorry in the slightest.

'What do you want?'

'To continue our conversation.'

'We're done.'

'I don't think we are.'

Before he could even think about striding past her and getting the hell out of his room, with its huge bed squatting there like some giant neon sign advertising sex, she'd walked towards him and planted her palms flat on his chest.

'What are you doing?' he said, every muscle in his body freezing while he burned where she touched him.

'I'd have thought it was obvious,' she murmured, moving her hands up over the muscles of his chest while staring at his mouth.

His jaw clenched and his fists tightened. 'I'd advise you to stop.'

'Why?'

Yes, why? his body screamed while his brain fought to be heard. 'Because you're playing with fire.'

'I'm more than happy to be burned.'

'You've been ill.'

'I'm much better now.'

But she still had some way to go. He'd done the research and witnessed her occasional off day. She was by no means totally well yet. 'That's irrelevant.'

'All that's relevant right now is that I want you and you want me.'

Not much point in denying it, really. He needed her so badly he was in physical pain and it was becoming blatantly obvious. Nevertheless…

'What I want doesn't come into it,' he muttered though gritted teeth.

'Yet here we are, all partnered up.'

'For the sake of our son.'

She tilted her head as she lifted her gaze to his, her brown eyes shimmering in the soft light. 'Are you sure about that?'

He had been once. Right now he wasn't sure he could even remember his own name. Her scent and her warmth were destroying his faculties. All he could think of was how good it had been between them and how desperately he wanted to find out if it still could be. 'One hundred per cent.'

'So selfless,' she said with the hint of a smile.

'Don't patronise me.'

'The tension is driving you nuts, isn't it?'

'What tension?' he ground out.

'We could make it go away. *I* could make it go away.'

She ran her hands along his shoulders and down his arms and he shuddered. He had to take a step back, out of her orbit. He had to break the spell she was weaving around him. His thundering heart couldn't take much more and his self-control was fast unravelling. But he couldn't move. His feet appeared to have taken root. And his grip on his sanity, already loosened by weeks of frustration, was slipping away.

'Leave me alone, Georgie,' he said, but the protest was weak and he knew she knew it.

'Give me one last shot and, if you really insist, then I'll go.'

He couldn't speak for trying to drum up the will to insist she leave, regardless of what she did next, and she seemed to take his silence as assent, which maybe it foolishly and recklessly was, because before he knew what she was planning, before he could brace himself for what she might say or do, she'd let go of him, reached down, and gripped the hem of her top.

And as she whipped it off and tossed it to the floor, exposing her lace-covered breasts and inches of beautiful, creamy skin to his ravenous gaze, Finn felt what was left of his resistance crumble and the last remaining vestiges of his self-control shatter.

When, suddenly galvanised into action after minutes of rock-solid stillness, Finn hauled her into his arms and his mouth crashed down on hers, Georgie's first thought was, oh, thank heavens for that. She hadn't known what she would have done next had he rejected her bold move. Back away and flee, most probably, because there was taking a leaf out of his book and not stopping until one got what one wanted, and then there was harassment.

Now, though, as he held her tightly and kissed her as if his life depended on it, she couldn't think at all. Her head was swimming and the electricity zinging through her as a result of his chest hair rubbing against her sensitised skin was enough to power the national grid. She'd forgotten how very good he was at this, how good they were together, and she kissed him back with equal fervour.

When at last Finn lifted his head, his eyes were so dark they were almost black and his breathing was as ragged as hers. 'You really don't play fair,' she heard him murmur harshly over the thunder of her heart.

'You're a hard man to crack.'

'You have no idea how hard I've been.'

She arched her back, pressing her hips more firmly to his, and gave him a quick grin. 'I think I may have some.'

His gaze bored into hers and she shivered. 'Are you sure about this?'

'Yes.'

'What exactly do you want from me?' he persisted.

'Not sex.'

He stilled for a moment and eased back, his expression tortured. 'OK, then,' he said, clearly grappling to contain his surprise and disappointment. 'OK.' And then, hoarsely, 'Out of interest, why not?'

'It's too risky,' she clarified swiftly to put him out of his misery. 'We were careful the last time and look what happened. I can't get pregnant a second time. I can't go through the last six months all over again. Ever. We can do everything else though.'

As her words sank in he shuddered with visible relief. 'Thank God for that.'

'I'm sure you know things I've never even heard of.'

'Based on past experience, I very much doubt that.'

'Is that OK?' she added, suddenly worried that it might not be enough for him.

'I'll take anything you're willing to give.'

Phew. 'Then we're going to be busy.'

'Fine by me.'

He turned with her still in his arms and backed her up towards the bed until her knees hit the edge of it. Together they fell onto the mattress, his hard-muscled weight pinning her down in the most breathtakingly lovely way.

'That's better,' he muttered, lowering his head and capturing her mouth with his in a kiss that blew her mind all over again.

Caught up in a maelstrom of soul-shattering sensation, Georgie gave up thinking and let instinct take over. She lifted her hands to his shoulders, smoothing them over his muscles, feeling them bunch and flex as he held himself off her just enough to prevent crushing her.

He dragged his mouth along her jaw to her ear, nipping at a spot that made her groan as heat sizzled through her, and she gasped, 'You remembered.'

'I remember everything.'

Shifting slightly onto his side, Finn put one large, warm hand on her waist, making her jump and shudder, and then slid it behind her back to unclip her bra. After slipping it off her and throwing it aside he cupped her breast, and with a soft moan she instinctively arched her back to press herself further into his hand. He bent his head and caught one tight nipple between his lips and she whimpered as sparks shot through her. Her hands tightened in his hair, although whether to hold him still or push him lower she couldn't tell. She didn't want the exquisite torment he was subjecting her to to stop but on the other hand she wanted that clever mouth of his all over her. It was the most delicious of dilemmas.

Abandoning her breast, he slid his hand lower, easing beneath the waistband of her shorts and knickers, and she lifted her hips to help him push them down.

'Beautiful,' he muttered gruffly, his gaze singeing her skin as he moved his hand back up her calf, her knee, her thigh, taking his time and lingering in places that had her quivering. When he reached the juncture of her thighs and covered her where she was so hot and needy she cried out. He parted her with his fingers and stroked, and jolts of excitement streaked through her. Her breath caught and her heart thundered and when she reached down to touch him through his jeans his breath shot out in one long hiss.

Unable to lie there impassively while Finn was still partly clothed and doing everything, and desperately wanting to feel him without denim between them, she nudged him to encourage him to roll over, but he stopped her.

'No,' he said roughly, his entire body vibrating with tension. 'You're first.'

Noble, she thought with a shudder at the thought of the pleasure to come. But no. That wasn't happening. Not when she owed him for the whipping-her-top-off moment. 'Who said we have to take turns?'

He went still for a moment and then his eyes darkened and his mouth curved into a slow, smouldering smile. 'Good point.'

He flipped onto his back, taking her with him, and she wriggled down his body. Her hands were trembling as she unbuckled his belt, so much so that she couldn't actually undo the buttons of his fly. He batted her aside to do it himself and the sight of his capable hands with their strong fingers that could cause so much devastation within her liquefied her stomach.

He kicked off his jeans and shorts and then planted his hands on her waist to manoeuvre her into a position in which she was facing his feet and he was gripping her hips and lifting her to where he wanted her and where she wanted to be. Supporting herself on her elbows, she wrapped her fingers around his long, thick, hard length and heard him groan, and then gave a reciprocal one of her own when his tongue touched her sensitive flesh and sent sensation coursing through her.

As she moved her hand up and down the velvety steel of him, and he found her clitoris and licked, her eyelids fluttered shut, her entire body filling with molten heat. She was shaking all over, but not nearly as much as he was when she took him into her mouth. When she started moving her head he moaned against her, and the vibrations sent tiny shock waves shooting through her.

His response stoked hers, making her move faster, which drove him to increase the pressure and the intensity of what he was doing to her and she was fast spiralling out of control. She could feel the tension building inside her, the heat and pleasure winding tight and scrambling her senses, and she seemed to be in synch with him because he was now shifting his hips and thrusting into her mouth as she moved, and his breathing was hot and ragged against her.

Desire soared within her, igniting a desperate ache, and she was just about to reach a hand down to where his tongue was buried to hurry him along, when, as if able to read her mind, he held her still and thrust two fingers inside her and curled them so that they hit that exact spot, and that was it. She flew apart, her orgasm crashing into her, a white-hot burst of pleasure spinning through her like a Catherine wheel. And as stars whirled round her head she took him deep, and with a harsh groan he grabbed her head, tensed and then pulsated hard, spilling into her mouth until neither of them had anything left.

Feeling utterly drained, Georgie eased herself off him and flopped back, lying top to tail against him while waiting for her heartbeat to regulate.

'God, we're good at this,' she said when she had enough breath to speak.

Finn rolled onto his side, and regarded her, his gaze dark and glittering and his face flushed. 'Just think how much better we could be with a bit of practice.'

A sharp shiver raced through her, electrifying her nerve endings all over again. 'I don't know if I'd survive.'

The smile he gave her was slow and full of wicked promise. 'Oh, you'll survive.'

CHAPTER EIGHT

THEY PRACTISED A LOT, and got so good that a week later Georgie thought it was just as well that the walls were soundproofed. Finn was very inventive and, as she'd suspected, he knew things to do with positions and accessories and devices that she'd never even seen before, let alone deployed.

He just had to look at her and she became flushed and aroused. Every night as soon as Josh had been put to bed—indecently soon, actually—Finn took her hand and led her into the nearest bedroom, where they stayed until either day broke or their son woke. She'd lost count of how many orgasms she'd had and she was fast becoming addicted to the things he could do to her.

She wasn't just surviving the way he handled her body, she was thriving on it, as the entries in her diary detailed, which only went to show that oxytocin and dopamine and the endorphins that accompanied them really were good for the brain. And if something was occasionally missing, if she sometimes felt a bit hollow on her way down from the bliss and sort of wished she could have all of him, well, that was the compromise she just had to make, in the same way that all this lovely nocturnal activity came at the cost of the conversation she'd been so keen to encourage.

Her days now had structure and routine and she and Finn were getting on splendidly, and she had absolutely nothing to complain about. However, in the absence of stress and anxiety and sexual frustration, she found that now all she had to wonder about was if and when he was going to introduce her to his friends as promised. He'd shown no indication of it so far, and she couldn't help wondering why not. They were in every night, so it wasn't as if a hectic schedule prevented it. So was it something to do with her, then? With their situation? Or did he see her as unfit for anywhere other than the bedroom?

There was only one way to find out.

'So when am I going to meet your friends?' she asked him one night as they lay sprawled across his enormous bed, the moonlight streaking through the windows and bathing everything in a silvery glow. 'It's been weeks. Are you in some way ashamed of me?'

'What?' he replied, his words muffled by the pillow he'd flopped onto only moments ago. 'Don't be ridiculous.'

Hmm. That wasn't exactly an answer. 'Don't get me wrong,' she said, trying to keep her voice light, 'your attention is very flattering but a girl could get a complex.' Especially a girl like her, with anxieties and insecurities that she knew could pop up at any time.

'She shouldn't.'

'She might.'

He turned his head to the side and levelled her with a long, hot look. 'Really?'

She nodded. 'Really.'

'I'll set something up.'

'Thank you,' she said with a grin.

'You're welcome.'

'I shall cook.'

'There's no need. We'll go out. Or have something sent up.'

'No, I'd like to. I used to love cooking and I can't keep eating all the food the kitchens provide. It's too easy, too convenient and way too delicious. Much more of it and I'll be as big as a house.'

His gaze slowly roamed over her, setting her on fire wherever he let it linger. 'You're fine,' he said, his smile fading and his eyes darkening as he reached for her yet again. 'You're beautiful. And I am in absolutely no way ashamed of you.'

And that was how, the following Friday evening, she and Finn played hosts to his friends, Theo and Kate Knox, and her friend Carla. Finn and Theo had known each other professionally for a couple of years, and socially for one of those, more so since Theo had met Kate and settled down. Kate, his wife of three months, was tall, statuesquely beautiful and heavily pregnant.

Over drinks and nibbles, a starter of salmon and asparagus and a main course of slow-roasted lamb, Georgie listened to the conversation that flowed easily, picking up anything she could about Finn, however tiny, and filing it away for later consideration. She smiled and laughed and made contributions where necessary, but for the most part she found herself surreptitiously watching Kate and trying not to envy her.

The other woman's clear enjoyment of her pregnancy and the serenity and radiance that she emanated were things that had been denied to Georgie, and that filled her with regret and sadness. If only she'd known she was pregnant, things could have been so different. It was hard not to feel cheated.

And then there was the immense love that Kate was lucky enough to bask in. In all honesty Georgie found Theo faintly aloof and more than a bit intimidating, but when he looked at his wife the hard lines of his face softened and the blazing emotion that warmed in his eyes stole her breath. What would it feel like to be on the receiving end of such love and such passion? Would she ever know? It didn't seem likely, given the hand of cards she'd been dealt.

'So how did you and Theo meet?' Carla asked, and Georgie made herself shake off the gloom and focus.

Kate put down her glass of elderflower *pressé* and gave her husband a look of wry amusement. 'I made myself available on an escort agency website and Theo took against it.'

Goodness, thought Georgie. That she hadn't known.

Theo arched an eyebrow, although a faint smile played at his mouth. 'Indeed,' he said, his dark gaze taking in Finn and Georgie. 'How about you?'

'Georgie picked Finn up in a bar,' Carla said with a wide grin.

'I wouldn't put it quite like that,' Georgie muttered, feeling herself blush.

'Why not?' said Finn, the glance he slid her holding a wicked glint. 'You did.'

'I don't remember you putting up much of a protest.'

'I put up no protest at all.'

'The sparks flying off the two of them could have set fire to a forest,' Carla said, taking a sip of champagne. 'I went up to them to see if Georgie was OK and had to back off for fear of getting singed.'

Oh? 'I don't remember you doing that.'

'I'm not surprised. The fire alarm could have gone off with sprinklers and everything and you'd have been oblivious.'

'And how do you two know each other?' asked Kate, indicating her and Carla.

'Our parents lived on the same commune for a while when we were teenagers,' said Georgie, remembering how excited she'd been at hearing the news of the latest arrivals.

'We clicked instantly,' said Carla. 'Took a few walks together on the wild side. Even after my family moved on we stayed in touch.'

'She's my best friend,' said Georgie.

'Back at you,' said Carla.

'Thank you,' said a suddenly serious Finn

to Carla, who, to Georgie's astonishment, blushed.

'You're very welcome.'

'I'll make coffee, shall I?' said Georgie before either of the too-sharp-for-their-own-good Knoxs could voice the curiosity that was filling their expressions.

'I'll help,' said Carla.

Feeling oddly peculiar, Georgie practically ran into the kitchen, with Carla hot on her heels.

'God, Finn really is divine,' said her friend, faux fanning herself with a hand while Georgie turned on the boiling water tap and filled a cafétière. 'All that intensity and focus on you. Blazing. The vibes are extraordinary. Watching you two together *and* Kate and Theo almost makes me want to give up singledom.'

'Finn and I aren't like that, as you know perfectly well,' said Georgie, her chest nevertheless tightening.

'Then what are you like?'

'I'm not entirely sure.'

But she had the suspicion that she knew exactly what she might want it to be like, and she stuck a lid on it because there was absolutely no point chasing rainbows.

And it was a good thing she did too, because it meant that at breakfast a couple of days after the dinner party when Finn made his unexpected announcement she was able to handle it. Josh was squashing a piece of banana between his fingers as he tried to cram it into his mouth. Finn was devouring a croissant and looking so dishevelled and sexy from her early-morning ministrations that Georgie, who was sipping coffee, felt her heart turn over, as it was increasingly wont to do whenever she looked at him.

'I have to go to Paris next weekend,' he said, jolting her out of her reverie and causing the mouthful of coffee she'd just taken to go down the wrong way. 'The Bellevue is finally opening. There's a launch party.'

She coughed and spluttered and banged her chest.

'Are you all right?' he asked with a faint frown of concern.

'Yes,' she said, thumping her chest one last time. 'Fine.'

She was just surprised, that was all. The Bellevue was finished? Well, that was excellent news. She knew a bit from him about how long the works had been going on and how stressful they'd been. She had no reason to feel stung by the fact that Finn had never mentioned the imminent launch of the hotel or the party, a party that must have been planned for weeks, if not months. Or by the lack of an invitation. He owed her nothing. The debt went entirely the other way. She'd be of no benefit to him at such an event anyway.

'When are you going?'

'Saturday.'

In six days. Gutting. Her period was due imminently, which would put a temporary halt to orgasms—for her at least—a halt that would now apparently last longer than she'd hoped. But she'd handle it. It wasn't as if she wouldn't survive without the pleasure he evoked in her. In fact, the delay would make his return all the sweeter.

'That's a shame,' she said, deciding to attribute the disappointment she nevertheless felt to PMT.

'Why?'

'Because I'll miss…'

You.

Well. She certainly wasn't going to tell him that. She'd sound pathetic. Besides, she was already too vulnerable when it came to him. He held all the cards. She held none. So she pulled herself together and lowered her voice, even though Josh was way too young to understand, and finished '…what we've been doing.'

His blue eyes gleamed. 'You don't have to.'

She looked at him quizzically. What did he have in mind? Phone sex? That was something they hadn't tried yet. Could be fun. 'What do you mean?'

'Come with me.'

Her heart skipped a beat and then began to race. 'Really?'

'Why not? Think of it as a belated mini honeymoon.'

Hmm. She'd be better off *not* thinking that actually, since, whatever they were doing, it wasn't romance and she'd be wise not to forget it. 'For how long?'

'A couple of days, maybe three. The party's on the Saturday night and I have some business on the Monday and Tuesday. We'd be back by Tuesday evening at the latest.'

'What about Josh?'

'He can stay here with Mrs Gardiner.'

As usual Finn had all the answers and he made it sound not only easy but also unbelievably tempting. Three days on her own with him in Paris, strolling through the parks and sitting in divine restaurants that had white tablecloths, sparkling crystal and soft, flickering candles...

Or perhaps not, since he'd probably be in meetings most of the time, but whatever. She could see it now—the party, the luxury and the almost-sex that would have an added frisson, given that it was Paris—and to her shame she wanted it all quite desperately.

But could she really do it? Wouldn't it be the height of selfishness to leave behind her tiny son to go off gallivanting around one of the most romantic cities in the world in search of pleasure, oblivion and her old self?

Well, maybe it would and maybe many would judge her for that, but maybe she ought to give herself a break. Didn't she deserve some fun? And how badly would her absence actually affect Josh? She'd only be away for three days max. Would he even notice? And if he did, would it scar him for life? She didn't think so. She had the utmost faith in Mrs Gardiner, which was ironic when she thought about how suspicious of the whole idea of having a nanny she'd been initially, and there was always the phone. It wasn't exactly difficult to get back from Paris, should for some reason she need to.

'Well?' Finn queried with an arch of an eyebrow that sent thrills of excitement skidding along her veins and a lovely warmth spreading through her body.

'Oui, d'accord,' she said, feeling the beginnings of a wide, silly smile spread across her face despite her best efforts to contain it. 'I'd love to.'

* * *

At ten o'clock on the following Saturday evening—French time—Georgie was floating on the most incredible high.

She and Finn had arrived in Paris earlier, having caught the train in London and travelled first class. A car had picked them up at the station and had then smoothly whisked them to the latest addition to the Calvert Collection portfolio.

When they'd pulled up outside the Hotel Bellevue on the Rue du Faubourg Saint-Honoré she'd had trouble keeping her jaw from hitting the floor. The pale, sand-coloured stone of the six-storey building gleamed in the afternoon sun. Each room had a black wrought-iron balcony from which spilled rich red flowers. Some had their red and white striped blinds down, some had their doors open to let in the warm spring breeze. Above the revolving glass and gold front door was a fine black awning, and either side of it stood a tub containing a perfectly clipped ball of a laurel tree. The doorman who tipped his black top hat to them as they approached was wearing a dark coat decorated with gold braid and polished brass. Inside, everything was soft whites and elegant *eau-de-nil*, marble floors and sparkling crystal. Beyond the reception desk, through a pair of huge patio doors, Georgie had seen a terrace where tables with bright white parasols had been placed around an area of emerald-green grass bordered with low, neat hedging.

'What do you think?' Finn had asked as they'd gone up in the lift to their suite.

'Breathtakingly stunning.'

'I couldn't agree more,' he'd replied, giving her a direct look that sent heat and desire stealing through her.

The honeymoon suite, which had been put at their disposal, was equally as beautiful with its calming off-white and taupe décor and gorgeous antique furniture. Disappointingly, Finn had disappeared pretty much immediately to go off and do things that, as owner of the hotel, he had to do. But Georgie had managed to occupy herself by exploring the vast suite and terrace, before kicking off her shoes and flopping onto the enormous bed to call Mrs Gardiner for quite possibly the twentieth time.

It hadn't been easy leaving Josh. It had actually been rather more of a wrench than she'd expected. For one dithering moment, just before she'd walked out of the penthouse back in London, she'd genuinely considered going downstairs to where Finn was waiting and telling him to go ahead without her. But Mrs Gardiner had shooed her off, practically locking the door behind her, and so she'd slunk off, torn between wanting to go and guilt at leaving.

That guilt, which had accompanied her throughout the journey to Paris, hadn't fully gone away but she'd been assured during every call she'd subsequently made that her son seemed to be taking their absence in his stride, and finally she'd been able to relax and enjoy the party.

And what a party it was. Five hundred guests, who'd earlier been divided into small groups and given an exclusive tour, now mingled in the ballroom. Members of the waiting staff wove through the journalists, upmarket travel company owners and anyone else lucky enough to have received a coveted invitation, offering up exquisite signature cocktails and the tiniest, most delicious canapés Georgie had ever tasted. She'd laughed and chatted all evening, remembering how much she'd once loved socialising and going giddy with the realisation that it was all coming back to her.

Having Finn at her side helped. His proximity was as reassuring as it was intoxicating. He looked so incredibly handsome this evening in his impeccably tailored navy suit that matched his eyes and a pale blue shirt. His imposing height and the impressive breadth of his shoulders stood him apart from everyone else, and then there was the aura of confidence and power that surrounded him and sent shivers of anticipation rippling through her.

Georgie had only really ever seen Finn the father or Finn the deliverer of outstanding orgasms. She'd never experienced this side of him, the utterly compelling, totally in command, billionaire tycoon. It was dazzling being with him, knowing he was hers, and she was no more immune to his effect than any of the other couple of hundred or so women present this evening.

However, it wasn't the luxury of her surroundings or the endless supply of champagne or even Finn's presence beside her that was causing Georgie's state of heightened excitement. Nor was it the memory of him raising the privacy partition in the car as they'd made their way from the station to the hotel, then sliding his hand up her skirt and making her come silently and hard within minutes, which kept slipping into her head and making her blush. It wasn't even the euphoric relief at knowing she was truly better and could therefore stop taking her medication, a plan she'd implemented this morning.

No.

What was responsible for the dizzying delight whipping through her was the unexpected yet shattering conclusion she'd come to while having her hair and make-up done this afternoon in the hotel's very exclusive salon.

To get there she'd had to pass the hotel's *pharmacie*, which was as elegantly designed as the rest of the building. As she'd settled back to have her hair washed, she'd found herself idly wondering what sort of pharmaceutical things a guest might need while staying in such a hotel but may not have. A forgotten toothbrush perhaps. A plaster or an aspirin. Or something they might possibly need unexpectedly, such as a tampon or, if they were very lucky, a condom. This naturally had got her to thinking about sex, with Finn, how much she longed to do it and what a crying shame it was that they couldn't.

And then it had struck her like a breath-stealing blow to the chest that maybe they could. Her period had finished yesterday—no unexpected need for a tampon—and her cycle was long. So the chances of getting pregnant at this stage of it were remote. Really remote.

And therefore if she and Finn were extra-careful, she'd thought, her head spinning and her heart thumping while the stylist lathered her up, what was stopping them from having full-on sex tonight? What was stopping them from making up for lost time and having full-on sex *the entire weekend*?

As far as she could tell, absolutely nothing. It would be virtually risk-free. Certainly risk-free enough for her to consider it an excellent idea. The only potential obstacle was Finn, but surely he wouldn't object. While unravelling her in the car he'd murmured that he'd found the last week impossibly frustrating, despite her extreme and selfless generosity on that front, so presumably he'd be as thrilled with her proposal as she was.

And so, once she was all styled and made up and fairly bubbling over with excitement and anticipation, Georgie had gone back to the pharmacy to acquire supplies for what she hoped would be at least forty-eight hours of mind-blowing sex, give or take a meeting or two, and returned to her room to get dressed as if floating on air.

For the duration of the party she'd hugged her plan to herself, but it wasn't for much longer. In an hour or so the party would surely begin to wind down and they'd be done, and then she and Finn would head upstairs and with any luck start burning up his one thousand thread-count sheets properly.

And, quite frankly, she couldn't wait.

CHAPTER NINE

THERE WAS SOMETHING different about Georgie tonight, Finn thought, watching through narrowed eyes as she chatted and laughed with a small group of guests. And it wasn't just the way she looked, although that was pretty magnificent. The dress she had on was strapless and tight, knee-length and of a forest-green velvety sort of fabric, the kind of dress he wanted to peel off her with his teeth. Nor was it the relaxed ease with which she interacted with people, which reminded him of the vibrant, sexy woman he'd originally met.

Over the last couple of weeks, that Georgie, the one he recognised, had showed increased signs of returning, and he was glad for her sake. And also his, if he was being honest. They might not be having full sex—slightly frustrating although completely understandable—but what they did get up to blew his mind every time. She was so responsive. So enthusiastic. A fascinating and inventive distraction, and just what he'd needed, in fact. Again. Because, what with work and Josh and her, he'd barely had time to think about the progress his investigation agency wasn't making. Nor did he have the head space to continue to mentally rage at Jim and Alice.

The tension that had been gripping him for what felt like decades had begun to lessen and life had become marginally easier in other respects too. While many of the circumstances surrounding his adoption remained painfully confusing, some of the chaos seemed to be settling. He was no longer short with his colleagues and subordinates. He scowled less and his behaviour had become less unpredictable. Only yesterday he'd made a snap decision without even having to think about it, and he was one hundred per cent certain that this was all down to the release he found with Georgie.

Tonight, however, frustratingly, that tension was back. Georgie might look unbelievably beautiful and achingly hot but she kept smiling to herself and drifting off into her own little world, which he found deeply unsettling. He couldn't work out what might have put that sparkle of mischief in her eyes. It couldn't have been the interlude in the car when he hadn't been able to resist touching her. Hours had passed since then. So what was it? He didn't know and he hated it.

But he wouldn't remain in the dark for much longer, he assured himself, his jaw tight. He'd had enough of trying to second guess what Georgie may or may not be planning. All evening he'd been in work mode, ruthlessly focused on the launch, but now the party was coming to an end and he was getting answers.

Taking her elbow and muttering their excuses, he drew her away from the throng and manoeuvred her behind one thick, towering pillar, into the shadows and out of the sight of prying eyes. He backed her up against it, pressed himself close, and she didn't seem to mind.

'What are you up to?' he murmured, planting one hand on the pillar beside her head while wondering where on her body to put the other.

She arched an eyebrow in a way that sent darts of desire shooting through him and smiled up at him coyly. 'What makes you think I'm up to anything?'

'You have a look about you.'

'What kind of a look?'

'As if you're keeping a secret.'

'Maybe I am.'

'I don't like secrets,' he muttered, deciding that high on the curve of her waist with access to the lower side of her breast would be a good place for his hand. He ran his thumb over the soft swell there and the pulse at the base of her neck fluttered.

'You'll like this one,' she said, her voice husky and her eyes darkening.

'What is it?'

'You'll see.' Her gaze dropped to his mouth and he heard her breath catch. 'Are we done here?'

'Nearly.'

'Because I think we should go upstairs. Now.'

'Why?'

'I've recently thought of something else we can try. Something new.'

His pulse thudded heavily and heat infused every inch of him. Something else? Wasn't what they'd already done enough? Was she trying to kill him? 'Like what?' he asked, his body hardening unbearably.

Without taking her eyes off his, she opened her bag, took something out and pressed it into his hand. He glanced down and saw a condom packet in his palm and his heart lurched. 'What's this?'

'Do you really need me to explain?'

Yes, as a matter of fact. 'I thought sex was off the table.'

'It was. But I've reconsidered. I realised this afternoon that it's all about the timing.'

'Which is now?'

She gave a nod. 'It is. And it will be for a couple of days.'

A couple of days? Halle-bloody-lujah. 'Are you sure?'

'Very much so.'

'Then we're going to need a lot more than one.'

'I bought out the pharmacy.'

She was truly unbelievable. 'You know what?' he muttered, practically passing out with the strength of the need now drumming through him. 'I think we're done here.'

To Finn's intense frustration, however, leaving the party took a while. As he strode towards the exit, just about resisting the temptation to drag Georgie along behind him and instead maintaining a civilised although determined speed, people kept coming up to him wanting to chat. Infuriatingly, no one seemed to be deterred either by the electricity he knew was rolling off him or the curtness of his replies. How he managed to refrain from telling everyone to move the hell out of his way so he could get upstairs and ravish the woman at his side he had no idea. The five minutes during which they had to stop and pose for a series of press photographs were quite possibly the longest of his life.

By the time they made it into the lift Finn's jaw was tight and he ached all over with the effort of restraint. Once inside, Georgie took up a position on one mirrored side of the car and he leaned against the opposite wall. Any closer and he might not be able to wait for privacy. He didn't even trust himself to speak, just kept his hand in his pocket, touching the condom, as if not doing so might make it a figment of his imagination. But he didn't take his eyes off her and she didn't stop looking at him, their gazes and their bodies communicating in a way that rendered words unnecessary.

Time passed agonisingly slowly, the space between them filling with tension and vibrating with need, but eventually the lift arrived at their floor. The minute the doors whooshed open, Finn grabbed Georgie's hand and strode towards their room. As soon as he got her inside he had her up against the door and in his arms, their mouths meeting in a hot clash of teeth and tongues that went on and on until his head emptied of everything but her and the clawing need to be inside her.

He ran his hands down her body, moulding them to her shape while she tugged furiously at his shirt. At the feel of her hands on the skin of his back he shuddered and for a moment wanted to pause and revel in her touch, but he wasn't to be distracted. Nothing was going to stop him from ridding of clothes the parts of her he wanted naked.

When he reached her mid-thigh and the fabric of her dress had some give he bunched it in his fists and shoved it up. With a soft, encouraging moan that turned him to granite she edged her legs apart and pushed her hips forwards. He skimmed his hand over the delicate lace of her knickers and she gasped, and when he slipped his fingers beneath the thin waistband her breathing became shallow, her breasts heaving against the restrictive bodice of her dress.

'You're so hot,' he muttered. 'So wet.'

'Stop talking,' she panted.

'No foreplay?'

'Haven't we had enough of that already?'

'More than enough.'

'Then hurry. I'm not sure how much longer I can wait and I *really* want you inside me when I come.'

The desperation he could hear in her voice stoked his desire like a can of petrol being tossed on a bonfire, and the flames raged within him. Shaking slightly, he eased away to yank his trousers and shorts off and roll the condom on while she pushed her knickers down and kicked them to one side. And then he was back in front of her, wrapping his hands around the backs of her thighs and lifting her up.

Their gazes locked as he thrust up and she pushed down, and he saw something hot and unidentifiable flare in the depths of her eyes before she closed them with a soft, ragged groan. Her head thudded against the door as she dropped it back and he couldn't help moving.

Driven on by an urgency and total lack of control he'd never felt before, Finn buried his head in her neck and pulled out of her and then thrust back in, as deep as he could go. He did it again and again, harder and faster, until she was clinging on to his shoulders, her legs tight around his waist, her breath coming in short, sharp pants as she muttered little cries of, 'Oh, God, yes.'

And then suddenly he could feel his orgasm rush towards him with the speed and force of a tsunami and he was too far gone to hold back. Everything inside him tightened, the pressure coiling in his groin so intense that it almost hurt. And when, with a cry, Georgie shattered, trembling in his arms and convulsing around him, he thrust one last time, hard and deep, and erupted as the pleasure hit and spun through him like a starburst.

How long he spent slumped against her in the quiet darkness, his heart thundering in time with hers, he had no idea. After what could well have been the most intense experience of his life, he wasn't capable of thought, much less reason. All he could do was drop his forehead to hers, his breathing harsh and his control in pieces, and whisper, 'You are incredible.'

The following morning when she woke, Georgie stretched and grinned like the cat who'd got the cream, or a woman whose body had been put to thoroughly good use.

Muscles deep inside her ached. She felt all soft and languid and buzzy. Last night had been brilliant. She hadn't realised how frustrating not having full sex had been, but it had clearly been very frustrating indeed, because with the flourishing of that condom she'd unleashed a beast in both of them that had kept going until the early hours of the morning, when they'd both collapsed into a sated, sleepy tangle of sheets. Hard and fast, soft and sensuous, on the bed, in the shower, they'd done it all...

But it wasn't just the mind-blowing sex that had made the night so amazing. It was the realisation she'd just come to that, after months of darkness, there was finally light. Everything was falling into place and, to her giddy relief and delight, the shadows were fading and it felt as if *she* was back.

And, while she didn't know about being incredible, she certainly felt invincible right now, which was in no small part down to the man stretched out beside her, who was sliding a hand down her body and doing a very good job of making her forget everything but him and her and the way he made her physically feel.

Or, rather, attempting to.

Because she wasn't quite so addled with desire that she'd forget about her son.

'I should call Mrs G and see how Josh is,' she murmured, determinedly ignoring the heat beginning to wind through her and reluctantly trying to ease away from him.

'He'll be fine,' Finn muttered against the sensitive skin of her neck that he was nuzzling as he clamped his hands on her hips to hold her still and then rolled over to pin her to the bed. 'I, on the other hand, am not,' he said, his eyes dark with need as he looked down into hers. 'I'm in pain.'

'You're insatiable.'

'That would make two of us, then.'

'A good mother would prioritise her son over sex.'

'You are a good mother.'

'You have to be kidding,' she said, staring up at him in disbelief. 'I've been a terrible mother.'

'Rubbish.'

'Have you forgotten how Josh and I came into your life?'

'You were ill.'

'Doesn't matter.'

Clearly realising that sex wasn't happening, although to his credit he didn't emit so much as a whisper of a resigned sigh, Finn lifted himself off her and lay on his side, propping himself up on his elbow beside her instead.

'Of course it does,' he said, with such certainty that she was almost convinced. 'How's he doing?'

She thought about her happy little boy and the way his tiny, chubby arms lifted up and reached for her when she walked into the room. About how, when she lifted him up, he actually snuggled into her. Josh's well-being couldn't *all* be down to Finn and Mrs Gardiner, could it?

'OK, so maybe I'm not so bad *now*,' she said as a different kind of warmth stole through her, 'but before...'

'Remember your bedsit?'

A picture of peeling paint and threadbare carpet flashed into her head and at the back of her throat she thought she could taste a trace of damp. 'I'd rather not,' she muttered with a shudder, pulling the sheet up to dispel the flurry of goosebumps.

'You weren't going to let me take Josh without you.'

'Well, no, but—'

'Trust me. You're doing fine. And you're around,' he added. 'Which is a plus.'

A shadow flitted across the lean lines of his face and her heart twanged in her chest. 'How did you cope without your mother?'

'I have no idea.'

'But you did.'

'Of course.'

Oh, to have his confidence, she thought wistfully. To not be in doubt about anything or anyone. She'd never met anyone so sure of himself and it was hard not to envy him. 'I was so jealous of you, you know,' she said, shooting him a quick smile.

'When?' he asked with a faint frown.

'Those first few days after we came to stay. When I walked into your kitchen the morning after we arrived and found you feeding Josh so adeptly. There was a time when I couldn't work out which bottle to use or how to mix formula. And then later, being with him, playing with him… You just automatically seemed to know what you were doing and I resented that.'

'Believe me, I didn't.'

'Really?'

'I've never had such a steep learning curve.'

Oh. 'Weirdly, that's good to know. It's easy to assume everyone else has it sorted while you feel like you're floundering, and I floundered more than most for what felt like the longest time.'

'What happened once you got to hospital, Georgie?'

A chill ran through her and she shivered. 'You don't want to know.'

'I do.'

Hmm, that was all very well, but what purpose would it serve either of them? She could see no advantage in rehashing the past. Much of it, blessedly, she couldn't even remember.

And, while sharing might have been recommended as therapy, as far as she could see she was doing perfectly well without it. 'Why?'

'I want to know everything about you.'

Oh.

Well.

That was different, then, she thought, her heart slowly turning over as she scoured his eyes, looking for signs of flippancy and finding none. That was shifting this…whatever this was…to another level. And as her heart melted and her resistance evaporated, quite suddenly she wanted to tell him. She wanted him to tell him everything. She didn't want anything to remain between them. He could handle it. He'd handled everything so far with rock-solid strength and complete equanimity, and she rather thought that, even if they hadn't been legally joined, he'd stick it out. She'd trusted him with her body. Surely she could trust him with her secrets.

'It's not pretty,' she warned, nevertheless scarcely able to believe she was going to open the door for him on what had been for her the darkest of times.

'I won't judge.'

'If you did, you'd find me guilty.'

'None of it was your fault.'

'I know that, but that doesn't lessen it.' She

swallowed hard to ease the tightness in her throat and took a deep breath. 'I never mentioned how I ended up in hospital in the first place, did I?'

'No.'

'While I was staying with Carla and everything started to fall apart, not only did I begin to behave erratically and have delusions, but I also found myself beginning to really resent Josh. I started to believe that his arrival had ruined everything and...' She paused, momentarily unable to continue, hating herself for what she was about to reveal but reminding herself that it had been a symptom of her illness. 'I didn't want him,' she finished shakily. 'I fantasised about how much easier things would be without him. I became obsessed with leaving him somewhere like outside the hospital and just walking away. One night I even got as far as the bus stop.'

'What happened?'

'Carla showed up and when I told her I was going to the hospital said she'd take me herself. Only when we arrived she had me sectioned.'

'That must have been distressing,' he said, his voice gruff.

'It was. I sort of knew that it was the right thing to be doing but I also hated her for it.

The diagnosis that followed was a double-edged sword. On the one hand it was a relief to know there was an explanation for what I was doing and thinking and feeling, but on the other it was a struggle to make sense of it all.' She shook her head and frowned. 'I was supposed to be so *together*. Something like that was never supposed to happen to me. And then it got worse.'

'How?' he asked, his gaze darkening with a concern that heated the chill in her blood and eased the pain of her memories.

'I naively assumed that when it began, the treatment would instantly sort everything out and I'd be better. But it didn't. I was all over the place. For days I'd feel full of energy and be buzzing, convinced that I was doing fantastically. I clearly remember a week or so when my thoughts zipped along, hopping from one to another at incredible speed, and it was so exhilarating to be able to think so fast and so brilliantly. But then I'd suddenly crash to unbelievable lows. I had the most unimaginably horrible hallucinations.'

'About what?'

'Death,' she said. 'My death mainly. I kept having visions of a bunch of doctors and nurses decked out in scrubs and face masks approaching my bed in order to lift me off and put me into the coffin that sat beside it.'

'My God,' he murmured, visibly blanching.

'I did warn you it wasn't pretty,' she said, watching his jaw tighten and his Adam's apple bob as he fought for...well...something. 'The periods in between were filled with the many anxieties I had over Josh. Because of the medication I was on I couldn't breastfeed him. I couldn't interact with him most of the time and I became obsessively worried about how that was going to affect him. Like how he wasn't going to achieve his milestones and things because I wasn't capable of teaching him anything. How badly I was letting him down. I was also terrified I was going to in some way harm him. Or myself.'

'But that never happened.'

'No.'

'It never would have happened.'

'I have to think not,' she said, determined to believe it. 'Eventually the medication kicked in and suppressed the mania but even that wasn't easy to deal with because it put me in a fog of nothingness which was almost as horrible as what had gone on before. At least then I had the ups.' She fell back against the pillows and gave a sigh of regret and sorrow. 'Looking back, I don't recognise any part of myself. I have no idea who I was. I totally lost me and that makes me sad because I'll never be the person I was before again, and I rather liked her. She was fun and fearless. I'm not even sure who I am now.'

'Josh knows who you are,' he said with quiet conviction.

'That's what the doctors told me. It's taken a while to believe it myself. And to believe that I will be, that I *am*, OK.'

'Are you?'

'I think so,' she said, casting him a small smile. 'But I've been here before. A relapse isn't out of the question. And I worry about getting depression. I've been warned that women who've had post-partum psychosis can end up with bipolar disorder.'

'If any of that happens, I'll be there to catch you. I'll keep you safe.'

He would, wouldn't he? 'Thank you.'

'I should be the one thanking you,' he said gruffly. 'But in all honesty I really don't know what to say.'

'Then why don't you kiss me instead?'

'That I can do.'

He reached out and wrapped a hand around the back of her neck as she moved towards him, and captured her mouth in a soft, soul-stealing kiss that slowly swept away the memories and the anguish and replaced them with a rush of heat and want.

'I'm sorry,' he murmured when they broke for breath.

'What for?'

'Not being there for you.'

'You couldn't have known.'

'The morning after the night we met, just before you left, I was going to suggest we exchange numbers.'

Her eyes widened. 'Were you?'

'I thought about asking you to dinner.'

'Did you? Why?'

'I liked you.'

'It was just sex.'

'No, it wasn't.'

She had to agree, and when she fleetingly thought about what could have been if only she'd had his number her heart squeezed with regret. 'Hindsight is pointless,' she said quietly. 'That me doesn't exist anymore.'

'Yes, she does.'

'She's battered and bruised.'

'She's brave and resilient and stronger than anyone I've ever met.'

God, someone should bottle him. 'I bet you say that to all the girls.'

'You'd be surprised,' he murmured. 'And in

any case, there hasn't been anyone else since I first met you a year and a half ago.'

For a moment she just stared at him. 'Are you serious?'

'Why would I lie?'

A good point. 'Why not?'

'It's been a turbulent time.'

'Your father's illness?'

He hesitated and sympathy tugged at her heart.

'You don't have to talk about it if you don't want to.'

'I would if I could,' he said, looking utterly, hopelessly tortured.

'But you can't so you shan't?'

'Something like that.'

'Too raw?'

He nodded and his eyes filled with bleakness. 'Shattering. In so many ways.'

Overwhelmed with the need to comfort him, to ease his torment in any way she could, Georgie shifted and rolled him onto his back, sliding her hand down the hard planes of his body and watching as the distress in his expression slowly disappeared.

'What happened to needing to know that Josh is OK?' he said, his voice thick with growing desire.

'We'll definitely call,' she said, giving him a slow smile. 'But later.'

It was quite a bit later when they finally made that call. Shortly afterwards, with great reluctance, Finn dragged himself out of bed and headed off for a meeting with the hotel management, which he had a feeling was going to be a challenge, when all he could think of was Georgie and how she continued to blow his mind.

She might not know who she was, but he did, and he was in awe. He'd never met anyone so insanely tough yet so unbelievably soft. So doggedly determined yet at times so achingly vulnerable. So generous and giving and fearless. Not of the struggles she'd had—those merited every bit of fear she'd felt—but of facing up to them. The way she was able to work through hugely difficult, personal, emotional topics and talk about them was staggering.

How did she *do* that? he wondered as he stepped into the lift and hit the ground floor button. Where did she find the strength to acknowledge her problems and confront them, her shoulders back and head high? He'd never figured out how to achieve any of that. Give him a complex strategic issue and he was all over it. Impossible deals and intransigent planning departments, no problem. A massive upheaval to his personal life, however, with all the tumultuous emotions that came with it, and he fell apart. After everything Georgie had told him about her experiences in hospital, he couldn't even talk about how he felt about Jim's death. He didn't know where to start.

Maybe he ought to ask her for tips. Maybe he ought to open up to her. A little. Because he might as well admit it, he thought, striding through Reception and walking into the meeting room, where a dozen of his staff shot to their feet, it wasn't just sex that had made his life less tense and stressful and somehow better over the last couple of weeks. It was her.

CHAPTER TEN

GEORGIE WHILED AWAY the hours Finn was out mostly by wafting around the suite and reflecting on her Parisian adventure so far, starting with the sex, which had surpassed her wildest expectations, and she'd had a fair few. The night they'd met had been scorching, but now... Well, now, in addition to the red-hot physical chemistry, there was knowing and feeling and, dare she say it, *liking*.

What would have happened if he *had* taken her number that morning? she wondered as she lathered up in the shower and tingled at the memory of Finn's hands on her body. Would they have dated? Would he have somehow noticed what she'd failed to? Could her pregnancy have been as it should have been? It was a pointless exercise if ever there was one, but that didn't stop her imagination playing out the various scenarios or her heart squeezing in response.

Conversely, what if she *hadn't* found him the evening she'd gone looking for him? She liked to think that she'd have muddled through somehow and that she and Josh would have been all right, but life was so much richer, so much brighter for having Finn in it.

Reliving the harrowing details of her stay in hospital had been agonisingly difficult, but ultimately she was glad she'd told him everything. She had no secrets left now and nothing more to hide, and, while she'd taken a massive risk and made herself incredibly vulnerable, she had no doubt that he'd take care of what she'd given him. Not only was he the sexiest man she'd ever met, he was also the most patient and the most understanding.

And then there were the glimpses of his soul that she caught through the tiny cracks that appeared in his armour from time to time. Beneath his brusque and aloof exterior lay a seething mass of emotion, she was sure. The issues he clearly had surrounding the death of his father made her heart wrench every time she recalled how desolate and devastated he'd looked, lying there next to her.

He was everything she could possibly ask for in a co-parent or a lover yet the things she found most attractive about him had nothing to do with Josh or his devastating looks and wicked bedroom skills and everything about who he fundamentally was. He took his responsibilities seriously. His support was steadfast. She had no doubt she would always be able to depend on him.

Little wonder, then, that she was beginning to fall for him.

And, as if all that wasn't enough to make her heart melt like butter over heat, Finn was now feeding her. When he'd returned from his meeting he'd announced that he was taking her out to lunch and told her to hop to it.

It was a glorious spring day so they'd walked, taking in the gardens and the parks and lingering in the Jardin des Tuileries, before being seated on the terrace of the fanciest restaurant she'd ever been to. While a string quartet nearby played something light and uplifting Finn tucked into a plate of seabass and she tried not to devour her delicious seared tuna too greedily.

The weekend was turning out to be as wonderful and romantic as Georgie had imagined, maybe even more so, and she was so overwhelmed by it that she thought she'd best stick to business before she did something unwise like tell him how she was beginning to feel about him.

'So, was the launch considered to be a success?' she asked, putting her fork down on her empty plate and taking a sip of crisp chilled Chablis in an effort to appear cool and collected.

'Yes.'

'Is anything you do *not* a success?'

He flashed her a quick smile that set off fireworks in the pit of her stomach. 'Rarely.'

'And again, I envy you,' she said with a sigh.

'Why?'

'It feels like a long time since anything I did was successful.'

'Not from where I'm sitting,' he said, giving a nod of thanks to the waiter who cleared their table, then sitting back and eyeing her thoughtfully. 'You know, we're very similar, you and I.'

She felt her eyebrows shoot up. Seriously? Finn was a put-together billionaire who knew exactly who he was and where he was going. She was still a bit of a mess who knew next to nothing about anything. She could see no similarity whatsoever. 'Are we?' she said sceptically. 'How?'

'We're both survivors.'

'I suppose,' she said, although she still didn't really know enough about him to judge.

'But that's not all. We're both determined.

Both ambitious. We've both come a long way and done it with little outside support.'

Hmm. 'Well, I might have been all that once upon a time,' she conceded, wondering whether that might be why she felt such a strong sense of recognition whenever she looked at him. 'But I'm not sure about now.'

'You will be again.'

'Not in the field of law,' she said, nevertheless warmed by his belief in her. 'My career in that is pretty much over, I suspect. I was sectioned. I haven't looked into it but it wouldn't surprise me if that didn't disqualify me from practising. And I doubt I'd get a glowing reference from my last company anyway.'

'Want me to take them on?'

'Why not?' she said with a grin.

'I mean it.'

Her grin faltered and her heart gave a great thump. 'Would you do that?'

'All you have to do is say the word and they're history.'

As if she needed a reminder of his power and influence or another reason to fall a little bit more in love with him. 'Thank you, but no.'

'Sure?'

'Yes.'

'Shame.'

'I'll figure something out workwise,' she said, forcing herself to focus on something other than how giddy she felt at having someone on her side for possibly the first time in her life, at being part of a team. 'Maybe I'll retrain and do something to help people who are going through what I did. I had amazing care. I'd like to give something back. Maybe I could fundraise or something.'

'Let me know what I can do to help.'

He already had, more than he could possibly know. 'I will,' she said with a smile.

His gaze dropped to her mouth then, his eyes darkening in a way that never failed to render her hot and breathless. 'Let's have dessert back at the hotel,' he said, and called for the bill.

Quite some time later, as Georgie lay sprawled across the bed, unable to move for lazy lethargy, it occurred to her that the thing that had been bubbling away inside her all day, filling her with light and hope, was happiness. She was happy. Actually happy. Her confidence and self-esteem were soaring and it felt as though her demons were finally in retreat, which only went to show how very good for her Finn was.

She'd had the best day, and now, as she listened to the sound of the shower and contemplated joining him in it, she couldn't help wondering if there was anything stopping them from turning this relationship that had started for the benefit of Josh into one that also benefited them. Because not only was she happy, but Finn too seemed remarkably content with the way things were. He was certainly less stressed and more relaxed than he'd been a month or so ago.

They appeared to be on the same wavelength and there was lust and there was trust and possibly even the beginnings of love, so who knew? Their relationship could go anywhere, and she cautiously examined the heart-thumping idea that the tight, stable, supportive family unit she'd always longed for might actually be within her grasp for the first time in her life.

Closing her eyes, she tried envisaging it, and it wasn't that hard because her common sense was no match for the allure of that which she craved deep inside. Within minutes she had herself and Finn and Josh living in a gorgeous house in the country filled with laughter and lust and love in a place where it was perpetual summer and the birds didn't stop singing.

It was a heady, if utterly unreal, bubble and one that kept expanding preposterously until it abruptly burst when Finn's phone started buzzing its way across the bedside table. The phone fell to the floor before she could reach it, but she leaned down to pick it up anyway, and as she did so, out of the corner of her eye, she caught sight of the caller.

Osborne Investigations.

The name sparked something in the dusty recesses of her memory.

What was it?

Hmm…

Oh, yes.

The night he'd scooped her and Josh up and whisked them to his hotel. The night she'd been left with no option but to tell him where she'd been and what she'd been doing because if she hadn't he'd have had an investigating agency on to it so fast it would make her head spin.

That was it.

But what could Finn possibly need investigating? she wondered, replacing his phone on the bedside table and lying back against the pillows. Was it something to do with work? A person? A company? Or something else entirely? It was none of her business, of course, yet she couldn't help but be curious. She was curious about everything to do with him.

'Why do you have an investigation agency working for you?' she asked when he emerged from the bathroom in a cloud of steam and a fluffy white towel wrapped around his hips, a sight she didn't think she'd ever tire of.

He visibly tensed, and all the little hairs at the back of her neck stood up in response to the conclusion that she was on to something interesting. 'Why do you ask?'

'Your phone vibrated and then fell on the floor, so I picked it up. Their name was on the screen.'

He went even stiller and seemed to pale. 'Did you answer it?'

'Of course not.'

'When did they ring?'

'About a minute ago.'

'Right.' He tossed the towel onto the bed and, to her disappointment, since it clearly meant that some more of that lovely, head-board-banging sex was temporarily off the agenda, spun away to don a pair of jeans and a shirt.

'Well?' she prompted.

'Excuse me,' he muttered distractedly as he strode to the bedside table and grabbed his phone. 'I need to return that call.'

* * *

With the last twenty-four hot, intense and strangely perturbing hours instantly wiped from his mind, Finn stalked out of the bedroom, across the hall, and into the sitting room. He closed the door behind him with deliberate control, his gut churning and his pulse racing. Alexandra Osborne called him once a week, same time, same day, regardless of whether she'd made progress, and Sunday evening at six—or five p.m. back home—was neither that day nor that time.

Beginning to pace up and down, he located the missed call and returned it, and when she answered said, 'What do you have for me?'

'You might want to sit down,' she replied without preamble.

He drew to an abrupt halt and dropped into the nearest available chair. 'Go ahead.'

'Early last week one of the leads we've been working on finally came good.'

'In what way?'

'It's been established that your adoptive parents visited Argentina six months after you were born. They went on their own and returned with you.'

The world skidded to a standstill and his heart gave a great lurch. Argentina? What the hell?

'My contact managed to trace their movements while they were there,' Alex continued while Finn grappled for calm and forced himself to focus, 'and placed them in La Posada.'

'Which is what?'

'A small, abandoned village near the border with Bolivia. It consists mainly of a derelict orphanage and a handful of ruined houses. While most of it was looted years ago, the office of the orphanage had barely been touched, quite probably because the filing cabinets had been bolted to the walls. In amongst the papers they contained he found a number of birth certificates. We believe one of them to be yours.'

His lungs tightened. A punch of adrenaline kicked him in the chest and his pulse raced. 'How can you be sure?'

'The recorded date of birth is a match.'

'Does it have the names of the parents?'

'Yes. Juan Rodriguez and Maria Gonzalez. I'll email you a copy of everything we have. I apologise for it taking so long. The trail has been extremely well buried. We're still working on why that would be the case.' Alex paused, while Finn reeled, then said, 'There's something else.'

'What?'

'Are you still sitting down?'

'Yes.'

'There were two other birth certificates in the same file. Both boys. All of you born at around the same time on the same day.'

It took a second or two for the implication of what she was saying to sink in, but when it did the ground beneath his feet tilted violently. His vision blurred and he could hardly breathe. He felt as if he was about to pass out. 'I have brothers?'

'It would appear so. The evidence would suggest you're triplets.'

'Where are they? Are they alive?'

'Impossible to know at this stage.'

'Find them,' he said, his voice thick and his throat clogging. 'Whatever you have to do, however much you have to pay, find them.'

'We will.'

Finn ended the call and as the phone slipped out of his hand and fell to the floor, the calm front he'd presented to Alex shattered. Every bit of him started shaking. His heart was beating too fast. His stomach was roiling. He was going to throw up.

Blindly, he got to his feet and made it to the terrace doors, which he threw open, and gulped in some much needed air while the information he'd just been given went round and round in his thoughts.

He'd been born in South America. He'd spent time in an orphanage. He had parents, brothers, was one of a set of triplets. Identical? Non-identical? What had happened to the other two? Where were they and why had they been separated?

The ping of an incoming message on his phone pierced the fog swirling around in his head and he stumbled back to where he'd been sitting. With trembling fingers he bent down to pick the device up and then collapsed into the chair before his legs gave way. Somehow he managed to unlock it. Somehow he found the right app, tapped the email and, his heart thundering so fast and hard it hurt, opened the attachment.

It contained three birth certificates plus translations. All identical, save the times of birth and the names. Mateo. Diego. Juan. His parents, his brothers, his family.

But which was his? Who was he and where were the others? Above all, *why*? Why the adoption? Why the separation? And who'd known? Had Jim and Alice been aware he was one of three? Surely not. Surely they couldn't have been so cruel as to keep that from him. Yet no one had ever mentioned Argentina. He even had a hotel there. In Buenos

Aires. Jim had been at the opening six years ago and he'd never said a thing.

Having scoured the details and committed them to memory, Finn dropped the phone again, then rubbed his hands across his face and leaned forwards, his elbows resting on his knees, his head buried in his hands. How the hell was he going to deal with this? He'd assumed that with information would come clarity, but he was wrong. That assumption had been based on the most simple of explanations, yet the news Alex had just delivered threw up an explanation that was anything but simple.

Instead of being answered and filed away for cool, calm analysis, the questions were multiplying, ricocheting around his head faster and more chaotically and he couldn't sort any of them out. It was all too huge, too overwhelming.

As was the pain now beginning to slice through him as the shock-induced numbness faded. Thirty-one years he'd lost. Thirty-one years that he could potentially have known his siblings, his brothers. He could have had an entire other life. Would it have been better? Worse? It didn't matter. He'd been denied the choice because of Jim and Alice's silence, and the sense of betrayal that he assumed had abated now flayed him all over again, ripping open old wounds and stabbing at them afresh.

He'd thought he had it all under control, but he didn't. He had nothing under control. The pain powering through him was like a living thing, writhing around in his belly and thundering along his veins, leaving every inch of him raw and exposed and bleeding.

'Are you all right?'

At the sound of Georgie's voice, filled with concern, coming from far, far away, Finn froze. He hadn't heard the door open. He hadn't noticed the shadows lengthening across the floor. She couldn't see him like this, he thought frantically, a cold sweat breaking out all over his skin—weak, vulnerable and suffering, a man on the brink of collapse. He couldn't let her help. He couldn't allow her to push and prod as she was wont to do. It would drive him over the edge.

'Get out,' he said, his voice hoarse and cracked.

'What's happened?' she said, walking into the room and dropping to her knees beside the chair in which he was sitting, crowding his space and his thoughts, too close, too dangerous.

'I said, get out.'

'I know. But you're white as a sheet and shaking. I'm worried about you.'

'I'm fine.'

'Talk to me.'

'It has nothing to do with you,' he said sharply, desperately, seeing her flinch, which only added to his torment.

'Try.'

His strength was failing. His control was unravelling. He didn't have much time. 'No.'

'Yes.'

'All right,' he said harshly, his resistance crumbling beneath the need to get her out of his space before he completely lost it. 'How's this? Last November I discovered that I was adopted at the age of six months and that my entire life has been a lie. Fifteen minutes ago I learned that not only was I born in Argentina and left in an orphanage, but that I also have two brothers. We're triplets. As you may be able to understand, it's quite a lot to take in. I need some time and space to process it. So I'd appreciate it if you would respect that and leave me the hell alone.'

Wow.

Just wow.

For the briefest of moments all Georgie could do was stare at Finn as the frustration and torment rolled off him in waves and engulfed her, the shock of what he'd told her and how brutally he'd delivered it rendering her immobile. She could barely process it. He'd been adopted? He'd just found out he had a family he'd known nothing about? No wonder he was in such a spin.

When she'd seen the man she was in love with hunched over like that, clearly hurting, clearly in pain, her heart had twisted, and even though she hadn't known what was troubling him, she'd just felt a clamouring urge to race over and give him a hug. All she wanted to do was help. Genuinely.

But he didn't want it, she realised, the breath catching in her throat as her chest tightened. He didn't want comfort. He didn't want anything from her, as was clear not only from his words but also from the way he was jerking to his feet, turning away from her and stalking over to the window, a blunt, brutal dismissal that sliced her in two.

To think she'd been worried about him, she thought, her eyes stinging and hurt scything through her as she pushed herself to her feet and took a shaky step back. That all the time she'd spent showering and dressing while the minutes ticked slowly by she'd been wondering whether he was all right. What a waste of time and effort that had been.

He didn't want her and he certainly didn't need her. He probably never had. He was wholly self-contained. And as for the idea that they might be embarking on something resembling a proper relationship, what had she been *thinking*?

There may be lust but there was certainly no trust. Not on his side anyway. He must have been carrying the burden of his adoption for months, and the discovery of it, the uncertainty surrounding his identity, must have been cataclysmic. And he hadn't said a word. She'd told him virtually everything there was to know about her, warts and all, and he'd revealed practically nothing.

Every time he'd asked her something about herself she'd spouted like a fountain. She'd told him things, this morning in particular, that she'd never told anyone, things that she'd only just begun to acknowledge. Yet when the tables were turned and she dared to ask him anything even *remotely* personal he deflected it. She knew next to nothing about his upbringing or his parents or how he felt about any of it. How had she let that happen?

And why had he never told her that he was adopted? He'd told her that he didn't like secrets, but he'd been harbouring a massive one of his own, and on top of everything else that made him a hypocrite. So who else knew? Was she the only one who didn't? Why hadn't he wanted to talk about it with her? What was wrong with her? Was it the state of her mental health? Was that why he'd told her he wanted to know everything about her when they'd been talking this morning? She'd seen his interest as a sign their relationship was shifting to another, more intimate level but perhaps he'd just been looking out for Josh by trying to find out how stable she really was?

They had no relationship and no connection, she realised as she stalked into the bedroom, blinking rapidly to ease the prickling in her eyes, and she'd been a fool to even begin to think otherwise. Everything she'd stupidly imagined they'd shared was entirely one-sided. Even this weekend, which had meant so much to her, would now be nothing more than a permanently tarnished memory.

She'd been falling for an illusion, a man who didn't exist, a man she'd conjured up out of her own imagination because that was what she needed. She'd been delusional, which wasn't a word she used lightly, and worse, naive. What would someone like Finn with his gorgeous looks and confidence and billions in the bank ever see in a woman like her anyway? How could her judgement still be so off?

Well, no more, she thought grimly, grabbing her suitcase and depositing it on the bed. Enough of the imbalance. Enough of being the pathetic, soppy drip she turned into around him. If she didn't want to end up being even more hurt, perhaps even irreparably so, she could afford neither.

Nor was she having her recently rediscovered confidence and self-esteem knocked by Finn and his stick-his-head-in-the-sand attitude. She had to protect herself, although how she was going to do that now that they were civilly partnered and therefore stuck with each other and living in close proximity she had no idea. But she'd think of something. She'd have to.

In the meantime there was no way she was hanging around like a punchbag for all the emotions he must be feeling and clearly couldn't handle. She was packing up and going back to London. Back to her son, who, unlike Finn, *did* need her. And then Finn would have all the space and time to think that he wanted.

CHAPTER ELEVEN

FINN STOOD AT the window and stared blankly onto the streets of Paris stretching out far below, the silence telling him that Georgie had finally done what he'd needed her to do and in the nick of time. Treachery, hurt and sadness had wound their tendrils along every vein and around every cell, and he felt shattered, broken, as though he was being pummelled to within an inch of his life.

He had to calm down, he told himself desperately, forcing himself to take a deep, shuddering breath and loosen his white-knuckled fists. He had to stop. For the sake of his blood pressure and the woman he'd sent away, who was no doubt cursing him with every breath she took. He couldn't go on like this, snapping and snarling in a way he thought he'd long since buried. He'd hated that man. He wouldn't allow himself to regress again.

As he battled to control the pandemonium

churning him up inside, he thought too how he hated the way he'd responded to Georgie's offer of help. How savagely he'd lashed out at her. At the memory of the way in which he'd spoken to her, he inwardly cringed. She'd done nothing to deserve such treatment. All she'd wanted was to help.

And maybe, despite his assertions to the contrary, he needed it. Because he didn't hold much hope of sorting the turmoil out on his own. He didn't exactly have a great track record on that front. He'd bottled up how he'd felt about his mother's death. He'd pushed aside his father's diagnosis initially with alcohol and sex and, subsequently, work. He'd responded to the discovery of his adoption by being unpleasantly short and rude to anyone who had the misfortune of finding themselves in his vicinity.

What he hadn't done was talk about it. Any of it. To anyone. He didn't do talking. He never had done. His father had been the stoical, stiff-upper-lip type, unable to show emotion. Even when Finn's mother had died, he'd hidden his grief behind a wall of impenetrability. As a result, when it came to feelings, Finn had always been self-reliant, a master of internalisation, choosing to box up what he felt so as not to have to deal with the inevitable messy fallout.

Only this morning—God, was it only this morning?—he'd considered perhaps asking Georgie for tips, and if ever there was an occasion to do so, this was it. Who better to talk to? She knew what it was like to stumble around blindly, looking for answers. She knew him. And, more to the point, for some unfathomable reason he *wanted* her to know. They were a team. In this thing, whatever it was, together.

He was under no illusion that it would be easy. It would probably be hell on earth, even assuming that Georgie was receptive to the idea, which was doubtful, given how he'd dismissed her. But it was worth a shot. He had to do *something* that made sense. And at the very least he owed her an apology.

Finally finding a path through the chaos, Finn spun round and strode out of the sitting room and into the bedroom, only to come to an abrupt halt at the sight of Georgie packing a suitcase.

'What are you doing?' he said, his brows snapping together in a deep frown.

She didn't look at him, just carried on folding the stunning green dress she'd worn last night and which he'd peeled off her what felt like a lifetime ago.

'What does it look like?' she said, her voice utterly devoid of the warmth and concern with which she'd asked him what was wrong back there in the sitting room.

'You're packing.'

'Yes.'

'Why?'

'You wanted space. You wanted time. I plan to give you both.'

What? 'I meant I needed a couple of minutes,' he said. 'Ten. Maybe fifteen. I didn't mean for you to leave.'

'Well, there seems little point in hanging around.'

At the realisation that she actually meant it he felt a sharp stab of something to the chest, and for a moment he thought, well, of course she was. Leaving was what people who he cared about or who were supposed to care about him did, after all. But he shoved it aside in order to focus because this was one occasion at least in which he *did* have the power to take control. 'Don't go.'

'Give me one good reason not to.'

'You were right. I think I probably should talk to someone.'

She flung her hairbrush into the case, then

whirled round to scoop up her make-up that was scattered on the dressing table. 'So find a therapist,' she said, dumping it in there too.

'But you're here.'

'Right.'

'Please. I'm sorry for lashing out,' he said, his jaw clenching as he recalled how he'd spoken to her. 'I didn't handle things well.'

'It's fine.'

'It isn't.'

She shrugged. 'You'd had a shock.'

That was an understatement. 'Nevertheless, it's no excuse,' he said gruffly. 'I really am sorry.'

'Apology accepted. Now, if you wouldn't mind…'

'Please, Georgie.'

She must have heard the note of torment in his voice because she stopped what she was doing, *finally*, and gave a great sigh. 'OK, fine,' she said, abruptly sitting on the bed and looking at him, her eyes wary and her expression cool. 'God knows you've had to listen to me prattle on enough.' *Prattle?* he thought with a frown. She did *not* prattle. 'So if you want to talk I'll listen.'

With a rush of relief, Finn stalked into the room and leaned against the edge of the dressing table she'd just cleared. He rubbed his hands over his face and then shoved them into the pockets of his jeans. He cleared his throat and braced himself.

'So it turns out that I find it hard to process big things,' he began, inwardly wincing at how pathetic he sounded. 'Especially big *emotional* things. I have a tendency to lock things down.'

'That's understandable. Although probably not very healthy.'

'No.' It wasn't healthy at all. God only knew the damage he'd caused his nervous system recently. It also smacked of hypocrisy because it had just occurred to him that by withholding the truth from her and obfuscating he'd been behaving like Jim and Alice, which did not sit well.

'Have you always done it?'

He gave a short nod. 'Ever since my mother—Alice—died.'

'That's a long time.'

'Yes.' Too long, with hindsight. 'I bottled up how I felt about that for years. I was only ten. I didn't know what the hell was going on. Jim—my father—or, rather, my adopted father—did the best he could but he wasn't one for emoting either.'

Her eyebrows lifted. 'You didn't talk to anyone? A counsellor? A teacher?'

He shook his head. 'No one. Not until the lid of the pressure cooker flew off when I was a teenager.'

'What happened then?'

'Nothing all that dramatic. I got into a couple of fights when I was sixteen. Spent a night in jail for being drunk and disorderly.'

'And then you had therapy?'

'Of a kind. The officer in charge that night asked what I was thought I was doing and it all came out. She gave me some good advice. The incident turned out to be a huge wake-up call. However, it turns out that internalising things is a hard habit to break.'

'We all have our ways of coping.'

Yes, well, unlike hers, his weren't working out so well. 'Jim's diagnosis was something else I didn't talk about,' he said, forcing himself to keep going because she needed to know everything in order to be able to help.

'Did no one ask?'

'Not many knew. I told the people who did that everything was fine.'

'So how did you find out you were adopted?'

'I was going through Jim's papers after he died. The certificate was in a box that had been stored in the attic of his house.'

'That must have been devastating.'

'It was. I was in the middle of a full-blown identity crisis when you turned up with the news about Josh.'

'No wonder you were so insistent on rescuing him. He's your only flesh and blood.'

'As far as I know.'

She frowned and gave a faint nod. 'Right.'

Unable to bear the intensity of her scrutiny or suppress the restlessness whipping around inside him any longer, Finn pushed himself off the dressing table. 'It's been a disorientating time,' he said, shoving his hands through his hair as he began to pace. 'I feel as if I've been manipulated. As though everything about me has to be redefined and renegotiated. I'm thirty-one. It's been tough trying to work out how much of my life has been real and how much a lie. I can't figure out why Jim never said anything, especially after Alice died, and it's been driving me mad.'

Georgie gave a loud sigh of what sounded like exasperation. 'Oh, for the love of God, will you *please* stop calling them that?' she said heatedly.

Stunned at her tone, wondering where the hell the sympathy he'd been expecting was, Finn came to an abrupt halt and whipped round to stare at her. 'What?'

Her colour was high and her eyes were

blazing and the need that suddenly streaked through him nearly knocked him off his feet. 'Look, Finn, I get that you feel let down and betrayed. And, believe me, I know what it's like to have your whole world turned upside down and your identity stripped away. But Jim and Alice were, to all intents and purposes, your parents.'

He ruthlessly quashed the desire and frowned at her, denial reeling through him. 'I fail to see how.'

'Biology doesn't automatically grant parental rights,' she said bluntly. 'Nor does it guarantee the ability to parent successfully. Look at mine. They're hardly an advert for parents of the year. They never gave a toss about me, not properly, and they still don't. Carla's looked out for me far more than they ever did. She's the reason I was able to find you all those weeks ago. If she hadn't made me send her a photo of you along with your name the night we met, things could have turned out very differently. You had two people who loved and cared for you. And, yes, then, tragically, only one, but nevertheless you had someone on your side for *years*, someone who by your own admission never failed to support and champion you when it mattered most. You honestly don't know how lucky you were.'

'What if my mother's death wasn't an accident?' The question shot out of his mouth before he could stop it and he froze, every muscle in his body as taut as a bow string.

'What do you mean?' she asked carefully and he suddenly found himself on a knife edge.

He could easily deflect the question, he knew, but what would be the point of that? He needed her perspective and her insight into things he couldn't make head or tail of, and that meant unlocking the doors on his greatest concerns and flinging them open, so he took a deep breath and said, 'What if she killed herself deliberately because of me, because of what I was or wasn't?'

He hated the catch he could hear in his voice, but he didn't regret the question because her face softened and, ah, there was the sympathy he'd been in need of. 'Do you really believe that?'

'I don't know.'

'What do you remember of her?'

He scrolled back twenty years, searching for memories that were faded and hazy but nevertheless still there. 'She smelled of roses,' he said eventually. 'She taught me poker and played football with me. Every Saturday she'd bake brownies.'

'She sounds lovely,' Georgie said, a trace of wistfulness flitting across her face.

'She was.'

'Did she make you eat your vegetables?'

'Yes.'

'Make you do your homework and go to bed on time?'

'Yes.'

'Were you ever sent to your room or grounded?'

'Frequently.'

'Then she loved you,' she said with quiet conviction. 'Very much. Take it from someone who knows what it feels like not to matter. They must have wanted you very much too, to go all the way to Argentina to fetch you. And they must have had their reasons for keeping it from you.'

'I guess I'll never know,' he said, his throat oddly tight.

'Unless your investigation agency digs something up.'

'Maybe not even then.'

'So much in life we just have to accept.'

'As I'm discovering.'

'Me too.'

With a strangely sad sort of smile she

pushed herself off the bed and returned her attention to the suitcase, and as he watched her pull the top down and zip it up it hit him like a blow to the chest that, despite everything he'd just revealed, nothing had changed.

'You're still planning to leave?' he asked, the blade of rejection slicing through him like a knife.

'I have to get back to Josh.' She shot him a quick glance, full of something he was too stung, too busy reeling, to identify. 'Unless there's any other reason for me to stay?'

'No, nothing,' he said, coolly, calling himself a fool for wanting her to stay, for thinking that he was good enough for her, for believing that they were in this together. 'Go. Please. Don't let me stop you.'

All she'd wanted was for him to say that he wanted her to stay, thought Georgie numbly as she stepped off the train at St Pancras and, dragging her wheelie case behind her, went in search of a taxi. That they were a team. A tightly knit unit. That she mattered to him as much as he mattered to her, despite her best efforts to deny it.

But he'd let her go with such ease, and that hurt unbelievably badly. So much for thinking that she could somehow avoid more pain, that she could protect herself. Or that she was only beginning to fall for him. She already had. There could be little doubt about it. She had to be head over heels in love with him for his indifferent dismissal to cause this much agony.

But however much it hurt, the pain wouldn't last because that love hadn't been real. Finn wasn't the man she'd thought him to be. She'd given him attributes—loyalty, honesty, integrity—that he didn't have, and really she had no one to blame but herself. She was the one who'd placed him on a pedestal so high and wobbly that it was inevitable he should fall off it. She was the one who'd misread every look and every word, reading things into his actions that simply hadn't been there. This whole mess was entirely her fault.

The train journey from Paris had lasted two and a half hours and every minute of it she'd spent analysing their relationship, such as it was. And she could see now that she'd been a fool. Finn had never wanted her. Not really. All he wanted was Josh. She came as part of the package and was handy for sex, but that was about it.

She knew this to be true because right from the start she'd been the one in the driving seat. In the bar the night they'd first met she'd been the one to approach him, and then the one to proposition him by telling him she wanted to leave, with him. He hadn't chosen her that night. She'd chosen him.

And so it had been ever since.

She'd given him no option but to take up the role of father and provide his support. What else could he have done in the circumstances? How could she have forgotten the reluctance with which he'd taken her in along with Josh? How she'd made him spend his evenings with her and then virtually forced him into going to bed with her by following him into his room the night he'd told her to put on a dressing gown and whipping her top off? Ditto when she'd pressed the condom into his hand at the party last night and told him she wanted sex. He hadn't even planned to take her to Paris. The invitation had been last-minute and he'd only asked her because of what they'd been getting up to after dark.

And then take this evening, when he'd finally opened up to her about how he felt about his parents and the revelations surrounding his adoption. He'd only done that because she was there. Because she was convenient. He hadn't particularly wanted to talk to *her*.

He'd volunteered nothing willingly, she could see now. He obviously didn't see her as an equal in this relationship. Maybe not in anything. They weren't partners in any sense of the word. They were nothing. She was nothing. And so, frankly, what was the point in them continuing with this ridiculous charade?

CHAPTER TWELVE

FINN SPENT THE torturous hours following Georgie's departure railing at himself while ploughing through half a bottle of Scotch. He'd been a fool for telling her everything. He'd made himself insanely vulnerable and unacceptably weak. He'd invested too much in the power of her response, and, unlike any other he'd ever made, that investment had badly backfired. The hurt and disappointment that roared through him when he recalled how carelessly she'd left him were precisely why he didn't share. How could he have forgotten that? At what point had he recklessly decided to ignore what he knew to be true—that other people's behaviour was incalculable and that the only person he could rely on was himself? What had he been thinking?

All in all, he was glad she'd gone. He had a hectic schedule over the next couple of days and he needed to focus. He did not need extra stress and he did not need Georgie. He was perfectly capable of working through everything going on in his head on his own. It might take some time, but he was going to let it play out and eventually he'd get there. He had to obliterate the ridiculous feelings of rejection and abandonment, and regroup.

However, with increasing frequency, he found himself revisiting their conversation, assessing what Georgie had said and stripping the words of emotion. Grudgingly, he came to the conclusion that she'd had a point. Possibly even more than one. Because the truth was that, however hard he looked, however much money he threw at the investigation, he may never get the answers he sought.

So what was he going to do? He couldn't spend the rest of his life being bitter and resentful. He had to accept that he'd become the man he was now because of Jim and Alice, who *had* been his parents in all ways that counted. The memories he had of his mother were warm and happy. The photos they'd taken of him had filled dozens of albums. His father had not once let him down while alive. He'd been an unfailing tower of strength. Only in death had he turned out to have feet of clay. But as neither of them was around to defend or explain their actions and decisions, what had gone before was beyond Finn's control.

How he went forward, however, *was* within his control. Whatever the reasons for his adoption and the subsequent secrecy surrounding it, he had to forgive his parents, his father in particular. He could understand now a paternal determination to protect a child to the exclusion of all else. To not let anything upset the status quo. Whatever else he might think, he had to understand that none of it was anything to do with him and believe it. His parents had done their best and they'd been good people, and Georgie was right: he had been lucky. It was all right to regret that his father had never got to meet Josh and it was all right to resume the grieving process that had been interrupted with the discovery of that certificate.

He had to let it go and focus on the family he did have instead of chasing relentlessly after wisps of the one he may or may not have elsewhere. He had so much to appreciate. So much to value.

Especially Georgie.

Who, despite her apparent rejection, despite his attempts to put her out of his mind, he was missing more than he could have ever imagined. He'd got used to having her around, in his home and in his bed, and he felt her absence like a physical loss. It was more than just the phenomenal sex he missed. He missed her wit and her smile, her wisdom, the way she challenged him and made him face up to things he'd rather ignore, and the conversations that had relaxed and deepened with time. Their relationship might have started out as one of convenience for the sake of Josh but it wasn't any longer. They knew every inch of each other's bodies. And minds. He'd trusted her with his secrets and she'd trusted him with hers, her honesty so raw that it had torn at his soul and filled him with even more burning regret that his support had come so late.

Finn had never been in love before. He'd never even so much as thought about it, so he had nothing with which to compare the feelings that were swirling around inside him, feelings that were so intense, so powerful they couldn't be locked away even if he tried. Nevertheless he was now pretty sure that the way his heart leapt whenever she walked into the room, the unrelenting need, the respect and admiration he had for her, and the hammering desire to protect her and grow old with her met the definition of it. So too did the happiness and sense of rightness that spread through him whenever she entered his head, which was virtually all the time. And when he thought about the shimmering warmth with which he occasionally caught her looking at him and the way her eyes sparkled when she was with him he was equally sure that she felt the same way about him.

Or at least she had done.

Until he'd behaved like an idiot and let her go. Even if he hadn't realised at the time quite why he needed her, he should have come up with a reason for her to stay. As she'd asked. A request, which, now he thought about it, now he could clearly recall how she'd put it, had been made with the answer she wanted in mind. Of course, it was entirely possible that she *had* simply wanted to get back to Josh. But equally, what if she'd wanted something else entirely? What if he'd allowed his insecurities to dominate and had overreacted? What if she hadn't been rejecting *him*, but the abominable way he'd behaved? More importantly, what might have happened if he hadn't let her go?

As Finn strode out of the hotel on Tuesday afternoon and climbed into the car he thought with grim determination that there was only one way to find out whether or not he'd ruined things with Georgie for good. And, since he was now through with boxing up emotion and ignoring it, however difficult, he was going to take it.

Finn had texted her earlier to say that he was on his way home and had given her an ETA, but Georgie, who was sitting cross-legged on the sofa and staring into space, couldn't summon up the energy to care. The last couple of days hadn't been easy. In fact, apart from the time she spent with Josh, they'd been miserable. She felt so cold, so tired. What with all the thinking she'd been doing about her and Finn, she hadn't been sleeping too well, and watching out for Josh, who'd started crawling and was constantly getting to places he shouldn't, was exhausting. This morning she'd barely managed to haul herself out of bed when her son had called for her for the fifth time in as many hours.

Contrary to her expectations, the disappointment and sadness she felt at knowing that the man she'd fallen in love with didn't exist hadn't faded. Everything had worsened and then amalgamated and now thrashed around in the pit of her stomach, giving her no respite. The delirious happiness she'd once thought she felt had been nothing but an illusion. The realisation that the secure, loving

family unit she craved was as distant a possibility as it ever had been was devastating.

Nothing she did alleviated the gloom. She'd
tried writing about how she felt in her journal
but the last two days' pages were blank. She
didn't know where to begin. Going out and
getting some fresh air seemed like a huge effort, so she hadn't bothered. Even venturing
onto the terrace presented a mammoth challenge. She certainly hadn't had the energy to
pack up with Josh and leave, as she'd originally planned. And in any case, where would
she have gone? She could hardly move into
a different hotel room, and Carla would ask
too many questions that Georgie wouldn't be
able to answer. Besides, she and Finn needed
to unpick this disaster of an arrangement and
sooner rather than later.

She fed Josh and changed him and played
with him, but she felt oddly disengaged, as
if she was simply going through the motions.
And, while a tiny part of her recognised that
how she was feeling wasn't normal and was
concerned by it, the greatest part of her was
too drained to pay any attention. Finn would
be back soon anyway, and when he was he
could take over, so she could crawl into bed
and stay there for a month, at which point
maybe they could then talk. In fact, she

thought dully as the sound of the front door opening reached her, here he was now.

She felt the air shift, and glanced up from the journal that was sitting open and empty in her lap to find Finn standing in the doorway and emanating a weird sort of taut determination, his face set and his eyes dark.

'Hi,' he said, removing his jacket and rolling the sleeves of his shirt up with an efficient competency that not so long ago would have had her quivering with desire but now left her distressingly unmoved.

'Hi.'

'How have you been?'

Freezing, actually. But spring could be like that. Maybe she ought to have turned the heating on. 'Fine.'

'Why are you sitting in the dark?' He stalked over to a lamp in the corner and switched it on.

'I didn't realise it was so late,' she said, blinking at the sudden light.

'How's Josh?'

'He's fine. He's asleep.' Finally. 'He started crawling yesterday.'

'Did he? I'm sorry I missed that.'

'He's fast,' she said, attempting a weak smile. 'I envy his energy.'

Finn sat down on the ottoman, leaning forwards and resting his elbows on his knees, and peered at her, his eyes narrowing slightly. 'Are you all right?' he asked. 'You look tired.'

'Josh has another tooth coming through. It's been keeping us both up at night.'

'Where's Mrs Gardiner?'

'I gave her a couple of days off.'

His dark brows snapped together. 'Why?'

'It was her granddaughter's birthday. She lives in Wales. Mrs G was keen to go.' And she'd been keen to have her go because even conversation had started being hard work.

'When is she back?'

'I'm not sure.'

'I'll give her a call later.'

'How were your meetings?'

'Fine,' he said, his gaze locking with hers and not letting it go. 'But I don't want to talk about my meetings.'

Of course he didn't. He didn't want to talk to her about anything. Why would he?

'I want to talk about us.'

Oh, the irony. 'There is no us,' she said, her chest nevertheless squeezing.

He went very still, something she couldn't even begin to identify flickering in the depths of his eyes. 'Do you mean that?'

'Yes.'

'Why?'

'Because you clearly don't trust me.'

His eyebrows shot up. 'What?'

'You don't trust me.'

'Why would you think that?'

She closed the journal with a snap, a sudden hot rush of emotion obliterating the numbness and firing her deadened nerve-endings. 'I told you everything about me, Finn. Everything. Yet every time I asked you anything about your parents or anything even vaguely personal you brushed me aside. You told me nothing. Until you absolutely had no choice.'

'What are you talking about?'

'Your adoption. That huge thing that you didn't think to share with me.'

He stared at her, a tiny muscle in his jaw pulsating. 'I couldn't,' he said gruffly. 'I could barely make sense of it myself. I certainly couldn't have talked about it any sooner than I did. With you or anyone.'

'No one else knows?'

'You're the only person I've told. The only person I *wanted* to know, I've recently realised. You unlocked me in that respect. You made me re-evaluate the past and see things from a different perspective. I don't regret any of that. I do, however, regret how that conversation ended. I'm sorry. I let decades-old hang-ups get the better of me. I was an idiot for letting you leave.'

'If you'd told me that I mattered to you and that we were in this together I'd have stayed.'

A flicker of warmth and something that looked like hope leapt in the depths of his eyes. 'You *do* matter to me and we *are* in this together.'

'Because of Josh.'

His gaze intensified and heated. 'Not entirely.'

No, she thought acidly. It wouldn't do to forget the sex side of things, would it? Or to be careless and ignore the need to protect herself. 'Yes, well, I have regrets too.'

'What do you regret?'

'Everything,' she said with deliberate bluntness. 'Our entire relationship is completely wrong.'

He paled. 'In what way?'

'In every way,' she said. 'Would you have chosen to be with me if it wasn't for Josh?'

'That's a wholly unfair question,' he said, his jaw tightening as a flash of wariness flitted across his face. 'Not to mention impossible to answer.'

Which meant no. And only went to prove her point. 'Right from the beginning I've forced you into doing things you can't possibly have wanted to do.'

'Such as?'

'Being a father. Accommodating me and Josh, me in particular. Giving up your evenings. Taking me to bed. The dinner with friends I made you have. Then Paris. The sex. The talking. You name it, I've made you do it.'

He looked at her as though she'd come from another planet. 'That's ridiculous.'

'Is it?'

'Are you serious?'

'Deadly.'

'I have never done anything even remotely reluctantly in my entire life,' he said, his steady gaze fixed to hers. 'If I want to do something, I do it. If I don't, I don't. If I'd known about Josh sooner I'd have been right there with you every step of the way. The night you came into my room and took off your top I wanted you so badly I was at the end of my tether anyway. I wanted you from the first moment I saw you again. Why do you think I spent so much time out of the apartment when you and Josh first moved in?'

'Work?'

'Not work,' he said darkly. 'I spent every evening in the fitness suite trying to obliterate the need, much good that it did me. If you hadn't come to me that night I would have gone to you. You were just quicker, that's all.' He gave his head a quick shake and then rubbed his hands over his face. 'I didn't deliberately delay us having dinner with friends, although I will admit to wanting you to myself for a while longer. And I didn't need to take you with me to Paris. I've never taken anyone to Paris. Or anywhere else, for that matter. I didn't even need to be there myself. I don't usually. I prefer to stay in the background and let my extremely efficient PR company take care of that side of things.'

She swallowed hard, torn between wanting to believe him and not wanting to believe him. 'So why did you?'

He looked at her for a moment, as if the question had taken him by surprise. 'I wanted to show you my hotel,' he said with a faint smile. 'I wanted to show you off.'

'Not for the sex?'

'We weren't having it then. But I admit there may have been an element of that too. It had been a while.'

'Why didn't you call me?'

'When?'

'At any point over the last forty-eight hours. It occurred to me that you might be busy thinking about your other family.'

'I wasn't. I spent the hours I wasn't in meetings processing the grief for my father that was interrupted when I found that certificate. And then thinking about what you said, how right you were and trying to figure it all out in my head. Would you have answered if I had called?'

'Possibly not,' she had to admit.

He leaned forwards and peered at her closely, confusion swirling in the depths of his eyes, a deep frown creasing his forehead. 'What's going on, Georgie? Where is all this coming from?'

Wasn't it obvious? It was all coming from him. From their situation. From his lack of trust and her crushing disappointment that he wasn't the man she'd desperately wanted him to be. From the realisation that they had no relationship outside parenting Josh and never would. From his shattering of her heart and the subsequent fracturing of her dreams.

Or was it?

Finn was still staring at her, his gaze clear and unwavering, as if he was trying to see into her soul, his presence about the only solid thing she could fix on. And through the fog of nothingness in her head, there was a spark of…something.

Light.

Clarity.

A seed of doubt planted itself in her head,

its roots spreading fast and wide. That tiny voice of concern grew louder. And as fragments of what Finn had been saying spun through her thoughts, solidifying, gaining credence, gaining volume, those doubts exploded and she went icy cold.

Oh, God.

What if all this had come not from him but from *her*? From her insecurities, from her illness? What if this was the setback, possibly even the depression, she'd been fearing?

As she frantically analysed everything that had happened over the last couple of days, the way she'd been feeling, the suspiciousness, the hopelessness and the sadness, her heart began to race and a cold sweat broke out all over her skin.

She was right in the middle of it, she realised with a sickening jolt. One tug of the rug from beneath her feet, one toss of the sea and she'd tumbled into a return of the paranoia, a deadening lack of energy, of libido, and icy numbness.

That was all it had taken.

She wasn't better, she thought as a shaft of agony and despair cut through her and she began to tremble all over. She wasn't anywhere near better. She may never be. And it was crucifying.

'I'm sorry, I can't do this,' she said, her throat tight and her eyes stinging.

'Can't do what?'

'Whatever it is you think we're doing.'

His dark gaze didn't leave hers, but it did nothing to calm the distress suddenly whirling around inside her. 'I think we're building a relationship,' he said. 'A real relationship.'

'We aren't,' she said hoarsely. Even if he *was* the man she'd thought he was—and God, she didn't know which version to believe any more—they couldn't be. She wasn't capable of it. She wasn't strong enough. She didn't know if she ever would be. 'We never have been.'

'I disagree. Our civil partnership stopped being a pragmatic arrangement weeks ago. If it ever was in the first place.' He stopped and took a deep breath. 'I love you, Georgie.'

As the words hit her brain a bolt of panic shot through her, denial screaming at her. 'No.'

'Yes,' he said, his eyes suddenly blazing with a heat that only emphasised how cold and confused she felt. 'I am head over heels in love with you.'

How could he be when even she didn't know who she was anymore? 'You don't know me.'

'I do. I know exactly who you are. And I think you love me too.'

That was what she'd thought once too but now she didn't know what to think. 'I don't know you.'

'You know me better than anyone.'

'Even if I could believe that, even if you're right, I can't be what you want,' she said, her voice breaking. How could she possibly lumber him with her when she was like this? How fair on him would it be if she had a setback every time he did or said something unexpected? How long would it be before they were both walking on eggshells, communicating only about their son?

'Yes, you can. You already are.'

'Do you want more children?'

'Not if you don't.'

'I don't believe you.'

'OK, maybe I would like Josh to have siblings,' he said. 'Maybe I would like to be part of a bigger family. But there's surrogacy. Or, dare I say it, adoption?'

He'd already thought that far ahead? 'I'm sorry,' she said, growing cold with fear and desperation. 'I can't handle this right now. It's all too much.'

'Either way, Georgie, I'm not letting you go. I told you I'd keep you safe and I meant it. Whatever is going on we'll deal with it together.'

'No. We can't.'

'We can.'

'You don't understand.'

'I'm trying to.'

'It's impossible.'

'Nothing is impossible.'

This is, she thought, sadness and confusion pouring through her. *This is.*

'I need to go.'

He recoiled as if she'd slapped him. 'Where?'

'I don't know,' she said, scrambling to her feet and taking a shaky step back. 'Somewhere else.'

'Don't fight me,' he said, his voice cracking as he rose too. 'Fight *for* me. Like I'm trying to fight for you. For us.'

'I told you before, there is no us.'

'You don't mean that.'

'I do.'

'I've never begged for anything,' he said, his voice low and rough, 'but I'm begging you. If you won't stay for me, at least stay for our son.'

Why? What was the point? What good could she possibly be to anyone while still so ill? 'He'll be far better off with you than me.'

'He needs *you*. *I* need you. I love you.' He

raked his hands through his hair, his eyes wild with confusion and desperation. 'Georgie, you matter so much to me. The night we met I felt we had a connection that went far beyond chemistry. It was like something in me instinctively recognised something in you. And it's only grown since then. Everything about you fascinates me. The way you twist your hair and chew on your pen. The way you are with our son, your patience and your gentleness. You're the strongest, most incredible person I've ever met. You confront your fears and deal with them and you've made me do that too. You let me get away with nothing. You're beautiful and clever and funny and the woman I love. I've never felt like this about anyone ever. I don't want to be without you, Georgie. I can't.'

'I'm sorry,' she said, her eyes stinging and her throat tight as she stumbled back in the direction of the door.

'Don't do this. Please.'

'I have to.'

He moved towards her and put his hands on her shoulders, his expression fierce. 'You don't.'

'I do,' she cried, wrenching away.

'Where will you go?'

'I'll let you know.'

'It's late.'

'I'll be fine.'

'I won't let you do this, Georgie. I won't let you leave. Not this time.'

'This time,' she said, turning and heading for the door before the tears could spill over, 'you don't have any choice.'

CHAPTER THIRTEEN

As THE DOOR closing rang in his ears, Finn stood there rooted to the spot, reeling as torment and bewilderment spun through him.

What the hell had just happened?

He'd returned home, all fired up with ferocious determination and the hammering need to put things right, the rings he'd bought her in Paris burning a hole in his pocket. He didn't know what he'd expected to find on his arrival. He hadn't given it much thought. However, if he had, Georgie sitting on the sofa in the dark, pale and drawn, would not have been it. The sight of her had knocked him for six. Concern had slammed into him. But nothing had stunned him as much as the conversation that had then ensued.

He felt as if he'd stepped into an alternative universe, one in which there were no rules and nothing made sense. Did she really believe everything she'd said? he wondered, his head spinning and his gut churning. That they had no relationship and never would? How could she, after everything they'd been through together?

Yet that was how it seemed. The more he'd tried to convince her that they did have something, that he loved her, the more she'd backed off. It had been like trying to hold on to water and somehow, unintentionally and agonisingly, he'd made things worse.

Georgie was not in a good way—she'd walked out on *their son*—and his entire body began to ache with the knowledge that perhaps he couldn't help her. Perhaps he'd never be able to help her. Her despair, her desperation and the tears that she'd struggled to contain cut through him like a knife. He'd thought he could bind her to him with a civil partnership, but no ties were strong enough to overcome this. Nor was how he felt about her, because he'd tried everything. He'd tried reasoning with her and then pleaded with her and it had made no difference. He didn't know how to fix this. Never had he felt so powerless. It was agony. It was terrifying.

But there was one thing he did know. When she'd told him he didn't have a choice she'd been wrong. Dead wrong. It was pretty much the only thing he did have right now, and, despite not having a clue about anything, he was making it because he was *not* losing her again.

Georgie fled down the hall, the tears that she'd been wretchedly holding back spilling over and streaking down her cheeks. With every step she took the knife slicing her heart to pieces struck harder and faster, the pain flowing through her veins unbearable.

Why was this happening to her? she thought with a desperate sniff. Why was life, her illness, so cruel? What had she ever done to deserve any of it? Why couldn't she be happy? Why couldn't she be normal?

Reaching the lift, she pressed the button with one trembling finger, but the lift seemed to be as broken as she was because nothing happened, no matter how much she jabbed away at it. And she really needed it to work because she had to escape. She had to find somewhere to hole up and lick her wounds, wounds that were raw and deep and indelible.

But what if there was no escape? a little voice inside her head cried. What if no matter how far she ran, how hard she tried, this was always going to be her reality? What if she was destined to be dogged by what had happened for the rest of her life, never happy, never normal? She couldn't run for ever. She didn't want to be that person, constantly in fear of the present and the future, continually up and down, vulnerable and helpless. She *wasn't* that person. She wouldn't be. She had to face up to it.

Starting now.

What was she doing? she asked herself urgently, taking a step back from the lift, away from the edge. Where was she planning on heading? Was she *really* going to walk away from Josh? From Finn? Who claimed to love her? Who maybe *did* love her?

In the still quiet of the hall, the only sound in her ears the hammering of her heart, Georgie thought about the calm, steadfast way he'd countered all her accusations. About his strength and resilience in the face of her increasing panic. About everything he'd said and done over the last few months. If she accepted that she'd been in the grip of paranoia and doubt caused by her illness then she also had to accept that his version of events was the right one.

And God, she wanted it to be. She had to take a chance on them. She *wanted* to take a chance on them. Because she loved him back. He *was* the man she'd imagined him to be. She hadn't got that wrong. The happiness she'd felt hadn't been an illusion. Nor had any of the feelings she had before she'd left Paris. Everything had been real. Her hopes and dreams still lay within her grasp if only she was brave enough to grab them.

She would take control of this thing winding its wicked tendrils around her thoughts and emotions, she promised herself as she blew her nose and set her jaw. Come hell or high water, she *would* beat it. She'd seek help and go back on the medication. She should never have stopped taking it in the first place. What had she been thinking when she'd even been warned of the dangers of doing exactly that? She was going to fight for herself. And fight for Finn, for them, just as he'd asked her to.

With determination powering through her, Georgie spun on her heel and retraced her steps, only to slam to a halt a moment later at the sight of Finn striding down the hall towards her.

'This is not happening,' he said with a fierceness on his handsome face that heated all the places that had been so cold lately. 'You are not leaving me. You are not leaving Josh. I love you and you don't get to run away. I won't allow it. I know it's complicated but we'll figure it out. Together.'

'Yes,' she said simply, the emotion pummelling her on the inside practically wiping out her knees. There was much, *much* more that she wanted to say but her throat was so tight and the emotion so thick that she couldn't. All she could do was throw her arms around his neck and pull his head down to hers and kiss him with everything she was feeling.

With a harsh groan Finn whipped one arm around her waist and the other around her shoulders, pulling her tightly against him as he kissed her back with equal heat and need and desperation.

'God, Georgie,' he muttered when he eventually lifted his head, his breath ragged, his heart pounding against hers.

'I'm so sorry,' she said, hearing the catch in her voice and swallowing hard. 'I had a relapse and panicked. I convinced myself that you weren't who I thought you were. I've been so confused. So lost.'

'So have I,' he said passionately. 'But we belong together. We belong to each other.'

'I don't want to live without Josh. Or you. I love you.'

He rested his forehead against hers and she could feel him shaking with emotion. 'I think I fell in love with you the moment you walked up to me in my club and asked me if you could join me. You were dazzling.'

'I'm not that person any longer.'

'You're all that and more.'

'I still need help.'

'We'll get it,' he said, stroking his thumbs over her cheeks to smooth away the tracks of her tears and the remnants of her fears. 'I will always be there for you, Georgie, whatever happens.'

'And I'll always be there for you.'

He kissed her again, this time more gently, more deeply, and by the time he lifted his head, the sense of peace and hope and joy that had been beginning to spin through her filled her to the brim, overwhelming her all over again.

'Don't cry,' he said, kissing away the tears. 'It'll be all right.'

'Will it?'

'Of course,' he said gruffly. 'I bought you these,' he added, digging his hand briefly into his pocket and then sliding a plain gold band and then a stunning diamond solitaire onto the third finger of her left hand. 'In Paris.'

'They're beautiful,' she said, her throat tightening and her heart swelling as she placed her hand over his heart and looked at them.

'You're beautiful.'

'I'm a mess.'

'You're mine.'

'Your lift is broken,' she said with a watery sniff.

'I had it stopped.'

'You had it stopped?'

'I couldn't risk losing you again,' he said, his eyes darkening with emotion, his hold on her strong and secure.

'You won't.'

'Promise?'

She nodded. 'I promise.'

EPILOGUE

Ospedale San Giovanni,
Venice

PROPPED UP IN bed in the dark, quiet private hospital room where his shattered body was gradually healing, Federico Rossi stared one last time at the image on the screen, a photo of a couple at the recent launch of the seven-star Hotel Bellevue in Paris—at one Finn Calvert in particular, a man who was the spitting image of himself but without the scars and the broken nose—and slowly, thoughtfully, closed the lid of his laptop.

* * * * *

The Author

GUY VANDERHAEGHE was born in Esterhazy, Saskatchewan, in 1951. He received his B.A. (1971) and his M.A. (1975) from the University of Saskatchewan and his B.Ed. (1978) from the University of Regina.

In his first volume of fiction, twelve stories gathered together under the title *Man Descending* (1982), Vanderhaeghe recounts the dilemmas and the humiliations of a variety of male characters, ranging in age from childhood to old age. The collection won the Governor General's Award for Fiction and went on to receive the Faber Prize in Great Britain. In his subsequent fiction, which includes two more collections of short stories and four novels, he has won further awards and acclaim, his recent novels being historical fiction of the west.

In addition to his fiction, Vanderhaeghe has also written two plays: *I Had a Job I Liked. Once.*, which premiered in 1991, and *Dancock's Dance*, which premiered in 1995.

Guy Vanderhaeghe lives in Saskatoon, Saskatchewan.

Guy Vanderhaeghe

MAN DESCENDING

With an Afterword by Leo McKay Jr.

M&S

This book was first published by Macmillan of Canada in 1982
New Canadian Library edition 2004

National Library of Canada Cataloguing in Publication

Vanderhaeghe, Guy, 1951-
Man descending / Guy Vanderhaeghe ;
with an afterword by Leo McKay.

First published: Toronto : Macmillan, 1982.
Includes bibliographical references.
ISBN 0-7710-8690-3

I. Title.

PS8593.A5386M3 2004   c813'.54   C2004-901149-9

We acknowledge the financial support of the Government of Canada
through the Book Publishing Industry Development Program and that of
the Government of Ontario through the Ontario Media Development
Corporation's Ontario Book Initiative. We further acknowledge the
support of the Canada Council for the Arts and the Ontario Arts Council
for our publishing program.

Typeset in Minion by M&S, Toronto
Printed and bound in Canada

McClelland & Stewart Ltd.
The Canadian Publishers
481 University Avenue
Toronto, Ontario
M5G 2E9
www.mcclelland.com/NCL

1 2 3 4 5   08 07 06 05 04

Contents

The Watcher

I SUPPOSE it was having a bad chest that turned me into an observer, a watcher, at an early age.

"Charlie has my chest," my mother often informed friends. "A real weakness there," she would add significantly, thumping her own wishbone soundly.

I suppose I had. Family lore had me narrowly escaping death from pneumonia at the age of four. It seems I spent an entire Sunday in delirium, soaking the sheets. Dr. Carlyle was off at the reservoir rowing in his little skiff and couldn't be reached – something for which my mother illogically refused to forgive him. She was a woman who nursed and tenaciously held dark grudges. Forever after that incident the doctor was slightingly and coldly dismissed in conversation as a "man who betrayed the public's trust."

Following that spell of pneumonia, I regularly suffered from bouts of bronchitis, which often landed me in hospital in Fortune, forty miles away. Compared with the oxygen tent and the whacking great needles that were buried in my skinny rump there, being invalided at home was a piece of cake. Coughing and hacking, I would leaf through catalogues and read comic books until my head swam with print-fatigue. My diet was largely of my own whimsical choosing – hot chocolate and graham wafers were supplemented by sticky sweet coughdrops, which I downed one after another until my stomach could take no more, revolted, and tossed up the whole mess.

With the first signs of improvement in my condition my mother moved her baby to the living-room chesterfield, where she and the radio could keep me company. The electric kettle followed me and was soon burbling in the corner, jetting steam into the air to keep my lungs moist and pliable. Because I was neither quite sick nor quite well, these were the best days of my illnesses. My stay at home hadn't yet made me bored and restless, my chest no longer hurt when I breathed, and that loose pocket of rattling phlegm meant I didn't have to worry about going back to school just yet. So I luxuriated in this steamy equatorial climate, tended by a doting mother as if I were a rare tropical orchid.

My parents didn't own a television and so my curiosity and attention were focused on my surroundings during my illnesses. I tried to squeeze every bit of juice out of them. Sooner than most children I learned that if you kept quiet and still, and didn't insist on drawing attention to yourself as many kids did, adults were inclined to regard you as being one with the furniture, as significant and sentient as a hassock. By keeping mum I was treated to illuminating glances into an adult world of conventional miseries and scandals.

I wasn't sure at the age of six what a miscarriage was, but I knew that Ida Thompson had had one and that now her plumbing was buggered. And watching old lady Kuznetzky hang her washing, through a living-room window trickling with condensed kettle steam, I was able to confirm for myself the rumour that the old girl eschewed panties. As she bent over to rummage in her laundry basket I caught a brief glimpse of huge, white buttocks that shimmered in the pale spring sunshine.

I also soon knew (how I don't remember exactly) that Norma Ruggs had business with the Liquor Board Store when she shuffled by our window every day at exactly 10:50 a.m. She was always at the store door at 11:00 when they unlocked and opened up for business. At 11:15 she trudged home again, a pint of ice cream in one hand, a brown paper bag disguising a bottle of fortified wine in the other, and her blotchy complexion painted a high colour of shame.

"Poor old girl," my mother would say whenever she caught sight of Norma passing by in her shabby coat and sloppy man's overshoes. They had been in high school together, and Norma had been class brain and valedictorian. She had been an obliging, dutiful girl and still was. For the wine wasn't Norma's – the ice cream was her only vice. The booze was her husband's, a vet who had come back from the war badly crippled.

All this careful study of adults may have made me old before my time. In any case it seemed to mark me in some recognizable way as being "different" or "queer for a kid." When I went to live with my grandmother in July of 1959 she spotted it right away. Of course, she was only stating the obvious when she declared me skinny and delicate, but she also noted in her vinegary voice that my eyes had a bad habit of never letting her go, and that I was the worst case of little pitchers having big ears that she had ever come across.

I ended up at my grandmother's because in May of that year my mother's bad chest finally caught up with her, much to her and everyone else's surprise. It had been pretty generally agreed by all her acquaintances that Mabel Bradley's defects in that regard were largely imagined. Not so. A government-sponsored X-ray program discovered tuberculosis, and she was packed off, pale and drawn with worry, for a stay in the sanatorium at Fort Qu'Appelle.

For roughly a month, until the school year ended, my father took charge of me and the house. He was a desolate, lanky, drooping weed of a man who had married late in life but nevertheless had been easily domesticated. I didn't like him much.

My father was badly wrenched by my mother's sickness and absence. He scrawled her long, untidy letters with a stub of gnawed pencil, and once he got shut of me, visited her every weekend. He was a soft and sentimental man whose eyes ran to water at the drop of a hat, or more accurately, death of a cat. Unlike his mother, my Grandma Bradley, he hadn't a scrap of flint or hard-headed common sense in him.

But then neither had any of his many brothers and sisters. It was as if the old girl had unflinchingly withheld the genetic code for responsibility and practicality from her pin-headed offspring. Life for her children was a series of thundering defeats, whirlwind calamities, or, at best, hurried strategic retreats. Businesses crashed and marriages failed, for they had – my father excepted – a taste for the unstable in partners marital and fiscal.

My mother saw no redeeming qualities in any of them. By and large they drank too much, talked too loudly, and raised ill-mannered children – monsters of depravity whose rudeness provided my mother with endless illustrations of what she feared I might become. "You're eating just like a pig," she would say, "exactly like your cousin Elvin." Or to my father, "You're neglecting the belt. He's starting to get as lippy as that little snot Muriel."

And in the midst, in the very eye of this familial cyclone of mishap and discontent, stood Grandma Bradley, as firm as a rock. Troubles of all kinds were laid on her doorstep. When my cousin Criselda suddenly turned big-tummied at sixteen and it proved difficult to ascertain with any exactitude the father, or even point a finger of general blame in the direction of a putative sire, she was shipped off to Grandma Bradley until she delivered. Uncle Ernie dried out on Grandma's farm and Uncle Ed hid there from several people he had sold prefab, assemble-yourself, crop-duster airplanes to.

So it was only family tradition that I should be deposited there. When domestic duties finally overwhelmed him, and I complained too loudly about fried-egg sandwiches for dinner again, my father left the bacon rinds hardening and curling grotesquely on unwashed plates, the slut's wool eddying along the floor in the currents of a draft, and drove the one hundred and fifty miles to the farm, *right then and there.*

My father, a dangerous man behind the wheel, took any extended trip seriously, believing the highways to be narrow, unnavigable ribbons of carnage. This trip loomed so dangerously in his mind that, rather than tear a hand from the wheel, or an eye from the road, he had me, *chronic sufferer of lung disorders*, light his cigarettes and place them carefully in his dry lips. My mother would have killed him.

"You'll love it at Grandma's," he kept saying unconvincingly, "you'll have a real boy's summer on the farm. It'll build you up, the chores and all that. And good fun too. You don't know it now, but you are living the best days of your life right now. What I wouldn't give to be a kid again. You'll love it there. There's chickens and *everything*."

It wasn't exactly a lie. There were chickens. But the *everything* – as broad and overwhelming and suggestive of possibilities as my father tried to make it sound – didn't cover much. It certainly didn't comprehend a pony or a dog as I had hoped, chickens being the only livestock on the place.

It turned out that my grandmother, although she had spent most of her life on that particular piece of ground and eventually died there, didn't care much for the farm and was entirely out of sympathy with most varieties of animal life. She did keep chickens for the eggs, although she admitted that her spirits lifted considerably in the fall when it came time to butcher the hens.

Her flock was a garrulous, scraggly crew that spent their days having dust baths in the front yard, hiding their eggs, and, fleet and ferocious as hunting cheetahs, running down scuttling lizards which they trampled and pecked to death while their shiny, expressionless eyes shifted dizzily in their stupid heads. The only one of these birds I felt any compassion for was Stanley the rooster, a bedraggled male who spent his days tethered to a stake by a piece of baler twine looped around his leg. Poor Stanley crowed heart-rendingly in his captivity; his comb drooped pathetically, and he was utterly crestfallen as he lecherously eyed his bantam beauties daintily scavenging. Grandma kept him in this unnatural bondage to prevent him fertilizing the eggs and producing blood spots in the yolks. Being a finicky eater I approved this policy, but nevertheless felt some guilt over Stanley.

No, the old Bradley homestead, all that encompassed by my father's *everything*, wasn't very impressive. The two-storey house, though big and solid, needed paint and shingles. A track had been worn in the kitchen linoleum clean through to the floorboards and a long rent in the screen door had been stitched shut with waxed thread. The yard was little more than a tangle of thigh-high ragweed and sowthistle to which the chickens repaired for shade. A windbreak of spruce on the north side of the house was dying from lack of water and the competition from Scotch thistle. The evergreens were no longer green; their sere needles fell away from the branches at the touch of a hand.

The abandoned barn out back was flanked by two mountainous rotted piles of manure which I remember sprouting button mushrooms after every warm soaker of a rain. That pile of shit was the only useful thing in a yard full of junk: wrecked cars, old wagon wheels, collapsing sheds. The barn itself was mightily decayed. The paint had been stripped from its planks by rain, hail, and dry, blistering winds, and the roof sagged like a tired nag's back. For a small boy it was an ominous place on a summer day. The air was still and dark and heavy with heat. At the sound of footsteps rats squeaked and scrabbled in the empty mangers, and the sparrows which had spattered the rafters white with their dung whirred about and fluted ghostly cries.

In 1959 Grandma Bradley would have been sixty-nine, which made her a child of the gay nineties – although the supposed gaiety of that age didn't seem to have made much impress upon the development of her character. Physically she was an imposing woman. Easily six feet tall, she carried a hundred and eighty pounds on her generous frame without prompting speculation as to what she had against girdles. She could touch the floor effortlessly with the flat of her palms and pack an eighty-pound sack of chicken feed on her shoulder. She dyed her hair auburn in defiance of local mores, and never went to town to play bridge, whist, or canasta without wearing a hat and getting dressed to the teeth. Grandma loved card games of all varieties and considered anyone who didn't a mental defective.

A cigarette always smouldered in her trap. She smoked sixty a day and rolled them as thin as knitting needles in an effort at economy. These cigarettes were so wispy and delicate they tended to get lost between her swollen fingers.

And above all she believed in plain speaking. She let me know that as my father's maroon Meteor pulled out of the yard while we stood waving goodbye on the front steps.

"Let's get things straight from the beginning," she said without taking her eyes off the car as it bumped toward the grid road. "I don't chew my words twice. If you're like any of the rest of them I've had here, you've been raised as wild as a goddamn Indian. Not one of my grandchildren have been brought up to mind. Well, you'll mind around here. I don't jaw and blow hot air to jaw and blow hot air. I belted your father when he needed it, and make no mistake I'll belt you. Is that understood?"

"Yes," I said with a sinking feeling as I watched my father's car disappear down the road, swaying from side to side as its suspension was buffeted by potholes.

"These bloody bugs are eating me alive," she said, slapping her arm. "I'm going in."

I trailed after her as she slopped back into the house in a pair of badly mauled, laceless sneakers. The house was filled with a half-light that changed its texture with every room. The venetian blinds were drawn in the parlour and some flies carved Immelmanns in the dark air that smelled of cellar damp. Others battered their bullet bodies *tip-tap*, *tip-tap* against the window panes.

In the kitchen my grandmother put the kettle on the stove to boil for tea. After she had lit one of her matchstick smokes, she inquired through a blue haze if I was hungry.

"People aren't supposed to smoke around me," I informed her. "Because of my chest. Dad can't even smoke in our house."

"That so?" she said genially. Her cheeks collapsed as she drew on her butt. I had a hint there, if I'd only known it, of how she'd look in her coffin. "You won't like it here then," she said. "I smoke all the time."

I tried a few unconvincing coughs. I was ignored. She didn't respond to the same signals as my mother.

"My mother has a bad chest, too," I said. "She's in a T.B. sanatorium."

"So I heard," my grandmother said, getting up to fetch the whistling kettle. "Oh, I suspect she'll be right as rain in no time with a little rest. T.B. isn't what it used to be. Not with all these new drugs." She considered. "That's not to say though that your father'll ever hear the end of it. Mabel was always a silly little shit that way."

I almost fell off my chair. I had never thought I'd live to hear the day my mother was called a silly little shit.

"Drink tea?" asked Grandma Bradley, pouring boiling water into a brown teapot.

I shook my head.

"How old are you anyway?" she asked.

"Eleven."

"You're old enough then," she said, taking down a cup from the shelf. "Tea gets the kidneys moving and carries off the poisons in the blood. That's why all the Chinese live to be so old. They all live to be a hundred."

"I don't know if my mother would like it," I said. "Me drinking tea."

"You worry a lot for a kid," she said, "don't you?"

I didn't know how to answer that. It wasn't a question I had ever considered. I tried to shift the conversation.

"What's there for a kid to do around here?" I said in an unnaturally inquisitive voice.

"Well, we could play cribbage," she said.

"I don't know how to play cribbage."

She was genuinely shocked. "What!" she exclaimed. "Why, you're eleven years old! Your father could count a cribbage hand when he was five. I taught all my kids to."

"I never learned how," I said. "We don't even have a deck of cards at our house. My father hates cards. Says he had too much of them as a boy."

At this my grandmother arched her eyebrows. "Is that a fact? Well, hoity-toity."

"So, since I don't play cards," I continued in a strained manner I imagined was polite, "what could I do – I mean, for fun?"

"Make your own fun," she said. "I never considered fun such a problem. Use your imagination. Take a broomstick and make like Nimrod."

"Who's Nimrod?" I asked.

"Pig ignorant," she said under her breath, and then louder, directly to me, "Ask me no questions and I'll tell you no lies. Drink your tea."

And that, for the time being, was that.

It's all very well to tell someone to make their own fun. It's the making of it that is the problem. In a short time I was a very bored kid. There was no one to play with, no horses to ride, no gun to shoot gophers, no dog for company. There was nothing to read except the *Country Guide* and *Western Producer*. There was nothing or nobody interesting to watch. I went through my grandmother's drawers but found nothing as surprising there as I had discovered in my parents'.

Most days it was so hot that the very idea of fun boiled out of me and evaporated. I moped and dragged myself listlessly around the house in the loose-jointed, water-boned way kids have when they can't stand anything, not even their precious selves.

On my better days I tried to take up with Stanley the rooster. Scant chance of that. Tremors of panic ran through his body at my approach. He tugged desperately on the twine until he jerked his free leg out from under himself and collapsed in the dust, his heart bumping the tiny crimson scallops of his breast feathers, the black pellets of his eyes glistening, all the while shitting copiously. Finally, in the last extremes of chicken terror, he would allow me to stroke his yellow beak and finger his comb.

I felt sorry for the captive Stanley and several times tried to take him for a walk, to give him a chance to take the air and broaden his limited horizons. But this prospect alarmed him so much that I was always forced to return him to his stake in disgust while he fluttered, squawked and flopped.

So fun was a commodity in short supply. That is, until something interesting turned up during the first week of August. Grandma Bradley was dredging little watering canals with a hoe among the corn stalks on a bright blue Monday morning, and I was shelling peas into a colander on the front stoop, when a black car nosed diffidently up the road and into the yard. Then it stopped a good twenty yards short of the house as if its occupants weren't sure of their welcome. After some time, the doors opened and a man and woman got carefully out.

The woman wore turquoise-blue pedal-pushers, a sloppy black turtleneck sweater, and a gash of scarlet lipstick swiped across her white, vivid face. This was my father's youngest sister, Aunt Evelyn.

The man took her gently and courteously by the elbow and balanced her as she edged up the front yard in her high heels, careful to avoid turning an ankle on a loose stone, or in an old tire track.

The thing which immediately struck me about the man was his beard – the first I had ever seen. Beards weren't popular in 1959 – not in our part of the world. His was a randy, jutting, little goat's-beard that would have looked wicked on any other face but his. He was very tall and his considerable height was accented by a lack of corresponding breadth to his body. He appeared to have been racked and stretched against his will into an exceptional and unnatural anatomy. As he walked and talked animatedly, his free hand fluttered in front of my aunt. It sailed, twirled and gambolled on the air. Like a butterfly enticing a child, it seemed to lead her hypnotized across a yard fraught with perils for city-shod feet.

My grandmother laid down her hoe and called sharply to her daughter.

"Evvie!" she called. "Over here, Evvie!"

At the sound of her mother's voice my aunt's head snapped around and she began to wave jerkily and stiffly, striving to maintain a tottering balance on her high-heeled shoes. It wasn't hard to see that there was something not quite right with her. By the time my grandmother and I reached the pair, Aunt Evelyn was in tears, sobbing hollowly and jamming the heel of her palm into her front teeth.

The man was speaking calmly to her. "Control. Control. Deep, steady breaths. Think sea. Control. Control. Control. Think sea, Evelyn. Deep. Deep. Deep," he muttered.

"What the hell is the matter, Evelyn?" my grandmother asked sharply. "And who is *he*?"

"Evelyn is a little upset," the man said, keeping his attention focused on my aunt. "She's having one of her anxiety attacks. If you'd just give us a moment we'll clear this up. She's got to learn to handle stressful situations." He inclined his head in a priestly manner and said, "Be with the sea, Evelyn. Deep. Deep. Sink in the sea."

"It's her damn nerves again," said my grandmother.

"Yes," the man said benignly, with a smile of blinding condescension. "Sort of."

"She's been as nervous as a cut cat all her life," said my grandmother, mostly to herself.

"Momma," said Evelyn, weeping. "Momma."

"Slide beneath the waves, Evelyn. Down, down, down to the beautiful pearls," the man chanted softly. This was really something.

My grandmother took Aunt Evelyn by her free elbow, shook it, and said sharply, "Evelyn, shut up!" Then she began to drag her briskly towards the house. For a moment the man looked as if he had it in mind to protest, but in the end he meekly acted as a flanking escort for Aunt Evelyn as she was marched into the house. When I tried to follow, my grandmother gave me one of her looks and said definitely, "You find something to do out here."

I did. I waited a few minutes and then duck-walked my way under the parlour window. There I squatted with my knobby shoulder blades pressed against the siding and the sun beating into my face.

My grandmother obviously hadn't wasted any time with the social niceties. They were fairly into it.

"Lovers?" said my grandmother. "Is that what it's called now? Shack-up, you mean."

"Oh, Momma," said Evelyn, and she was crying, "it's all right. We're going to get married."

"You believe that?" said my grandmother. "You believe that geek is going to marry you?"

"Thompson," said the geek, "my name is Thompson,

Robert Thompson, and we'll marry as soon as I get my divorce. Although Lord only knows when that'll be."

"That's right," said my grandmother, "Lord only knows." Then to her daughter, "You got another one. A real prize off the midway, didn't you? Evelyn, you're a certifiable lunatic."

"I didn't expect this," said Thompson. "We came here because Evelyn has had a bad time of it recently. She hasn't been eating or sleeping properly and consequently she's got herself run down. She finds it difficult to control her emotions, don't you, darling?"

I thought I heard a mild yes.

"So," said Thompson, continuing, "we decided Evelyn needs some peace and quiet before I go back to school in September."

"School," said my grandmother. "Don't tell me you're some kind of teacher?" She seemed stunned by the very idea.

"No," said Aunt Evelyn, and there was a tremor of pride in her voice that testified to her amazement that she had been capable of landing such a rare and remarkable fish. "Not a teacher. Robert's a graduate student of American Literature at the University of British Columbia."

"Hoity-toity," said Grandmother. "A graduate student. A graduate student of American Literature."

"Doctoral program," said Robert.

"And did you ever ask yourself, Evelyn, what the hell this genius is doing with you? Or is it just the same old problem with you – elevator panties? Some guy comes along and pushes the button. Up, down. Up, down."

The image this created in my mind made me squeeze my knees together deliciously and stifle a giggle.

"Mother," said Evelyn, continuing to bawl.

"Guys like this don't marry barmaids," said my grandmother.

"Cocktail hostess," corrected Evelyn. "I'm a cocktail hostess."

"You don't have to make any excuses, dear," said Thompson pompously. "Remember what I told you. You're past the age of being judged."

"What the hell is that supposed to mean?" said my grandmother. "And by the way, don't start handing out orders in my house. You won't be around long enough to make them stick."

"That remains to be seen," said Thompson.

"Let's go, Robert," said Evelyn, nervously.

"Go on upstairs, Evelyn, I want to talk to your mother."

"You don't have to go anywhere," said my grandmother. "You can stay put."

"Evelyn, go upstairs." There was a pause and then I heard the sound of a chair creaking, then footsteps.

"Well," said my grandmother at last, "round one. Now for round two – get the hell out of my house."

"Can't do that."

"Why the hell not?"

"It's very difficult to explain," he said.

"Try."

"As you can see for yourself, Evelyn isn't well. She is very highly strung at the moment. I believe she is on the verge of a profound personality adjustment, a breakthrough." He paused dramatically. "Or breakdown."

"It's times like this that I wished I had a dog on the place to run off undesirables."

"The way I read it," said Thompson, unperturbed, "is that at the moment two people bulk very large in Evelyn's life. You and me. She needs the support and love of us both. You're not doing your share."

"I ought to slap your face."

"She has come home to try and get a hold of herself. We have to bury our dislikes for the moment. She needs to be handled very carefully."

"You make her sound like a trained bear. *Handled.* What

that girl needs is a good talking to, and I am perfectly capable of giving her that."

"No, Mrs. Bradley," Thompson said firmly in that maddeningly self-assured tone of his. "If you don't mind me saying so, I think that's part of her problem. It's important now for you to just let Evelyn *be*."

"Get out of my house," said my grandmother, at the end of her tether.

"I know it's difficult for you to understand," he said smoothly, "but if you understood the psychology of this you would see it's impossible for me to go; or for that matter, for Evelyn to go. If I leave she'll feel *I've* abandoned her. It can't be done. We're faced with a real psychological balancing act here."

"Now I've heard everything," said my grandmother. "Are you telling me you'd have the gall to move into a house where you're not wanted and just . . . just *stay there*?"

"Yes," said Thompson. "And I think you'll find me quite stubborn on this particular point."

"My God," said my grandmother. I could tell by her tone of voice that she had never come across anyone like Mr. Thompson before. At a loss for a suitable reply, she simply reiterated. "My God."

"I'm going upstairs now," said Thompson. "Maybe you could get the boy to bring in our bags while I see how Evelyn is doing. The car isn't locked." The second time he spoke his voice came from further away; I imagined him paused in the doorway. "Mrs. Bradley, please let's make this stay pleasant for Evelyn's sake."

She didn't bother answering him.

When I barged into the house some time later with conspicuous noisiness, I found my grandmother standing at the bottom of the stairs staring up the steps. "Well, I'll be damned," she said under her breath. "I've never seen anything like that. Goddamn freak." She even repeated it several times under her breath. "Goddamn freak. Goddamn freak."

Who could blame me if, after a boring summer, I felt my chest tighten with anticipation? Adults could be immensely interesting and entertaining if you knew what to watch for.

At first things were disappointingly quiet. Aunt Evelyn seldom set forth outside the door of the room she and her man inhabited by squatters' right. There was an argument, short and sharp, between Thompson and Grandmother over this. The professor claimed no one had any business prying into what Evelyn did up there. She was an adult and had the right to her privacy and her own thoughts. My grandmother claimed *she* had a right to know what was going on up there, even if nobody else thought she did.

I could have satisfied her curiosity on that point. Not much was going on up there. Several squints through the keyhole had revealed Aunt Evelyn lolling about the bedspread in a blue housecoat, eating soda crackers and sardines, and reading a stack of movie magazines she had had me lug out of the trunk of the car.

Food, you see, was beginning to become something of a problem for our young lovers. Grandma rather pointedly set only three places for meals, and Evelyn, out of loyalty to her boyfriend, couldn't very well sit down and break bread with us. Not that Thompson didn't take such things in his stride. He sauntered casually and conspicuously about the house as if he owned it, even going so far as to poke his head in the fridge and rummage in it like some pale, hairless bear. At times like that my grandmother was capable of looking through him as if he didn't exist.

On the second day of his stay Thompson took up with me, which was all right as far as I was concerned. I had no objection. Why he decided to do this I'm not sure exactly. Perhaps he was looking for some kind of an ally, no matter how weak. Most likely he wanted to get under the old lady's skin. Or maybe he just couldn't bear not having anyone to tell how wonderful he was. Thompson was that kind of a guy.

I was certainly let in on the secret. He was a remarkable fellow. He dwelt at great length on those things which made him such an extraordinary human being. I may have gotten the order of precedence all wrong, but if I remember correctly there were three things which made Thompson very special and different from all the other people I would ever meet, no matter how long or hard I lived.

First, he was going to write a book about a poet called Allen Ginsberg which was going to knock the socks off everybody who counted. It turned out he had actually met this Ginsberg the summer before in San Francisco and asked him if he could write a book about him and Ginsberg had said, Sure, why the hell not? The way Thompson described what it would be like when he published this book left me with the impression that he was going to spend most of the rest of his life riding around on people's shoulders and being cheered by a multitude of admirers.

Second, he confessed to knowing a tremendous amount about what made other people tick and how to adjust their mainsprings when they went kaflooey. He knew all this because at one time his own mainspring had gotten a little out of sorts. But now he was a fully integrated personality with a highly creative mind and a strong intuitive sense. That's why he was so much help to Aunt Evelyn in her time of troubles.

Third, he was a Buddhist.

The only one of these things which impressed me at the time was the bit about being a Buddhist. However, I was confused, because in the *Picture Book of the World's Great Religions* which we had at home, all the Buddhists were bald, and Thompson had a hell of a lot of hair, more than I had ever seen on a man. But even though he wasn't bald, he had an idol. A little bronze statue with the whimsical smile and slightly crossed eyes which he identified as Padma-sambhava. He told me that it was a Tibetan antique he had bought in San Francisco as an object of veneration and an aid to his meditations. I asked him what a meditation was and he offered to teach me one. So I learned to recite with great seriousness and flexible intonation one of his Tibetan meditations, while my grandmother glared across her quintessentially Western parlour with unbelieving eyes.

I could soon deliver, "A king must go when his time has come. His wealth, his friends and his relatives cannot go with him. Wherever men go, wherever they stay, the effect of their past acts follows them like a shadow. Those who are in the grip of desire, the grip of existence, the grip of ignorance, move helplessly round through the spheres of life, as men or gods or as wretches in the lower regions."

Not that an eleven-year-old could make much of any of *that*.

Which is not to say that even an eleven-year-old could be fooled by Robert Thompson. In his stubbornness, egoism and blindness he was transparently un-Buddhalike. To watch him and my grandmother snarl and snap their teeth over that poor, dry bone, Evelyn, was evidence enough of how firmly bound we all are to the wretched wheel of life and its stumbling desires.

No, even his most effective weapon, his cool benevolence, that patina of patience and forbearance which Thompson displayed to Grandmother, could crack.

One windy day when he had coaxed Aunt Evelyn out for a walk I followed them at a distance. They passed the wind-break of spruce, and at the sagging barbed-wire fence he gallantly manipulated the wires while my aunt floundered over them in an impractical dress and crinoline. It was the kind of dippy thing she would decide to wear on a hike.

Thompson strode along through the rippling grass like a wading heron, his baggy pant-legs flapping and billowing in the wind. My aunt moved along gingerly behind him, one hand modestly pinning down her wind-teased dress in the front, the other hand plastering the back of it to her behind.

It was only when they stopped and faced each other that I realized that all the time they had been traversing the field they had been arguing. A certain vaguely communicated agitation in the attitude of her figure, the way his arm stabbed at the featureless wash of sky, implied a dispute. She turned toward the house and he caught her by the arm and jerked it. In a fifties calendar fantasy her dress lifted in the wind, exposing her panties. I sank in the grass until their seed tassels trembled against my chin. I wasn't going to miss watching this for the world.

She snapped and twisted on the end of his arm like a fish on a line. Her head was flung back in an exaggerated, antique display of despair; her head rolled grotesquely from side to side as if her neck were broken.

Suddenly Thompson began striking awkwardly at her exposed buttocks and thighs with the flat of his hand. The long, gangly arm slashed like a flail as she scampered around him, the radius of her escape limited by the distance of their linked arms.

From where I knelt in the grass I could hear nothing. I was too far off. As far as I was concerned there were no cries and no pleading. The whole scene, as I remember it, was shorn of any of the personal idiosyncrasies which manifest themselves in violence. It appeared a simple case of retribution.

That night, for the first time, my aunt came down to supper and claimed her place at the table with queenly graciousness. She wore shorts, too, for the first time, and gave a fine display of mottled, discoloured thighs which reminded me of bruised fruit. She made sure, almost as if by accident, that my grandmother had a good hard look at them.

Right out of the blue my grandmother said, "I don't want you hanging around that man any more. You stay away from him."

"Why?" I asked rather sulkily. He was the only company I had. Since my aunt's arrival Grandmother had paid no attention to me whatsoever.

It was late afternoon and we were sitting on the porch watching Evelyn squeal as she swung in the tire swing Thompson had rigged up for me in the barn. He had thrown a length of stray rope over the runner for the sliding door and hung a tire from it. I hadn't the heart to tell him I was too old for tire swings.

Aunt Evelyn seemed to be enjoying it though. She was screaming and girlishly kicking up her legs. Thompson couldn't be seen. He was deep in the settled darkness of the barn, pushing her back and forth. She disappeared and reappeared according to the arc which she travelled through. Into the barn, out in the sun. Light, darkness. Light, darkness.

Grandma ignored my question. "Goddamn freak," she said, scratching a match on the porch rail and lighting one of her rollies. "Wait and see, he'll get his wagon fixed."

"Aunt Evelyn likes him," I noted pleasantly, just to stir things up a bit.

"Your Aunt Evelyn's screws are loose," she said sourly. "And he's the son of a bitch who owns the screwdriver that loosened them."

"He must be an awful smart fellow to be studying to be a professor at a university," I commented. It was the last dig I could chance.

"One thing I know for sure," snapped my grandmother. "He isn't smart enough to lift the toilet seat when he pees. There's evidence enough for that."

After hearing that, I took to leaving a few conspicuous droplets of my own as a matter of course on each visit. Every little bit might help things along.

I stood in his doorway and watched Thompson meditate. And don't think that, drenched in *satori* as he was, he didn't know it. He put on quite a performance sitting on the floor in his underpants. When he came out of his trance he pretended to be surprised to see me. While he dressed we struck up a conversation.

"You know, Charlie," he said while he put on his sandals (I'd never seen a grown man wear sandals in my entire life), "you remind me of my little Padma-sambhava," he said, nodding to the idol squatting on his dresser. "For a while, you know, I thought it was the smile, but it isn't. It's the eyes."

"Its eyes are crossed," I said, none too flattered at the comparison.

"No they're not," he said good-naturedly. He tucked his shirt-tail into his pants. "The artist, the maker of that image, set them fairly close together to suggest – aesthetically speaking – the intensity of inner vision, its concentration." He picked up the idol and, looking at it, said, "These are very watchful eyes, very knowing eyes. Your eyes are something like that. From your eyes I could tell you're an intelligent boy." He paused, set Padma-sambhava back on the dresser, and asked, "Are you?"

I shrugged.

"Don't be afraid to say it if you are," he said. "False modesty can be as corrupting as vanity. It took me twenty-five years to learn that."

"I usually get all A's on my report card," I volunteered.

"Well, that's something," he said, looking around the room for his belt. He picked a sweater off a chair and peered under it. "Then you see what's going on around here, don't you?" he asked. "You see what your grandmother is mistakenly trying to do?"

I nodded.

"That's right," he said. "You're a smart boy." He sat down on the bed. "Come here."

I went over to him. He took hold of me by the arms and looked into my eyes with all the sincerity he could muster.

"You know, being intelligent means responsibilities. It means doing something worth while with your life. For instance, have you given any thought as to what you would like to be when you grow up?"

"A spy," I said.

The silly bugger laughed.

It was the persistent, rhythmic thud that first woke me, and once wakened, I picked up the undercurrent of muted clamour, of stifled struggle. The noise seeped through the beaverboard wall of the adjoining bedroom into my own, a storm of hectic urgency and violence. The floorboards of the old house squeaked; I heard what sounded like a strangled curse and moan, then a fleshy, meaty concussion which I took to be a slap. Was he killing her at last? Choking her with the silent, poisonous care necessary to escape detection?

I remembered Thompson's arm flashing frenziedly in the sunlight. My aunt's discoloured thighs. My heart creaked in my chest with fear. And after killing her? Would the madman stop? Or would he do us all in, one by one?

I got out of bed on unsteady legs. The muffled commotion was growing louder, more distinct. I padded into the hallway. The door to their bedroom was partially open, and a light showed. Terror made me feel hollow; the pit of my stomach ached.

They were both naked, something which I hadn't expected, and which came as quite a shock. What was perhaps even more shocking was the fact that they seemed not only oblivious of me, but of each other as well. She was slung around so that her head was propped on a pillow resting on the foot-board of the bed. One smooth leg was draped over the edge of the bed and her heel was beating time on the floorboards (the thud which woke me) as accompaniment to Thompson's plunging body and the soft, liquid grunts of expelled air which he made with every lunge. One of her hands gripped the footboard and her knuckles were white with strain.

I watched until the critical moment, right through the growing frenzy and ardour. They groaned and panted and heaved and shuddered and didn't know themselves. At the very last he lifted his bony, hatchet face with the jutting beard to the ceiling and closed his eyes; for a moment I thought he was praying as his lips moved soundlessly. But then he began to whimper and his mouth fell open and he looked stupider and weaker than any human being I had ever seen before in my life.

"Like pigs at the trough," my grandmother said at breakfast. "With the boy up there too."

My aunt turned a deep red, and then flushed again so violently that her thin lips appeared to turn blue.

I kept my head down and went on shovelling porridge. Thompson still wasn't invited to the table. He was leaning against the kitchen counter, his bony legs crossed at the ankles, eating an apple he had helped himself to.

"He didn't hear anything," my aunt said uncertainly. She whispered conspiratorially across the table to Grandmother. "Not at that hour. He'd been asleep for hours."

I thought it wise, even though it meant drawing attention to myself, to establish my ignorance. "Hear what?" I inquired innocently.

"It wouldn't do any harm if he had," said Thompson, calmly biting and chewing the temptress's fruit.

"You wouldn't see it, would you?" said Grandma Bradley. "It wouldn't matter to you what he heard? You'd think that was manly."

"Manly has nothing to do with it. Doesn't enter into it," said Thompson in that cool way he had. "It's a fact of life, something he'll have to find out about sooner or later."

Aunt Evelyn began to cry. "Nobody is ever pleased with me," she spluttered. "I'm going crazy trying to please you both. I can't do it." She began to pull nervously at her hair. "He made me," she said finally in a confessional, humble tone to her mother.

"Evelyn," said my grandmother, "you have a place here. I would never send you away. I want you here. But he has to go. I want him to go. If he is going to rub my nose in it that way he has to go. I won't have that man under my roof."

"Evelyn isn't apologizing for anything," Thompson said. "And she isn't running away either. You can't force her to choose. It isn't healthy or fair."

"There have been other ones before you," said Grandma. "This isn't anything new for Evelyn."

"Momma!"

"I'm aware of that," he said stiffly, and his face vibrated with the effort to smile. "Provincial mores have never held much water with me. I like to think I'm above all that."

Suddenly my grandmother spotted me. "What are you gawking at!" she shouted. "Get on out of here!"

I didn't budge an inch.

"Leave him alone," said Thompson.

"You'll be out of here within a week," said Grandmother, "I swear."

"No," he said smiling. "When I'm ready."

"You'll go home and go with your tail between your legs. Last night was the last straw," she said. And by God you could tell she meant it.

Thompson gave her his beatific Buddha-grin and shook his head from side to side, very, very slowly.

A thunderstorm was brewing. The sky was a stew of dark, swollen cloud and a strange apple-green light. The temperature stood in the mid-nineties, not a breath of breeze stirred, my skin crawled and my head pounded above my eyes and through the bridge of my nose. There wasn't a thing to do except sit on the bottom step of the porch, keep from picking up a sliver in your ass, and scratch the dirt with a stick. My grandmother had put her hat on and driven into town on some unexplained business. Thompson and my aunt were upstairs in their bedroom, sunk in a stuporous, sweaty afternoon's sleep.

Like my aunt and Thompson, all the chickens had gone to roost to wait for rain. The desertion of his harem had thrown the rooster into a flap. Stanley trotted neurotically around his tethering post, stopping every few circuits to beat his bedraggled pinions and crow lustily in masculine outrage. I watched him for a bit without much curiosity, and then climbed off the step and walked toward him, listlessly dragging my stick in my trail.

"Here Stanley, Stanley," I called, not entirely sure how to summon a rooster, or instil in him confidence and friendliness. I did neither. My approach only further unhinged Stanley. His stride lengthened, the tempo of his pace increased, and his head began to dart abruptly from side to side in furtive despair. Finally, in a last desperate attempt to escape, Stanley upset himself trying to fly. He landed in a heap of disarranged, stiff, glistening feathers. I put my foot on his string and pinned him to the ground.

"Nice pretty, pretty Stanley," I said coaxingly, adopting the tone that a neighbour used with her budgie, since I wasn't sure how one talked to a bird. I slowly extended my thumb to stroke his bright-red neck feathers. Darting angrily, he struck the ball of my thumb with a snappish peck and simultaneously hit my wrist with his heel spur. He didn't hurt me, but he did startle me badly. So badly I gave a little yelp. Which made me feel foolish and more than a little cowardly.

"You son of a bitch," I said, reaching down slowly and staring into one unblinking glassy eye in which I could see my fate looming larger and larger. I caught the rooster's legs and held them firmly together. Stanley crowed defiantly and showed me his wicked little tongue.

"Now, Stanley," I said, "relax, I'm just going to stroke you. I'm just going to stroke you. I'm just going to pet Stanley."

No deal. He struck furiously again with a snake-like agility, and bounded in my hand, wings beating his poultry smell into my face. A real fighting cock at last. Maybe it was the weather. Perhaps his rooster pride and patience would suffer no more indignities.

The heat, the sultry menace of the gathering storm, made me feel prickly, edgy. I flicked my middle finger smartly against his tiny chicken skull, hard enough to rattle his pea-sized brain. "You like that, buster?" I asked, and snapped him another one for good measure. He struck back again, his comb red, crested, and rubbery with fury.

I was angry myself. I turned him upside down and left him dangling, his wings drumming against the legs of my jeans. Then I righted him abruptly; he looked dishevelled, seedy and dazed.

"Okay, Stanley," I said, feeling the intoxication of power. "I'm boss here, and you behave." There was a gleeful edge to my voice, which surprised me a little. I realized I was hoping this confrontation would escalate. Wishing that he would provoke me into something.

Strange images came into my head: the bruises on my aunt's legs; Thompson's face drained of life, lifted like an empty receptacle toward the ceiling, waiting to be filled, the tendons of his neck stark and rigid with anticipation.

I was filled with anxiety, the heat seemed to stretch me, to tug at my nerves and my skin. Two drops of sweat, as large and perfectly formed as tears, rolled out of my hairline and splashed onto the rubber toes of my runners.

"Easy, Stanley," I breathed to him, "easy," and my hand crept deliberately towards him. This time he pecked me in such a way, directly on the knuckle, that it actually hurt. I took up my stick and rapped him on the beak curtly, the prim admonishment of a schoolmarm. I didn't hit him very hard, but it was hard enough to split the length of his beak with a narrow crack. The beak fissured like the nib of a fountain pen. Stanley squawked, opened and closed his beak spasmodically, bewildered by the pain. A bright jewel of blood bubbled out of the split and gathered to a trembling bead.

"There," I said excitedly, "now you've done it. How are you going to eat with a broken beak? You can't eat anything with a broken beak. You'll starve, you stupid goddamn chicken."

A wind that smelled of rain had sprung up. It ruffled his feathers until they moved with a barely discernible crackle.

"Poor Stanley," I said, and at last, numbed by the pain, he allowed me to stroke the gloss of his lacquer feathers.

I wasn't strong enough or practised enough to do a clean and efficient job of wringing his neck, but I succeeded in finishing him off after two clumsy attempts. Then, because I wanted to leave the impression that a skunk had made off with him, I punched a couple of holes in his breast with my jack knife and tried to dribble some blood on the ground. Poor Stanley produced only a few meagre spots; this corpse refused to bleed in the presence of its murderer. I scattered a handful of his feathers on the ground and buried him in the larger of the two manure piles beside the barn.

"I don't think any skunk got that rooster," my grandmother said suspiciously, nudging at a feather with the toe of her boot until, finally disturbed, it was wafted away by the breeze.

Something squeezed my heart. How did she know?

"Skunks hunt at night," she said. "Must have been some-body's barn cat."

"You come along with me," my grandmother said. She was standing in front of the full-length hall mirror, settling on her hat, a deadly-looking hat pin poised above her skull. "We'll go into town and you can buy a comic book at the drugstore."

It was Friday and Friday was shopping day. But Grandma didn't wheel her battered De Soto to the curb in front of the Brite Spot Grocery, she parked it in front of Maynard & Pritchard, Barristers and Solicitors.

"What are we doing here?" I asked.

Grandma was fumbling nervously with her purse. Smalltown people don't like to be seen going to the lawyer's. "Come along with me. Hurry up."

"Why do I have to come?"

"Because I don't want you making a spectacle of yourself for the half-wits and loungers to gawk at," she said. "Let's not give them too much to wonder about."

Maynard & Pritchard, Barristers and Solicitors, smelled of wax and varnish and probity. My grandmother was shown into an office with a frosted pane of glass in the door and neat gilt lettering that announced it was occupied by D.F. Maynard, Q.C. I was ordered to occupy a hard chair, which I did, battering my heels on the rungs briskly enough to annoy the secretary into telling me to stop it.

My grandmother wasn't closeted long with her Queen's Counsel before the door opened and he glided after her into the passageway. Lawyer Maynard was the neatest man I had ever seen in my life. His suit fit him like a glove.

"The best I can do," he said, "is send him a registered letter telling him to remove himself from the premises, but it all comes to the same thing. If that doesn't scare him off, you'll have to have recourse to the police. That's all there is to it. I told you that yesterday and you haven't told me anything new today, Edith, that would make me change my mind. Just let him know you won't put up with him any more."

"No police," she said. "I don't want the police digging in my family's business and Evelyn giving one of her grand performances for some baby-skinned constable straight out of the depot. All I need is to get her away from him for a little while, then I could tune her in. I could get through to her in no time at all."

"Well," said Maynard, shrugging, "we could try the letter, but I don't think it would do any good. He has the status of a guest in your home; just tell him to go."

My grandmother was showing signs of exasperation. "But he *doesn't* go. That's the point. I've told him and told him. But he *won't.*"

"Mrs. Bradley," said the lawyer emphatically, "Edith, as a friend, don't waste your time. The police."

"I'm through wasting my time," she said.

Pulling away from the lawyer's office, my grandmother began a spirited conversation with herself. A wisp of hair had escaped from under her hat, and the dye winked a metallic red light as it jiggled up and down in the hot sunshine.

"I've told him and told him. But he won't listen. The goddamn freak thinks we're involved in a christly debating society. He thinks I don't mean business. But I mean business. I do. There's more than one way to skin a cat or scratch a dog's ass. We'll take the wheels off his little red wagon and see how she pulls."

"What about my comic book?" I said, as we drove past the Rexall.

"Shut up."

Grandma drove the De Soto to the edge of town and stopped it at the Ogdens' place. It was a service station, or rather had been until the B.A. company had taken out their pumps and yanked the franchise, or whatever you call it, on the two brothers. Since then everything had gone steadily downhill. Cracks in the windowpanes had been taped with masking tape, and the roof had been patched with flattened tin cans and old licence plates. The building itself was surrounded by an acre of wrecks, sulking hulks rotten with rust, the guts of their upholstery spilled and gnawed by rats and mice.

But the Ogden brothers still carried on a business after a fashion. They stripped their wrecks for parts and were reputed to be decent enough mechanics whenever they were sober enough to turn a wrench or thread a bolt. People brought work to them whenever they couldn't avoid it, and the rest of the year gave them a wide berth.

The Ogdens were famous for two things: their meanness and their profligacy as breeders. The place was always aswarm with kids who never seemed to wear pants except in the most severe weather, and tottered about the premises, their legs smeared with grease, shit, or various combinations of both.

"Wait here," my grandmother said, slamming the car door loudly enough to bring the two brothers out of their shop. Through the open door I saw a motor suspended on an intricate system of chains and pulleys.

The Ogdens stood with their hands in the pockets of their bib overalls while my grandmother talked to them. They were quite a sight. They didn't have a dozen teeth in their heads between them, even though the oldest brother couldn't have been more than forty. They just stood there, one sucking on a cigarette, the other on a Coke. Neither one moved or changed his expression, except once, when a tow-headed youngster piddled too close to Grandma. He was lazily and casually slapped on the side of the head by the nearest brother and ran away screaming, his stream cavorting wildly in front of him.

At last, their business concluded, the boys walked my grandmother back to the car.

"You'll get to that soon?" she said, sliding behind the wheel.

"Tomorrow all right?" said one. His words sounded all slack and chewed, issuing from his shrunken, old man's mouth.

"The sooner the better. I want that seen to, Bert."

"What seen to?" I asked.

"Bert and his brother Elwood are going to fix that rattle that's been plaguing me."

"Sure thing," said Elwood. "Nothing but clear sailing."

"What rattle?" I said.

"What rattle? What rattle? The one in the glove compartment," she said, banging it with the heel of her hand. "That rattle. You hear it?"

Thompson could get very edgy some days. "I should be working on my dissertation," he said, coiled in the big chair. "I shouldn't be wasting my time in this shit-hole. I should be working!"

"So why aren't you?" said Evelyn. She was spool knitting. That and reading movie magazines were the only things she ever did.

"How the christ do I work without a library? You see a goddamn library within a hundred miles of this place?"

"Why do you need a library?" she said calmly. "Can't you write?"

"Write," he said, looking at the ceiling. "Write, she says. What the hell do you know about it? What the hell do you know about it?"

"I can't see why you can't write."

"Before you write, you research. That's what you do, you *research.*"

"So bite my head off. It wasn't my idea to come here."

"It wasn't me that lost my goddamn job. How the hell were we supposed to pay the rent?"

"You could have got a job."

"I'm a student. Anyway, I told you, if I get a job my wife gets her hooks into me for support. I'll starve to death before I support that bitch."

"We could go back."

"How many times does it have to be explained to you? I don't get my scholarship cheque until the first of September. We happen to be broke. Absolutely. In fact, you're going to have to hit the old lady up for gas and eating money to get back to the coast. We're stuck here. Get that into your empty fucking head. The Lord Buddha might have been able to subsist on a single bean a day; I can't."

My grandmother came into the room. The conversation stopped.

"Do you think," she said to Thompson, "I could ask you to do me a favour?"

"Why, Mrs. Bradley," he said, smiling, "whatever do you mean?"

"I was wondering whether you could take my car into town to Ogdens' to get it fixed."

"Oh," said Thompson. "I don't know where it is. I don't think I'm your man."

"Ask anyone where it is. They can tell you. It isn't hard to find."

"Why would you ask me to do you a favour, Mrs. Bradley?" inquired Thompson complacently. Hearing his voice was like listening to someone drag their nails down a blackboard.

"Well, you can be goddamn sure I wouldn't," said Grandma, trying to keep a hold on herself, "except that I'm right in the middle of doing my pickling and canning. I thought you might be willing to move your lazy carcass to do something around here. Every time I turn around I seem to be falling over those legs of yours." She looked at the limbs in question as if she would like to dock them somewhere in the vicinity of the knee.

"No, I don't think I can," said Thompson easily, stroking his goat beard.

"And why the hell can't you?"

"Oh, let's just say I don't trust you, Mrs. Bradley. I don't like to leave you alone with Evelyn. Lord knows what ideas you might put in her head."

"Or take out."

"That's right. Or take out," said Thompson with satisfaction. "You can't imagine the trouble it took me to get them in there." He turned to Evelyn. "She can't imagine the trouble, can she, dear?"

Evelyn threw her spool knitting on the floor and walked out of the room.

"Evelyn's mad and I'm glad," shouted Thompson at her back. "And I know how to tease her!"

"Charlie, come here," said Grandma. I went over to her. She took me firmly by the shoulder. "From now on," said my grandma, "my family is off limits to you. I don't want to see you talking to Charlie here, or to come within sniffing distance of Evelyn."

"What do you think of that idea, Charlie?" said Thompson. "Are you still my friend or what?"

I gave him a wink my grandma couldn't see. He thought that was great; he laughed like a madman. "Superb," he said. "Superb. There's no flies on Charlie. What a diplomat."

"What the hell is the matter with you, Mr. Beatnik?" asked Grandma, annoyed beyond bearing. "What's so goddamn funny?"

"Ha ha!" roared Thompson. "What a charming notion! Me a beatnik!"

Grandma Bradley held the mouthpiece of the phone very close to her lips as she spoke into it. "No, it can't be brought in. You'll have to come out here to do the job."

She listened with an intent expression on her face. Spotting me pretending to look in the fridge, she waved me out of the kitchen with her hand. I dragged myself out and stood quietly in the hallway.

"This is a party line," she said, "remember that."

Another pause while she listened.

"Okay," she said and hung up.

I spent some of my happiest hours squatting in the corn patch. I was completely hidden there; even when I stood, the maturing stalks reached a foot or more above my head. It was a good place. On the hottest days it was relatively cool in that thicket of green where the shade was dark and deep and the leaves rustled and scraped and sawed dryly overhead.

Nobody ever thought to look for me there. They could bellow their bloody lungs out for me and I could just sit and watch them getting uglier and uglier about it all. There was some satisfaction in that. I'd just reach up and pluck myself a cob. I loved raw corn. The newly formed kernels were tiny, pale pearls of sweetness that gushed juice. I'd munch and munch and smile and smile and think, why don't you drop dead?

It was my secret place, my sanctuary, where I couldn't be found or touched by them. But all the same, if I didn't let them intrude on me – that didn't mean I didn't want to keep tabs on things.

At the time I was watching Thompson stealing peas at the other end of the garden. He was like some primitive man who lived in a gathering culture. My grandma kept him so hungry he was constantly prowling for food: digging in cupboards, rifling the refrigerator, scrounging in the garden.

Clad only in Bermuda shorts he was a sorry sight. His bones threatened to rupture his skin and jut out every which way. He sported a scrub-board chest with two old pennies for nipples, and a wispy garland of hair decorated his sunken breastbone. His legs looked particularly rackety; all gristle, knobs and sinew.

We both heard the truck at the same time. It came bucking up the approach, spurting gravel behind it. Thompson turned around, shaded his eyes and peered at it. He wasn't much interested. He couldn't get very curious about the natives.

The truck stopped and a man stepped out on to the runningboard of the '51 IHC. He gazed around him, obviously looking for something or someone. This character had a blue handkerchief sprinkled with white polka dots tied in a triangle over his face. Exactly like an outlaw in an Audie Murphy western. A genuine goddamn Jesse James.

He soon spotted Thompson standing half-naked in the garden, staring stupidly at this strange sight, his mouth bulging with peas. The outlaw ducked his head back into the cab of the truck, said something to the driver, and pointed. The driver then stepped out on to his runningboard and, standing on tippy-toe, peered over the roof of the cab at Thompson. He too wore a handkerchief tied over his mug, but his was red.

Then they both got down from the truck and began to walk very quickly towards Thompson with long, menacing strides.

"Fellows?" said Thompson.

At the sound of his voice the two men broke into a stiff-legged trot, and the one with the red handkerchief, while still moving, stooped down smoothly and snatched up the hoe that lay at the edge of the garden.

"What the hell is going on here, boys?" said Thompson, his voice pitched high with concern.

The man with the blue mask reached Thompson first. One long arm, a dirty clutch of fingers on its end, snaked out and caught him by the hair and jerked his head down. Then he kicked him in the pit of the stomach with his work boots.

"Okay, fucker," he shouted, "too fucking smart to take a fucking hint?" and he punched him on the side of the face with several short, snapping blows that actually tore Thompson's head out of his grip. Thompson toppled over clumsily and fell in the dirt. "Get fucking lost," Blue Mask said more quietly.

"Evelyn!" yelled Thompson to the house. "Jesus Christ, Evelyn!"

I crouched lower in the corn patch and began to tremble. I was certain they were going to kill him.

"Shut up," said the man with the hoe. He glanced at the blade for a second, considered, then rotated the handle in his hands and hit Thompson a quick chop on the head with the blunt side. "Shut your fucking yap," he repeated.

"Evelyn! Evelyn! Oh God!" hollered Thompson, "I'm being murdered! For God's sake, somebody help me!" The side of his face was slick with blood.

"I told you shut up, cock sucker," said Red Mask, and kicked him in the ribs several times. Thompson groaned and hugged himself in the dust.

"Now you get lost, fucker," said the one with the hoe, "because if you don't stop bothering nice people we'll drive a spike in your skull."

"Somebody help me!" Thompson yelled at the house.

"Nobody there is going to help you," Blue Mask said. "You're all on your own, smart arse."

"You bastards," said Thompson, and spat ineffectually in their direction.

For his defiance he got struck a couple of chopping blows with the hoe. The last one skittered off his collar-bone with a sickening crunch.

"That's enough," said Red Mask, catching the handle of the hoe. "Come on."

The two sauntered back towards the truck, laughing. They weren't in any hurry to get out of there. Thompson lay on his side staring at their retreating backs. His face was wet with tears and blood.

The man with the red mask looked back over his shoulder and wiggled his ass at Thompson in an implausible imitation of effeminacy. "Was it worth it, tiger?" he shouted. "Getting your ashes hauled don't come cheap, do it?"

This set them off again. Passing me they pulled off their masks and stuffed them in their pockets. They didn't have to worry about Thompson when they had their backs to him: he couldn't see their faces. But I could. No surprise. They were the Ogden boys.

When the truck pulled out of the yard, its gears grinding, I burst out of my hiding place and ran to Thompson, who had got to his knees and was trying to stop the flow of blood from his scalp with his fingers. He was crying. Another first for Thompson. He was the first man I'd seen cry. It made me uncomfortable.

"The sons of bitches broke my ribs," he said, panting with shallow breaths. "God, I hope they didn't puncture a lung."

"Can you walk?" I asked.

"Don't think I don't know who's behind this," he said, getting carefully to his feet. His face was white. "You saw them," he said. "You saw their faces from the corn patch. We got the bastards."

He leaned a little on me as we made our way to the house. The front door was locked. We knocked. No answer. "Let me in, you old bitch!" shouted Thompson.

"Evelyn, open the goddamn door!" Silence. I couldn't hear a thing move in the house. It was as if they were all dead in there. It frightened me.

He started to kick the door. A panel splintered. "Open this door! Let me in, you old slut, or I'll kill you!"

Nothing.

"You better go," I said nervously. I didn't like this one little bit. "Those guys might come back and kill you."

"Evelyn!" he bellowed. "Evelyn!"

He kept it up for a good five minutes, alternately hammering and kicking the door, pleading with and threatening the occupants. By the end of that time he was sweating with exertion and pain. He went slowly down the steps, sobbing, beaten. "You saw them," he said, "we have the bastards dead to rights."

He winced when he eased his bare flesh onto the hot seat-covers of the car.

"I'll be back," he said, starting the motor of the car. "This isn't the end of this."

When Grandma was sure he had gone, the front door was unlocked and I was let in. I noticed my grandmother's hands trembled a touch when she lit her cigarette.

"You can't stay away from him, can you?" she said testily.

"You didn't have to do that," I said. "He was hurt. You ought to have let him in."

"I ought to have poisoned him a week ago. And don't talk about things you don't know anything about."

"Sometimes," I said, "all of you get on my nerves."

"Kids don't have nerves. Adults have nerves. They're the only ones entitled to them. And don't think I care a plugged nickel what does, or doesn't, get on your nerves."

"Where's Aunt Evelyn?"

"Your Aunt Evelyn is taken care of," she replied.

"Why wouldn't she come to the door?"

"She had her own road to Damascus. She has seen the light. Everything has been straightened out," she said. "Everything is back to normal."

He looked foolish huddled in the back of the police car later that evening. When the sun began to dip, the temperature dropped rapidly, and he was obviously cold dressed only in his Bermuda shorts. Thompson sat all hunched up to relieve the strain on his ribs, his hands pressed between his knees, shivering.

My grandmother and the constable spoke quietly by the car for some time; occasionally Thompson poked his head out the car window and said something. By the look on the constable's face when he spoke to Thompson, it was obvious he didn't care for him too much. Thompson had that kind of effect on people. Several times during the course of the discussion the constable glanced my way.

I edged a little closer so I could hear what they were saying.

"He's mad as a hatter," said my grandmother. "I don't know anything about any two men. If you ask me, all this had something to do with drugs. My daughter says that this man takes drugs. He's some kind of beatnik."

"Christ," said Thompson, drawing his knees up as if to scrunch himself into a smaller, less noticeable package, "the woman is insane."

"One thing at a time, Mrs. Bradley," said the RCMP constable.

"My daughter is finished with him," she said. "He beats her, you know. I want him kept off my property."

"I want to speak to Evelyn," Thompson said. He looked bedraggled and frightened. "Evelyn and I will leave this minute if this woman wants. But I've got to talk to Evelyn."

"My daughter doesn't want to see you, mister. She's finished with you," said Grandma Bradley, shifting her weight from side to side. She turned her attention to the constable. "He beats her," she said, "bruises all over her. Can you imagine?"

"The boy knows," said Thompson desperately. "He saw them. How many times do I have to tell you?" He piped his voice to me. "Didn't you, Charlie? You saw them, didn't you?"

"Charlie?" said my Grandmother. This was news to her.

I stood very still.

"Come here, son," said the constable.

I walked slowly over to them.

"Did you see the faces of the men?" the constable asked, putting a hand on my shoulder. "Do you know the men? Are they from around here?"

"How would he know?" said my grandmother. "He's a stranger."

"He knows them. At least he saw them," said Thompson. "My little Padma-sambhava never misses a trick," he said, trying to jolly me. "You see everything, don't you, Charlie? You remember everything, don't you?"

I looked at my grandmother, who stood so calmly and commandingly, waiting.

"Hey, don't look to her for the answers," said Thompson nervously. "Don't be afraid of her. You remember everything, don't you?"

He had no business begging me. I had watched their game from the sidelines long enough to know the rules. At one time he had imagined himself a winner. And now he was asking me to save him, to take a risk, when I was more completely in her clutches than he would ever be. He forgot I was a child. I depended on her.

Thompson, I saw, was powerless. He couldn't protect me. God, I remembered more than he dreamed. I remembered how his lips had moved soundlessly, his face pleading with the ceiling, his face blotted of everything but abject urgency. Praying to a simpering, cross-eyed idol. His arm flashing as he struck my aunt's bare legs. Crawling in the dirt, covered with blood.

He had taught me that "Those who are in the grip of desire, the grip of existence, the grip of ignorance, move helplessly round through the spheres of life, as men or gods or as wretches in the lower regions." Well, he was helpless now. But he insisted on fighting back and hurting the rest of us. The weak ones like Evelyn and me.

I thought of Stanley the rooster and how it had felt when the tendons separated, the gristle parted and the bones crunched under my twisting hands.

"I don't know what he's talking about," I said to the constable softly. "I didn't see anybody."

"Clear out," said my grandmother triumphantly. "Beat it."

"You dirty little son of a bitch," he said to me. "You mean little bugger."

He didn't understand much. He had forced me into the game, and now that I was a player and no longer a watcher he didn't like it. The thing was that I was good at the game. But he, being a loser, couldn't appreciate that.

Then suddenly he said, "Evelyn." He pointed to the upstairs

window of the house and tried to get out of the back seat of the police car. But of course he couldn't. They take the handles off the back doors. Nobody can get out unless they are let out.

"Goddamn it!" he shouted. "Let me out! She's waving to me! She wants me!"

I admit that the figure was hard to make out at that distance. But any damn fool could see she was only waving goodbye.

Reunion

IT WAS a vivid countryside they drove through, green with new wheat, yellow with random spatters of wild mustard, blue with flax. The red and black cattle, their hides glistening with the greasy shine of good pasture, left off grazing to watch the car pass, pursued by a cloud of boiling dust. Poplar bluffs in the distance shook in the watery heat haze with a crazy light, crows whirled lazily in the sky like flakes of black ash rising from a fire.

The man, his wife, and their little boy were travelling to a Stiles family reunion. It was the woman who was a Stiles, had been *born* a Stiles rather. Her husband was a Cosgrave.

The boy wasn't entirely certain who he was. Of course, most times he was a Cosgrave. That was his name, Brian Anthony Cosgrave, and he was six years old and could spell every one of his names. But in the company of his mother's people, somehow he became a Stiles. None of them saw anything but his mother in him: hair, eyes, nose, mouth – all were so like hers they might have been borrowed, relatives exclaimed. Since his father had no people (at least none that mattered enough to visit), Brian Anthony Cosgrave had never heard the other side of the story.

"For God's sake, Jack," Edith Cosgrave said, "stay away from the whiskey for once. It's a warm day. If they offer you whiskey ask for a beer instead. On a hot day it isn't rude to ask for a beer."

"Yes, mother dear," her husband said, eyes fixed on the grid road. "No, mother. If you please, mother. Christ."

"You know as well as I do what happens when you drink whiskey, Jack. It goes down too easy and you lose count of how many you've had. I don't begrudge you your beers. It's that damn whiskey," she said angrily.

"It tastes twice as good when I know the pain it costs a Stiles to put it on the table."

"Or me to watch you guzzle it."

"Shit."

The Cosgrave family had the slightly harried and shabby look of people who, although not quite poor, know only too well and intimately the calculations involved in buying a new winter coat, eyeglasses, or a pair of shoes. Jack Cosgrave's old black suit was sprung taut across his belly, pinched him under the armpits. It also showed a waxy-white scar on the shoulders where it had hung crookedly on a hanger, untouched for months.

His wife, however, had tried to rise to the occasion. This involved an attempt to dress up a white blouse and pleated skirt with two purchases: a cheap scarlet belt cinched tightly at her waist and a string of large red beads wound round her throat.

The boy sat numbly on the back seat in a starched white shirt, strangled by a clip-on bow tie and itching in his one pair of "good" pants – heavy wool trousers.

"They're not to be borne without whiskey," Cosgrave muttered, "your family."

"And you're not to be borne with it in you," she answered sharply. But relented. Perhaps it did not pay to keep at him today. "Please, Jack," she said, "let's have a nice time for once. Don't embarrass me. Be a gentleman. Let me hold my head up. Show some respect for my family."

"That's all *I* ask," he said, speaking quickly. "I'd like a little respect from *them*. They all look at me as if I was something the goddamn cat dragged in and dropped in the front parlour." Saying this, he gave an angry little spurt to the gas pedal for emphasis and the car responded by slewing around in the loose gravel on the road, pebbles chattering on the undercarriage.

So like Jack, she thought, to be a bit reckless. A careless, passionate man. It was what drew her to him in the beginning. His recklessness, his charming ways, his sweet cunning. So different from what she had learned of the male character from observing her brothers: slow, apple-faced men who plodded about their business, the languor of routine steeped deep into their heavy limbs.

Edith Cosgrave glanced at her husband's face. A face dark with furious blood, dark as a plum. He was right in believing her family didn't think much of him. She could not deny it. A man meant to work for wages all his life, that was how her brothers would put it. She only wished Jack had not failed in that first business. It had been his one chance, bought with the little money his father had left him. He was unsuited to taking orders, job after job had proved that. Now he found himself a clerk, standing behind a counter in a hardware store, courtly and gallant to women, patient with children, sullen and rude to men. Faithful to his conception of what a man owed to pride.

"It's not as bad as all that," she said. "Don't get your Irish up."

He smiled suddenly, a crooked, delighted grin. "If one of them, just one of them, happens to mention – as they always do, the bastards – that this car is getting long in the tooth, why, my dear, that Stiles sleeps tonight cold in the ground with a clay comforter, I swear. Who gives a shit if my car is nine years old? I don't. Nineteen forty-six was a very good year for Fords. A good year in general, wasn't it, mother?"

"You're a fool," she said. It was the year they had married. "And whether it was a good year or not depends on how you look at it." Still, she was glad to see his dark mood broken, and couldn't help smiling back at him with a mixture of relief and indulgence. The man could smile, she had to grant him that.

"How long is this holy, blessed event, this gathering of the tribe Stiles, to continue?" he asked with the heavy irony that had become second nature whenever he spoke of his in-laws.

"I don't have the faintest. When you're ready to leave just say so."

"Oh no. I'm not bearing that awful responsibility. I can see them all now, casting that baleful Stiles look, the one your father used to give me, certain that I'm tearing you against your will out of the soft, warm bosom of the family. Poor Edith."

"Jack."

"What we need is a secret signal," Cosgrave said, delighted as always by any fanciful notion that happened to strike him. "What if I stamp my foot three times when I want to go home? Like this." He pounded his left foot down on the floorboards three times, slowly and deliberately, like a carnival horse stamping out the solution to an arithmetic puzzle for the wondering, gaping yokels.

Brian laughed exuberantly.

"No, no," his father declared, glancing over his shoulder at the boy, playing to his audience, "that won't do. If I know your mother she'd just pretend to think that my foot had gone to sleep and ignore me. I know her ways, the rascal."

"Watch the road or you'll murder us all."

"What if I hum a tune? That would be the ticket. Who'd catch on to that?"

"Goodnight Irene," his wife suggested, entering into the spirit of the thing. "You used to sing it to me when you left me on the doorstep when we were going out." She winked at Brian. He flung his torso over the front seat, wriggled his shoulders, and giggled.

"Mind your shirt buttons," his mother warned him, "or you'll tear them off."

"My dear woman, you must have me confused with what's his name, Arnold Something-or-other. He was the type to croon on doorsteps. I was much more forward. If you remember."

"Jack, watch your mouth. Little pitchers have big ears."

"Anyway," he carried on, " 'Goodnight Irene' isn't it. How about 'God Save the Queen'? Much more appropriate to conclude a boring occasion. Standard fare to bring to an end any gathering in this fair Dominion. After all, it's one of your favourites, Edith. I'll pay a little vocal tribute to Her Majesty, Missus the Duke, by the Grace of God, etc. How does that strike you, honey?"

He was teasing her. For although the Stileses' hard-headed toughness ran deep in his wife, she had a romantic weakness for the royal family. There was her scrapbook of coronation pictures, her tears for Captain Townsend and the Princess. And, most treasured of all, a satin bookmark with Edward VIII's abdication speech printed on it. She had been a girl when he relinquished the crown and it had seemed to her that Edward's love for Mrs. Simpson was something so fine, so beyond earthly considerations, that the capacity for such feelings had to be the birthright of kings. Only a king could love like that.

"Don't tease, Jack," she said, lips tightening.

Brian flung himself back against the back seat, sobered by the knowledge she meant business. The game, the light-heartedness, were at an end.

"Oh, for Christ's sake," his father said testily, "now we're offended for the bloody Queen."

"You never know when enough is enough, do you? You've always got to push it. So what if I feel a certain way about the Queen? Or my family? Why can't you respect that?"

The car rushed down into a little valley where a creek had slipped its banks and puddled on the bay flats, bright as mercury. The Ford ground up the opposing hills. Swearing and double-clutching, his father had to gear down twice to make the grade. A few miles on, a sign greeted them. Brian, who read even cornflakes boxes aloud, said carefully: "Welcome to Manitoba."

The town was an old one judged by prairie standards and had the settled, completed look that most lack. Where Brian lived there were no red-brick houses built by settlers from Ontario, fewer mountain ashes or elms planted on the streets. The quality of the shade these trees cast surprised him when he stepped from the car. It swam, glided over the earth. It was full of breezes and sudden glittering shifts of light. Yet it was deeper, cooler, bluer than any he could remember. He threw his head back and stared, perplexed, into a net of branches.

His mother took him by the hand, and, his father follow-ing, they started up the walk to what had been her father's house and now was her eldest brother's. A big house, two storeys of mustard-coloured stucco, white trim, and green shingles, it stood on a double lot. The lawn was dotted with relatives.

"They must have emptied the jails and asylums for the occasion," his father observed. "Quite a turnout."

"Jack," Edith said perfunctorily as she struggled with the gate latch.

Brian could sense the current of excitement running in his mother's body and he felt obscurely jealous. To see the famil-iar faces of aunts, uncles, brothers, and the cousins with whom she had idled away the summers of childhood had made his mother shed the tawdry adult years like a snake sheds an old and worn skin. Every one of them liked her. She was a favourite with them all. Even more so now that they felt sorry for her.

"Edith!" they cried when they hugged and kissed her. Brian had his hair rumpled and, in a confusion of adult legs, his toes stepped on once. An uncle picked him up, hefted him judiciously, pretended to guess his weight. "This is a big one!" he shouted. "A whopper! A hundred and ninety if he's a pound!"

Jack Cosgrave stood uncomfortably a little off from the small crowd surrounding his wife, smiling uneasily, his hands thrust in his pockets. He took refuge in lighting a cigarette and appearing to study the second-storey windows of the house. He had spent one night up there in the first year of their marriage. But never again. That same year he had come to his father-in-law with a business proposition when the shoe store failed. A business proposition the miserable old shit had turned down flat. None of the rest of those Stileses needed to think things wouldn't have been different for Jack Cosgrave if he had got a little help when he really needed it. If he had, he'd have been in clover this minute instead of walking around with his ass practically hanging out of his pants and nothing in his pockets to jingle but his balls.

"Brian," said Edith, her arm loosely circling a sister-in-law's waist, "you run along and play with your cousins. Over there, see?" She pointed to a group of kids flying around the lawn, chanting taunts to one another as they played tag. "*Can't catch me for a bumble bee!*" squealed a pale girl with long, coltish legs.

"Just be careful you don't get grass stains on your pants, okay, honey?"

The boy felt forlorn at this urging to join in. His mother, returned to her element, sure of the rich sympathies of blood, could not imagine the desolation he felt looking at those children's strange faces.

"Bob, dear," said Edith, turning to a brother, "keep an eye on Jack, won't you? See that he doesn't get lonely without me." They all laughed. Among the stolid Stileses Edith had a reputation as a joker. Jack Cosgrave, looking at his wife's open, relaxed face, seeing her easiness among these people, felt betrayed.

"Sure, sure thing, Edith," replied her brother. He turned to Cosgrave, seemed to hesitate, touched him on the elbow. "Come along and say hello to the fellows, Jack." He indicated a card table set under a Manitoba maple around which a group of men were sitting. They started for it together.

"Jack," said Bob, "these are my cousins from Binscarth, Earl and George. You know Albert, of course." Jack Cosgrave knew Albert. Albert was Edith's youngest brother and the one who had the least use for him. "This here is Edith's husband, Jack Cosgrave."

"Hi, Jack, take a load off," said one of the men. Earl, he thought it was. Cosgrave nodded to the table, but before he took a seat his eye was caught by his son standing, arms dangling hopelessly as he watched his cousins race across the grass. The boy was uncertain about the etiquette of entering games played by strangers in strange towns, on strange lawns.

"Pour Jack a rye."

"You want 7-Up or Coke?" asked Albert, without a trace of interest in his voice.

"What?" The question had startled Cosgrave out of his study of his son.

"Coke or 7-Up."

"7-Up." He sat down, took the paper cup, and glanced at the sky. The blue had been burned out of it by a white sun. No wonder he was sweating. He loosened his tie and said the first thing that came to mind, "Well, this'll make the crops come, boys."

"What will?" asked Albert.

"This here sun," said Jack, turning his palm up to the sky. "This heat."

"Make the weeds come on my summer fallow. That's what it'll do," declared Earl.

"Don't you listen to Earl," confided Bob. "He's got the cleanest summer fallow in the municipality. You could eat off it."

"Is that so?" said Jack. "I'd like to see that."

"Go on with you," said Earl to no one in particular. He was pleased.

The conversation ran on, random and disconnected. There was talk of the hard spring, calf scours, politics, Catholics, and curling. Totting up the score after four drinks, Jack concluded hard springs, calf scours, politics, and Catholics weren't worth a cup of cold piss. That seemed to be the consensus. Curling, however, was all right. Provided a fellow didn't run all over the province going to bonspiels and neglect his chores.

Jack helped himself to another drink and watched the tip of the shadow of a spruce advance slowly across the lawn. It's aimed at my black heart, he thought, and speculated as to when it would reach it.

"I would have got black," said Albert of his new car with satisfaction, "but you know how black shows dust. It's as bad as white any day."

"Maybe next year for me," said George. "An automatic for sure. I could teach the wife to drive with an automatic."

"Good reason not to get it," said someone.

"Albert's got power steering," Bob informed Jack. "I told him he was crazy to pay extra for that. I said, 'The day a man hasn't got the strength to twist his own steering-wheel . . . ,' well, I don't know." He shook his head at how the very idea had rendered him speechless.

"What you driving now, Jack?" Albert asked smoothly, leaning across the table.

You conniving, malicious shit, thought Cosgrave. Still doing your level best to show me up. "The same car I had last year, and the year before that, and the year before that. In fact, as I said to Edith coming down here, I bought that car the year we got married." He stared at Albert, defiance in his face.

"I wouldn't have thought it was that old," said Albert.

"Oh yes it is, Bert," said Cosgrave. "That car *is* old. Older than dirt. Why, I've had that car almost as long as you've had the first nickel you ever made. And I won't part with it. No, sir. I'd as soon part with that car as you would with your first nickel."

"Ha ha!" blurted out cousin Earl. Then, embarrassed at breaking family ranks, he took a Big Ben pocket watch out of his trousers and looked at it, hard.

Jack Cosgrave was drunk and he knew it. Drunk and didn't care. He reached for the whiskey bottle and, as he did, spotted Brian sitting stiffly by himself on the porch steps, his white shirt blazing in the hot sunshine.

"Brian!" he called. "Brian!"

The boy climbed off the steps and made his way slowly across the lawn. Cosgrave put his arm around him and drew him up against his side. His father's breath was hot in the boy's face. The sharp medicinal smell repelled him.

"Why aren't you playing?"

Brian shrugged. Shyness had paralysed him; after a few half-hearted feints and diffident insults which had been ignored by the chaser, he had given up.

Jack Cosgrave saw that the other boys were now wrestling. Grappling, twisting and fencing with their feet, they flung one another to the grass. He pulled Brian closer to him, put his mouth to the boy's ear and whispered: "Why don't you get in there and show them what a Cosgrave can do? Whyn't you toss a Stiles on his ass, eh?"

"Can't," mumbled Brian in an agony of self-consciousness.

"Why?"

"Mum says I have to keep my pants clean."

"Sometimes your mother hasn't got much sense," Cosgrave said, baffled by the boy's reluctance. Was he scared? "She's got you all dressed up like Little Lord Fauntleroy and expects you to have a good time. Give me that goddamn thing," he said, pulling off the boy's bow tie and putting it in his pocket. "Now go and have some fun."

"These are my good pants," Brian said stubbornly.

"Well, we'll take them off," said his father. "It's a hot day."

"*No!*" The child was shocked.

"Don't be such a christly old woman. You've got boxer shorts on. They look like real shorts."

"Jesus, you're not going to take the kid's pants off, are you?" inquired Albert.

Cosgrave looked up sharply. Albert wore the concentrated, stubborn look of a man with a grievance. "I am. What's it to you?"

"Well, Jesus, we're not Indians here or anything to have kids roaming around with no pants on."

"No, I don't want to," whispered Brian.

"For chrissakes," said Jack. "You've embarrassed the kid now. Why'd you do that? He's only six years old."

"It wasn't him that wanted to take his pants off, was it? I don't know how you were brought up, or dragged up maybe, but we were taught to keep our pants on in company. Isn't that so, Bob?"

Bob didn't reply. He composed his face and peered down into his paper cup.

"Bert," said Jack, "you're a pain in the arse. You're also one hell of a small-minded son of a bitch."

"I don't think there's any need –" began Bob.

"No, no," said Albert. He held his hand up to silence his brother. "Jack feels he's got things to get off his chest. Well, so do I. He thinks I'm small-minded. Maybe I am. I guess in his books a small-minded man is a man that lets a debt go for four years without once mentioning it. A man that never tries to collect. Is that a small-minded man, Jack? Is it? Because if it is, I plead guilty. And what do you call a man who doesn't pay up? Welsher?"

"*I* never borrowed money from you in my life," said Cosgrave thickly. "What *she* does is her business. I told her not to write and ask for money."

"You're a liar."

"Hey, fellows," said Bob anxiously, "this is a family occasion. No trouble, eh? There's women and kids here."

"I told her not to write! I can't keep track of everything she does! I didn't want your goddamn money!"

"In this family we know better," said Albert Stiles. "We know who does and doesn't hide behind his wife's skirts. We know that in our family."

Edith Cosgrave came down the porch steps just as her husband lunged to his feet, snatched a handful of her brother's shirt and punched clumsily at his face. Albert's folding chair tipped and the two of them spilled over in an angular pinwheel of limbs. It was only when sprawled on the grass that Jack finally did some damage by accidentally butting Albert on the bridge of the nose, sending a gush of blood down his lips. Then they were separated.

By the time Edith had run across the grass, ungainly on her heels, Bob was leading Albert to the house. Albert was holding his nose with his fingers, trying to stanch the blood which dripped on his cuffs and saying, "Son of a bitch, they're going to have to cauterize this. Once my nose starts bleeding . . ."

A few women and children were standing some distance off, mute, staring. Jack was trying to button his suit jacket with trembling fingers. "That'll hold him for a while, loudmouthed –" he began to say when he saw his wife approaching.

"Shut up," she said in a level voice. "Shut your mouth. Your son is listening to you, for God's sake." She was right. The boy was listening and looking, face white and curdled with fright. "And if you hadn't noticed, the others are politely standing over there, gawking at the wild colonial boy. You're drunk and you're disgusting."

"I'm not drunk."

She slapped him hard enough to make his eyes water, his ears ring. "Christ," he said, stunned. She had never hit him before.

"You're a drunken, stupid pig," she said. "I'm sick of the sight of you."

"Don't you ever hit me again, you bitch." He wiped his lips with the back of his hand.

"Don't you ever give me reason to again. Stop ruining my life."

"You don't want to hear my side. You never do."

"I've heard it for nine years."

"He was yapping about that hundred dollars you borrowed. I said it wasn't any of my affair. I want you to tell him I didn't have anything to do with it."

"Nothing at all. No, you didn't have anything to do with it. You just ate the groceries it bought."

"I didn't ask him for anything. I wouldn't ask him for sweet fuck all."

"Don't fool yourself. You don't like being hungry any better than I do. Don't pretend you didn't want me to ask him for the money. Don't fool yourself. You needed my brother Albert because you couldn't take care of your family. Could you?"

Cosgrave straightened himself and touched the knot of his tie. "We're going," he said, as if he hadn't heard her last words, "get the boy ready."

"The hell we are! I want you to apologize to Albert. Families don't forgive things like this."

"It'll be a frosty fucking Friday in hell the day I apologize to Albert Stiles. We're leaving."

"No we aren't. Brian and I are staying. This is my day and I'm having it."

"All right, it's your day. Welcome to it. But it sure isn't mine. If you don't come now, don't expect me back."

His wife said nothing.

It was only when he turned up the street and headed for the beer parlour, his shoulders twisted in his black suit, feet savage on the gravel, that Brian trotted after him, uncertainly, like a dog. The short legs stumbled; the face was pale, afflicted.

His father stopped in the road. "Go back!" he shouted, made furious by his son's helplessness, his abjectness. "Get back there with your mother! Where you both belong!" And then, without thinking, Cosgrave stooped, picked up a tiny pebble and flung it lightly in the direction of his son, who stood in the street in his starched white shirt and prickly wool pants, face working.

By nine o'clock that night the last dirty cup had been washed and the last Stiles had departed. Edith, Brian, Bob and his wife went out to sit in the screened verandah.

It was one of those nights in early summer when the light bleeds drowsily out of the sky, and the sounds of dogs and children falter and die suddenly in the streets when darkness comes. In the peace of such evenings, talk slumbers in the blood, and sentences grow laconic.

Edith mentioned him first. "He may not be back, you know," she said. "You may be stuck with us, Bob."

"His car's still in the street."

"What I mean is, he won't come to the house. And if he sits in the car I won't go to him."

"It's your business, Edith. You know you're welcome."

"He's always lied to himself, you know?" she said calmly. "It's that I get tired of mostly. Big ideas, big schemes. He won't be what he is. I don't complain about the other. He doesn't drink as much as people think. You're mostly wrong about him, all of you, on that count."

Brian sat, his legs thrust stiffly out in front of him, eyes fixed on the street where the dark ran thickest and swiftest under the elms.

"You should cry," suggested her sister-in-law. "Nobody would mind."

"I would. I did all my crying the first year we were married. One thing about him, he's obvious. I saw it all the first year. Forewarned is forearmed. But if he blows that horn he can go to hell. *If he blows it.* I never hit him before," she said softly.

They sat for a time, silent, listening to the moths batter their fat, soft bodies against the naked bulb over the door. It was Brian who saw him first, making his way up the street. "Mum," he said, pointing.

They watched him walk up the street with that precarious precision a drunk adopts to disguise his drunkenness.

"He won't set foot on this place. He's too proud," said Edith. "And if he sits in the car I won't go to him. I've had it up to here."

Cosgrave walked to the front of the property and faced the house. For the people on the verandah it was difficult to make him out beneath the trees, but he saw his wife and son sitting in a cage of light, faces white and burning under the glare of the lightbulb, their features slightly out of focus behind the fine screen mesh. He stood without moving for a minute, then he began to sing in a clear, light tenor. The words rang across the lawn, incongruous, sad.

"Jesus Christ," said Bob, "the man's not only drunk, he's crazy."

Edith leaned forward in her chair and placed her hand against the screen. The vague figure whose face she could not see continued to sing to her across the intervening reaches of night. He sang without a trace of his habitual irony. Where she would have expected a joke there was none. The voice she heard was not the voice of a man in a cheap black suit, a man full of beer and lies. She had, for a fleeting moment, a lover serenading her under the elms. It was as close as he would ever come to an apology or an invitation. Jack Cosgrave was not capable of doing any more and she knew it.

> *God save our gracious Queen,*
> *Long live our noble Queen,*
> *God save the Queen.*

Send her victorious,
  Happy and glorious . . .

Edith Cosgrave was not deluded. Not really. She was a Stiles, had been born a Stiles rather. She got to her feet and took Brian by the hand. "Well," she said to her brother, "I guess I can take a hint as well as the next person. I think the bastard is saying he wants to go home."

How the Story Ends

CARL Tollefson was what people, only a short time ago, commonly used to refer to as a *nice, clean old bachelor*. In any event, that was the manner in which Little Paul's mother, Tollefson's niece, chose to characterize him to Big Paul while their guest unpacked in his room upstairs.

"I was so pleased to see he was a *nice, clean old bachelor*," she said, buttering toast for her husband, who refused to go to bed on an empty stomach. "Most old men get awful seedy if they don't marry. And I really had no idea what to expect. I hadn't seen him since I was a little girl – I couldn't have been more than ten. Eleven maybe."

"Christ, Lydia," said Big Paul, "don't you think they keep them clean in that T.B. sanatorium? They don't have no choice about bathing in a place like that. They make them. Sure he looks clean. *Now*."

"Did you notice he wears elastic sleeve garters to keep his cuffs even? When was the last time you saw somebody wear sleeve garters, Paul?" She slid the plate deftly in front of him. "I think it's real cute."

"You make sure he has his own plate and cup," said Big Paul, who was mortally afraid of illness. "And make sure it's a different colour from the dish set. I don't want his stuff getting mixed with ours. I'm not eating off no goddamn T.B. plate."

"You know better than to talk such ignorance," his wife answered him. "He'd die of embarrassment. Anyway, he isn't contagious. Do you think he'd get a foot in the door if he was?"

She tilted her head and lifted an eyebrow ever so slightly in the direction of their son, as if to say: Do you really think I'd put him in jeopardy?

Little Paul stood with his thin shoulders jammed against the wall, and a harried look on his face as he scratched the red scale of eczema which covered his hands. His hair, which had been cropped short because of the skin disorder, appeared to have been gnawed down to his skull by a ravenous rodent, rather than cut, and made the scalp which showed through the fine hair seem contused and raw.

He was six years old and slow to read, or count, or do most things people seemed to expect of him. In school he gave the impression of a small, pale spider hung in the centre of a web of stillness, expecting at any moment to feel one of the fragile threads vibrate with a warning.

"Give him a chipped plate then," said Big Paul around a mouthful of toast. "You can keep track of that easy enough. He'll never notice."

"You might buy three or four weanling pigs," his wife replied, ignoring him, "and he could look after them. I'm sure he wouldn't mind doing light chores for his room and board. We could feed them garden trash. It would keep him busy pottering around until he found a place."

"Where's he going to find a place?" asked Big Paul with that easy contemptuousness which had first attracted his wife to him. "Nobody is going to hire an old fart like him."

"He's not so *old*. Sixty-six isn't *so* old. And it's not as if farm work is all bull labour any more. He could get on with a dairy farm and run the milking machines, say. Or maybe work a cattle auction. He knows cattle, he said so himself."

"Anybody can say anything. Saying something doesn't make it so."

"Tollefsons were never blowhards nor braggers."

"One lung," said Big Paul moodily, "he won't last long. You saw him. The old bugger looks like death warmed over."

"Paul," his wife returned sharply, "not in front of the boy."

"Why did he come here?" whined Little Paul, who felt something vaguely like jealousy, and decided he could exercise it now that his presence had been formally recognized.

"To die in my upstairs bed," his father said unhappily, apparently speaking to himself, "that's why. To die on a goddamn spanking-new box-spring mattress."

"Don't listen to your father," said his mother. "He's only joking."

"What do you want?" Tollefson said, startled to see the silent, solemn boy standing in the doorway dressed in pyjamas. He tried hard to remember the child's name. He couldn't.

"That's my dad's bed," Little Paul said pointing to where Tollefson sat. "He owns it."

"Yes." The old man took exception to what he read as a note of belligerence in the boy's voice. "And this is my room. Nobody is welcome here who doesn't knock." Little Paul's settled gaze made him uncomfortable. He supposed it was being shirtless and exposing the scar of his operation – an L of ridged, plum-coloured tissue, the vertical of which ran alongside his spine, the horizontal directly beneath and parallel to the last bone of his rib cage. Whenever Tollefson thought of his missing lung he felt empty, hollow, unbalanced. He felt that way now.

"Why can't I come in here without knocking?" the boy demanded listlessly, his eyes shifting about the room, looking into things, prying. "This is my dad's house."

"Because I have certain rights, After all, I'm sixty-six and you're only . . ." He didn't know. "How old are you anyway?"

"Almost seven."

"Almost seven," Tollefson said. He extended one blunt-fingered hand scrolled with swollen blue veins, grasped a corner of the dresser and dragged himself upright. Then he unzipped a cracked leather case and removed two old-fashioned gentleman's hairbrushes which he slipped on his hands.

"What are you doing?" said the boy, advancing cautiously into the room. He thrust his tattered head from side to side like some wary buzzard fledgling.

What an ugly child, Tollefson thought, and was immediately ashamed. He glanced at the hairbrushes on his hands and remembered he had originally intended to have them initialled. *Vanity of vanities, saith the preacher, vanity of vanities, all is vanity* rang in his mind.

What exactly had his married sister, Elizabeth, said to him forty-five years ago on the occasion of his twenty-first birthday party?

"Carlie," she had sung in the lilting voice he had been pleased to hear her daughter Lydia had inherited, "you're a handsome young devil. You do know that, don't you?"

No. He hadn't. Never dreamed it. The notion had surprised and confounded him. He would have liked to ask someone else's opinion on the matter, but that was hardly the thing a person did.

This startling information, however, did lead him to begin to take great pains with his appearance. He refused any longer to let his father cut his hair. Instead, he went to the barber in town for a "trim" and his first baptism with bay rum. His sideburns crept past his ear-lobes; his hair appeared to be trying to mount a plausible pompadour. He bought elastic-sided boots, took to looking at himself in store windows when he sauntered past, and lounged on street corners with his thumbs hooked in his belt loops. Carl Tollefson began to suspect more than one girl of being in love with him.

Nobody told him any different until, in a moment of fanciful speculation, insane even for him, he remarked to his brother-in-law Roland that he thought the butcher's wife had her "eye on me."

Elizabeth spoke to him a second time. "Carlie, you remember what I said to you about being a handsome devil? I'm sorry, but I only meant to give you a little confidence – you're so shy around girls. The thing is, Carlie, there never was a Tollefson born who was anything but plain. I swear to God Roland married me out of charity. Still, I learned some time ago that nothing much helps; you can't make a silk purse out of a sow's ear. So let me give you a little advice – the girls around here don't much run to hair oil and elastic-sided boots. What they want is steady, and God knows you're steady. Just remember, Carlie, we're all in the same boat – there never was a Tollefson who turned a head with his profile."

"You think I don't know that," he had replied with a tight, pinched laugh. "What kind of fool do you think I am?"

Studying his face in the mirror he was puzzled by the mystery of how he had been able to believe in his supposed good looks, even for a second. Evidence to the contrary stared out at him from the mirror as it had every one of those mornings forty-five years ago as he had so carefully shaved.

Of course, age hadn't improved him. But, by and large, it was the same old face, only a little more used up. An indifferent kind of face: mild blue eyes which in a certain light appeared unfocused; a limp mouth which he often caught himself breathing through; a decent, ordinary, serviceable nose for a decent, ordinary face; and a set of small, neat ears which lay close to his skull and gave him the surprised look of a man caught in a fierce wind.

Perhaps it was from the moment he realized what he *was* in comparison with what he hoped to *be* that he turned in upon himself. And although he bore no resentment against his sister for planting the seed that flowered in his humiliation, he always sensed that the story of his life might have been very different if she had never said what she had. Not better, only different.

After all, he did not renounce all of what he had come to be; that would have been an admission that everything stemmed from self-delusion, and he was too proud to do that. The sideburns disappeared and the never-to-be-completed edifice of his pompadour crumbled from neglect, but the elastic-sided boots and the trips to the barber endured.

Nor did he dare court the local girls, imagining that they scorned the memory of his debonair days and thought him a poor thing, likely simple. Yet when the chrome-backed hairbrushes he had ordered from the catalogue finally arrived, he hadn't returned them and requested a refund. He was not quite the same young man he had been before his twenty-first birthday.

"What are you doing?" said Little Paul again, with greater emphasis.

"I'm going to brush my hair," Tollefson told him, cocking his head and looking at himself in the glass from a different angle.

"And then what?"

"I'll get myself ready for breakfast. Like you should. I'll wash my face and hands."

"Why?"

"Cleanliness is next to godliness."

"Why can't I come to your room without knocking?" the boy asked again.

"Because I might be doing something I don't want anybody to see."

"Like what?"

"Praying. Having my private talks with God that nobody has any business butting into," said Tollefson sternly. "For Jesus told us: 'When thou prayest, enter into thy closet, and when thou hast shut thy door, pray to thy Father which is in secret; and thy Father which seeth in secret shall reward thee openly.'"

"Here? In this room? God would come here in this room?" the boy said excitedly, his fingers digging and twisting at the crotch of his pyjamas. "Come here and talk to you?"

"Yes, in a way He would."

Little Paul thought for a moment, sucking his bottom lip. "I don't believe you," he said. "God wouldn't fit in such a little room. Jesus might fit, but not God."

"Same thing, son," said Tollefson, slipping into his shirt.

Little Paul appeared to be sceptical of Tollefson's contention, but he let the subject drop. "My dad's buying you pigs," he informed the old man.

"That a fact?"

"Can I help you look after them pigs?"

"You can if you promise not to come here in my room without knocking any more."

"All right." He climbed on to the bed and crossed and locked his legs.

"Why don't you go to the bathroom, son?"

"Don't need to."

"Suit yourself. But no accidents on my bed, eh?"

Little Paul giggled at the idea. Somehow Tollefson heard this as a plaintive sound. The boy didn't seem to have acquired the knack of laughter. Tollefson began to do up his shirt.

"Why did you come here?" the boy asked abruptly.

Tollefson paused at his collar-button. He always did up his collars. He was that kind of man. "I never thought about it," he said. "I suppose because there was no place else to go." He considered further. "No, God brought me here," he decided at last.

"To die in this upstairs bed," added Little Paul conversationally, patting the bedclothes with a hand crusted with eczemic lesions.

That terrible spring Big Paul often inquired of Tollefson, "Did you bring this goddamn miserable weather with you, or what?" He made a point of the goddamn, always careful to stress it after he learned from Lydia that her uncle had turned "churchy" some time during the past twenty years.

"I don't remember hearing anything about his being religious from Mom," she said. "He didn't catch it from home; I know that for sure. Grandpa Tollefson's acquaintance with church was of the marrying and burying variety."

"Why do they have to creep?" said Big Paul. "He minces around like he was walking on eggs. They all walk the same and they all talk the same. They're so jeezly *nice*. I never thought there'd come a day when I'd have to sidle past some creeping christer slipping and sliding around my house."

"There's nothing the matter with religion," declared his wife. "You could do with a little yourself."

"What really frosts my ass about guys like him," said Big Paul, who found anything out of the ordinary offensive, "is they got no idea of what's *normal*. Take him. He wouldn't say shit if his mouth was full of it. Yesterday he fell down in that slop in the corral. Know what he says?"

"Can't imagine."

"'Oh Lord, how long?' he says. 'How long what?' I asks. 'Oh Lord, how long will it rain?' he says, and then laughs like he was in his right mind. That's his idea of a joke!"

"If God happens to answer his question, let me in on the secret," said Lydia. "I want to hang washing some time this week."

But April was not a month to hang washing. April was a month of cruel rains. The eaves on the house choked on ice water; the poplars behind the cow sheds glistened in an agony of chilling sweats; and sparrows shrank to black clots of damp feathers which rode telephone wires that vibrated dolefully in the wind.

Big Paul's farmyard swam in water. The early calves were dropped from the warm bath of the womb into numbing puddles – where four drowned before they found the strength to gain their feet. Others shook in the steady drizzles until they contracted hemorrhagic septicemia, shat blood, and died between their mother's legs.

Under the pressure of circumstances, Tollefson tried to do more than he was capable of. The muck in the corrals sucked the strength out of his legs and left him trembling from head to foot, his single lung straining, the blood surging in his temples. When the old man stumbled in pursuit of new-born calves, his mouth gaped in a mute appeal for oxygen; his breath was barely visible in the cold as a thin, exhausted vapour. The wound on his back became a fiery letter, and one grey day in the mindlessness of utter fatigue, trying to wrestle a struggling calf to shelter in a pelting rain, he found himself muttering over and over, "L . . . , L . . . , L . . . ," in cadence with the thrumming of the blood in his ears and scar.

In mid-month, on April 18, the temperature dropped and the rain resolved itself into a stinging sleet which came driving out of a flat, impassive sky and froze to whatever it struck. Fence posts were sheathed in ice; barbed wire turned to glass, its spikes to frosty thorns. The cattle humped their backs to the bitter onslaught and received it dumbly, until their coats crackled when they stirred uneasily during lulls in the wind.

Big Paul and Tollefson began to search the bushes behind the cowsheds for calves when it became clear, after an hour, that the storm was not going to abate. They panted over deadfalls, forced their way through blinds of saskatoon and chokecherry bushes, slogged through the low spots where the puddles lay thick and sluggish, a porridge of ice crystals.

Within half an hour Tollefson's flannel shirt stuck to his back, heavy and damp with a sickly sweat. Thirty minutes later he had the feeling that his legs were attempting to walk out from underneath him. They felt as light and airy as balsa wood; it was only by an exertion of great will that he made them carry him. At some point, however, the cold gnawed through the gristle of his resolve and concentration, his mind wandered, his legs did what they wished – and folded under him. Tollefson was surprised to find himself kneeling in mud and slush, the wet seeping through his pant-legs and draining slowly into his boots, while he listened to his heart ticking over, and felt the scar blaze on his back.

"I found him," Big Paul would tell the beer parlour crowd later, "else he'd have froze stiff as a tinker's dink. It was just behind my barley bin, about a quarter-mile from where he says his legs gave out. I guess the old bugger got pooped out and sat down for a minute, and then his legs cramped with the cold and he couldn't get up. When I seen him he was just a lump of snow by the granary skids. He must have had horseshoes up his ass, because I could have easy missed him. I looked twice, mind you.

"But as I was saying, I saw this bump and first thing I says to myself is, 'That's another christly calf down and sure as Carter's got liver pills he's dead, son of a bitch.' I nearly crapped my drawers when I got close up and saw it wasn't no calf but the wife's uncle. I hadn't seen him for an hour, but I'd figured he'd got cold and went back to the house.

"He didn't have a thing left in him. He was on his side with an arm over his face to keep the sleet off. He could have been sleeping. Didn't hear me until I was practically standing on him.

"'Hey!' I hollered. 'Hey!' I figured he was tits up. I wasn't too crazy about touching a dead man. But he wasn't dead. 'You found me,' he says, real quiet. Then he takes his arm off his face. No teeth. He lost his teeth somewhere.

"'You broke a leg, or what?' I says. 'Can you get up?'

"'No, I can't get up,' he mumbles. 'I'm beat.' He didn't talk so good without his teeth and he was so tired I could barely make out what he was saying. I yelled at him: 'You broke a leg or had a heart attack or what?'

"'I'm tired,' he says. 'My legs give up on me.'

"Now he's old but he ain't light, and I was thinking how the hell was I going to get him out of there? He seen I was wondering how I was going to pack his arse out of there. I couldn't get a truck in there; she'd go down to the axles.

"'Go hook the stoneboat to the Ford tractor,' he says, 'and pull me out of here.' He had it all figured out. Of course, he had plenty of time, didn't he?

"'I got a pile of manure on it!' I hollers. 'I'll have to throw it off first!'

"'I can't wait,' he says. 'I can't feel my toes.' Then he says, 'You bring her in here and load me on. That Ford can pull a double load of b.s., can't it?' And he laughs. I tell you, I figure he was pretty far gone for him to say that. That's pretty strong stuff for that old man. He's a regular Bible-banger. I never heard him say so much as damn before that.

"So that's how I dragged him out of there. Rolled him onto a pile of cow shit and pulled him up to the house. He just lay there with his arms flung out on either side, the sleet coming down in his face. He didn't even try to cover up. I don't think he cared for nothing at that point."

Eric, who was seated across the table from Paul, said: "You say he crawled a half-mile? You ought to race him against Charlie's kid," he laughed, poking Charlie. "I was over to his place yesterday, and his rug rat can really rip. I'd put a dollar on him."

"I paced it off next day," Big Paul said, and his voice hinted at wonder. "That was what it was, just under a quarter-mile. And he gets the pension. I didn't think he had it in him."

"How's he now?" asked Charlie.

"Seems he's okay. We brought him home from the hospital a week ago. He spends most of the day laying in bed, then he reads to the kid when he comes home from school. Reads him mostly Bible stories. The old bird ain't nothing if he ain't odd. Lydia thinks it helps the kid. He don't do much at school."

"Sounds just like his old man," said Eric, "a regular little shit-disturber."

"No," said Big Paul, honesty itself, "he just don't learn."

"He won't grow up to be a shit-disturber with a preacher in the house," said Charlie, draining his glass.

"You ought to seen the kid," Big Paul said, suddenly struck by the recollection. "The things he comes up with. The things he thinks of. The other day I come in from feeding the stock and Little Paul's traipsing around the kitchen with a towel tied on his head and a piece of butcher's tape stuck on his chin for a beard.

"'Who the hell are you?' I says.

"'Moses leading the Jews out of Egypt,' he says. Do you believe that? Moses leading the Jews out of Egypt.

"'Well, lead the bastards over the nearest cliff,' I says." Big Paul winked at his companions and rubbed his palms on his knees. "'Over the nearest cliff,' I says," he repeated, laughing.

"A preacher in the house," said Eric, shaking his head. "That's trouble. You know what they say about preachers. Hornier than a two-peckered owl is what my old man used to say. Watch that old bugger; he might preach the pants off the wife."

"Keep him away from the goats," snorted Charlie. "He'll turn the cheese."

Big Paul hated it when they teased him. Every time they started in on him he began to feel confused and helpless. "Ah, not him," he said nervously, "for chrissakes show some respect. He's her uncle, for crying out loud."

"Any port in a storm," said Eric, poking Charlie.

"He don't like women much," said Big Paul, "he never got married." He paused, and, suddenly inspired, saw a solution. "You know," he said, "if anything, he's a little fruity. He's got fruity ways. Irons his own shirts. Cleans his fingernails every day before dinner. Queer, eh?"

"That reminds me," said Charlie. "Did you ever hear the one about the priest and the altar boy?"

"What?" said Big Paul sharply.

Tollefson's four volumes of *Bible Tales for Children* were twenty years old. He had bought them for his own edification weeks after his conversion at a Pentecostal meeting he had been taken to by a widow who had thoughts of marriage. She never landed that fish, but Jesus did.

Tollefson bought the books for two reasons. He admired the bright illustrations, particularly the angels who were sweetness itself; and he thought that in those children's books the great mysteries of the Trinity, the Incarnation, and the Resurrection would be so simply and obviously stated that his perplexities on those matters would evaporate. He found they helped.

Now the first volume lay open on the scarlet counterpane that covered Tollefson's bed and Little Paul was huddled beside him, his head drawn into his bony shoulders, his face intent.

"But why did God ask Abraham to do that?" the boy demanded, his voice much too loud for the narrow bedroom.

"Can't you wait for nothing?" said Tollefson. "The book'll say. It'll all come out in the end." The old man resumed reading, his words muffled and moist because his lost teeth had not been found.

"*So Abraham took his only son Isaac, whom he loved more than life itself, two trusty servants, a donkey, and bundles of sticks to make a fire, and began his journey to the land of Moriah where God had told him he would point out the mountain on which he was to sacrifice his son Isaac to God.*"

Tollefson paused and wiped at his slack lips with the back of his hand. Little Paul wound his fingers together and grimaced suddenly, like a small ape displaying his teeth.

"Why is God doing this?" he said nervously. "Little Isaac is scared, I bet."

"He doesn't know," Tollefson reminded him.

"Why is God doing this?" the boy said. "Why?"

"Wait and see, it's like a mystery. Wait until the end of the story. Listen now," he said, beginning to read in a flat, uninspired monotone. "*Can you imagine what pain was in Abraham's heart when he watched Isaac skipping lightheartedly beside him? How he longed to disobey God?*"

"He won't do it," Little Paul said under his breath. "Isaac's daddy won't do it. Not when he sees how scared he is."

"*And all through the trip,*" Tollefson read, "*Isaac kept repeating one question over and over again. 'Father,' he said, 'we are carrying these big bundles of sticks to make a fire, but what will we offer to the Lord our God, since we have forgotten a lamb to sacrifice?'*

"*But Abraham ignored the question, because he could not tell his son that he was the sacrifice.*"

Little Paul stared down at the stark print; for the first time in his life his mind wrestled with the hard words. He wanted to spell out the conclusion to this fearsome puzzle. He hated the story. He hated the book. He hated all books. They said he could read if he wanted to. That he could count. *Your tests prove it*, they said. *You could read if you'd try.* But he wouldn't. Little Paul was not going down that long tunnel. Count maybe.

His head could count. One, two, three, four . . . on and on you could go. Numbers never stopped. But they would never find out he counted in his head. He just would never say the numbers out loud.

"*After many weary days and thirsty miles Isaac and Abraham arrived at the mountain in Moriah, Abraham climbed it with oh so sad a heart, his son beside him. When they arrived at the top they gathered stones and built an altar.*"

Little Paul had begun to rock himself on the bed, his arms clasping his knees tightly. He slowly waggled his prison-camp head with its shorn hair and scent of powerful medication from side to side. "No," he said softly, his lips carefully forming before he sounded the word, "no-o-o, he won't."

Tollefson, his ears numbed by the singsong cadences of his own voice, did not hear Little Paul. He had a picture of his own forming behind his eyes. A great golden angel crouched behind a rock on a barren, sandy mountain top. Rescue. Unconsciously, his voice began to rise with his own excitement. "*Suddenly, after the last stone was lifted, Abraham seized his son, bound him, placed him on the altar amongst the sticks, and lifted his sharp dagger high, high above his head!*"

A sob, a darting hand, and the page was torn. The old man, stunned, caught Little Paul; but the boy's body wriggled violently upward, his eyes staring, his mouth a pocket of blackness – a diver with bursting lungs breaking the surface. For a moment the boy's body throbbed with inchoate fury as he strained silently in Tollefson's grasp, speechless, and full of wonder at what had passed through his mind. Then he screamed: "It's stupid! It's stupid! You're stupid!"

"Paul! Stop it!"

"He killed him!" shouted Little Paul. "The little boy is dead! There's nothing left of him! He's all gone! All of him!"

"No," said Tollefson, and he said it with such assurance and sincerity that the boy went quiet in his hands. "No, he isn't. The little boy's alive. There's an angel, and the angel tells Abraham not to kill Isaac, and there's a ram in the thicket," he went on quickly, "and they sacrifice that instead. The little boy . . . Isaac, he isn't dead."

"Yes?"

"Yes," said Tollefson. Once more on familiar ground, he was recovering his stride and filling with annoyance. "What kind of performance was that?" he asked, handling the book. "You can't get away with stunts like that. You know, people won't stand for it. Look at the book."

Little Paul was not interested in the book. "Why did God tell him to kill the little boy? Was he bad?"

"No, he wasn't bad. God told Abraham to kill Isaac to see if

Abraham loved God enough to obey. And Abraham did love God enough. He loved God so much that he was willing to sacrifice his only son, just as God was willing to sacrifice his only son, Jesus, because He so loved the world and wished to wash it clean of sin, as white as snow, by the saving mercy of His blood."

Little Paul could see blood. Pails and pails of blood were needed to wash away the sins of the world. He had seen his father catch blood in a pail to make sausage. Blood pumping hot out of a slashed throat in bright jets. Later, when it cooled, it turned black and thick like pudding.

"And because Abraham loved God," said Tollefson, "he would do anything God asked. No matter how hard."

"Would you?"

"I'd try very hard. We must always try our hardest to please God. You must too, Paul, because He loves you."

"Did he love Isaac?"

"Of course. He loves all his children."

"I don't like the story."

"Oh, you didn't at first," said Tollefson, "because you didn't wait for the end. But everything came out all right in the end, didn't it? That's the point."

It didn't seem the point to Little Paul. It seemed to him that God, being who he was, could have as easily ended the story the other way. That, to Little Paul, seemed the point.

"What do you mean," said Big Paul, "he wet the bed?"

"He wet the bed, that's what I mean. And keep your voice down."

"Jesus, he's seven years old."

"It's the nightmares," Lydia said. "They all have them at his age. Myrna's youngest had them for months and then, just like that, they stopped."

Big Paul felt uneasy. "He never plays with other kids. He's always with that sick old man. It's as if he's afraid to take his eyes off him. No wonder the goddamn kid has nightmares."

"Maybe if you didn't talk about Uncle dying in front of Paul, he wouldn't have bad dreams."

"Shit."

"And he spends time with Uncle because of the pigs. He likes to help him."

"That's another thing. I told you to tell that kid those pigs weren't supposed to become pets. That they were going to be butchered. Yesterday I go down to the pens and he shows me how they'll roll over to have their bellies scratched. Jesus H. Murphy, doesn't anybody listen to me around here any more?"

"He knows they've got to be butchered. I've told him and told him."

"And something else," Big Paul said, his voice rising with outrage, "the old boy is butchering those pigs. I'm not looking like a shit-head in my kid's eyes killing those pigs. I didn't teach them cute tricks!"

"My God, Paul, are you jealous?" Lydia asked, surprised and a little pleased at the notion.

"And last of all," he yelled, "tell that old son of a bitch to leave the bedroom door open when he's in there with Little Pauly! Better still, keep the kid out of there!"

"You *pig*," she said.

"What are you telling Uncle?" Little Paul whispered, his head twisting at the keyhole in a futile attempt to see more of Tollefson's bedroom.

"Don't you listen, Uncle Carl," he muttered fiercely. "Don't you listen to him."

Through the keyhole the boy could see only part of the room, and that part contained Tollefson's bed, by which the old man knelt praying, his bare back turned to the door, and the scar, faded by time, a faint letter formed by a timid hand.

What was out of view, in that portion of the bedroom that

contained the unseen wardrobe, toward which Tollefson's head was beseechingly turned, Little Paul could only imagine.

The old man and the boy picked their way between the dusty rows of garden vegetables under a stunning August sun, collecting refuse for the pigs. Little Paul trudged along listlessly behind Tollefson, pulling a wagon heaped with old pea vines; tiny, sun-scalded potatoes; beet and carrot tops. Their two shadows, black as pitch, crept over the dry, crumbling soil; shattered on the plant tops shaking in the breeze; squatted, stooped, and stretched.

Tollefson was admitting to himself he was a sinful man, a deceitful man. For months, ever since the April storm in which he had collapsed, he had known he was incapable of any longer earning his way in the world. His working days were over. He really was an old man, and in his talks with God he had come to realize that he was close to death. Yet he had pretended it was only a matter of time before he regained his strength and left to find work. But this deception was no longer enough. His niece and her husband were becoming impatient with him. Perhaps they would soon invite him to leave.

Tollefson didn't want to leave. He was an old man with nowhere to go. A man with no place of his own; no people of his own. All his life he had lived in other men's houses; played with other men's children; even, on occasion, slept with other men's wives before he had come to know Jesus. He was lonely and frightened.

That was why he had hit on the idea of making Little Paul the beneficiary of his will. He had worked very hard all his life and saved more money than anybody would suspect. Thirty-nine thousand dollars. When he told Lydia what he was going to do, they wouldn't dare ask him to leave for fear he would take the boy out of his will. What had Jesus said? "*Or what man is there of you, whom if his son ask bread, will he give him a stone? Or if he ask a fish, will he give him a serpent?*"

Big Paul might hate his guts, but he wouldn't deny his son a stake in thirty-nine thousand dollars. He was sure of that.

Tollefson looked down at Paul grubbing under a tomato plant for wormy fruit. Lydia had told him the child was suffering from bad dreams and nervous diarrhea.

The boy glanced up at him with his flat, guarded eyes. "Tomorrow will be too hot to kill pigs," he said out of the blue. Although Little Paul hadn't phrased his sentence as a question, Tollefson knew it was. For a week the boy had heard his father and Tollefson discuss whether they would soon have "killing weather" – cooler temperatures and a wind to prevent flies swarming on the pigs as they were scalded and gutted.

"Can't wait any longer," said Tollefson matter-of-factly, shading his eyes and studying the glowing blue glaze of the sky. "Your dad made a booking to have the meat cut and wrapped at the locker plant tomorrow afternoon. I'll have to do the pigs in the morning." The old man paused, adjusted his shirt sleeves, and then inquired, "Are you going to give me a hand?"

"It's too hot to kill pigs," the boy said sullenly.

"You got to learn some time," Tollefson said, "if you want to be a farmer. I told you all along them pigs would be butchered, and your mother told you. You knew it. That's a farmer's job to grow things for people to eat. Now, you like bacon, don't you? Where do you think bacon comes from?"

"God," said Little Paul automatically. He thought he'd learned how to please Tollefson.

His answer took the old man momentarily aback. "Well yes . . . that's right. But pigs is what I meant. It comes from pigs. It's pork. But you're right. Everything God made, he made for a reason. He made pigs for men to eat."

"I'd puke," said Little Paul vehemently. "I'd puke it all up."

Tollefson took off his long-billed cap and peered into it as if he expected to find there an answer to his predicament. "Listen," he said at last, taking the boy by the shoulders and looking directly into his face, "you got to learn to see things through. Believe me when I tell you it's the most important thing in life. You can't feed a pig and keep a pig and grow a pig and then leave the end, the dirty part, for another man to do. You had the fun of it all, and now you don't want the rest. It isn't right, Little Paul," he said. "You got to learn that. Remember when I read you the story of Abraham and Isaac? You didn't want to hear the end of the story because you thought it didn't suit. Just the way now you think butchering those pigs doesn't suit. But it does. There's nothing finer in God's eyes than a farmer, because the work he does, it does good for all people. A farmer feeds people and that's good. Don't you see?" he pleaded to the pale, intractable face.

"No." The boy's shoulders twisted under his hand. "No."

"God wants them pigs butchered," said Tollefson, trying to make sense of it for the boy. "They won't feel nothing. I'm a top-notch pig shot. I shot hundreds."

"You talk to him," said the boy, speaking very quickly, his face a strained mask. "You two got secrets from me. I talk and talk but he doesn't answer me what you got planned for me. I asked and asked and asked. But it's a secret. Why don't he tell me!"

"Who?" said Tollefson, reaching for the boy, alarmed by the fear which had lain in the shallows of the child's eyes all those months, but which he recognized only then, for the first time.

"Is he hungry?" implored Little Paul. "Is he hungry? Please, is that how the story ends?"

What I Learned From Caesar

THE OLDEST story is the story of flight, the search for greener pastures. But the pastures we flee, no matter how brown and blighted – these travel with us; they can't be escaped.

My father was an immigrant. You would think this no penalty in a nation of immigrants, but even his carefully nurtured, precisely colloquial English didn't spare him much pain. Nor did his marriage to a woman of British stock (as we called it then, before the vicious-sounding acronym Wasp came into use). That marriage should have paid him a dividend of respectability, but it only served to make her suspect in marrying him.

My father was a lonely man, a stranger who made matters worse by pretending he wasn't. It's true that he was familiar enough with his adopted terrain, more familiar than most because he was a salesman. Yet he was never really *of* it, no matter how much he might wish otherwise. I only began to understand what had happened to him when I, in my turn, left for greener pastures, heading east. I didn't go so far, not nearly so far as he had. But I also learned that there is a price to be paid. Mine was a trivial one, a feeling of mild unease. At odd moments I betrayed myself and my beginnings; I knew that I lacked the genuine ring of a local. And I had never even left my own country.

Occasionally I return to the small Saskatchewan town near the Manitoba border where I grew up. To the unpractised eye of an easterner the countryside around that town might appear undifferentiated and monotonous, part and parcel of that great swath of prairie that vacationers drive through, pitying its inhabitants and deploring its restrooms, intent only on leaving it all behind as quickly as possible. But it is just here that the prairie verges on parkland, breaking into rolling swells of land, and here, too, that it becomes a little greener and easier on the eye. There is still more sky than any country is entitled to, and it teases the traveller into believing he can never escape it or find shelter under it. But if your attention wanders from that hypnotic expanse of blue and the high clouds drifting in it, the land becomes more comfortable as prospects shorten, and the mind rests easier on attenuated distances. There is cropland: fields of rye, oats, barley, and wheat; flat, glassy sloughs shining like mirrors in the sun; a solitary clump of trembling poplar; a bluff that gently climbs to nudge the sky.

When I was a boy it was a good deal bleaker. The topsoil had blown off the fields and into the ditches to form black dunes; the crops were withered and burnt; there were no sloughs because they had all dried up. The whole place had a thirsty look. That was during the thirties when we were dealt a doubly cruel hand of drought and economic depression. It was not a time or place that was kindly to my father. He had come out of the urban sprawl of industrial Belgium some twenty-odd years before, and it was only then, I think, that he was beginning to come to terms with a land that must have seemed forbidding after his own tiny country, so well tamed and marked by man. And then this land played him the trick of becoming something more than forbidding; it became fierce, and fierce in every way.

It was in the summer of 1931, the summer that I thought was merely marking time before I would pass into high school, that he lost his territory. For as long as I could remember I had been a salesman's son, and then it ended. The company he worked for began to feel the pinch of the depression and moved to merge its territories. He was let go. So one morning he unexpectedly pulled up at the front door and began to haul his sample cases out of the Ford.

"It's finished," he said to my mother as he flung the cases on to the lawn. "I got the boot. I offered to stay on – strictly commission. He wouldn't hear of it. Said he couldn't see fit to starve two men where there was only a living for one. I'd have starved that other sonofabitch out. He'd have had to hump his back and suck the hind tit when I was through with him." He paused, took off his fedora and nervously ran his index finger around the sweat-band. Clearing his throat, he said, "His parting words were 'Good luck, Dutchie!' I should have spit in his eye. Jesus H. Christ himself wouldn't dare call me Dutchie. The bastard."

Offence compounded offence. He thought he was indistinguishable, that the accent wasn't there. Maybe his first successes as a salesman owed something to his naivete. Maybe in good times, when there was more than enough to go around, people applauded his performance by buying from him. He was a counterfeit North American who paid them the most obvious of compliments, imitation. Yet hard times make people less generous. Jobs were scarce, business was poor. In a climate like that, perceptions change, and perhaps he ceased to be merely amusing and became, instead, a dangerous parody. Maybe that district manager, faced with a choice, could only think of George Vander Elst as Dutchie. Then again, it might have been that my father just wasn't a good enough salesman. Who can judge at this distance?

But for the first time my father felt as if he had been exposed. He had never allowed himself to remember that he was a foreigner, or if he had, he persuaded himself he had been wanted. After all, he was a northern European, a Belgian. They had been on the preferred list.

He had left all that behind him. I don't even know the name of the town or the city where he was born or grew up. He always avoided my questions about his early life as if they dealt with a distasteful and criminal past that was best forgotten. Never, not even once, did I hear him speak Flemish. There were never any of the lapses you might expect. No pet names in his native language for my mother or myself; no words of endearment which would have had the comfort of childhood use. Not even when driven to one of his frequent rages did he curse in the mother tongue. If he ever prayed, I'm sure it was in English. If a man forgets the cradle language in the transports of prayer, love, and rage – well, it's forgotten.

The language he did speak was, in a sense, letter-perfect, fluent, glib. It was the language of wheeler-dealers, and of the heady twenties, of salesmen, high-rollers, and persuaders. He spoke of people as live-wires, go-getters, self-made men. Hyphenated words to describe the hyphenated life of the seller, a life of fits and starts, comings and goings. My father often proudly spoke of himself as a self-made man, but this description was not the most accurate. He was a remade man. The only two pictures of him which I have in my possession are proof of this.

The first is a sepia-toned photograph taken, as nearly as I can guess, just prior to his departure from Belgium. In this picture he is wearing an ill-fitting suit, round-toed, clumsy boots, and a cloth cap. The second was taken by a street photographer in Winnipeg. My father is walking down the street, a snap-brim fedora slanting rakishly over one eye. His suit is what must have been considered stylish then – a three-piece pin-stripe – and he is carrying an overcoat casually over one arm. He is exactly what he admired most, a "snappy dresser," or, since he always had trouble with his p's, a "snabby dresser." The clothes, though they mark a great change, aren't really that important. Something else tells the story.

In the first photograph my father stands rigidly with his arms folded across his chest, unsmiling. Yet I can see that he is a young man who is hesitant and afraid; not of the camera, but of what this picture-taking means. There is a reason why he is having his photograph taken. He must leave something of himself behind with his family so he will not be forgotten, and carry something away with him so that he can remember. That is what makes this picture touching; it is a portrait of a solitary, an exile.

In the second picture his face is blunter, fleshier: nothing surprising in that, he is older. But suddenly you realize he is posing for the camera – not in the formal, European manner of the first photograph but in a manner far more unnatural. You see, he is pretending to be entirely natural and unguarded; yet he betrays himself. The slight smile, the squared shoulder, the overcoat draped over the arm, all are calculated bits of a composition. He has seen the camera from a block away. My father wanted to be caught in exactly this negligent, unassuming pose, sure that it would capture for all time his prosperity, his success, his adaptability. Like most men, he wanted to leave a record. And this was it. And if he had coached himself in such small matters, what would he ever leave to chance?

That was why he was so ashamed when he came home that summer. There was the particular shame of having lost his job, a harder thing for a man then than it might be today. There was the shame of knowing that sooner or later we would have to go on relief, because being a lavish spender he had no savings. But there was also the shame of a man who suddenly discovers that all his lies were transparent, and everything he thought so safely hidden had always been in plain view. He had been living one of those dreams. The kind of dream in which you are walking down the street, meeting friends and neighbours, smiling and nodding, and when you arrive at home and pass a mirror you see for the first time you are stark naked. He was sure that behind his back he had always been Dutchie. For a man with so much pride a crueller epithet would have been kinder; to be hated gives a man some kind of status. It was the condescension implicit in that diminutive, its mock playfulness, that made him appear so undignified in his own eyes.

And for the first time in my life I was ashamed of him. He didn't have the grace to bear an injustice, imagined or otherwise, quietly. At first he merely brooded, and then like some man with a repulsive sore, he sought pity by showing it. I'm sure he knew that he could only offend, but he was under a compulsion to justify himself. He began with my mother by explaining, where there was no need for explanation, that he had had his job taken from him for no good reason. However, there proved to be little satisfaction in preaching to the converted, so he carried his tale to everyone he knew. At first his references to his plight were tentative and oblique. The responses were polite but equally tentative and equally oblique. This wasn't what he had hoped for. He believed that the sympathy didn't measure up to the occasion. So his story was told and retold, and each time it was enlarged and embellished until the injustice was magnified beyond comprehension. He made a damn fool of himself. This was the first sign, although my mother and I chose not to recognize it.

In time everyone learned my father had lost his job for no good reason. And it wasn't long before the kids of the fathers he had told his story to were following me down the street chanting, "No good reason. No good reason." That's how I learned my family was a topical joke that the town was enjoying with zest. I suppose my father found out too, because it was about that time he stopped going out of the house. He couldn't fight back and neither could I. You never can.

After a while I didn't leave the house unless I had to. I spent my days sitting in our screened verandah reading old copies of *Saturday Evening Post* and *Maclean's*. I was content to do anything that helped me forget the heat and the monotony, the shame and the fear, of that longest of summers. I was thirteen then and in a hurry to grow up, to press time into yielding the bounty I was sure it had in keeping for me. So I was killing time minute by minute with those magazines. I was to enter high school that fall and that seemed a prelude to adulthood and independence. My father's misfortunes couldn't fool me into believing that maturity didn't mean the strength to plunder at will. So when I found an old Latin grammar of my mother's I began to read that too. After all, Latin was the arcane language of the professions, of lawyers and doctors, those divinities owed immediate and unquestioning respect. I decided I would become either one, because respect could never be stolen from them as it had been from my father.

That August was the hottest I can remember. The dry heat made my nose bleed at night, and I often woke to find my pillow stiff with blood. The leaves of the elm tree in the front yard hung straight down on their stems; flies buzzed heavily, their bodies tip-tapping lazily against the screens, and people passing the house moved so languidly they seemed to be walking in water. My father, who had always been careful about his appearance, began to come down for breakfast barefoot, wearing only a vest undershirt and an old pair of pants. He rarely spoke, but carefully picked his way through his meal as if it were a dangerous obstacle course, only pausing to rub his nose thoughtfully. I noticed that he had begun to smell.

One morning he looked up at me, laid his fork carefully down beside his plate and said, "I'll summons him."

"Who?"

"Who do you think?" he said scornfully. "The bastard who fired me. He had no business calling me Dutchie. That's slander."

"You can't summons him."

"I can," he said emphatically. "I'm a citizen. I've got rights. I'll go to law. He spoiled my good name."

"That's not slander."

"It is."

"No it isn't."

"I'll sue the bastard," he said vaguely, looking around to appeal to my mother, who had left the room. He got up from the table and went to the doorway. "Edith," he called, "tell your son I've got the right to summons that bastard."

Her voice came back faint and timid, "I don't know, George."

He looked back at me. "You're in the same boat, sonny. And taking sides with them don't save you. When we drown we all drown together."

"I'm not taking sides," I said indignantly. "Nobody's taking sides. It's facts. Can't you see . . . ," but I didn't get a chance to finish. He left, walked out on me. I could hear his steps on the stairway, tired, heavy steps. There was so much I wanted to say. I wanted to make it plain that being on his side meant saving him from making a fool of himself again. I wanted him to know he could never win that way. I wanted him to win, not lose. He was my father. But he went up those steps, one at a time, and I heard his foot fall distinctly, every time. Beaten before he started, he crawled back into bed. My mother went up to him several times that day, to see if he was sick, to attempt to gouge him out of that room, but she couldn't. It was only later that afternoon, when I was reading in the verandah, that he suddenly appeared again, wearing only a pair of undershorts. His body shone dully with sweat, his skin looked grey and soiled.

"They're watching us," he said, staring past me at an empty car parked in the bright street.

Frightened, I closed my book and asked who was watching us.

"The relief people," he said tiredly. "They think I've got money hidden somewhere. They're watching me, trying to catch me with it. The joke's on them. I got no money." He made a quick, furtive gesture that drew attention to his almost naked body, as if it were proof of his poverty.

"Nobody is watching us. That car's empty."

"Don't take sides with them," he said, staring through the screen. I thought someone from one of the houses across the street might see him like that, practically naked.

"The neighbours'll see," I said, turning my head to avoid looking at him.

"See what?" he asked, surprised.

"You standing like that. Naked almost."

"There's nothing they can do. A man's home is his castle. That's what the English say, isn't it?"

And he went away laughing.

Going down the hallway, drawing close to his door that always stood ajar, what did I hope? To see him dressed, his trousers rolled up to mid-calf to avoid smudging his cuffs, whistling under his breath, shining his shoes? Everything as it was before? Yes. I hoped that. If I had been younger then and still believed that frogs were turned into princes with a kiss, I might even have believed it could happen. But I didn't believe. I only hoped. Every time I approached his door (and that was many times a day, too many), I felt the queasy excitement of hope.

It was always the same. I would look in and see him lying on the tufted pink bedspread, naked or nearly so, gasping for breath in the heat. And I always thought of a whale stranded on a beach because he was such a big man. He claimed he slept all day because of the heat, but he only pretended to. He could feel me watching him and his eyes would open. He would tell me to go away, or bring him a glass of water; or, because his paranoia was growing more marked, ask me to see if they were still in the street. I would go to the window and tell him, yes, they were. Nothing else satisfied him. If I said they weren't, his jaw would shift from side to side unsteadily and his eyes would prick with tears. Then he imagined more subtle and intricate conspiracies.

I would ask him how he felt.

"Hot," he'd say, "I'm always hot. Can't hardly breathe. Damn country," and turn on his side away from me.

My mother was worried about money. There was none left. She asked me what to do. She believed women shouldn't make decisions.

"You'll have to go to the town office and apply for relief," I told her.

"No, no," she'd say, shaking her head. "I couldn't go behind his back. I couldn't do that. He'll go himself when he feels better. He'll snap out of it. It takes a little time."

In the evening my father would finally dress and come downstairs and eat something. When it got dark he'd go out into the yard and sit on the swing he'd hung from a limb of our Manitoba maple years before, when I was a little boy. My mother and I would sit and watch him from the verandah. I felt obligated to sit with her. Every night as he settled himself onto the swing she would say the same thing. "He's too big. It'll never hold him. He'll break his back." But the swing held him up and the darkness hid him from the eyes of his enemies, and I like to think that made him happy, for a time.

He'd light a cigarette before he began to swing, and then we'd watch its glowing tip move back and forth in the darkness like a beacon. He'd flick it away when it was smoked, burning a red arc in the night, showering sparks briefly, like a comet. And then he'd light another and another, and we'd watch them glow and swing in the night.

My mother would lean over to me and say confidentially, "He's thinking it all out. It'll come to him, what to do."

I never knew whether she was trying to reassure me or herself. At last my mother would get to her feet and call to him, telling him she was going up to bed. He never answered. I waited a little longer, believing that watching him I kept him safe in the night. But I always gave up before he did and went to bed too.

The second week of September I returned to school. Small differences are keenly felt. For the first time there was no new sweater, or unsharpened pencils, or new fountain pen whose nib hadn't spread under my heavy writing hand. The school was the same school I had gone to for eight years, but that day I climbed the stairs to the second floor that housed the high school. Up there the wind moaned more persistently than I remembered it had below, and intermittently it threw handfuls of dirt and dust from the schoolyard against the windows with a gritty rattle.

Our teacher, Mrs. MacDonald, introduced herself to us, though she needed no introduction since everyone knew who she was – she had taught there for over ten years. We were given our texts and it cheered me a little to see I would have no trouble with Latin after my summer's work. Then we were given a form on which we wrote a lot of useless information. When I came to the space which asked for Racial Origin I paused, and then, out of loyalty to my father, numbly wrote in "Canadian."

After that we were told we could leave. I put my texts away in a locker for the first time – we had had none in public school – but somehow it felt strange going home from school empty-handed. So I stopped at the library door and went in. There was no school librarian and only a few shelves of books, seldom touched. The room smelled of dry paper and heat. I wandered around aimlessly, taking books down, opening them, and putting them back. That is, until I happened on Caesar's *The Gallic Wars*. It was a small, thick book that nestled comfortably in the hand. I opened it and saw that the left-hand pages were printed in Latin and the right-hand pages were a corresponding English translation. I carried it away with me, dreaming of more than proficiency in Latin.

When I got home my mother was standing on the front step, peering anxiously up and down the street.

"Have you seen your father?" she asked.

"No," I said. "Why?"

She began to cry. "I told him all the money was gone. I asked him if I could apply for relief. He said he'd go himself and have it out with them. Stand on his rights. He took everything with him. His citizenship papers, baptismal certificate, old passport, bank book, everything. I said, 'Everyone knows you. There's no need.' But he said he needed proof. Of what? He'll cause a scandal. He's been gone for an hour."

We went into the house and sat in the living-room. "I'm a foolish woman," she said. She got up and hugged me awkwardly. "He'll be all right."

We sat a long time listening for his footsteps. At last we heard someone come up the walk. My mother got up and said, "There he is." But there was a knock at the door.

I heard them talking at the door. The man said, "Edith, you better come with me. George is in some trouble."

My mother asked what trouble.

"You just better come. He gave the town clerk a poke. The constable and doctor have him now. The doctor wants to talk to you about signing some papers."

"I'm not signing any papers," my mother said.

"You'd better come, Edith."

She came into the living-room and said to me, "I'm going to get your father."

I didn't believe her for a minute. She put her coat on and went out.

She didn't bring him home. They took him to an asylum. It was a shameful word then, asylum. But I see it in a different light now. It seems the proper word now, suggesting as it does refuge, a place to hide.

I'm not sure why all this happened to him. Perhaps there is no reason anyone can put their finger on, although I have my ideas.

But I needed a reason then. I needed a reason that would lend him a little dignity, or rather, lend me a little dignity; for I was ashamed of him out of my own weakness. I needed him to be strong, or at least tragic. I didn't know that most people are neither.

When you clutch at straws, anything will do. I read my answer out of Caesar's *The Gallic Wars*, the fat little book I had carried home. In the beginning of Book I he writes, "Of all people the Belgae are the most courageous. . . ." I read on, sharing Caesar's admiration for a people who would not submit but chose to fight and see glory in their wounds. I misread it all, and bent it until I was satisfied. I reasoned the way I had to, for my sake, for my father's. What was he but a man dishonoured by faceless foes? His instincts could not help but prevail, and like his ancestors, in the end, on that one day, what could he do but make the shadows real, and fight to be free of them?

Drummer

YOU'D THINK my old man was the Pope's nephew or something if you'd seen how wild he went when he learned I'd been sneaking off Sundays to Faith Baptist Church. Instead of going to eleven o'clock Mass like he figured I was.

Which is kind of funny. Because although Mom is solid R.C. – eight o'clock Mass and saying a rosary at the drop of a hat – nobody ever accused Pop of being a religious fanatic by no means. He goes to confession regular like an oil change, every five thousand miles, or Easter, whichever comes first.

Take the Knights of Columbus. He wouldn't join those guys for no money. Whenever Mom starts in on him about enlisting he just answers back that he can't afford the outlay on armour and where'd we keep a horse? Which is his idea of a joke. So it isn't exactly as if he was St. Joan of Arc himself to go criticizing me.

And Pop wouldn't have been none the wiser if it wasn't for my older brother Gene, the prick. Don't think I don't know who told. But I can't expect nothing different from that horse's ass.

So, as I was saying, my old man didn't exactly take it all in stride. "Baptists! *Baptists!* I'm having your head examined. Do you hear me? I'm having it *examined*! Just keep it up and see if I don't, you crazy little pecker. They roll in the aisles. Baptists, for chrissakes!"

"I been three times already and nobody rolled in an aisle once."

"Three times? *Three times?* Now it all comes out. Three, eh?" He actually hits himself in the forehead with the heel of his palm. Twice. "Jesus Christ Almighty, I'm blessed with a son like this? What's the matter with you? Why can't you ever do something I can understand?"

"Like wrecking cars?" This is a swift kick in the old fun sack. Pop's just getting over Gene's totalling off the first new car he's bought in eight years. A 1966 Chevy Impala.

"Shut your smart mouth. Don't go dragging your brother into this. Anyway, what he done to the car was *accidental*. But not you. Oh no, you marched into that collection of religious screwballs, holy belly-floppers, and linoleum-beaters under your own steam. *On purpose.* For God's sake, Billy, that's no religion that – it's *exercise*. Stay away from them Baptists."

"Can't," I says to him.

"Can't? *Can't?* Why the hell not?"

"Matter of principle."

They teach us that in school, matters of principle. I swear it's a plot to get us all slaughtered the day they graduate us out the door. It's their revenge, see? Here we are reading books in literature class about some banana who's only got one oar in the water to start with, and then he pops it out worrying about principles. Like that Hamlet, or what's his name in *A Tale of Two Cities*. Ever notice how many of those guys are alive at the end of those books they teach us from?

"I'll principle you," says the old man.

The only teacher who maybe believes all that crock of stale horseshit about principles is Miss Clark, who's fresh out of wherever they bake Social Studies teachers. She's got principles on the brain. For one thing, old Clarkie has pretty nearly wallpapered her room with pictures of that Negro, Martin

Luther King, and some character who's modelling the latest in Wabasso sheets and looks like maybe he'd kill for a hamburger – Gandhi is his name – and that hairy old fart Tolstoy, who wrote the books you need a front-end loader to lift. From what Clarkie tells us, I gather they're what you call non-violent shit-disturbers.

Me too. Being a smart-ass runs in the Simpson family. It's what you call hereditary, like a disease. That's why all of a sudden, before I even *think* for chrissakes, I hear myself lecturing the old man in this fruity voice that's a halfway decent imitation of old Clarkie, and I am using the exact words which I've heard her say myself.

"Come, come, surely by this day and age everybody has progressed to the point where we can all agree on the necessity of freedom of worship. If we can't agree on anything else, at least we can agree on that."

I got news for her. My old man don't agree to no such thing. He up and bangs me one to the side of the head. A backhander special. You see, nobody in our house is allowed an opinion until they're twenty-one.

Of course, I could holler Religious Persecution. Not that it would do any good. But it's something I happen to know quite a bit about, seeing as Religious Persecution was my assignment in Social Studies that time we studied Man's Inhumanity to Man. The idea was to write a two-thousand-word report proving how everybody has been a shit to everybody else through the ages, and where did it ever get them? This is supposed to improve us somehow, I guess.

Anyway, as usual anything good went fast. Powbrowski got A. Hitler, Keller put dibs on Ivan the Terrible, Langly asked for Genghis Khan. By the time old Clarkie got around to me there was just a bunch of crap left like No Votes For Women. So I asked, please, could I do a project on Mr. Keeler? Keeler is the dim-witted bat's fart who's principal of our school.

For being rude, Miss Clark took away my "privilege" of picking and said I had to do Religious Persecution. Everybody was avoiding that one like the plague.

Actually, I found Religious Persecution quite interesting. It's got principles too, number one being that whatever you're doing to some poor son of a bitch – roasting his chestnuts over an open fire, or stretching his pant-leg from a 29-incher to a 36-incher on the rack – why, you're doing it for his own good. So he'll start thinking right. Which is more or less what my old man was saying when he told me I can't go out of the house on Sundays any more. He says to me, "You aren't setting a foot outside of that door [he actually points at it] of a Sunday until you come to your senses and quit with all the Baptist bullshit."

Not that that's any heavy-duty torture. What he don't know is that these Baptists have something called Prayer, Praise and Healing on Wednesday nights. My old man hasn't locked me up Wednesday nights yet by no means.

I figure if my old man wants somebody to blame for me becoming a Baptist he ought to take a peek in my older brother Gene's direction. He started it.

Which sounds awful funny if you know anything about Gene. Because if Gene was smart enough to have ever thought about it, he'd come out pretty strong against religion, since it's generally opposed to most things he's in favour of.

Still, nobody thinks the worse of my brother for doing what he likes to do. They make a lot of excuses for you in a dinky mining town that's the arsehole of the world if you bat .456 and score ninety-eight goals in a thirty-five-game season. Shit, last year they passed the hat around to all the big shots on the recreation board and collected the dough for one of Gene's liquor fines and give it to him on the q.t.

But I'm trying to explain my brother. If I had to sum him

up I'd probably just say he's the kind of guy doesn't have to dance. What I mean is, you take your average, normal female: they slobber to dance. The guys that stand around leaning against walls are as popular to them as syphilis. You don't dance, you're a pathetic dope – even the ugly ones despise you.

But not Gene. He don't dance and they all cream. You explain it. Do they figure he's too superior to be bothered? Because it's not true. I'm his brother and I know. The dink just can't dance. That simple. But if I mention this little fact to anybody, they look at me like I been playing out in the sun too long. Everybody around here figures Mr. Wonderful could split the fucking atom with a hammer and a chisel if he put his mind to it.

Well, almost everybody. There's a born doubter in every crowd. Ernie Powers is one of these. He's the kind of stupid fuck who's sure they rig the Stanley Cup and the Oscars and nobody even went up in space. Everything is a hoax to him. Yet he believes professional wrestling is on the up and up. You wonder – was he dropped on his head, or what? Otherwise you got to have a plan to grow up that ignorant.

So it was just like Einstein to bet Gene ten dollars he couldn't take out Nancy Williams. He did that while we were eating a plate of chips and gravy together in the Rite Spot and listening to Gene going on about who's been getting the benefit of his poking lately. Powers, who is a very jealous person because he's going steady with his right hand, says, oh yeah sure, maybe her, but he'd bet ten bucks somebody like Nancy Williams in 11B wouldn't even go out with Gene.

"Get serious," says my brother when he hears that. He considers himself irresistible to the opposite sex.

"Ten bucks. She's strictly off-limits even to you, Mr. Dreamboat. It's all going to waste. That great little gunga-poochy-snuggy-bum, that great matched set. Us guys in 11B, you know what we call them? The Untouchables. Like on TV."

"What a fucking sad bunch. Untouchables for you guys, maybe. If any of you queers saw a real live piece of pelt you'd throw your hat over it and run."

"Talk's cheap," says Ernie, real offended. "You don't know nothing about her. My sister says Miss High-and-Mighty didn't go out for cheerleading because the outfits was *too revealing*. My sister says Nancy Williams belongs to some religion doesn't allow her to dance. Me, I saw her pray over a hard-boiled egg for about a half-hour before she ate it in the school lunch-room. Right out where anybody could see, she prayed. No way somebody like that is going to go out with you, Simpson. If she does I'll eat my shorts."

"Start looking for the ten bucks, shitface, and skip dinner, because I'm taking Nancy Williams to the Christmas Dance," my brother answers him right back. Was Gene all of a sudden hostile or was he hostile? I overheard our hockey coach say one time that my brother Gene's the kind of guy rises to a challenge. The man's got a point. I lived with Gene my whole life, which is sixteen years now, and I ought to know. Unless he gets mad he's useless as tits on a boar.

You better believe Gene was mad. He called her up right away from the pay phone in the Rite Spot. It was a toss-up as to which of those two jerks was the most entertaining. Powers kept saying, "There's no way she'll go out with him. No way." And every time he thought of parting with a ten-spot, a look came over his face like he just pinched a nut or something. The guy's so christly tight he squeaks when he walks. He was sharing *my* chips and gravy, if you know what I mean?

And then there was Gene. I must say I've always enjoyed watching him operate. I mean, even on the telephone he looks so sincere I could just puke. It's not unconscious by no means. My brother explained to me once what his trick is. To look that way you got to think that way is his motto. "What I do, Billy," he told me once, "is make myself believe, really believe, say . . . well, that an H-bomb went off, or that some kind of disease which only attacks women wiped out every female on the face of the earth but the one I'm talking to. That makes her the last piece of tail on the face of the earth, Billy! It's just natural then to be extra nice." Even though he's my brother, I swear to God he had to been left on our doorstep.

Of course, you can't argue with success. As soon as Gene hung up and smiled, Powers knew he was diddled. Once. But my brother don't show much mercy. Twice was coming. Nancy Williams had a cousin staying with her for Christmas vacation. She wondered if maybe Gene could get this cousin a date? When Powers heard that, he pretty nearly went off in his pants. Nobody'll go out with him. He's fat and he sweats and he never brushes his teeth, there's stuff grows on them looks like the crap that floats on top of a slough. Even the really desperate girls figure no date is less damaging to their reputations than a date with Powers. You got to hold the line somewhere is how they look at it.

So Ernie's big yap cost him fifteen dollars. He blew that month's baby bonus (which his old lady gives him because he promises to finish school) and part of his allowance. The other five bucks is what he had to pay when Gene sold him Nancy Williams' cousin. It damn near killed him.

All right. Maybe I ought to've said something when Gene marched fat Ernie over to the Bank of Montreal to make a withdrawal on this account Powers has had since he was seven and started saving for a bike. He never got around to getting the bike because he couldn't bring himself to ever see that balance go down. Which is typical.

Already then I knew Ernie wasn't taking the cousin to no Christmas Dance. I'd heard once too often from that moron how Whipper Billy Watson would hang a licking on Cassius Clay, or how all the baseball owners get together in the spring to decide which team will win the World Series in the fall. He might learn to keep his hole shut for once.

The thing is *I'd* made up my mind to take the cousin. For nothing. It just so happens that, Gene being mad, he'd kind of forgot he's not allowed to touch the old man's vehicle. Seeing as he tied a chrome granny knot around a telephone pole with the last one.

Gene didn't realize it yet but he wasn't going nowhere unless I drove. And I was going to drive because I'd happened to notice Nancy Williams around. She seemed like a very nice person who maybe had what Miss Clark says are principles. I suspected that if that was true, Gene for once was going to strike out, and no way was I going to miss *that*. Fuck, I'd have killed to see that. No exaggeration.

On the night of the Christmas Dance it's snowing like a bitch. Not that it's cold for December, mind you, but snowing. Sticky, sloppy stuff that almost qualifies for sleet, coming down like crazy. I had to put the windshield wipers on. In December yet.

Nancy Williams lives on the edge of town way hell and gone, in new company housing. The mine manager is the dick who named it Green Meadows. What a joke. Nobody lives there seen a blade of grass yet nor pavement neither. They call it Gumboot Flats because if it's not frozen it's mud. No street-lights neither. It took me a fuck of a long time to find her house in the dark. When I did I shut off the motor and me and Gene just sat.

"Well?" I says after a bit. I was waiting for Gene to get out first.

"Well what?"

"Well, maybe we should go get them?"

Gene didn't answer. He leans across me and plays "Shave and a haircut, two bits" on the horn.

"You're a geek," I tell him. He don't care.

We wait. No girls. Gene gives a couple of long, long blasts on the hooter. I was wishing he wouldn't. This time somebody pulls open the living-room drapes. There stands this character in suspenders, for chrissakes, and a pair of pants stops about two inches shy of his armpits. He looked like somebody's father and what you'd call belligerent.

"I think he wants us to come to the door."

"He can want all he likes. Jesus Murphy, it's snowing out there. I got no rubbers."

"Oh, Christ," I says. "I'll go get them, Gene. It's such a big deal."

Easier said than done. I practically had to present a medical certificate. By the time Nancy's father got through with me I was starting to sound like that meatball Chip on *My Three Sons*. Yes sir. No sir. He wasn't too impressed with the horn-blowing episode, let me tell you. And then Nancy's old lady totes out a Kodak to get some "snaps" for Nancy's scrapbook. I didn't say nothing but I felt maybe they were getting evidence for the trial in case they had to slap a charge on me later. You'd have had to see it to believe it. Here I was standing with Nancy and her cousin, grinning like I was in my right mind, flash bulbs going off in my face, nodding away to the old man, who was running a safe-driving clinic for yours truly on the sidelines. Gene, I says to myself, Gene, you're going to pay.

At last, after practically swearing a blood oath to get his precious girls home, *undamaged*, by twelve-thirty, I chase the women out the door. And while they run through the snow, giggling, Stirling Moss delays me on the doorstep, in this blizzard, showing me for about the thousandth time how to pull a car out of a skid on ice. I kid you not.

From that point on everything goes rapidly downhill.

Don't get me wrong. I got no complaints against the girls. Doreen, the cousin, wasn't going to break no mirrors, and she sure was a lot more lively than I expected. Case in point. When I finally get to the car, fucking near frozen, what do I see? Old Doreen hauling up about a yard of her skirt, which she rolled around her waist like the spare tire on a fat guy. Then she pulled her sweater down to hide it. You bet I was staring.

"Uncle Bob wouldn't let me wear my mini," she says. "Got a smoke? I haven't had one for days."

It seems she wasn't the only one had a bit of a problem with the dress code that night. In the back seat I could hear Nancy apologizing to Gene for the outfit her mother had made her special for the dance. Of course, I thought Nancy looked quite nice. But with her frame she couldn't help, even though she was got up a bit peculiar. What I mean is, she had on this dress made out of the same kind of shiny material my mother wanted for drapes. But the old man said she couldn't have it because it was too heavy. It'd pull the curtain rods off the wall.

I could tell poor old Nancy Williams sure was nervous. She just got finished apologizing for how she looked and then she started in suckholing to Gene to please excuse her because she wasn't the world's best dancer. As a matter of fact this was her first dance ever. Thank heavens for Doreen, who was such a good sport. She'd been teaching her to dance all week. But it takes lots and lots of practice to get the hang of it. She hoped she didn't break his toes stepping on them. Ha ha ha. Just remember, she was still learning.

Gene said he'd be glad to teach her anything he figured she needed to know.

Nancy didn't catch on because she doesn't have that kind of mind. "That would be sweet of you, Gene," she says.

The band didn't show because of the storm. An act of God they call it. I'll say. So I drove around this dump for about an hour while Gene tried to molest Nancy. She put up a fair-to-middling struggle from what I could hear. The stuff her dress was made of was so stiff it crackled when she moved. Sort of like tin foil. Anyway, the two of them had it snapping and crackling like a bonfire there in the back seat while they fought a pitched battle over her body. She wasn't having none of that first time out of the chute.

"*Gene!*"

"Well for chrissakes, relax!"

"Don't take the Lord's name in vain."

"What's that supposed to mean?"

"Don't swear."

"Who's swearing?"

"Don't snag my nylons, Gene. Gene, what in the world are you . . . *Gene!*"

"Some people don't know when they're having a good time," says Doreen. I think she was a little pissed I hadn't parked and give her some action. But Lord knows what might've happened to Nancy if I'd done that.

Then, all of a sudden, Nancy calls out, sounding what you'd call desperate, "Hey, everybody, who wants a Coke!"

"Nobody wants a Coke," mumbles Gene, sort of through his teeth.

"Well, maybe we could go some place?" Meaning somewhere well-lit where this octopus will lay off for five seconds.

"I'll take you some place," Gene mutters. "You want to go somewhere, we'll go to Zipper's. Hey Billy, let's take them to Zipper's."

"I don't know, Gene . . ."

The way I said that perked Doreen up right away. As far as she was concerned, anything was better than driving around with a dope, looking at a snowstorm. "Hey," she hollers, "that sounds like *fun!*" Fun like a mental farm.

That clinched it though. "Sure," says Gene, "we'll check out Zipper's."

What could I say?

Don't get me wrong. Like everybody else I go to Zipper's and do stuff you can't do any place else in town. That's not it. But I wouldn't take anybody nice there on purpose. And I'm not trying to say that Zipper and his mother are bad people neither. It's just that so many shitty things have happened to those two that they've become kind of unpredictable. If you aren't used to that it can seem pretty weird.

I mean, look at Zipper. This guy is a not entirely normal human being who tries to tattoo himself with geometry dividers and India ink. He has this home poke on his arm which he claims is an American bald eagle but looks like a demented turkey or something. He did it himself, and the worst is he doesn't know how homely that bird is. The dumb prick shows it to people to admire.

Also, I should say a year ago he quits school to teach himself to be a drummer. That's all. He doesn't get a job or nothing, just sits at home and drums, and his mother, who's a widow and doesn't know any better, lets him. I guess that that's not any big surprise. She's a pretty hopeless drunk who's been taking her orders from Zipper since he was six. That's when his old man got electrocuted out at the mine.

Still, I'm not saying that the way Zipper is is entirely his fault. Though he can be a real creep all right. Like once when he was about ten years old Momma Zipper gets a jag on and passes out naked in the bedroom, and he lets any of his friends look at his mother with no clothes on for chrissakes, if they pay him a dime. His own mother, mind you.

But in his defence I'd say he's seen a lot of "uncles" come and go in his time, some of which figured they'd make like the man of the house and tune him in. For a while there when he was eleven, twelve maybe, half the time he was coming to school with a black eye.

Now you take Gene, he figures Zipper's house is heaven on earth. No rules. Gene figures that's the way life ought to be. No rules. Of course, nothing's entirely free. At Zipper's you got to bring a bottle or a case of beer and give Mrs. Zipper a few snorts, then everything is hunky-dory. Gene had a bottle of Five Star stashed under the back seat for the big Christmas Dance, so we were okay in that department.

But that night the lady of the house didn't seem to be around, or mobile anyway. Zipper himself came to the door, sweating like a pig in a filthy T-shirt. He'd been drumming along to the radio.

"What do you guys want?" says Zipper.

Gene holds up the bottle. "Party time."

"I'm practising," says Zipper.

"So you're practising. What's that to us?"

"My old lady's sleeping on the sofa," says Zipper, opening the door wide. "You want to fuck around here you do it in the basement." Which means his old lady'd passed out. Nobody sleeps through Zipper on the drums.

"*Gene.*" Nancy was looking a bit shy, believe me.

My brother didn't let on he'd even heard her. "Do I look particular? You know me, Zip."

Zipper looked like maybe he had to think about that one. To tell the truth, he didn't seem quite all there. At last he says, "Sure. Sure, I know you. Keep a cool tool." And then, just like that, he wanders off to his drums, and leaves us standing there.

Gene laughs and shakes his head. "What a meatball."

It makes me feel empty lots of times when I see Zipper. He's so skinny and yellow and his eyes are always weepy-looking. They say there's something gone wrong with his kidneys from all the gas and glue he sniffed when he was in elementary school.

Boy, he loves his drums though. Zipper's really what you'd call dedicated. The sad thing is that the poor guy's got no talent. He just makes a big fucking racket and he don't know any better. You see, Zipper really thinks he's going to make himself somebody with those drums, he really does. Who'd tell him any different?

Gene found some dirty coffee cups in the kitchen sink and started rinsing them out. While he did that I watched Nancy Williams. She hadn't taken her coat off, in fact she was hugging it tight to her chest like she figured somebody was going to tear it off of her. I hadn't noticed before she had on a little bit of lipstick. But now her face had gone so pale it made her mouth look bright and red and pinched like somebody had just slapped it, hard.

Zipper commenced slamming away just as the four of us got into the basement. Down there it sounded as if we were right inside a great big drum and Zipper was beating the skin directly over our heads.

And boy, did it *stink* in that place. Like the sewer had maybe backed up. But then there were piles of dirty laundry humped up on the floor all around an old wringer washing machine, so that could've been the smell too.

It was cold and sour down there and we had nothing to sit on but a couple of lawn chairs and a chesterfield that was all split and stained with what I think was you know what. Nancy looked like she wished she had a newspaper to spread out over it before she sat down. As I said before, you shouldn't never take anybody nice to Zipper's.

Gene poured rye into the coffee mugs he'd washed out and passed them around. Nancy didn't want hers. "No thank you," she told him.

"You're embarrassing me, Nancy," says Doreen. The way my date was sitting in the lawn chair beside me in her make-do mini I knew why Gene was all scrunched down on that wrecked chesterfield.

"You know I don't drink, Doreen." Let me explain that when Nancy said that it didn't sound snotty. Just quiet and well-mannered like when a polite person passes up the parsnips. Nobody in their right minds holds it against them.

"You don't do much, do you?" That was Gene's two bits' worth.

"I'll say," chips in Doreen.

Nancy doesn't answer. I could hear old Zipper crashing and banging away like a madman upstairs.

"You don't do much, *do you*?" Gene's much louder this time.

"I suppose not." I can barely hear her answer because her head's down. She's checking out the backs of her hands.

"Somebody in your position ought to try harder," Doreen pipes up. "You don't make yourself too popular when you go spoiling parties."

Gene shoves the coffee mug at Nancy again. "Have a drink." She won't take it. Principles.

"Have a drink!"

"Whyn't you lay off her?"

Gene's pissed off because he can't make Nancy Williams do what he says, so he jumps off the chesterfield and starts yelling at me. "Who's going to make me?" he hollers. "You? You going to make me?"

I can't do nothing but get up too. I never won a fight with my brother yet, but that don't mean I got to lay down and die for him. "You better take that sweater off," I says, pointing, "it's mine and I don't want blood on it." He always wears my clothes.

That's when the cousin Doreen slides in between us. She's the kind of girl loves fights. They put her centre stage. That is, if she can wriggle herself in and get involved breaking them up. Fights give her a chance to act all emotional and hysterical like she can't stand all the violence. Because she's so sensitive. Blessed are the peacemakers.

"Don't fight! Please, don't fight! Come on, Gene," she cries, latching on to his arm, "don't fight over her. Come away and cool down. I got to go to the bathroom. You show me where the bathroom is, Gene. Okay?"

"Don't give me that. You can find the bathroom yourself." Old Gene has still got his eyes fixed on me. He's acting the role. Both of them are nuts.

"Come on, Gene, I'm scared to go upstairs with that Zipper person there! He's so strange. I don't know what he might get it in his head to do. Come on, take me upstairs." Meanwhile this Doreen, who is as strong as your average sensitive ox, is sort of dragging my brother in the direction of the stairs. Him pretending he don't really want to go and have a fuss made over him, because he's got this strong urge to murder me or cripple me or something.

"You wait," is all he says to me.

"Ah, quit it or I'll die of shock," I tell him.

"Please, Gene. That Zipper person is *weird*."

At last he goes with her. I hear Gene on the stairs. "Zipper ain't much," he says, "I know lots of guys crazier than him."

I look over to Nancy sitting quietly on that grungy chesterfield, feet together, hands turned palms up on her lap. Her dress kind of sticks out from under the hem of her coat all stiff and shiny and funny-looking.

"I shouldn't have let her make me this dress," she says, angry. "We ought to have gone downtown and bought a proper one. But she had this *material*." She stops, pulls at the buttons of her coat and opens it. "Look at this thing. No wonder Gene doesn't like it, I bet."

At first I don't know what to say when she looks at me like that, her face all white except for two hot spots on her cheekbones. Zipper is going nuts upstairs. He's hot tonight. It almost sounds like something recognizable. "Don't pay Gene any attention," I say, "he's a goof."

"It's awful, this dress."

She isn't that dumb. But a person needs a reason for why things go wrong. I'm not telling her she's just a way to win ten dollars and prove a point.

"Maybe it's because I wouldn't drink that whiskey? Is that it?"

"Well, kind of. That's part of it. He's just a jerk. Take it from me, I know. Forget it."

"I never even thought he knew I was alive. Never guessed. And here I was, crazy about him. Just crazy. I'd watch him in the hallway, you know? I traded lockers with Susan Braithwaite just to get closer to his. I went to all the hockey games to see him play. I worshipped him."

The way she says that, well, it was too personal. Somebody oughtn't to say that kind of a thing to a practical stranger. It was worse than if she'd climbed out of her clothes. It made me embarrassed.

"And funny thing is, all that time he really did think I was cute. He told me on the phone. But he never once thought to ask me out because I'm a Baptist. He was sure I couldn't go. Because I'm a Baptist he thought I couldn't go. But he thought I was cute all along."

"Well, yeah."

"And now," she says, "look at this. I begged and begged Dad to let me come. I practically got down on my hands and knees. And all those dancing lessons and everything and the band doesn't show. Imagine."

"Gene wouldn't have danced with you anyway. He doesn't dance."

Nancy smiled at me. As if I was mental. She didn't half believe me.

"Hey," I says, just like that, you never know what's going to get into you, "Nancy, you want to dance?"

"Now?"

"Now. Sure. Come on. We got the one-man band, Zipper, upstairs. Why not?"

"What'll Gene say?"

"To hell with Gene. Make him jealous."

She was human at least. She liked the idea of Gene jealous. "Okay."

And here I got a confession to make. I go on all the time about Gene not being able to dance. Well, me neither. But I figured what the fuck. You just hop around and hope to hell you don't look too much like you're having a convulsion.

Neither of us knew how to get started. We just stood gawking at one another. Upstairs Zipper was going out of his tree. It sounded like there was four of him. As musical as a bag of hammers he is.

"The natives are restless tonight, Giles," I says. I was not uncomfortable. Let me tell you another one.

"Pardon?"

"Nothing. It was just dumb."

Nancy starts to sway from side to side, shuffling her feet. I figure that's the signal. I hop or whatever. So does she. We're out of the gates, off and running.

To be perfectly honest, Nancy Williams can't dance for shit. She gets this intense look on her face like she's counting off in her head, and starts to jerk. Which gets some pretty interesting action out of the notorious matched set but otherwise is pretty shoddy. And me? Well, I'm none too co-ordinated myself, so don't go getting no mental picture of Fred Astaire or whoever.

In the end what you had was two people who can't dance, dancing to the beat of a guy who can't drum. Still, Zipper didn't know no better and at the time neither did we. We were just what you'd call mad dancing fools. We danced and danced and Zipper drummed and drummed and we were all together and didn't know it. Son of a bitch, the harder we danced the hotter and happier Nancy Williams' face got. It just smoothed the unhappiness right out of it. Mine too, I guess.

That is, until all of a sudden it hit her. She stops dead in her tracks and asks, "Where's Doreen and Gene?"

Good question. They'd buggered off in my old man's car. Zipper didn't know where.

The rest of the evening was kind of a horror story. It took me a fair while to convince Nancy they hadn't gone for Cokes or something and would be right back. In the end she took it like a trooper. The only thing she'd say was, "That Doreen. *That Doreen*," and shake her head. Of course she said it about a thousand times. I was wishing she'd shut up or maybe give us a little variety like "*That Gene*." No way.

I had a problem. How to get Cinderella home before twelve-thirty, seeing as Gene had the family chariot. I tried Harvey's Taxi but no luck. Harvey's Taxi is one car and Harvey, and both were out driving lunches to a crew doing overtime at the mine.

Finally, at exactly twelve-thirty, we struck out on foot in this blizzard. Jesus, was it snowing. There was slush and ice water and every kind of shit and corruption all over the road. Every time some hunyak roared by us we got splattered by a sheet of cold slop. The snow melted in our hair and run down our necks and faces. By the time we went six blocks we were soaked. Nancy was the worst off because she wasn't dressed too good with nylons and the famous dress and such. I seen I had to be a gentleman so I stopped and give her my gloves, and my scarf to tie around her head. The two of us looked like those German soldiers I seen on TV making this death march out of Russia, on that series *Canada at War*. That was a very educational series. It made you think of man's inhumanity to man quite often.

"I could just die," she kept saying. "Dad is going to kill me. This is my last dance ever. I could just die. I could just die. *That Doreen.* Honestly!"

When we stumbled up her street, all black because of the lack of street-lights, I could see that her house was all lit up. Bad news. I stopped her on the corner. Just then it quits snowing. That's typical.

She stares at the house. "Dad's waiting."

"I guess I better go no further."

Nancy Williams bends down and feels her dress where it sticks out from under her coat. "It's soaked. I don't know how much it cost a yard. I could just die."

"Well," I says, repeating myself like an idiot, "I guess I better go no further." Then I try and kiss her. She sort of straight-arms me. I get the palm of my own glove in the face.

"What're you doing?" She sounds mad.

"Well, you know —"

"I'm not *your* date," she says, real offended. "I'm your brother's date."

"Maybe we could go out some time?"

"I won't be going anywhere for a long time. Look at me. He's going to kill me."

"Well, when you do? I'm in no hurry."

"Don't you understand? Don't you understand? Daddy will never let me go out with anybody named Simpson again. Ever. Not after tonight."

"Ever?"

"I can't imagine what you'd have to do to redeem yourself after this mess. That's how Daddy puts it — you've got to redeem yourself. I don't even know how *I'm* going to do it. And none of it's my fault."

"Yeah," I says, "he'll remember me. I'm the one he took the picture of."

She didn't seem too upset at not having me calling. "Everything is ruined," she says. "If you only knew."

Nancy Williams turns away from me then and goes up that dark, dark street where there's nobody awake except at her house. Wearing my hat and gloves.

Nancy Williams sits third pew from the front, left-hand side. I sit behind her, on the other side so's I can watch her real close. Second Sunday I was there she wore her Christmas Dance dress.

Funny thing, everything changes. At first I thought I'd start going and maybe that would *redeem* myself with her old man. Didn't work. He just looks straight through me.

You ought to see her face when she sings those Baptist hymns. It gets all hot and happy-looking, exactly like it did when we were dancing together and Zipper was pounding away there up above us, where we never even saw him. When her face gets like that there's no trouble in it, by no means.

It's like she's dancing then, I swear. But to what I don't know. I try to hear it. I try and try. I listen and listen to catch it. Christ, somebody tell me. What's she dancing to? Who's the drummer?

Cages

HERE IT IS, 1967, the Big Birthday. Centennial Year they call it. The whole country is giving itself a pat on the back. Holy shit, boys, we made it.

I made it too for seventeen years, a spotless life, as they say, and for presents I get, in my senior year of high school, my graduating year for chrissakes, a six-month suspended sentence for obstructing a police officer, and my very own personal social worker.

The thing is I don't need this social worker woman. She can't tell me anything I haven't already figured out for myself. Take last Wednesday. Miss Krawchuk, who looks like the old widow chicken on the Bugs Bunny show, the one who's hot to trot for Foghorn Leghorn, says to me: "You know, Billy, your father loves you just as much as he does Gene. He doesn't have a favourite."

Now I can get bullshit at the poolroom any time I want it – and without having to keep an appointment. Maybe Pop *loves* me as much as he does Gene, but Gene is still his favourite kid. Everybody has a favourite kid. I knew that much already when I was only eight and Gene was nine. I figured it out right after Gene almost blinded me.

Picture this. There the two of us were in the basement. It was Christmas holidays and the old man had kicked us downstairs to chuck darts at this board he'd give us for a present. Somehow, I must've had horseshoes up my ass. I'd beat Gene six games straight. And was he pissed off! He never loses to me at nothing ever. And me being in such a real unique situation, I was giving him the needle-rooney.

"What's that now?" I said. "Is that six or seven what I won?"

"Luck," Gene said, and he sounded like somebody was slowly strangling him. "Luck. Luck. Luck." He could hardly get it out.

And that's when I put the capper on it. I tossed a bull's-eye. "Read'er and weep," I told him. That's what the old man says whenever he goes out at rummy. It's his needle-rooney. "Read'er and weep."

That did it. The straw what broke the frigging camel's back. All I saw was his arm blur when he let fly at me. I didn't even have time to *think* about ducking. Bingo. Dead centre in the forehead, right in the middle of the old noggin he drills me with a dart. And there it stuck. Until it loosened a bit. Then it sagged down real slow between my eyes, hung for a second, slid off of my nose, and dropped at my feet. I hollered bloody blue murder, you better believe it.

For once, Pop didn't show that little bastard any mercy. He took after him from room to room whaling him with this extension cord across the ass, the back of the legs, the shoulders. Really hard. Gene, naturally, was screaming and blubbering and carrying on like it was a goddamn axe murder or something. He'd try to get under a bed, or behind a dresser or something, and get stuck halfway. Then old Gene would really catch it. He didn't know whether to plough forward, back up, shit, or go blind. And all the time the old man was lacing him left and right and saying in this sad, tired voice: "You're the oldest. Don't you know no better? You could of took his eye out, you crazy little bugger."

But that was only justice. He wasn't all that mad at Gene. Me he was mad at. If that makes any sense. Although I have to admit he didn't lay a hand on me. But yell? Christ, can that man yell. Especially at me. Somehow I'm the one that drives him squirrelly.

"Don't you *never*, *never* tease him again!" he bellowed and his neck started to swell. When the old man gets mad you can see it swell, honest. "You know he can't keep a hold of himself. One day you'll drive him so goddamn goofy with that yap of yours he'll do something terrible! Something he'll regret for the rest of his life. And it'll all be your fault!" The old man had to stop there and slow down or a vein would've exploded in his brain, or his arsehole popped inside out, or something. "So smarten up," he said, a little quieter, finally, "or you'll be the death of me and all my loved ones."

So there you are. I never pretended the world was fair, and I never bitched because it wasn't. But I do resent the hell out of being forced to listen to some dried-up old broad who gets paid by the government to tell me it is. Fuck her. She never lived in the Simpson household with my old man waiting around for Gene to do that *terrible thing*. It spoils the atmosphere. Makes a person edgy, you know?

Of course, Gene has done a fair number of *bad things* while everybody was waiting around for him to do the one great big *terrible thing*; and he's done them in a fair number of places. That's because the old man is a miner, and for a while there he was always telling some foreman to go piss up a rope. So we moved around a lot. That's why the Simpson household has a real history. But Gene's is the best of all. In Elliot Lake he failed grade three; in Bombertown he got picked up for shoplifting; in Flin Flon he broke some snotty kid's nose and got sent home from school. And every grade he goes higher, it gets a little worse. Last year, when we were both in grade eleven, I'm sure the old man was positive Gene was finally going to pull off the *terrible thing* he's been worrying about as long as I can remember.

It's crazy. Lots of times when I think about it, I figure I

don't get on with the old man because I treat him nice. That I try too hard to make him like me. I'm not the way Gene is, I respect Pop. He slogs it out, shift after shift, on a shitty job he hates. Really hates. In fact, he told me once he would have liked to been a farmer. Which only goes to show you how crazy going down that hole day after day makes you. Since we moved to Saskatchewan I've seen lots of farmers, and if you ask me, being one doesn't have much to recommend it.

But getting back to that business of being nice to Dad. Last year I started waiting up for him to come home from the afternoon shift. The one that runs from four p.m. in the afternoon until midnight. It wasn't half bad. Most nights I'd fall asleep on the chesterfield with the TV playing after Mom went to bed. Though lots of times I'd do my best to make it past the national news to wait for Earl Cameron and his collection of screwballs. Those guys kill me. They're always yapping off because somebody or something rattled their chain. Most of those characters with all the answers couldn't pour piss out of a rubber boot if they read the instructions printed on the sole. They remind me of Gene; he's got all the answers too. But still, quite a few of them are what you'd call witty. Which Gene is in his own way too.

But most times, as I say, I'd doze off. Let me give you a sample evening. About twelve-thirty the lights of his half-ton would come shooting into the living-room, bouncing off the walls, scooting along the ceiling when he wheeled into the driveway like a madman. It was the lights flashing in my eyes that woke me up most nights, and if that didn't do it there was always his grand entrance. When the old man comes into the house, from the sound of it you'd think he never heard of door knobs. I swear sometimes I'm sure he's taking a battering-ram to the back door. Then he thunks his lunch bucket on the kitchen counter and bowls his hard hat into the landing. This is because he always comes home from work mad. Never once in his life has a shift ever gone right for that man. Never. They could pack his pockets with diamonds and send him home two hours early and he'd still bitch. So every night was pretty much the same. He had a mad on. Like in my sample night.

He flicked on the living-room light and tramped over to his orange recliner with the bottle of Boh. "If you want to ruin your eyes, do it on school-books, not on watching TV in the goddamn dark. It's up to somebody in this outfit to make something of themselves."

"I was sleeping."

"You ought to sleep in bed." *Keerash!* He weighs two hundred and forty-four pounds and he never sits down in a chair. He falls into it. "Who's that? Gary Cooper?" he asked. He figures any movie star on the late show taller than Mickey Rooney is Cooper. He doesn't half believe you when you tell him they aren't.

"Cary Grant."

"What?"

"Cary Grant. Not Gary Cooper. Cary Grant."

"Oh." There he sat in his recliner, big meaty shoulders sagging, belly propped up on his belt buckle like a pregnant pup's. Eyes red and sore, hair all mussed up, the top of his beer bottle peeking out of his fist like a little brown nipple. He has cuts all over those hands of his, barked knuckles and raspberries that never heal because the salt in the potash ore keeps them open, eats right down to the bone sometimes.

"How'd it go tonight?"

"Usual shit. We had a breakdown." He paused. "Where's your brother? In bed?"

"Out."

"Out? Out? *Out?* What kind of goddamn answer is that? Out where?"

I shrugged.

"Has he got his homework done?" That's the kind of question I get asked. *Has your brother got his homework done?*

"How the hell would I know?"

"I don't know why you don't help him with his school-work," the old man said, peeved as usual.

"You mean do it for him."

"Did I say that? Huh? I said help him. Didn't I say that?" he griped, getting his shit in a knot.

He thinks it's that easy. Just screw the top off old Gene and pour it in. No problem. Like an oil change.

"He's got to be around to help," I said.

That reminded him. He jumped out of the chair and gawked up and down the deserted street. "It's almost one o'clock. On a school night. I'll kick his ass." He sat down and watched the screen for a while and sucked on his barley sandwich.

Finally, he made a stab at acting civilized. "So how's baseball going?"

"What?"

"Baseball. For chrissakes clean out your ears. How's it going?"

"I quit last year. Remember?"

"Oh yeah." He didn't say nothing at first. Then he said: "You shouldn't have. You wasn't a bad catcher."

"The worst. No bat and no arm – just a flipper. They stole me blind."

"But you had the head," said the old man. And the way he said it made him sound like he was pissed at me for mean-mouthing myself. That surprised me. I felt kind of good about that. "You had the head," he repeated, shaking his own. "I never told you but Al came up to me at work and said you were smart back there behind the plate. He said he wished Gene had your head."

I can't say that surprised me. Gene is one of those cases of a million-dollar body carrying around a ten-cent head. He's a natural. Flop out his glove and, smack, the ball sticks. He's like Mickey Mantle. You know those stop-action photos where they caught Mickey with his eyes glommed onto the bat, watching the ball jump off the lumber? That's Gene. And he runs like a Negro, steals bases like Maury Wills for chrissake.

But stupid and conceited? You wouldn't believe the half of it. Give him the sign to bunt to move a runner and he acts as if you're asking him to bare his ass in public. Not him. He's a big shot. He swings for the fence. Nothing less. And old Gene is always in the game, if you know what I mean? I don't know what happens when he gets on base, maybe he starts thinking of the hair pie in the stands admiring him or something, but he always dozes off at the wheel. Once he even started to comb his hair at first base. Here it is, a 3 and 2 count with two men out, and my brother forgets to run on the pitch because he's combing his hair. I could have died. Really I could have. The guy is such an embarrassment sometimes.

"He can have my head," I said to Pop. "If I get his girls."

That made the old man wince. He's sure that Gene is going to knock up one of those seat-covers he takes out and make him a premature grandpa.

"You pay attention to school. There's plenty of time later for girls." And up he jumped again and stuck his nose against the window looking for Gene again. Mom has to wash the picture window once a week; he spots it all up with nose grease looking for Gene.

"I don't know why your mother lets him out of the house," he said. "Doesn't she have any control over that boy?"

That's what he does, blames everybody but himself. Oh hell, maybe nobody's to blame. Maybe Gene is just Gene, and there's nothing to be done about it.

"I don't know what she's supposed to do. You couldn't keep him in if you parked a tank in the driveway and strung barbed wire around the lot."

Of course that was the wrong thing to say. I usually say it.

"Go to bed!" he yelled at me. "You're no better than your brother. I don't see you in bed neither. What'd I do, raise alley cats or kids? Why can't you two keep hours like human beings!"

And then the door banged and we knew the happy wanderer was home. Gene makes almost as much noise as the old man does when he comes in. It's beneath his dignity to sneak in like me.

Dad hoisted himself out of the chair and steamed off for the kitchen. He can move pretty quick for a big guy when he wants to. Me, I was in hot pursuit. I don't like to miss much.

Old Gene was hammered, and grinning from ass-hole to earlobes. The boy's got a great smile. Even when he grins at old ladies my mother's age you can tell they like it.

"Come here and blow in my face," said my father.

"Go on with you," said Gene. All of a sudden the smile was gone and he was irritated. He pushed past Pop, took the milk out of the fridge and started to drink out of the container.

"Use a glass."

Gene burped. He's a slob.

"You stink of beer," said the old man. "Who buys beer for a kid your age?"

"I ain't drunk," said Gene.

"Not much. Your eyes look like two piss-holes in the snow."

"Sure, sure," said Gene. He lounged, he swivelled over to me and lifted my Players out of my shirt pocket. "I'll pay you back tomorrow," he said, taking out a smoke. I heard that one before.

"I don't want to lose my temper," said Dad, being patient with him as usual, "so don't push your luck, sunshine." The two of them eyeballed it, hard. Finally Gene backed down, looked away and fiddled with his matches. "I don't ride that son of a bitch of a cage up and down for my health. I do it for you two," Dad said. "But I swear to God, Gene, if you blow this year of school there'll be a pair of new work boots for you on the back step, come July 1. Both of you know my rules. Go to school, work, or pack up. I'm not having bums put their feet under my table."

"I ain't scared of work," said Gene. "Anyways, school's a pain in the ass."

"Well, you climb in the cage at midnight with three hours of sleep and see if *that* ain't a pain in the ass. Out there nobody says, please do this, please do that. It ain't school out there, it's life."

"Ah, I wouldn't go to the mine. The mine sucks."

"Just what the hell do you think you'd do?"

"He'd open up shop as a brain surgeon," I said. Of course, Gene took a slap at me and grabbed at my shirt. He's a tough guy. He wasn't really mad, but he likes to prevent uppityness.

"You go to bed!" the old man hollered. "You ain't helping matters."

So off I went. I could hear them wrangling away even after I closed my door. You'd wonder how my mother does it, but she sleeps through it all. I think she's just so goddamn tired of the three of us she's gone permanently deaf to the sound of our voices. She just don't hear us any more.

The last thing I heard before I dropped off was Pop saying: "I've rode that cage all my life, and take it from me, there wasn't a day I didn't wish I'd gone to school and could sit in an office in a clean white shirt." Sometimes he can't remember what he wants to be, a farmer or a pencil-pusher.

The cage. He's always going on about the cage. It's what the men at the mine call the elevator car they ride down the shaft. They call it that because it's all heavy reinforced-steel mesh. The old man has this cage on the brain. Ever since we were little kids he's been threatening us with it. *Make something of yourself,* he'd warn us, *or you'll end up like your old man, a monkey in the cage!* Or: *What's this, Gene? Failed arithmetic? Just remember dunces don't end up in the corner. Hell no, they end up in the cage! Look at me!* My old man really hates that cage and the mine. He figures it's the worst thing you can threaten anybody with.

I was in the cage, once. A few years ago, when I was fourteen, the company decided they'd open the mine up for tours. It was likely the brainstorm of some public relations tit sitting in head office in Chicago. In my book it was kind of like taking people into the slaughterhouse to prove you're kind to the cows. Anyway, Pop offered to take us on one of his days off. As usual, he was about four years behind schedule. When we were maybe eleven we might have been nuts about the idea, but just then it didn't thrill us too badly. Gene, who is about as subtle as a bag of hammers, said flat out he wasn't interested. I could see right away the old man was hurt by that. It isn't often he plays the buddy to his boys, and he probably had the idea he could whiz us about the machines and stuff. Impress the hell out of us. So it was up to me to slobber and grin like some kind of half-wit over the idea, to perk him up, see? Everybody suffers when the old man gets into one of his moods.

Of course, like always when I get sucked into this good-turn business, I shaft myself. I'd sort of forgotten how much I don't like tight places and being closed in. When we were younger, Gene used to make me go berserk by holding me under the covers, or stuffing a pillow in my face, or locking me in the garage whenever he got the chance. The jerk.

To start with, they packed us in the cage with twelve other people, which didn't help matters any. Right away my chest got tight and I felt like I couldn't breathe. Then the old cables started groaning and grinding and this fine red dust like chili powder sprinkled down through the mesh and dusted our hard hats with the word GUEST stencilled on them. It was rust. Kind of makes you think.

"Here we go," said Pop.

We went. It was like all of a sudden the floor fell away from under my boots. That cage just dropped in the shaft like a stone down a well. It rattled and creaked and banged. The bare light bulb in the roof started to flicker, and all the faces around me started to dance and shake up and down in the dark. A wind twisted up my pant-legs and I could hear the cables squeak and squeal. It made me think of big fat fucking rats.

"She needs new brake shoes," said this guy beside me and he laughed. He couldn't fool me. He was scared shitless too, in his own way.

"It's not the fall that kills you," his neighbour replied. "It's the sudden stop." There's a couple of horses' patoots in every crowd.

We seemed to drop forever. Everybody got quieter and quieter. They even stopped shuffling and coughing. Down. Down. Down. Then the cage started to slow, I felt a pressure build in my knees and my crotch and my ears. The wire box started to shiver and clatter and shake. *Bang!* We stopped. The cage bobbed a little up and down like a yo-yo on the end of a string. Not much though, just enough to make you queasy.

"Last stop, Hooterville!" said the guide, who thought he was funny, and threw back the door. Straight ahead I could see a low-roofed big open space with tunnels running from it into the ore. Every once in a while I could see the light from a miner's helmet jump around in the blackness of one of those tunnels like a firefly flitting in the night.

First thing I thought was: *What if I get lost? What if I lose the group? There's miles and miles and miles of tunnel under here.* I caught a whiff of the air. It didn't smell like air up top. It smelled used. You could taste the salt. *I'm suffocating,* I thought. *I can't breathe this shit.*

I hadn't much liked the cage but this was worse. When I was in the shaft I knew there was a patch of sky over my head with a few stars in it and clouds and stuff. But all of a sudden I realized how deep we were. How we were sort of like worms crawling in the guts of some dead animal. Over us were billions, no, trillions, of tons of rock and dirt and mud pressing down. I could imagine it caving in and falling on me, crushing my chest, squeezing the air out slowly, dust fine as flour trickling into my eyes and nostrils, or mud plugging my mouth so I couldn't even scream. And then just lying there in the dark, my legs and arms pinned so I couldn't even twitch them. For a long time maybe. Crazy, lunatic stuff was what I started to think right on the spot.

My old man gave me a nudge to get out. We were the last.

"No," I said quickly and hooked my fingers in the mesh.

"We get out here," said the old man. He hadn't caught on yet.

"No, I can't," I whispered. He must have read the look on my face then. I think he knew he couldn't have pried me off that mesh with a gooseneck and winch.

Fred, the cage operator, lifted his eyebrows at Pop. "What's up, Jack?"

"The kid's sick," said Pop. "We'll take her up. He don't feel right." My old man was awful embarrassed.

Fred said, "I wondered when it'd happen. Taking kids and women down the hole."

"Shut your own goddamn hole," said the old man. "He's got the flu. He was up all last night."

Fred looked what you'd call sceptical.

"Last time I take you any place nice," the old man said under his breath.

The last day of school has always got to be some big deal. By nine o'clock all the dipsticks are roaring their cars up and down main street with their goofy broads hanging out their windows yelling, and trying to impress on one another how drunk they are.

Dad sent me to look for Gene because he didn't come home for supper at six. I found him in the poolroom playing dollar-a-hand poker pool.

"Hey, little brother," he waved to me from across the smoky poolroom, "come on here and I'll let you hold my cards!" I went over. He grinned to the goofs he was playing with. "You watch out now, boys," he said, "my little brother always brings me luck. Not that I need it," he explained to me, winking.

Yeah, I always brought him luck. *I* kept track of the game. *I* figured out what order to take the balls down. *I* reminded him not to put somebody else out and to play the next guy safe instead of slamming off some cornball shot. When *I* did all that Gene won – because I brought him luck. Yeah.

Gene handed me his cards. "You wouldn't believe these two," he said to me out of the corner of his mouth, "genuine plough jockeys. These boys couldn't find their ass in the dark with both hands. I'm fifteen dollars to the good."

I admit they didn't look too swift. The biggest one, who was *big*, was wearing an out-of-town team jacket, a Massey-Ferguson cap, and shit-kicker wellingtons. He was maybe twenty-one, but his skin hadn't cleared up yet by no means. His pan looked like all-dressed pizza, heavy on the cheese. His friend was a dinky little guy with his hair designed into a duck's ass. The kind of guy who hates the Beatles. About two feet of a dirty comb was sticking out of his ass pocket.

Gene broke the rack and the nine went down. His shot.

"Dad's looking for you. He wants to know if you passed," I said.

"You could've told him."

"Well, I didn't."

"Lemme see the cards." I showed him. He had a pair of treys, a six, a seven, and a lady. Right away he stopped to pocket the three. I got a teacher who always talks about thought processes. Gene doesn't have them.

"Look at the table," I said. "Six first and you can come around up here," I pointed.

"No coaching," said Pizza Face. I could see this one was a poor loser.

Gene shifted his stance and potted the six.

"What now?" he asked.

"The queen, and don't forget to put pants on her." I paused. "Pop figured you were going to make it. He really did, Gene."

"So tough titty. I didn't. Who the hell cares? He had your suck card to slobber over, didn't he?" He drilled the lady in the side pocket. No backspin. He'd hooked himself on the three. "Fuck."

"The old man is on graveyard shift. You better go home and face the music before he goes to work. It'll be worse in the morning when he needs sleep," I warned him.

"Screw him."

I could see Gene eyeballing the four. He didn't have any four in his hand, so I called him over and showed him his cards. "You can't shoot the four. It's not in your hand."

"Just watch me." He winked. "I've been doing it all night. It's all pitch and no catch with these prizes." Gene strolled back to the table and coolly stroked down the four. He had shape for the three which slid in the top pocket like shit through a goose. He cashed in on the seven. "That's it, boys," he said. "That's all she wrote."

I was real nervous. I tried to bury the hand in the deck but the guy with the runny face stopped me. He was getting tired of losing, I guess. Gene doesn't even cheat smart. You got to let them win once in a while.

"Gimme them cards," he said. He started counting the cards off against the balls, flipping down the boards on the felt. "Three." He nodded. "Six, seven, queen. I guess you got them all," he said slowly, with a look on his face like he was pissing ground glass.

That's when Duck Ass chirped up. "Hey, Marvin," he said, "that guy shot the four. He shot the four."

"Nah," said Gene.

Marvin studied on this for a second, walked over to the table and pulled the four ball out of the pocket. Just like little Jack Horner lifting the plum out of the pie. "Yeah," he said. "You shot the four."

"Jeez," said Gene, "I guess I did. Honest mistake. Look, here's a dollar for each of you." He took two bills out of his shirt pocket. "You got to pay for your mistakes is what I was always taught."

"I bet you he's been cheating all along," said Duck Ass.

"My brother don't cheat," I said.

"I want all my money back," said Marvin. Quite loud. Loud enough that some heads turned and a couple of tables stopped playing. There was what you would call a big peanut gallery, it being the beginning of vacation and the place full of junior high kids and stags.

"You can kiss my ass, bozo," said Gene. "Like my brother here said, I never cheated nobody in my life."

"You give us our money back," threatened Marvin, "or I'll pull your head off, you skinny little prick."

Guys were starting to drift towards us, curious. The manager, Pat Bert, was easing his guts out from behind the cash register.

"Give them their money, Gene," I said, "and let's get out of here."

"No."

Well, that was that. You can't change his mind. I took a look at old Marvin. As I said before, Marvin was *big*. But what was worse was that he had this real determined look people who aren't too bright get when they finally dib on to the fact they've been hosed and somebody has been laughing up his sleeve at them. They don't like it too hot, believe me.

"Step outside, shit-head," said Marvin.

"Fight," somebody said encouragingly. A real clump of ring-siders was starting to gather. "Fight." Bert came hustling up, bumping his way through the kids with his bay window. "Outside, you guys. I don't want nothing broke in here. Get out or I'll call the cops."

Believe me, was I tense. Real tense. I know Gene pretty well and I was sure that he had looked at old Marvin's muscles trying to bust out everywhere. Any second I figured he was going to even the odds by pasting old Marv in the puss with his pool cue, or at least sucker-punching him.

But Gene is full of surprises. All of a sudden he turned

peacemaker. He laid down his pool cue (which I didn't figure was too wise) and said: "You want to fight over this?" He held up the four ball. "Over this? An honest mistake?"

"Sure I do," said Marvin. "You're fucking right I do, cheater."

"Cheater, cheater," said Duck Ass. I was looking him over real good because I figured if something started in there I'd get him to tangle with.

Gene shrugged and even kind of sighed, like the hero does in the movies when he has been forced into a corner and has to do something that is against his better nature. He tossed up the four ball once, looked at it, and then reached behind him and shoved it back into the pocket. "All right," he said, slouching a little and jamming his hands into his jacket pockets. "Let's go, sport."

That started the stampede. "Fight! Fight!" The younger kids, the ones thirteen and fourteen, were really excited; the mob kind of swept Marvin and Gene out the door, across the street and into the OK Economy parking lot where most beefs get settled. There's lots of dancing-room there. A nice big ring.

Marvin settled in real quick. He tugged the brim of his Massey-Ferguson special a couple of times, got his dukes up and started to hop around like he'd stepped right out of the pages of *Ring* magazine. He looked pretty stupid, especially when Gene just looked at him, and kept his hands rammed in his jacket pockets. Marvin kind of clomped from foot to foot for a bit and then he said: "Get 'em up."

"You get first punch," said Gene.

"What?" said Marv. He was so surprised his yap fell open.

"If I hit you first," said Gene, "you'll charge me with assault. I know your kind."

Marvin stopped clomping. I suspect it took too much coordination for him to clomp and think at the same time. "Oh no," he said, "I ain't falling for that. If I hit *you* first, you'll charge *me* with assault." No flies on Marvin. "*You* get the first punch."

"Fight. Come on, fight," said some ass-hole, real disgusted with all the talk and no action.

"Oh no," said Gene. "I ain't hitting *you* first."

Marvin brought his hands down. "Come on, come on, let fly."

"You're sure?" asked Gene.

"Give her your best shot," said Marvin. "You couldn't hurt a fly, you scrawny shit. Quit stalling. Get this show on the road."

Gene uncorked on him. It looked like a real pansy punch. His right arm whipped out of his jacket pocket, stiff at the elbow like a girl's when she slaps. It didn't look like it had nothing behind it, sort of like Gene had smacked him kind of contemptuous in the mouth with the flat of his hand. That's how it looked. It *sounded* like he'd hit him in the mouth with a ball-peen hammer. Honest to God, you could hear the teeth crunch when they broke.

Big Marvin dropped on his knees like he'd been shot in the back of the neck. His hands flew up to his face and the blood just ran through his fingers and into his cuffs. It looked blue under the parking-lot lights. There was an awful lot of it.

"Get up, you dick licker," said Gene.

Marvin pushed off his knees with a crazy kind of grunt that might have been a sob. I couldn't tell. He came up under Gene's arms, swept him off his feet and dangled him in the air, crushing his ribs in a bear hug.

"*Waauugh!*" said Gene. I started looking around right smartly for something to hit the galoot with before he popped my brother like a pimple.

But then Gene lifted his fist high above Marvin's head and brought it down on his skull, hard as he could. It made a sound like he was banging coconuts together. Marvin sagged a little at the knees and staggered. *Chunk! Chunk!* Gene hit him two more times and Marvin toppled over backwards. My brother landed on top of him and right away started pasting him left and right. Everybody was screaming encouragement. There was no invitation to the dick licker to get up this time. Gene was still clobbering him when I saw the cherry popping on the cop car two blocks away. I dragged him off Marvin.

"Cops," I said, yanking at his sleeve. Gene was trying to get one last kick at Marvin. "Come on, fucker," he was yelling. "Fight now!"

"Jesus," I said, looking at Gene's jacket and shirt, "you stupid bugger, you're all over blood." It was smeared all over him. Marvin tried to get up. He only made it to his hands and knees. There he stayed, drooling blood and saliva on the asphalt. The crowd started to edge away as the cop car bounced up over the curb and gave a long, low whine out of its siren.

I took off my windbreaker and gave it to Gene. He pulled off his jacket and threw it down. "Get the fuck out of here," I said. "Beat it."

"I took the wheels off his little red wagon," said Gene. "It don't pull so good now." His hands were shaking and so was his voice. He hadn't had half enough yet. "I remember that other guy," he said. "Where's his friend?"

I gave him a shove. "Get going." Gene slid into the crowd that was slipping quickly away. Then I remembered his hockey jacket. It was wet with blood. It also had flashes with his name and number on it. It wouldn't take no Sherlock Holmes cop to figure out who'd beat on Marvin. I picked it up and hugged it to my belly. Right away I felt something hard in the pocket. Hard and round. I started to walk away. I heard a car door slam. I knew what was in that pocket. The controversial four ball old Gene had palmed when he pretended to put it back. He likes to win.

I must have been walking too fast or with a guilty hunch to my shoulders, because I heard the cop call, "Hey you, the kid with the hair." Me, I'm kind of a hippy for this place, I guess. Lots of people mention my hair.

I ran. I scooted round the corner of the supermarket and let that pool ball fly as hard as I could, way down the alley. I never rifled a shot like that in my life. If coach Al had seen me trigger that baby he'd have strapped me into a belly pad himself. Of course, a jacket don't fly for shit. The bull came storming around the corner just as I give it the heave-ho. I was kind of caught with shit on my face, if you know what I mean?

Now a guy with half a brain could have talked his way out of that without too much trouble. Even a cop understands how somebody would try to help his brother. They don't hold it too much against you. And I couldn't really protect Gene. That geek Marvin would have flapped his trap if I hadn't. And it wasn't as if I hadn't done old Gene *some* good. After all, they never found out about that pool ball. The judge would have pinned Gene's ears back for him if he'd known he was going around thwacking people with a hunk of shatter-proof plastic. So Gene came out smelling like a rose, same suspended sentence as me, and a reputation for having hands of stone.

But at a time like that you get the nuttiest ideas ever. I watched them load Marvin in a squad car to drive him to the hospital while I sat in the back seat of another. And I thought to myself: *I'll play along with this. Let the old man come down to the cop shop over me for once. Me he takes for granted. Let him worry about Billy for a change. It wouldn't hurt him.*

So I never said one word about not being the guy who hopped Marvin. It was kind of fun in a crazy way, making like a hard case. At the station I was real rude and lippy. Particularly to a sergeant who was a grade A dink if I ever saw one. It was only when they took my shoe-laces and belt that I started to get nervous.

"Ain't you going to call my old man?" I asked.

The ass-hole sergeant gave me a real smile. "In the morning," he said. "All in good time."

"In the morning?" And then I said like a dope: "Where am I going to sleep?"

"Show young Mr. Simpson where he's going to sleep," said the sergeant. He smiled again. It looked like a ripple on a slop pail. The constable who he was ordering around like he was his own personal slave took me down into the basement of the station. Down there it smelled of stale piss and old puke. I kind of gagged. I got a weak stomach.

Boy, was I nervous. I saw where he was taking me. There were four cells. They weren't even made out of bars. Just metal strips riveted into a cross hatch you couldn't stick your hand through. They were all empty.

"Your choice," said the corporal. He was real humorous too, like his boss.

"You don't have to put me in one of them, sir," I said. "I won't run away."

"That's what all the criminals say." He opened the door. "Entrez-vous."

I was getting my old crazy feeling really bad. Really bad. I felt kind of dizzy. "I got this thing," I said, "about being locked up. It's torture."

"Get in."

"No – please," I said. "I'll sit upstairs. I won't bother anybody."

"You think you've got a choice? You don't have a choice. Move your ass."

I was getting ready to cry. I could feel it. I was going to bawl in front of a cop. "I didn't do it," I said. "I never beat him up. Swear to Jesus I didn't."

"I'm counting three," he said, "and then I'm applying the boots to your backside."

It all came out. Just like that. "*It was my fucking ass-hole brother Gene!*" I screamed. The only thing I could think of was, if they put me in there I'll be off my head by morning. I really will. "*I didn't do nothing! I never do nothing! You can't put me in there for him!*"

They called my old man. I guess I gave a real convincing performance. Not that I'm proud of it. I actually got sick on the spot from nerves. I just couldn't hold it down.

Pop had to sign for me and promise to bring Gene down in the morning. It was about twelve-thirty when everything got cleared up. He'd missed his shift and his ride in the cage.

When we got in the car he didn't start it. We just sat there with the windows rolled down. It was a beautiful night and there were lots of stars swimming in the sky. This town is small enough that street-lights and neon don't interfere with the stars. It's the only thing I like about this place. There's plenty of sky and lots of air to breathe.

"Your brother wasn't enough," he said. "You I trusted."

"I only tried to help him."

"You goddamn snitch." He needed somebody to take it out on, so he belted me. Right on the snout with the back of his hand. It started to bleed. I didn't try to stop it. I just let it drip on those goddamn furry seat-covers that he thinks are the cat's ass. "They were going to put me in this place, this cage, for him, for that useless shit!" I yelled. I'd started to cry. "No more, Pop. He failed! He failed on top of it all! So is he going to work? You got the boots ready on the back step? Huh? Is he going down in the fucking cage?"

"Neither one of you is going down in the cage. Not him, not you," he said.

"Nah, I didn't think so," I said, finally wiping at my face with the back of my hand. "I didn't think so."

"I don't have to answer to you," he said. "You just can't get inside his head. You were always the smart one. I didn't have to worry about you. You always knew what to do. But Gene..." He pressed his forehead against the steering-wheel, hard. "Billy, I see him doing all sorts of stuff. Stuff you can't imagine.

I see it until it makes me sick." He looked at me. His face was yellow under the street-light, yellow like a lemon. "I try so hard with him. But he's got no sense. He just does things. He could have killed that other boy. He wouldn't even think of that, you know." All of a sudden the old man's face got all crumpled and creased like paper when you ball it up. "What's going to happen to him?" he said, louder than he had to. "What's going to happen to Eugene?" It was sad. It really was.

I can never stay mad at my old man. Maybe because we're so much alike, even though he can't see it for looking the other way. Our minds work alike. I'm a chip off the old block. Don't ever doubt it.

"Nothing."

"Billy," he said, "you mean it?"

I knew what he was thinking. "Yes," I said. "I'll do my best."

Going to Russia

"A NOTHER of your letters arrived at my house yesterday," the doctor announces. "That makes four now." He says this in a colourless, insipid voice, in the way he says most things.

It is only the significant pause which follows that alerts me I am expected to respond, and distracts my attention from the scene outside his office window. For several minutes I have been watching two children as they tramp stiffly off into the distance. They lead me to think of my daughter, and to wonder if she misses my visits.

Here, we are on the outskirts of the city, where the new suburbs dwindle into prairie, and prairie into winter sky. The children, stuffed into bulky snowsuits, totter along, their arms stiffly extended like tiny astronauts foraging on the frozen cinder of a spent star.

Suburban tots often come to explore these splendid spaces. I have navigated them too, in my imagination, warm behind a double pane of glass. I find it strange that this blank sweep of land terrifies some of my fellow inmates and that they feel the need to keep their blinds down night and day. I like it. It makes me think of Russia.

"Yes?" I say finally, a little late, but nevertheless meaning to politely encourage him.

"Mr. Caragan, I thought when we met last Wednesday we agreed there would be no more letters."

The man has me there. But I am an impulsive fellow and that was Wednesday. By Thursday I felt I owed him some kind of explanation as to what had moved me to write the first three letters. "That's true," I admit, "that was the understanding."

"But?"

I shrug.

Dr. Herzl spreads a sheet of paper on his desk. His fingers rub diligently at the fold marks. When he is satisfied everything is shipshape, he begins to read to himself. I note a barely perceptible flicker in his upper lip. When he finishes, he looks up at me sharply. An old tactic that I recognize immediately. "This doesn't make much sense to me," he says.

"No?"

"Excuse me," he says, pausing. "I'm not a critic. . . ." The doctor smiles to signal me that this is an offering from his store of inexhaustible wit. "But I find your language rather ... formal, stilted," he says at last, finding the words he wants. "As if you are under great strain, as if you are trying to keep a lid on your feelings when you write me these letters." He searches the page. "For instance, there's this: 'I answer in writing because my thought will thus be more fully expressed, and more distinctly perceived, like a sound amid silence.' Doesn't that sound a bit unusual to you?"

"There's quotation marks around that."

"Pardon?"

"I didn't write that. There's quotation marks around that."

"Oh." The doctor hesitates. "Who *did* write it then?"

"Mikhail Osipovich Gershenzon."

A doubtful look passes over his face. He suspects me of pulling his leg. Dr. Herzl considers me a great joker, albeit an unbalanced, a lunatic one.

"It's true," I assure him.

"I am not familiar . . ."

"So who is? But then, you don't need to be," I say. "I explained it all in the letter. It's all in there. I used Gershenzon as an example. I was trying to help you see why I write –"

I am interrupted. "Yes, I'm sure. But you understand – fourteen pages in your tiny handwriting – I only skimmed it."

"Of course." I don't know whatever led me to believe he would profit from the story of the Corner-to-Corner Correspondence. Or that anyone else would, for that matter. When I told Janet, who is young, an artist, and believes herself to be in possession of a sensitive soul, about the series of letters exchanged between Gershenzon and Viacheslav Ivanovitch Ivanov while they recuperated in a rest-home in Russia, she said: "I don't get it. What's a corner-to-corner correspondence?"

"It was called that because each of the correspondents was in opposite corners of the same room. That's why it was called the Corner-to-Corner Correspondence," I said, ending my obvious explanation lamely.

"They couldn't talk? What was it, throat cancer?"

"No, as I said before, these guys were poets, philosophers, men of letters. Remember?" I prodded. "It was just that they felt more comfortable, surer of themselves, when writing. They had time to reflect on what they wanted to say, to test their ideas. To compose."

"That's the weirdest thing I ever heard – writing to someone in the same room," she said. "That sort of thing just gets in the way of real feelings. It's a kind of mask to hide who you really are, and what you're all about."

That was her final judgment, and from Janet's considered decisions there is no appeal, as I have learned to my sorrow. Still, I was almost in love, and at that precarious point one imagines it is important to be understood. So at our next planned meeting, two days later, I took along with me a passage I had copied from one of Gershenzon's letters. It was to demonstrate to her the subtleties which are the province of the written word, and, more importantly, to signal her what was going on in my mind.

"You see, honey," I said, trying to explain what Gershenzon meant to me, "he felt out of step with things going on around him. He might have said to old Ivanov: 'Viacheslav, what's the matter with me? I don't feel I belong, I don't feel right. Why is it I don't think what other people think, or feel what other people say they feel?' He could have put it that way. He could have, but he didn't. What he did do was write:

> This is the life I lead by day. But on a deeper level of consciousness I lead a different life. There, an insistent, persistent, hidden voice has been saying for years: No, no, this is not it! Some other kind of will in me turns away in misery and distaste from all of culture, from all that is being said and done around me. It finds all this tedious and vain, like a struggle of phantoms flailing away in a void; it seems to know another world, to foresee a different life, not yet to be found on earth but which will come and cannot fail to come, for only then will true reality be achieved. To me this voice is the voice of my real self. I live like a foreigner acclimatized in an alien land; the natives like me and I like them. I diligently work for their good, share their sorrows and rejoice in their joys, but at the same time I know that I am a stranger, I secretly long for the fields of my homeland, for its different spring, the smell of its flowers, and the way its women speak. Where is my homeland? I shall never see it, I shall die in foreign parts.

Of course, when I looked up from the page, it was only to discover that Janet had gone to the bathroom to apply her contraceptive foam.

"I hear that you're still refusing to see your wife," says Dr. Herzl, introducing a new topic.

"That's not entirely true. I said I wouldn't see her alone. If she brings our daughter with her, well, that's a different story."

"Why won't you speak with your wife alone?"

"I explained that in my second letter –"

"Why don't you explain it to me now. Face to face, without the pretences of these letters." There is a measure of asperity in the good doctor's voice. From the very beginning I knew he didn't like me. I do not have a confessional nature and he holds that against me.

I stare back stolidly.

"Is it because you're ashamed? Is that why you won't allow your wife to visit?"

"Yes." There is little harm in agreeing with him. He has made up his mind on this point long ago.

"Ashamed of what? Your affair? Or what you did at the gallery?"

Why not? "Both," I affirm, blithely shouldering a double load, the tawdry fardels of sexual guilt.

"Speaking of the gallery," says Dr. Herzl, "your wife agrees with me. She believes that the depiction of the penis was what triggered the incident there."

"She does, does she?"

"She thinks you felt it was undersized. She says you're prone to read a disproportionate significance into that sort of thing."

This is so like Miriam that I offer no complaint against this preposterous interpretation of my actions. I had my reasons.

Dr. Herzl clears his throat. "How am I to understand your silence?"

"The suggestion is too silly to grace with a comment."

"How did you feel when you did it?"

"Cold."

"I see," says the doctor, letting his fingers wander through the paper on his desk. "Well, I believe we've made some progress. We've begun to talk to one another, at any rate. Now is as good a time to stop as any." He closes my file. Perhaps the fact that it bulges with my correspondence reminds him. "You do see that writing letters is a way of avoiding the problem?" he asks hopefully.

"I want to see my daughter. You tell Miriam to bring Cynthia here."

"I'm sorry," says Dr. Herzl. "Mrs. Caragan says that would be impossible."

In my room I lie down on my bed and speculate how Miriam is making out. I know she is not starving. I am on full salary while incapacitated. The teachers' federation knows how to negotiate a collective agreement, and insanity is paid its rich deserts.

As far as the other things go – the neighbours' whispers, the long, woeful faces of acquaintances – the proud prow of Miriam's clipper can cleave those mundane waters. And her real friends, the ones that never liked me, will be intent on keeping her busy, or, as they would prefer, "involved."

For a number of years I was "involved" too. Miriam demanded it. She was terribly concerned that we didn't trade our ideals for a mortgage, that we didn't become ordinary people. The flight from ordinariness kept me on a pretty strenuous schedule. I'd get home from the high school where I teach something called social studies just in time to grab a cheese sandwich and receive a briefing while the paint dried on my placard. Then we'd all load into a Volkswagen van owned by a troll with a social conscience, a short, hairy guy who made pieces of knotty-pine furniture capacious and sturdy enough to stand up to hard use by the giants I assumed were his clients, and drive off to let our opinions be known.

But about four years ago, when Miriam and I were fighting about Cynthia, and I was drinking even more than I was just before I got tossed in here, I gave up being involved and began my own journey; and there is no way that I'm going to give Miriam the chance to coax me back to Canada, now that I'm safely here, on the borders of Russia.

There's an irony, too, in how my travels began. They commenced at one of Miriam's protest rallies. About a dozen lonely souls were picketing a Liberal Fund-Raising Dinner – the reason why I now fail to recollect. It was the usual dispirited occasion. I was a little drunk and bored. The cars kept pulling up to the front of the hotel and discharging Liberals who slunk tight-lipped through our righteous gauntlet. One particularly incensed woman of our number kept demanding to know whether the Liberals were dining on macaroni and cheese that night. "Are you?" she shrilled in their faces. "Are you eating macaroni and cheese tonight?" The implication being that her own feisty spirit was sustained solely on that starchy, plebeian fuel.

It was all going more or less our way until a large, ruddy, drunk, middle-aged Liberal turned a passionate eye on our assembly. He was very angry. He seemed to have missed the point about macaroni and cheese. He thought we were objecting to our country! "Hey, you bastards!" he bellowed, while his wife tried to drag him into the lobby. "I love my country! I love Canada!" he yelled, actually striking his chest with his fist. "And if you don't, why don't you get out! *Why don't you go to Russia if you don't like it here?*"

The poor man's obvious sincerity touched me as much as his logic bewildered me. Why did he presume those people had any interest in going to Russia? Didn't he know it was *Sweden* they wanted to get to? Volvos, guiltless sex, Bergman films, functional furniture. Hey, I wanted to shout back, these people would prefer Sweden! And realizing for the first time where my wife and her friends were bound, I admitted I didn't want to go along. I was the one the gentleman was addressing. Although at the time I didn't know my longing was for Russia.

Oh, not the Russia he meant. Not Soviet Russia. But nineteenth-century Russia, the Russia of Dostoevsky's saintly prostitutes and Alyosha; of Tolstoy's Pierre; and Aksionov, the sufferer in "God Sees the Truth But Waits." A country where the characters in books were allowed to ask one another the questions: How must I live to be happy? What is goodness? Why does man suffer? What is to be done?

I had set a timid foot on that Eurasian continent years ago when, as a student in a course on European literature in translation, I had read some of the Russian masters. I returned because I was unhappy and because I sensed that only in Russia does unhappiness find a meaning. Like Aksionov, who suffered in place of the real murderer and thief, I felt a hundred times worse, a hundred times more guilt. I don't suppose I let it show much. I punished Miriam by putting our daughter's framed photograph on the end table, by drinking too much, and by being rude to people she wished desperately to impress.

Still, I was faithful to her in a purely technical sense until I met Janet several months ago. Janet is a young artist who supports herself as a substitute teacher; we met in the staff-room of my high school. At the end of that particular day, a bitterly cold one late in November, I spotted her waiting at the bus stop, looking hypothermic in the kind of tatty old fur coat creative people buy at Salvation Army thrift stores. I offered her a ride. She, in turn, when I had driven her home, offered me coffee.

I think it was the splendour of the drawings and paintings lending life to her old, decaying, high-ceilinged apartment that attracted me to her. Perhaps I felt she could salvage any wreck and breathe life into it, as she had that apartment. *Here*, I thought, gazing at the fire on her walls, *is a Russian soul*.

I asked if I could come back another day to make a purchase. She assured me that I could, that she would be delighted. I returned, bought a drawing. Returned again and carried away a canvas. Simply put, one thing led to another. We became lovers. Regularly, on school-days between three-thirty and four-thirty, p.m., she screwed me with clinical detachment. If I close my eyes I can see her hard little jockey-body rocking above me, muscles strained and taut (I could pluck the cords on her neck) as she mutely galloped me hither and thither, while I snorted away under her like old Dobbin.

That it was nothing more than a little equestrian exercise I lacked the courage to see.

Dr. Herzl makes a point of telling me how pleased he is that there have been no more letters since last we met. He sits behind his desk, bathed in pale March sunshine and self-assurance. I am struck by his aseptic smile and unlined face, hardly the face of a man privy to so many sorrows. More than most men, certainly.

Out of the blue he asks: "I think we're ready to talk about the Opening. And Janet. Don't you?"

"We could." I clear my throat and look at my hands. They're very soft. The therapists here have tried to encourage me to take up handicrafts. However, if I cannot make boots like Tolstoy I will do nothing in that line.

"I'm interested to know the reasons why you posed for her. Particularly in light of what subsequently happened, it seems an odd thing for you to do."

"I didn't want to."

"But you did nevertheless."

"Obviously."

"Why?"

"Because she said she needed to sketch from life, and now that she wasn't a student she didn't get the opportunity. She couldn't afford to pay a model."

"So you wanted to help her with her work?"

"Yes." I knew how much it meant to her. Even then I knew what she was: a gifted, intense, ambitious girl, who was also a little bit stupid about things that had nothing to do with her art, and therefore did not concern her.

I can see by the look in the doctor's eyes that he is about to chance something. "Could it have been that modelling was a way of safely exposing yourself? Exposing yourself without having to fear consequences?"

"No."

He presses his hands together. "Why did you take such violent exception when you learned that the sketches were to be shown?" he asks softly.

"You can't be serious."

"Perfectly. I am perfectly serious. Tell me why."

"Because she didn't tell me," I say. I am unable to keep the anger out of my voice. "I saw it on a poster. 'Janet Markowsky: Studies in the Male Nude'."

"Any other reason?"

"Sure. This is a small city. I'm a teacher. Somebody would recognize me. How the hell could I walk into a classroom after every kid in the school had gone down to take a gander at old Caragan's wazoo?"

"You're exaggerating."

"And you don't know kids. Anyway, it was the principle of the thing. Don't you see?" My hands have begun to tremble, I trap them between my knees.

"Were you disturbed that there were drawings of other men?"

"No."

"Are you sure?"

"I went to Janet and I said, 'For God's sake, what are you doing to me? I can't take this right now. Please, take the sketches out of the show.'" It *was* a bad time for me. Cynthia's birthday was coming up and every year she gets older, the more her face haunts me.

"And?"

"She said she was very sorry but this opportunity had suddenly presented itself. A small gallery had an immediate opening because the artist slotted had decided to show in Calgary. Janet said she hadn't time to produce new work. She had to go with the drawings. With what she had. 'Janet,' I said, 'I'm a teacher, put a moustache on me. Anything!'

"'I can't touch them,' she said. 'I could screw them up really badly. You never can tell what you'll do when you start mucking around with things.'"

"I phoned Ms. Markowsky yesterday and I asked her a question," says Herzl severely.

"What question?" I am surprised.

"I asked her if you wanted her to change the penises. It was just a hunch," he says, very much the clever, smug detective. "She said you did. She said you wanted them made bigger."

I put my head in my hands. I should have known it. The little bitch is the type to make sure she gets even. She won't forgive me for ruining her Opening. Herzl, the moron, gave her the clue she needed to do it. Not that I really mind. "I wanted a moustache," I say tiredly.

Herzl is really on a roll now. "Why did you take all your clothes off and walk through the gallery, Mr. Caragan? Did you think you would frighten people with your penis? Do you think it is menacing?"

"Because I'm crazy," I say. "Because I thought Life should imitate Art."

The hospital is silent at night. Nothing like I would have imagined – no dim cries, or the muffled sounds of sleepers dreaming bad dreams. Everyone has sunk into the opaque slumber of the correctly dosed and medicated. Except me. I hide my pills under my tongue and make a magnificent show of swallowing.

I hear the night-duty nurse go by. The moon is so bright tonight, so full and white and gleaming, that I can write my fifth letter to Dr. Herzl without showing a light under my door and risking detection at three o'clock in the morning.

On my shaky plastic desk my books are piled. I have Herzen, Dostoevsky, Gogol, Turgenev, Lermontov, Soloviev, Leontiev, Gorky, Chekhov, Pushkin, Tolstoy and Rozanov to keep me company in exile. Day by day I feel a little of my guilt subside as I share her sentence. Like her father, Cynthia sleeps in an institution.

The people who care for her tell me she doesn't remember me from visit to visit. That is why Miriam never goes to visit the child. *It is pointless*, she says. *Cynthia is profoundly retarded, and nothing will ever change that. I refuse to feel guilt.*

But my daughter is four years old now. She is no longer a baby. She must remember me.

And whenever I look into her wise, calm eyes set like stones in their Asiatic folds, I sense the grandeur of Russia, the infinite, colossal steppes sleeping there.

A Taste for Perfection

"A NEW FACE," said Albert the orderly in a dispirited voice. He had spent twenty years in the navy, had his nose broken twice and his arms covered with an ornate green scrollwork of tattoos. That, a pension, and some bad memories were all he had to show for it. Now, much to his despair, he was an orderly in a hospital. He lingered by the bed and rustled the pages on his clipboard officiously. "Mr. Ogle? Is that it?" he said, concentrating on a sheet.

"Yes, that's right. Tom Ogle."

"B.M. this A.M.?" inquired Albert, his pen poised above the clipboard.

"I'm sorry," Ogle said, confused, unsure whether to trust his ears or not. "I didn't catch that."

"B.M.," said Albert, tapping the pen on his metal watch-band. *Click. Click. Click.* "B.M., B.M.," he said impatiently.

"Bowel movement," translated Morissey, the patient in the next bed. He was a rack of bones and loose skin moored to the narrow bed by transparent tubing stuck in his veins. Looking at him, Ogle estimated he couldn't weigh more than a hundred pounds. Morissey stared back with the saucer eyes of a famine victim glittering in his wizened face. His dentures slipped and cracked on shrunken gums. "Bowel movement, he means," Morissey repeated, sawing the air inappropriately with a bony hand whose nails were as yellow and ridged as a chicken's feet. "He's asking if you had a *shit* this morning."

"No," said Ogle, turning back to Albert, "I didn't."

Albert made a mark on the sheet and went out.

"I don't like that son of a bitch," said Morissey in a stage whisper that could have been heard in the next room. "He's rough – got no consideration. You should see the bastard put in a catheter. You'd think he was shoving a meat thermometer into a roast of beef. Jesus." He considered for a moment. "The other one though – David – he's okay." He paused. "He's a Jew."

"Yeah?" said Ogle.

"Imagine," said Morissey, "a Jew working in a hospital who ain't a doctor."

David the orderly, the bedpan-fetcher. David the polymath, whose mind was a blizzard of equations, snippets of verse from Heine and Browning, contending languages, and line scores from yesterday's baseball games. Perhaps as a consequence of the perpetual storm of information blowing in his head, he dropped urine specimens, upset trays, and generally careened recklessly among the beds.

But if his hands had no aptitude for graduated cylinders and bedpans, his own private tragedies and melancholy lent them gentleness whenever they came in contact with flesh. A refugee of post-war Europe, David had shunted through eight different countries, and finally, as Ogle later came to imagine, collapsed of nervous exhaustion in Canada. A cousin had drawn him to Saskatchewan, and now, marooned in the midst of the prairies, he yearned for the ancient sun-baked stones of Jerusalem, the oranges of Jaffa, the lithe and saucy sabras packing firearms.

Ultimately, however, his courage failed him and he never packed and left. No one in the hospital was sure why. People speculated that he sensed that the reality could never equal the bounty, the splendour, the milk and honey of the land of Canaan that he imagined. Better to be here, dreaming, than there, disillusioned.

"Yeah, David's okay," said Morissey. "Better than most, and believe me, I know them all. Everybody. Doctors, nurses, orderlies, aides. I should. I been here six months; ever since January three. I'm a regular. Seen three guys die in that bed," he said primly. "That's why I got a policy of not getting too friendly." He paused meaningfully. "With nobody."

He extricated his arm from a loop of intravenous tubing and turned over on his side, his back to Ogle. "Jesus," he said tiredly, staring out at the ragged green of the trees tearing the sunlight before it struck the lawn, and watching the clouds shred in the wind, "another day, another dollar. It's a great life if you don't weaken."

Ogle, who had been brought in the night before, after collapsing at work, felt panic strumming in his gut. His throat pinched and he felt damp invade his groin and slide down his spine into the small of his back.

"The doctors," he said, holding his voice steady, treading carefully the tightrope of his anxiety, "when do they make their rounds? When will I see my doctor?"

"Don't get your shit in a knot," Morissey replied. "In here you learn to wait. If your doctor is anything like the rest, he'll come when it suits. But don't start thinking about getting shut of this place in a hurry. They don't put nobody on this ward for a *tune-up*." And he snapped his false teeth in anger at the very idea.

Morissey was right. Ogle's doctor made infrequent appearances when it suited him. Nevertheless, Ogle spent the mornings perched on the edge of his bed while the doctors made their rounds, keeping a sharp watch and scrutinizing the hallways, daring to hope Dr. Bartlett would make an appearance, and, with the utterance of an incomprehensible medical term and a flourish of his healer's hand, dispel, like a necromancer, the terrible sentence of uncertainty. But four days of this and a battery of alternately painful, humiliating, and exhausting tests taught Ogle the rudiments of resignation. He was made aware also of something else.

Ogle was young – not yet thirty – and had never considered the ills to which the flesh is heir. He was not yet acquainted with sorrow and grief. But sitting on the edge of his bed he was introduced to the uninterrupted parade of disease and infirmity that crept and wheeled past his doorway. The participants in this cavalcade lurched by on canes, supported themselves against walls, tottered along clinging to the arms of nurses, rolled briskly past, pushed by orderlies. Senile old ladies with inquisitive, darting eyes and flickering vipers' tongues cried out for babies they had borne half a century before, their hair as white, startled, and on-end as a dandelion gone to seed. A victim of kidney disease rolled by, his mind overwhelmed by the poisons his body could no longer eliminate, calmly and silently smiling to himself, his monstrously swollen leg supported on a sheepskin and ripening to a shiny, mottled-purple iridescence. A coronary patient took his first post-convalescent, tremulous steps, his face vibrant with fear and his bathrobe fallen open to display a livid blue scar on his chest. A diabetic who had lost a leg to gangrene swung by on crutches, his face grey and wrinkled with anxiety and concentration.

And as Ogle watched them troop by, he wrung his wet palms together and shuffled his cold feet in his slippers. There was little else to do. There were no visitors to relieve the monotony because Ogle had never troubled to make friends. He was an essentially shy man who had early learned to disguise his timidity with rancour, and who had, given time and practice, transformed his mouth into a cynical gash in what otherwise would have been an open and frank face. He had the neurotic's partial vision of life, and a sense of the absurdity which adheres to all effort when observed in the light of a long enough perspective. This had never made him popular. Most people didn't care for his desperate, crabbed views. Of course, the people from the office had felt obligated to send him a get-well card and flowers (they couldn't ignore him; he had keeled over at their feet), but no one had troubled to visit him.

His days were spent waiting, being directed here and there, from X-ray to lab, from pillar to post. He dozed and ate and lived the elemental life of a prisoner, shaving with an exactitude that could never be duplicated outside the walls of the hospital, moving his bowels with the patience of Job, brushing each tooth many times over. He murdered each day minute by minute.

When night came he found he couldn't sleep. He hid this fact from the nurses to avoid medication. His only previous experience with sleeping-pills had left him with the feeling that he was toppling blindly into a grave.

By ten o'clock every night Morissey was dead to the world, enjoying, Ogle imagined, the dreamless sleep of the blessed. By eleven the ward came alive with the sounds of night terrors. The dying made broken cries; those made bitter by pain piped complaints to the staff in querulous voices. A stroke victim, never seen but much discussed by Morissey, tunelessly struck up "God Save the Queen" to ring down the curtain on the day, and a senile clergyman across the hall began a litany of blasphemies triggered out of his subconscious by a plaque-clogged artery in the brain.

During the course of a night Ogle slept by moments, but woke often with a start that jerked him upright in bed, shivering. His fingers trembled as he scrubbed his face and squeezed his eyelids tight. And every night at three o'clock he smelled the coffee percolating at the nurses' station as they took their shift break. By association, that aroma awakened another hunger. Ogle was prompted to swing his legs out of bed, pull open the drawer of his night table and take out a cigarette and matches. Then, his bare feet sticking to the linoleum, he padded across the room to the can, carefully skirted the foot of Morissey's bed, and paused for a moment at the window to look out on the city.

He was always surprised and a little exalted by the number of lighted windows burning so bravely in the night. What did they signify? A sick child? A tired domestic dispute lengthening, with tears and recriminations, past resolve? A happy, drunken party? A couple achingly grinding out the night's last session of love? He never speculated for long, but took a little comfort from those terrestrial, temporal stars in the night.

The sudden glare of the light in the bathroom glancing off rubbed enamel and spanking bright tiles hurt his eyes. The place smelled of antiseptic and somebody else's turds.

Ogle examined his face in the mirror over the sink. It seemed to him that the left side of his face had altered, although he couldn't be sure. There was a sensual droop to the eyelid, and the corner of his mouth felt a little slack and lacking in decision. He flexed the fingers of his left hand and made a weak fist; he felt faint.

He sat down on the toilet seat, lit his cigarette, entwined his long legs about one another and meditatively scratched his shin. All he wanted now was four ounces of Scotch, neat. That would make this an occasion. The cigarette smoke hovered around his head, a blue nimbus.

"A drink, a drink," he declaimed to the opposite wall, hoisting an imaginary glass, "my sterile, christly kingdom for a drink." Ogle attempted a suitably ironic smile but the stiff, resisting muscles of his face informed him he had failed and produced only a grimace. *There is something radically wrong here*, he thought.

On the other side of the door, Morissey spoke indistinctly to a character in his dreams.

"Die in your sleep, you old prick," Ogle answered him.

It had been brewing for some time. Ogle believed he hated his doctor. Dr. Bartlett didn't care for Ogle's attitude.

It might have had to do with the similarity in their ages. They had rubbed up against some of the same experiences, but had been weathered into very different shapes. Ogle, for all his cynicism, had carried placards denouncing the Vietnamese war and occupied a corporate recruiting office. He was sure Bartlett was the type who had watched these kinds of proceedings aloofly from a dormitory window. And convictions had had nothing to do with it.

Ogle had retained his pony-tail until economic necessity of the direst kind had forced him to relinquish it. Bartlett, with his unformed face of shaded planes, had attempted to distinguish and hearten a moist, indistinct mouth with a twitch of coppery hair on his upper lip. Ogle was convinced that growing it was the bravest thing Bartlett had ever done.

So, on the morning of the seventh day of his hospital stay, Ogle was waiting for Bartlett with the Gideon Bible resting open on his lap. He had taken to skimming it when all else failed to relieve his boredom. He had come across and marked a passage in 2 Chronicles with Bartlett in mind.

At about ten o'clock Bartlett stuck his head around the door jamb. "Good morning," he said, "I thought I'd just pop in on you for a minute." Popping in was the word for it.

"Good morning," said Ogle.

"Keeping busy, I see," said Bartlett professionally, indicating the Bible.

"Nothing like 'The Good Book,'" said Ogle, smiting the cover.

Bartlett, who was never sure when Ogle was pulling his leg, yet loath to offend religious sensibilities, said, "I suppose so."

"Take this here," said Ogle, clearing his throat. "'And Asa in the thirty and ninth year of his reign was diseased in his feet until his disease was exceeding great: yet in his disease he sought not to the Lord, but the physicians. And Asa slept with his fathers . . .' What do you make of that, Doc?" said Ogle, feigning naivete.

"Very amusing, Mr. Ogle," said Bartlett stiffly, removing a pen-light from his shirt pocket. He drew the blind at the window and went to work. "Follow the light, please," he said, bending over Ogle and breathing a gust of warm Sen-Sen into his face. Ogle chased the light until his eye ached. "The other now. Very good. Thank you." Bartlett snapped off the light.

"Gazing in the windows of the soul. And what *did* we see?" Ogle said glibly.

Bartlett extended a stubby hand with square, pink nails. "Squeeze my hand, please. Right first. Fine. Now the left."

Ogle bore down with his left hand and felt a stain of weakness radiate from his shoulder and lodge under his rib cage. His heart caught the contagion and began to drum. He shrugged apologetically to the doctor. "Not enough breakfast, I guess," he said, visibly discomfited.

"Yes," said Bartlett. "No better, eh? What about the dizzy spells? Any more faintness, weakness?"

"No," lied Ogle.

"Please stand up," said Bartlett. His square, strong hands pushed at Ogle's shoulders, attempting to throw them back into a military posture. "Heels together, hands at your side. Good. Good." He paused. "Now close your eyes."

"No tricks now, Doctor."

"Close your eyes, please."

He did. Something whirled in his head with crazy, wrenching speed, like a flywheel torn loose. His eyes sprang open in time to see the bed rush into his face. A muffled blow of mattress, pillows, bedclothes, and he was breathless, face down on the bed.

"Oh, how the mighty are brought low," he said in a choked voice.

"You're all right, aren't you?" said Bartlett with some concern. "I tried to catch you, but you went down too quickly."

Ogle turned over on his back and flung his forearm across his eyes. *What is this?* he asked himself. *What is wrong with me?*

"Yeah. Just fine. Hunky-dory."

"Well now, about dizzy spells . . ."

"I told a fib. Gee whiz, but I'm an incorrigible fibber."

"So you have had more?"

"Yeah."

"I wish you would show a little more confidence in me. It would make things easier. I can't diagnose without your help."

"You've got it," said Ogle. "So what *is* your diagnosis?"

"Be patient. I know it's difficult, but I'd like to do another series of tests. The last ones weren't conclusive."

Ogle tangled his legs in the sheets in frustration. His voice, ground to an edge against the whetstone of exasperation, was sharp, high, keen. "You have an *idea*. Give me an idea of what you *think*."

Bartlett shot his cuffs once or twice. "I don't think there would be any point to that. I might have to retract it. I wouldn't want to raise – or dash – your hopes."

"Hey, the last time I looked you were human. The first mistake is on me and no complaints."

"I have no intention of saying anything," said Bartlett with more firmness than Ogle had thought him capable of.

"Look then, Doctor," said Ogle, bargaining. "Leave a pass for me at the desk. I'm going crazy here. This place is driving me crazy." There it was. An undercurrent of fear, even mild hysteria, in his voice. *They're like dogs*, he thought. *They can smell it.* "If I could get out for a walk on the grounds . . . maybe I'd feel better. I wouldn't be so jumpy."

Bartlett caught his wheedling tone, sensed the desperation, and immediately recovered his equanimity. He had something this person wanted.

"Do you have someone to accompany you? A friend or relative?"

"No. I don't need someone to accompany me. I don't need training wheels. I just want to get out of here for a while. This place is getting to me."

"I'm sorry if you find us lacking," said Bartlett. He pocketed his pen-light and smoothed his white jacket with his palms, readying himself to depart. "But we're not a grand hotel. Bear with us."

"The pass," said Ogle, hating himself, but none the less begging.

"I'll leave one at the desk – on condition you're accompanied by someone." Bartlett showed his teeth in a medical smile. "Charm one of your friends into going for a stroll with you."

He went out.

Ogle lay without moving a muscle until he felt the shame drain out of his face. He supposed he had no choice. There was no one else. He got out of bed and went to the pay phone at the end of the hallway. He dialled Barbara's number. They had lived together for two years before separating six months ago on fairly amicable terms. She had simply had enough of him. Too much drinking, irresponsibility, and scorn.

Her voice conveyed no hint of alarm or even surprise as he explained what he wanted, his body involuntarily writhing and twisting on the hook of his embarrassment.

Yes, she would come.

No, not tomorrow. The day after. When she finished work.

No trouble. Take care.

Then there was nothing but a dial tone in his ear. He couldn't remember having said goodbye. Ogle put the receiver carefully back on the hook.

It was the following day that Ogle saw Morissey weighed for the first time. The weighing took place weekly and the results were meticulously recorded.

Morissey was afflicted with a rare metabolic disorder that was slowly making him waste away, imperceptibly killing him inch by inch, or rather, pound by pound. Nothing arrested the melting of the flesh from his bones, not the 2,400 liquid calories daily dripped into his veins by tubes, not the three hearty meals he dutifully choked down every day. For Morissey, every weighing marked a stage on his journey to extinction.

At eleven o'clock the scale was pushed into the room by Albert and David.

"Weigh-in time, champ," said Albert.

"Please, Mr. Morissey," said David, seeing the terror which crossed Morissey's face at the sight of the scale. "Co-operate. Relax."

This admonition was followed by an uneasy silence that made Ogle sit up in bed. The two orderlies were watching Morissey closely. He had burrowed down into the bedclothes and his bony hands were clinging to the metal railing of the bed. His eyes swivelled cautiously in their sockets.

"Ah, shit," said Albert. The old boy in 44 had tried to bite him earlier, and now he had to put up with this. "We got to go through all this again, champ?" he inquired bleakly.

"Bugger off with that scale," said Morissey. "Weigh your own fat, lazy ass with it."

David went to the bed and took him by the wrist, handling it as carefully as if it were made of balsa wood. "We'll just slide the railing down so you can get out a little easier," he said. A certain emphasis of pronunciation, vaguely foreign, lent his voice a lulling quality. His red hair, profuse and crested, bobbed in the sunshine as he worked on Morissey's grip.

"Ouch! Ouch! Ouch!" roared Morissey, "you're hurting me!"

He wasn't, of course, and David was affronted by the accusation. "*Mr. Morissey*," he said and clucked his tongue.

"Ouch! Ouch! Ouch!" yelled Morissey unconvincingly.

"Shut your gob," said Albert. "You're scaring the chickens."

A nurse stuck her head in the doorway. "Trouble, fellows?" she asked.

"Nah," said Albert, "we're just weighing the champ here. Same as always."

She nodded understandingly and went away.

Gradually, patiently, David had worked Morissey to a sitting position on the edge of the bed.

"Now," he said, "if you please, step down on the scale, Mr. Morissey." Old-world courtliness.

"Hop on," said Albert.

"Jump down a fucking well yourself," replied Morissey.

"It don't bite," said Albert. "What the hell is the problem?"

"I ain't climbing on that scale," said Morissey with trembling lips. "It ain't correct; it lies." Tears pricked his eyes and he snuffled.

"Okay," said David to Albert, "lift him now."

And a stunned Morissey was snatched off the mattress, hospital gown fluttering, and lowered onto the scale. He slumped purposely, a passive dead weight in David's arms. Albert manipulated the sliding weights and tried to shield the reading from Morissey's view.

"What is it?" implored Morissey, craning his neck. "I'm heavier, ain't I? I'm heavier, ain't I? Oh, God, sure I am."

"You're a regular jumbo," said Albert, tinkering. "But shut up for chrissake. I got enough trouble with this metric shit, without you making that noise."

"I seen it!" Morissey shouted. "I lost another pound! Oh, sweet Jesus, another pound!" He began to sob and fling his body around recklessly in David's arms. "I'm dying. Don't nobody know I'm dying?" he moaned.

David stroked his matchstick arms like a mother soothing a child. "Hush," he said. "We're almost through."

Morissey contorted himself in David's arms, flailing his bony limbs. "I'm dying!" he cried. "Don't you care, you bastards? Don't it signify?"

David turned to Ogle. "Help me, please," he said. "I can't hold him." But he read on Ogle's face Ogle's inward disturbance, the facial hieroglyphics of his own anxiety made manifest in Morissey's struggle to free himself from the prison of his disintegrating body.

"No," said Ogle numbly. "I can't." He turned his face away from Morissey's ugly head, each bone of the skull ridging the skin, each indigo vein a distinct, anxious swelling. He found his feet and scurried out the door. His bathrobe flapped around his calves as he marched down the corridor. In his agitation he dodged beds, lounge chairs, and wheelchairs loaded with patients. All these people had been removed from their rooms and left in the hallway while the cleaning staff plied mops, scrub brushes and floor polishers in a wholesale cleaning.

I don't belong here, thought Ogle. *It's a mistake. This doesn't make any kind of sense.*

Nothing was right. His leg felt funny; it seemed to trail along insensibly, clumsily. He stopped and leaned against the dead-green wall and kneaded the muscles of his thigh. Sweat glistened in his hairline.

"Edward."

What the hell is the matter with this leg? He pummelled it lightly with his fists.

"Edward."

It was the old woman in the wheelchair beside him.

Ogle looked down at her. She was restrained loosely in the chair by cotton straps that prevented her from falling out. These she hung against like a boxer on the ropes. Patches of pink, scurfy scalp showed through thin hair which had been subjected to attempts to resurrect its youthfulness by means of a rinse. Her mild blue eyes were rendered innocent by a glaze of cataracts, and a sprout of coarse white hairs on her chin made Ogle think of elderly Chinese gentlemen. What might have been a placid face was rendered angry by scabby sores which, shining with ointment, crept down her face to lose themselves in the wattles and creases of her neck.

"Edward!"

Suddenly it struck Ogle that she was speaking to him.

"Me?" he said. "Excuse me, ma'am. I'm not Edward."

She waggled her head and crooked a finger at him vigorously. He moved a little closer. A hand darted out and snared his sleeve.

"Edward, my dear," she said peevishly. "Where have you been?" She lost her train of thought and her eyes shifted unsteadily as she ransacked her memory. "Been. Been. Been," she repeated vaguely. "Look what they do to me," she said, seizing another subject and plucking at her cotton straps. "Untie me."

"Look, lady, you're mistaken. My name isn't Edward. It's Tom. Tom Ogle," he replied uneasily.

"Nonsense, Edward. Untie me this moment. And we'll go home."

"No, we won't," said Ogle, tugging gently against her grip, attempting to retrieve his sleeve.

"Very well," she said with a sigh. "As you wish. Home is, after all, where the heart is."

"A case of mistaken identity," explained Ogle.

"As if I don't know my Edward," she said. "Don't be silly, my dear man."

"Let go of me, lady. I mean it."

She began to cry brokenly. "Been. Been. Been," she sobbed. "Oh, don't go away. Where have you been all these years, Edward?"

He bent towards her, trying to work her fingers loose from his sleeve. Her other hand shot up and caught him at the nape of the neck.

"Kiss me, Edward," she said, "for old times' sake."

He thought he caught a whiff of a colostomy bag. He saw in detail the pitted, cracked sores, the old, milky eyes. "You can go to hell," he said. "You can all go to hell. I just want to be left alone. Just leave me alone. It's all I ask."

Barbara did not come the next day as she had promised. She did not come the following day. She did not come at all. Ogle did not trouble to phone her again; he was too proud.

He stood by the window and observed life go on outside the hospital as if he were watching a movie screen. The sprinklers waved majestic plumes of silver in the summer air, the green lawns sizzled cinematically in the heat. Nurses spread their sweaters on the grass and sat down on them to eat their lunches. At that distance their imperfections were obliterated. And Ogle desired their images, like those of starlets, fervently but abstractly.

He began to prowl the hospital hallways with his hands thrust belligerently in his bathrobe pockets. On his journeys he discovered a good many things: a burn ward where he heard the voices of scalded children crying in the distance, where visitors were fitted with surgical masks before being allowed to pay their visits. A room full of amputees who brandished the stumps of their arms like blunt antennae while they argued. And finally, the physical-therapy room.

The therapy room was almost empty when he came across it. A female therapist was sitting on a hard, straight-backed chair with her hands folded sedately in her lap while she watched a man with flopping, nerveless legs swing his body along between two parallel bars that stood at hip height.

The room was not provided with much equipment: an exercise bicycle stood against one wall; there was a system of weights and pulleys; some tumbling-mats. Ogle walked directly to a basketball lying in the middle of the floor and picked it up.

He relished the pebbly grain with his fingertips. He had played the game in high school and had loved its speed, grace and fluid, intricate ballet.

A hoop was fixed on the back wall. He launched a shot at it; the arc was all wrong, too flat. The ball bounded off the backboard and rattled the rim of the basket.

Jarred by the noise, the therapist unfolded her hands and

watched him quizzically. Ogle was stripping off his bathrobe. He wriggled out of his pyjama top and shucked off his slippers. Barefoot, he gathered up the ball, dribbled lazily around an imaginary key, feinted to his right and lofted a soft, one-handed jumper.

His left leg almost folded up under him when he came down. He kicked it out in front of him several times and waggled his ankle. With a look of determination on his face he squeezed the ball, deked, spun and drove for the basket. The leg did not respond properly; it felt weak and rubbery.

The therapist made up her mind. She started towards him. Ogle was massaging his thigh and muttering angrily under his breath. "Come on," he said. "Come on. Work."

"Excuse me," said the woman, "but I have no one on the list for eleven-thirty. Are you scheduled for eleven-thirty?"

Ogle looked up at her as if this question were an unpardonable imposition. His concern for his leg was verging on hysteria. "I've got a problem here," he said. "This damn leg isn't working right."

"Please," she said, "who told you to come here? Are you sure you were scheduled for eleven-thirty? Mr. Krantz needs my undivided attention. Sometimes I think they don't know what they are doing downstairs. They know Mr. Krantz needs my undivided attention."

"Fine," said Ogle. "You look after Mr. Krantz. Don't worry about me. I'll just shoot a few hoops."

"Who's your doctor?" she said, becoming suspicious.

"Zorba the Greek," said Ogle, turning his back on her and dragging his leg after him to the basketball.

"You're not supposed to be in here, are you?" she said. "You can't just walk in here. This isn't a games room, it's a *medical facility*."

"Oops," said Ogle, "there went Krantz."

She cast a desperate look over her shoulder at Krantz trying to haul himself back up on the bar, hand over hand, after a plunge to the mats. "If you're not out of here in one minute," she said, "I'm calling security."

"Sure thing," said Ogle, "but don't forget Humpty Dumpty over there. He wants your *undivided attention*." With that he lunged towards the basket and stumbled. All the feeling in his leg was gone. Nothing.

"One minute," she grimly reiterated.

"Hey, you dumb bitch!" he shouted in his fear and frustration. "Lay off, I got a fucking problem here. Don't you listen? I got a fucking problem!" *Couldn't she see? Couldn't she?*

She looked as if she had been slapped. "I won't tolerate that," she said. "I don't have to tolerate that."

Ogle slammed the ball into the floor. "I've had it!" he yelled. "You, lady, can go piss up a rope! I have had it with this fucking place!"

"You are obviously crazy," she said, turning away. "I'm calling security."

Ogle climbed onto the stationary bicycle and began to pedal. He buried his head between the handlebars like a racing cyclist and his legs spun. Occasionally his left foot slid off the pedal and he barked his shin, but he kept at it. His back began to shine with sweat; his lungs swelled and collapsed like bellows.

Krantz had hauled himself upright and was staring at him with a bemused look on his face.

"Hey, Krantz," yelled Ogle, "look at the world-famous bicycle racer sweep up the cobbled streets of Monte Carlo."

"Give her shit!" shouted Krantz gleefully.

Ogle jacked his butt in the air and began to really pump.

"Yahoo!" yelled Krantz, wobbling.

Ogle was determined to teach that leg its duty. But he did not feel one hundred per cent. He was not up to snuff. So when the therapist arrived with the security guard they found Krantz calling for help and Ogle in convulsions on the floor, his legs rhythmically drawing up and thrusting out again, like a galvanized frog on a laboratory table, swimming to God only knows what destination.

They opened his skull and took a look. The tumour was sequestered in the folds of the brain lobe in such a way that the surgeon lost all confidence in his scalpel. So they closed him up again and wheeled him back to the ward. The doctors wished to let the tumour "ripen." The very word led Ogle to imagine button mushrooms swelling in the humid night of some hothouse. He lay in his bed with his head swathed in yards of gauze, his eyes hooded, seldom speaking.

Morissey, perhaps heartened by what he surmised were signs of Ogle's imminent demise, took to conversation.

"You know what you put me in mind of?" he asked.

"A corpse."

"Oh, Jesus, what a thing to say," said Morissey cheerfully. "Nah, a what-you-call-it? A Hindu with a thingamajig – a turbine."

"Is that right?" said Ogle flatly.

"Yeah, there's one of them in here. A real black bugger with the washing wrapped around his head – a doctor."

"I'm tired," said Ogle. "I'm going to sleep now."

"Sure," said Morissey. "Keep up your strength."

But Ogle didn't even go through the pretence of dropping off. He neglected even to close his eyes. Instead he stared at the ceiling very hard and tried to remember what had gone through his mind during those convulsions. There had been something. He had been sure.

David tried to coax Ogle out of his depression. He described for him the glories of the Holy Land: a purifying sun like hot glass; the salinity of the Dead Sea; the holiness of the learned rabbis of Jerusalem – all as if Ogle were as ardent and as hopeful a prospective pilgrim as he. He stole a minute here, a minute there, to sit by Ogle's bed, to smoke a cigarette and extol the virtues of the Expos. Ogle's smokes had been taken away from him because he didn't have full control of his limbs and the nurses were afraid he would drop a cigarette and set the bedclothes on fire. So David shared his butt, holding it for him and allowing him an occasional drag that lent Ogle's face some of the beatific splendour of a nursing baby's.

David discovered that Ogle had the rudiments of chess, so on the night shift when things were slow they would play a game on David's little magnetic travelling board. The red head bobbed and weaved above the checkered square; his fingers snapped; he hummed the overture from *The Nutcracker*. His body writhed, and like a Hassid lost in the ecstasy of holy dance, he was transported. David was happy amidst the smell of stale urine, soiled bedclothes, fevers and agonies.

Ogle was not.

Sometimes he found himself in tears. David would pat his shoulder with a large, freckled hand, with bright, virile tufts of red hair on the knuckles. "There, there," he would say, and on the next move gratuitously surrender a knight to Ogle.

Once Ogle threw the chessboard against the wall in a fit of petulance at losing once again. "That's it," he said, burning with humiliation. "I'm finished with this goddamn game. Never again. There's no point in it. That's it."

David patiently picked the pieces off the floor and tidily stowed them in the board, which also folded into a case. One of the hinges of the case was bent from hitting the wall. The lid wouldn't close.

David looked at him reproachfully. "It doesn't close," he said.

"I don't give a shit," said Ogle, beginning to cry. "Do you think I give a shit about your christly chess case?"

"You are always causing trouble now," said David. "Why don't you behave like a gentleman? Yesterday you wet the bed. There is no reason for that. You are turning into an exhibitionist."

"I'm turning into a vegetable! A fucking vegetable!" shouted Ogle. "And nobody cares! Nobody does anything!"

"Did you ever consider that there is nothing to be done?" said David, grasping the chess case to his smock with both hands.

"Something can be done!" shouted Ogle. "Something can always be done!"

"Perhaps," said David.

"Yes," said Ogle, "yes, yes, yes."

David came to the bed. "Tom," he said, "be quiet. Get some rest."

"You shit," said Ogle. "You can do something for yourself. I can't. Why don't you bugger off to Israel? You're always yapping about it. Take the bull by the horns."

"It's not possible," said David.

"Oh God," said Ogle. "I can't feel my toes. I can't feel my toes."

"Be calm," said David. "Calm down."

"Like him," said Ogle, pointing to Morissey sleeping a heavy, drug-induced sleep. "Calm like him. I'm not croaking like that bastard. Not in my sleep. Not yet."

"You shouldn't carry on this way," said David.

"Why shouldn't I?" yelled Ogle. "This whole business has left one bad taste in my mouth. Your doctors, your hospital, everything."

David smoothed his trousers on his knee. "Please," he said earnestly, "don't be bitter. It doesn't help."

"It doesn't hurt," said Ogle. "I didn't live twenty-eight years to end up like this – a slab of meat."

"All right," said David, "I won't argue with you. But let me tell you a little story. Some time after the war – 1947 – I ended up in London. I lived with a Jewish tailor in the East End for a little while. I was very unhappy, very bitter. He left me to myself for a long time and then one day he told me a kind of parable. He said there were two kinds of bitterness: one that takes away the appetite and one that stimulates it. Pepper, he said, was of the first kind – it burns the tongue and nothing more. But horse-radish, though bitter, sharpens the hunger and makes a man impatient for the good things of the meal. So, he said, if a man becomes only bitter and downcast he goes no further. But a little bitterness, a little horse-radish, may give one an appetite for perfection."

"How quaint," said Ogle, "how undeniably folksy."

David shrugged and stood up.

"You haven't told me," Ogle said, "why, with all your good advice, you're still here and not in Israel? Physician, heal thyself."

"Why? Because I fell in love with and married a gentile," said David. He laughed. "She won't go. She was born here. This is home to her. So I suppose you could say that I have been forced to make the best of things. I had no choice about acquiring a taste for perfection. Besides, there are no Expos in Israel."

When it came time to clean his room according to the rotation schedule, Ogle found himself parked in the hallway in a wheelchair along with the other non-ambulatory patients. The walking wounded headed immediately for the television lounge.

Ogle sat in the hallway. He hadn't been shaved that morning and he scrubbed his beard with his hands. He enjoyed the tingling sensation in his palms. Ogle found that his hands were growing more insensitive with every passing day, and so he was constantly rubbing, battering and thumping them against any surface that would render up some feeling.

It seemed that everything was slipping away. David had showed Ogle his face in a hand mirror the day before while he was being shaved. The left side had sagged and wrinkled and collapsed like a rotten spot on a fruit.

A cleaning lady with swollen ankles and stockings rolled

down on her shoes shifted him to another spot where the sun shone directly in his face and made his eyes blink and water.

"Hey," he said, "the sun is in my face."

"Hold your horses," she said, "it will only be a minute." She waddled away. He held up his stronger hand, his right, and sheltered his eyes. But after only a minute or two his shoulder began to ache and he let the hand drop back into his lap.

He sat quietly for a moment with the sun full on his face. *I'm dying*, he said to himself for the first time. The idea surprised him, coming as it did apparently from nowhere. He looked about him and understood with a flash of revelatory perception that everyone on this ward was dying. Everyone was a terminal case. Morissey. The stroke victim who sang "God Save the Queen." The blasphemous clergyman. The demented old man who ate Kleenex and wet his bed. Everybody. No one was ever discharged. He couldn't remember a single case. As Morissey had said, three men had died in Ogle's bed and now Ogle saw that he would be the fourth. For a short time he had believed himself different. But there was no escaping this ward. Not even for a moment. Not even on a pass. *There was no outside.*

And Ogle ached, for the first time in his life, with pity for them all.

"Edward."

He swivelled in his wheelchair and, blinking the sun out of his eyes, saw the old woman.

"Edward, my dear, dear husband," she said, "where are the children? Where are Alma and John?"

Ogle began to sob. Each sob was torn, wrenched from his gut. "I don't know," he said. "Lost. I suppose they're lost." Even as he said these things he did not know what prompted him, except perhaps the desire to enter into a different world, to escape, at any cost, the present.

"Come here, dear," she said, and the sunlight was melted and diffused in her glazed eyes, "Come here."

Somehow he struggled across the hallway, the heels of his palms skidding on the rubber tires of his chair.

"We'll find them," she said.

"Sure," he said.

"And after we find them," she said, "we'll have a picnic. The perfect end to a perfect day."

"Fine," agreed Ogle, who had quite unexpectedly acquired a taste for perfection.

The Expatriates' Party

JOE WAS dreaming, and in his dream his wife and he were having an argument. She had chosen a bad time to start this one. There Joe was, rubbers buckled, overcoat buttoned to his chin, gloves pulled on – all ready to set out for school. He stood with his hand impatiently gripping the doorknob, prickly with heat and wool and anger, feeling the sweat begin to crawl down his sides, waiting for her to finish with her damn nonsense. He suspected she was going to make him late for class, and at this thought he felt very anxious indeed. In thirty-five years of teaching he had never been late more than once or twice that he could remember.

"Of course I'm pregnant," she said. "And you're the dirty old man who slipped the bun in my oven. At your age. Imagine."

"Don't be silly," he replied, doing his best to disguise his exasperation with her. "You're fifty-seven years old and women fifty-seven years old *don't* have babies."

"Well, if I don't have a bun in the oven, what do I have?" she inquired with a schoolgirlish petulance that made him feel slightly queasy, a trifle faint with disgust. This wasn't at all like Marie. And why did she keep using that idiotic euphemism?

"You know what you have," he said, angry with her for having it, and angry too that she refused to admit it. "You have a tumour on your uterus, and it's no good pretending it's a

169

baby. Old women don't have babies. It's a goddamn law of nature. It's a *fact*."

It was the steep descent of the plane that woke him. The sense of imbalance, of disorientation, of falling, snapped him abruptly out of the dream. Almost immediately he was conscious of where he was, of his surroundings. He seldom stumbled and groped his way out of sleep any more, but was often jarred out of his dreams in this way, catapulted into reality.

He sat absolutely still and upright, acknowledging the insistent pressure of the seat-belt on his bladder, uncomfortably aware of his damp, sticky shirt tucked up his back.

I never think of her when I'm awake, he thought. Is that why I dream? Is there a law of psychological compensation which I must pay?

The woman sitting beside him, realizing he was no longer asleep, said: "We're beginning our landing approach now."

Joe smiled and nodded to her while he took final stock of how she had fared on the flight. She had certainly boarded pert and powdered enough, but in the course of eight hours her make-up had been ravaged and she had undergone some changes for the worse. Everyone over forty had. At that age the body forgets how to forgive, thought Joe. Here we sit, swollen with gas, eyes raw from lack of sleep, legs cramped and toes afire with pins and needles, smiling amiably and socking back the charter-flight booze, prepared to cheerfully suffer the consequences and pay the penalties.

Joe turned and looked out his window. Rags of vapour tore past, luminous with a feeble, watery sunshine. He couldn't see land below, only a thick, undulating surface of cloud. Nor could he make out what the pilot was saying. His ears had blocked with the change in altitude.

"What's that? What's he saying?" he inquired of the woman beside him. He cocked his head to indicate deafness.

"The temperature is fifty-four degrees," she said, mouthing the words carefully. "Sweater weather."

"Good," he replied, acting as if it genuinely mattered to him.

"We'll be there in minutes," she commented, smoothing a plaid skirt down on her heavy thighs. "I can hardly wait to take a bath and crawl between clean sheets." The woman laughed uncomfortably and inexplicably. Was it the word sheets? "I'm staying at the Penta." She paused. "What about you? Where are you staying?"

Good God, woman, Joe thought.

"I'm staying with my son and daughter-in-law," he lied.

"In London?"

"Yes."

"Well, that's lovely, isn't it? You'll have a full schedule with them taking you around to see the sights, won't you?"

"Sure will." Hungry, hunting widow. At least she had *said* her husband was dead, explaining her ring. But how did you know? Nowadays women were liable to lie about that sort of thing.

The plane suddenly dropped out of the bank of clouds. They were much lower than Joe had suspected. Below him he saw a rush of hummocked, rank turf of such a startling green, a green so unprecedented in his experience, that it struck him as false, a tourist's hopeful, unrealistic vision. A tiny man toiled in his garden allotment, unconcerned as the plane bellied over him, sweeping him in its dark shadow, surrounding him in a shimmering bath of sound waves.

Joe's ears popped, clearing, and simultaneously he heard the pilot announce, seconds before the tires touched the tarmac – a fine display of a sense of the dramatic: "Ladies and gentlemen, welcome to England in Jubilee Year."

There was a ragged cheer of approval and a smattering of hand-clapping. Relief at journey's end, at escaping this aluminum tube, at being safe.

Joe smacked his hands together too. And old English teacher that he was, though out of harness, he muttered a line of Blake's that ran through his mind as swiftly and verdantly as the ground, only seconds before, had sped beneath him.

"*In England's green and pleasant land.*"

He was, wasn't he? In England's green and pleasant land?

His son, Mark, was waiting to meet him at Gatwick as he had promised, but Joe had difficulty in recognizing him at first. It had been two years since he had seen his son. Now he appeared sporting a fine fan of feathery beard, wearing a flat tweed cap and carrying a furled umbrella under his arm.

Like a bloody convert to Catholicism, Joe thought, more Catholic than the Pope. It appeared the boy had gone ersatz English on him. Joe felt a little embarrassed for his son, particularly when they hesitantly and clumsily shook hands. There was a first time for everything, Joe mused, even shaking hands with your father. You had to acquire the method.

Mark was obviously on edge. He kept fidgeting with his umbrella, stabbing the point at the toe of his shoe and saying, "You look great, Dad. Really fit. Just fine." His stay in England had clipped his speech and truncated his vowels.

"Fit for an old duffer, you mean," his father said, pinching up a roll of fat above his waistband.

They collected Joe's baggage and then, luggage banging their legs, sidled up to a wicket and bought tickets for Victoria Station from a black man. He felt cheated. He had expected his first Englishman to be more like Stanley Holloway. After boarding a third-class coach they stowed Joe's bags and seated themselves just as the train pulled out. It slid away so quietly and serenely from the platform that Joe wondered for a minute if he were hallucinating. Where were the jerks, bangs and metallic clangs he remembered from the CNR milk runs of his boyhood?

The train gathered speed, and through a window pane smudged with grease Joe watched, without apparent interest, the row houses and villas shudder past, while waiting for

Mark to have his say. To get all that off his chest. It wasn't long in coming. After pointing out a few sights and architectural oddities, Mark said: "I'm sorry we didn't make it, Dad. It wasn't right that you had to go through that yourself. But we were broke and it was a hell of a long way to go. I hope you see our point."

The train swayed past a school. A group of boys were huddling bleakly on a playing-field. What was it that Wellington had claimed? The battle of Waterloo was won on the playing-fields of Eton. Joe pitied those kids their grey flannel shorts and muddy knees. It must be damn cold standing there. On the platform he had felt a raw, wet wind that had cut to the bone.

He turned away from the window to his son. "I didn't expect you and Joan to come, Mark," he said softly. "I told you that on the phone. I don't want you to worry about that any longer. You know I never set much store on the formalities." Having said that, he reached inside his jacket and took out an envelope which he passed to his son. "I brought these pictures for you," he said. "I don't know if that was wise or not. I took them with the Polaroid and they didn't turn out all the best."

Joe wasn't sure why he had taken the snapshots. Funeral photographs had never been a family tradition, although some of the old-country Germans, Marie's people, had always taken coffin portraits. Perhaps that was where he had got the idea. Still, it wasn't like him. But then lately he had been acting in surprising ways that he could hardly credit. The world had changed since his wife had died.

Mark was tearing open the flap when Joe warned him. "I wouldn't look at those now," he said quietly. "Not here. Wait until you get home. She's in the coffin and I'll warn you – she doesn't look herself."

That was an understatement. The mortician's creation, that's what she was. A frenzy of grey Little Orphan Annie curls, hectic blotches of rouge on the cheeks, a pathetic, vain attempt at lending colour to a corpse. So thin, so thin. Eaten hollow by cancer, a fragile husk consumed by the worm within.

"What?"

"They are pictures of your mother in the coffin, of your mother's funeral," said Joe deliberately.

"Jesus Christ," Mark said, stuffing the envelope in his pocket and giving his father a strange, searching look. Or was it only his imagination? Joe had trouble reading his boy's bearded face. The strong, regular planes had been lost in the thick, curling hair, and only the mild eyes were familiar.

"And you're really making out all right on your own?" his son asked a little doubtfully. "Tell me the truth, Dad."

"Fine," said Joe.

"And the pension? It's okay, no problems there?"

"Full pension," said Joe.

"And the charges were dropped?"

"Yes."

"Jesus," said Mark, "you're a real tiger. What the hell got into you?"

Joe looked at his hand. What had gotten into him? He had broken that kid's jaw as easily as if he were snapping kindling.

"Too long in the trenches," he said, trying to smile. "Shell-shock."

"On to other topics," said Mark with feigned heartiness. "That's the past. It's dead, isn't it? Forgotten. And you're in England. You made it, Pop. After thirty years of talking about it, you made it."

"I made it," said Joe. He reflected that Mark would see this trip in a different light. He would remember the brochures read at the breakfast table, the magazines and travel books piled on the end table that slithered down in a cascade of shiny, slick paper at the slightest touch. All of them illustrated with quaint prospects, thatched cottages, the dark, mellow interior of old pubs with great adze-hewn beams.

But that wasn't what he had necessarily come looking for. Joe had never explained to anyone what this place meant to him. If he had had to, he would have said: water mostly, tame rivers, soft rain, mist, coolness, greenery and arbours, shady oaks. Things of refreshment and ease. Poetry, too. Yes. Things that cut the deepest thirst. Peace.

Of course, these notions had grown slowly over the years. They began in his first school in a small country place in southwestern Saskatchewan in 1937. He started in May as a replacement for a Scot who had shot himself in the teacher-age. Nobody knew exactly why.

It wasn't a happy place he had come to. The kids sat hunched in their desks and bit their dried lips and cast anxious glances out the window at dust devils that spun tortuously across the fields. They all looked tired and old and worried. The ceaseless wind rattled grit against the windows. Dust seeped in under the doors, crept under the sills, powdered them all with greyness and desperation. Their pinched faces and smudged eyes, irritated and bleary, watched him closely.

It was an accident his giving them what country folk wanted: a vision of water, of fecundity, of transparent plenty. He would never have planned it; he would have considered the idea cruel.

How still they had gone when he read:

> *On either side the river lie*
> *Long fields of barley and of rye,*
> *That clothe the wold and meet the sky;*
> *And thro' the field the road runs by*
> *   To many-towered Camelot.*

Even the littlest ones had seemed momentarily transported. Towers, sweet water, heavy crops. He had begun to comb his anthologies of British poetry and mark certain passages with little slips of paper. When they became restless or edgy as the wind scored the siding of the school or the stove-pipes began to hum and vibrate, Joe would read to them. He was a good reader. He knew that.

> *How pleasant thy banks and green valleys below,*
> *Where wild in the woodlands the primroses blow;*
> *There oft as mild evening weeps over the lea,*
> *The sweet scented birk shades my Mary and me.*

Looking back, he considered it a miracle. But then, you tempt people with the impossible.

> *O sound to rout the brood of cares,*
> *The sweep of scythe in morning dew,*
> *The gust that round the garden flew,*
> *And tumbled half the mellowing pears!*

Those kids were lucky to get a goddamn orange in their stockings at Christmas. Few ever did. Tumbling pears.

> *And brushing ankle-deep in flowers,*
> *We heard behind the woodbine veil*
> *The milk that bubbled in the pail,*
> *And buzzings of the honeyed hours.*

And gradually, with each of the succeeding thirty-odd years of small towns and stifling classrooms, these visions of refreshment sustained *him*, although the poetry stopped working for the students. He came to the conclusion that they no longer needed it or wanted it. With prosperity, their dreams became more elaborate, more opulent, less dictated by peculiar circumstances. Their desires were the conventional lusts of a consumer society.

But Joe needed the old visions during those sweltering

June days as he prepared class after class, row after row, face after face, for the Department of Education final examinations. Every year his head pounded and ached from the stunning sunlight, the smell of hot paper and dirty hair.

"*I heard the water lapping on the crag / And the long ripple washing in the reeds.*" It had always helped to imagine the cool sinuosity of moving water, the liquid coiling between green, lavish banks, the silken run so silent and so deep.

Perhaps, Joe thought, that is why I have come. For the healing waters. Like a nineteenth-century gentleman in search of a cure for what ails him. I have come to take the waters. I have come to be made whole.

Mark was speaking to him. "I made a reservation at the Bloomsbury Centre," he said. "We'll go there now so you can catch up on missed sleep. That jet-lag is a killer. I was a zombie for a week."

Joe nodded. It was a good idea. Already jet-lag was making it difficult for him to concentrate. He felt stretched on the rack of two continents. Physically here; in time, located some place back there.

"It's a good location," his son said. "It's within walking distance of the University of London and the British Museum, so we'll be able to meet easily. I can slip out of the Reading Room at noon and we can have lunch together in a pub or at your hotel."

"That's fine," said Joe equably. "I don't want to take you away from your work. Just go about your usual business." He was proud to have a son who was a scholar.

"You know," Mark said, shrugging apologetically, "we only have a bed-sitter. Not even our own bathroom. We'd put you up if we could, but there's no room. Joan's mortified. She's afraid you'll think she doesn't want you."

"Christ," said Joe, hurrying to interrupt him, "as if I didn't know? The shack your mother and I lived in when we were first married – a crackerbox. . . ." He trailed off, uncertain if the boy had flinched at mention of his mother. The beard was a mask he couldn't penetrate, the face couldn't be read.

"Look at that!" said Mark, suddenly fierce, diverting the conversation. "Bastards! The National Front thugs are at it again."

The train was slowing for a station. Brakes binding, it slid by a carious warehouse with skirts of broken-brick rubble, windows painted blind. A message several feet high was painted on the building in white letters. "No Wogs Here."

"It seems," said Joe, "that the sun has finally set on the British Empire."

"No," said Mark, his face intent, "the Empire's come home to roost."

Joe woke to hunger and the sound of voices speaking German in the hall outside his doorway. The glowing numerals of the clock on the dresser announced that it was two o'clock in the morning, but his belly informed him that if he were back in North America he would be sitting down to a meal. What meal – breakfast, dinner, supper – he couldn't say. He wasn't sure how to compute the time change.

The woman outside his door was drunk. There was an alcoholic, forced gaiety to her voice that couldn't be mistaken. And although Joe barely knew three words of German, he could guess that the man's guttural purr was directed towards convincing her to go to bed with him.

Joe got out of bed and flicked on the TV. The screen was empty. He ran quickly through the channel selections. BBC 1 and 2, ITV, all blank. Bathed in the aquatic, wavering blue light and kept company by the hum of the box, he sat on the foot of the bed and lit a cigarette.

Odd the often simple source of our most complex imaginings, our most disturbing dreams. The sounds of an attempted seduction heard in indistinct German and he had dreamed that his wife and her mother (dead these twenty years past) had been sitting talking the Deutsch in his living-room, just as they had in the first years of his marriage when the old girl was still alive.

He had always resented that. He had felt left out not being able to follow the conversation. He was suspicious that his mother-in-law asked questions and pried into their private life. He hadn't liked her much. Frieda was what his own father would have called a creeping christer. A woman of a narrow, fundamental piety and sour views who hadn't liked her daughter marrying outside the charmed circle of the *Kirche*.

But a dream has its own rules and logic and Joe had understood this conversation perfectly well. He knew that Frieda was trying to take Marie away with her. She was trying to persuade her to leave Joe and go away some place with her. Silly old bitch. The only thing was that Marie seemed half inclined to follow her mother's suggestions.

And while all this had been going on Joe had found himself unable to move out of his chair. He was paralysed, and no matter how he struggled to unlock his rigid limbs he could not do it. He was unable to stir a muscle, not even to speak.

He saw at last that they were in agreement. Marie got up and put on her coat. She went around the house turning out the lights as if he weren't there. Then she followed her mother out the door. But she forgot to close the door. That was strange.

And there Joe sat in an empty house, rooted in a chair, blinded with tears. Not even a decent goodbye.

The sounds outside intruded. Joe was sure that the man's voice seemed to be growing more insistent and demanding, and the woman's more encouraging in a sad, passive sort of way. The bargains struck, the diplomacy and language of love.

Joe made the rounds. He began as a proper tourist. He wound through the Jubilee-jammed streets of London on a tour bus. The banners were out, the buildings were being cleansed of a century of dirt and grime. The workmen exposed clean stone in patches; it shone through like white bone in an incinerated corpse. The windows in Oxford Street were stuffed with regal souvenirs; the crowds surged on the sidewalks.

Everything was done with haste. They disembarked for a thirty-minute gawk at St. Paul's, a stampede through the Tower, a whirl around Piccadilly Circus. Their female guide was disconcertingly brazen. She browbeat outlandishly large tips out of them. She claimed intimacy with famous people. Described a night out on the town with Lord Snowdon. She drove her charges relentlessly through the sacred places, hectoring, scolding, full of dire warnings not to be late, not to dawdle. Joe put up with the woman and his fellow tourists for two days; then he gave it up as a bad business, likely only to get worse.

It didn't take him long to realize that something was wrong. He was filled with anxiety. The long English faces with their bad teeth made him shift his shoulders uneasily when he looked at them. The streets were too full. The lure of royalty and the weak pound was a powerful attraction.

Joe was surprised to find that nothing much pleased him. Most things he saw made him feel sad, or lost, or lonely, or guilty. He was sorry to see the English look like the landlords of boarding-houses, possessors of a testy dignity, forced by straitened circumstances into a touchy hospitality.

Where were the healing waters? He might have said that he never expected to find them in London. They were in the Cotswolds. Or Kent. Or Norfolk. Or Yorkshire. But he knew that wasn't true. He knew that now. The great trees in Hyde Park should have been enough, but weren't.

He left off sightseeing and began to aimlessly wander the streets. Following his nose, he found himself drawn down narrow alleys daubed with graffiti and slogans. The messages disturbed him. He could see nothing suggestive of the vigour with which they were executed in the tired people he saw in the streets. "No Boks Here!" they said. "CFC Rule OK!" "David Essex Is King!" "Mick Is King!" "Arsenal Rule!" He was not sure why they made him angry, why they upset him. Most of them he couldn't even understand. Later he had to ask Mark to explain to him what they signified.

At first Joe had imagined them the work of senile, angry old men – they gave off the crazy intensity he associated with an old man's rage. But in time he came to believe them the handiwork of the bizarre creatures he sometimes came across lounging in subway stations like lizards, bathing themselves in the noise, smells and smuts. Horrible, self-mutilated young people. They flaunted safety-pins driven through their bottom lips, earlobes, nostrils. Bristling porcupine haircuts quivered on their heads, radiating electric rage and venom. They were clad in intricately torn T-shirts and dresses made of shiny green garbage-bags. Joe felt like the discoverer of a whole subterranean culture down in the tube, a whole crazed tribe intent on festooning itself with refuse and offal.

Staring bewildered at them for the first time in the harsh light of the station, he had been frightened, suspicious they might attack him. And then he found himself laughing when he thought of Dryden's lines:

> *These Adam-wits, too fortunately free,*
> *Began to dream they wanted liberty:*
> *And when no rule, no precedent was found,*
> *Of men by laws less circumscrib'd and bound*
> *They led their wild desires to woods and caves,*
> *And thought that all but savages were slaves.*

His edginess grew. He seemed drawn to the train stations with their dirt and noise and pigeons and stink and movement. He wandered the Embankment and stared at the sullen Thames filled with commerce. It seemed that this stretch of river bank was dotted with old men and old women bundled in unravelling sweaters and shapeless coats, some drunk, some crazy.

Joe began to drink. He sought out pubs seldom frequented by tourists. This was resented. But nevertheless he sat stubbornly in the midst of strangers who talked past him at the bar, who even occasionally made jokes about him while he drank his whiskeys and got falling-down drunk. At afternoon-closing the proprietors turned him out and he took to the streets again. He walked mile after mile, often losing himself entirely in the city. He tramped past the British Museum and its imposing portico with barely a glance. Inside, his son was reading documents. He ignored the blandishments of Madame Tussaud's, of the Victoria and Albert, of the National Gallery.

He felt he was on the verge of losing control as he had back home. When he was jostled and elbowed and pushed outside Harrods he had sworn viciously and even taken a kick at a man who had stepped on his foot. Yet his behaviour didn't particularly worry him. He decided that he didn't give a damn.

In the first week of his visit Joe spent two evenings at his son's. He climbed three flights of stairs past strange sounds and Asiatic smells to a bed-sitter you couldn't swing a cat in. His daughter-in-law cooked them pork pies in a tiny range and they drank whiskey that Joe brought with him. Mark and Joe sat at the table on the only chairs, and Joan, his daughter-in-law, sat on the couch with her plate on her knee. Conversation never ran the way it should have. Mark kept asking questions that Joe didn't consider any of his goddamn business and tried to avoid answering.

"So that thing with the kid is finished now, all cleared up?"

Joe splashed some whiskey in his glass. "Yes," he said. "It's finished and I prefer to leave it that way."

"Why did they decide to drop the charges?"

Joan coughed and gave Mark a warning look. It was funny, she seemed able to read him better than his own son could.

"They settled out of court for a thousand bucks. They said they felt sorry for me, my wife having just died. They talked about the poor kid walking around with wire-cutters in his back pocket, living on soup and milkshakes."

Mark's eyes had that squinty, harried look they got when he was worried. He had had that look even as a child. He hated trouble. "I don't know," he said. "I can't imagine you doing that."

"Maybe you don't know me as well as you think you do," said Joe.

He *had* surprised a lot of people: his principal, himself, the kid most of all. A lot was forgiven because it happened two weeks after the funeral. Everybody thought he had come back to work too soon. But Joe wasn't sure that he hadn't understood that would be the reaction before he did what he did. Maybe he had calculated the consequences. He couldn't remember now.

That particular kid, Wesjik, had been giving him trouble all year. Not that he was especially bad. He was representative of a type becoming more and more common. He did the usual insolent, stupid things: farting noises out of the side of his mouth while Joe read a poem, backchat, bothering people, arriving late for class, destruction of books and school property.

That day Joe had had to tell him at the beginning of class (as he had every day for the past four months) to sit at his desk and get his text out. The boy had given him a witheringly contemptuous smile and, slouching to his place, said: "You got it. Sure thing."

Joe had ignored him. "Open your books to page 130, Grade Twelve," he said, "and we'll begin the class with Tennyson's 'The Splendor Falls'." After the books had all thumped open and the banging and foot-shuffling had subsided, Joe gave a little hitch to his voice and read, "The splendor falls —"

And there he was interrupted by a voice from the back of the room, brazen and sullen, "on shit-house walls." There was laughter. Most of it nervous. Some encouraging.

Joe looked up from his book. He knew who had said that. "Mr. Wesjik," he said, "get your carcass out of this room."

"I didn't say nothing," the kid shot back, his face set in a mockery of innocence. "How could you know who said anything? You were reading." A courtroom lawyer.

Joe closed the book and carefully put it down. "You come along with me, Wesjik," he said. There were titters when the kid, grinning, followed him out of the room. A trip to the office. It didn't mean anything any more.

And that was where Joe had intended to take him when they set out. But there was something about the way the kid slouched along, lazily and indifferently swivelling his hips, that grated. Joe changed his mind on the way. He led Wesjik into the vestibule where the student union soft-drink machine was kept, and pulled the doors closed behind him.

"What's this?" said Wesjik. "How come I'm not going to the office?"

"You like talking to Mr. Cooper, don't you?" asked Joe, adopting an artificially pleasant tone. Cooper was a smooth-cheeked character with a master's degree in educational administration. Joe thought he was a dink, although he never mouthed off about Cooper in the staff-room the way some others did.

"Sure," said Wesjik sarcastically, "he's one honey of a guy. He *understands* me."

"Is that right?" said Joe.

"Hey," the kid said, "give me the Dutch-uncle treatment and let's get out of here. There's a draft. I'm getting cold."

"I'm sorry, Mr. Wesjik," said Joe. "What is it? Is it your hands that are cold?"

"Yeah," said the kid, smiling, "my hands are terribly cold. I think I got chilblains maybe."

"Put them in your pockets."

"What?"

"Put your goddamn hands in your pockets if they're cold," said Joe calmly. To himself he said, I don't give a shit any more. About anything. Let it ride.

"You swore," said Wesjik surprised. "You swore at me."

"Put your goddamn hands in your pockets, Wesjik," said Joe. Get them in there, Wesjik, he thought. I'm an old man. Get them in there.

He could see he was beginning to scare the kid. He didn't mind. Maybe the kid thought he was crazy. Wesjik put his hands slowly into his pockets, licked his lips and tried to freeze his smart-ass smile on his lips.

"How old are you, Wesjik?" he asked.

"What?"

"How *fucking old* are you, Wesjik? And the word is pardon."

"Eighteen."

"Is that right? Eighteen? Is that your correct age, eighteen?"

"Yes."

Joe could barely hear his answer. "I didn't hear that, Wesjik. How old?"

Wesjik cleared his throat. "Eighteen," he said a little more loudly.

"My brother was dead at your age," said Joe. "He died in Italy during the Second World War. Ever hear of the Second World War, Wesjik? Any knowledge of that little incident?"

"Yes." A whisper.

"Do you want to know something, Wesjik?" said Joe, his voice rising dangerously. "I'm so tired. I'm so goddamn tired. I wish I had had that fucking chance," he said. "I wish I could have died when I was eighteen." He looked around the vestibule, surprised by what he had said, as if searching for the source of that idea. But it was true. His saying it had made it true. "That's what I wish now, looking back. You know why?"

"Let me out of here," the kid said, whining. "You've got no business keeping me here, swearing at me!"

"Because I didn't know life was shit," said Joe, ignoring him. "I didn't know it was taking shit, year after year. I didn't know life was putting up with punks who crap on everything they can't understand, who piss on everything they can't eat or fuck – just to ruin it for someone else. To make it unusable."

"I'm sorry," said Wesjik. But Joe knew he wasn't. He was just afraid. Most of these kids thought they were the same thing. You were never sorry unless you were scared. Only when it paid.

"I want you to say this after me," said Joe. "So listen carefully, Wesjik. Here goes:

> "*The splendor falls on castle walls,*
> *And snowy summits old in story;*
> *The long light shakes across the lakes,*
> *And the wild cataract leaps in glory.*

"Now you say it, Mr. Wesjik – with feeling. Like I did."

"I can't," said Wesjik. "I don't remember. Let me out of here."

"You can't?" said Joe. "Why? Because you don't choose to, or because you're stupid?"

"I ain't stupid," said Wesjik sullenly. "You guys aren't allowed to call us stupid."

"Yes, you are," said Joe, doubling his hand behind his back into a fist. "You're stupid, Wesjik. Otherwise you wouldn't stand around somebody who is as pissed off at you as I am with your hands in your pockets." And that said, Joe hit the kid before he could drag his hands out of his pockets and cover up.

Of course he had been forced to resign. But that was no hardship. He was eligible for a pension. There was talk of a court case and that frightened him, but his lawyer smoothed it out. In a meeting with the parents and their lawyer, Joe had calmly said he had hit the kid because the kid had spat on him.

He could see that Mr. and Mrs. Wesjik weren't sure how far they could trust their kid, and that was an advantage. Their lawyer quite correctly pointed out that being spat on didn't justify a broken jaw. Joe was glad to see they had swallowed the lie. He consoled himself by convincing himself it was metaphorically true.

Joe didn't bother filling Mark in on any of the details. He could see his son didn't know what to make of the way he was acting. And the boy was particularly disturbed by the way he went at the bottle. He had never really seen his father drunk before and it set his teeth on edge.

"Jesus," he said, noting the level of liquid in the bottle of Scotch, "there isn't a prize at the bottom of that, Dad. It isn't Crackerjack. Slow down."

"That's where you're wrong, my boy," said Joe. "There's a prize. Oh yes, there certainly is." He poured himself another tumbler.

"Well, just remember you have to find your way home tonight," Mark said, trying to maintain a light tone and avoid sounding preachy.

"If worse comes to worst," said Joe, "I shall rely on the good offices of London's finest."

"Maybe you should just ease up a bit. Joan'll make some coffee."

"Joan is English," said Joe, suddenly belligerent. "What the hell does she know about making coffee?"

"And who the hell taught me my manners?" said Mark sharply.

The party held in Joe's honour was Mark's way of asking to be forgiven for the quarrel that had resulted. Joe's way of apologizing was to arrive in a taxi laden with gifts: several bottles of booze, roses for Joan, a canned ham, cheeses, pickles. He was careful to arrive sober.

The two tiny rooms were filled with Mark's and Joan's student friends. They were expatriates. There was an American couple and an Aussie studying to be an engineer, and the rest were Canadian graduate students mining the English libraries.

The atmosphere was a happy one. They greeted the arrival of the extra bottles with cheers. It was obvious that they were all a little hard-up and this wealth of liquor was unexpected and entirely appreciated.

But Joe knew it was a place where he didn't belong. They were polite. They asked his impressions of England. Gave him names of inexpensive restaurants. Made suggestions for day excursions outside of London. Reviewed the latest stage offerings. But he had really nothing in common with these young people. They were full of their work and anxious to regale friends with tales of the idiosyncrasies of thesis advisors or the smarminess of English students. More than ever before, Joe felt as if he were disconnected and out of touch with his surroundings. After introductions he willingly disengaged himself from their conversations and leaned against a wall with a drink in his hand, watching.

There was something that bothered him about his son and his friends. They didn't much like England. But they could leave it at that. Home was what bothered them, seemed to nag at them like a sore tooth. It seemed that as expatriates they were afraid the country they left behind was going to embarrass them, pull down its pants on the world stage. The American was the most afraid of this.

"Ford," he said. "Gerald Ford. I mean, there's a limit to it. Nixon was an unshaved weasel – but Ford! He hit somebody with a golf ball again the other day."

The girl from Edmonton who was studying at the Royal Academy said, "I heard it was a tennis ball. The BBC announcer said tennis ball. And then he gave that little knowing smile – the one that means only in America, folks."

They were allies here apparently.

"I don't know why the English press can't leave Margaret Trudeau alone," said a blocky girl who had a settled air of grievance about her. "They certainly kept their mouths shut about Mrs. Simpson and Edward, didn't they? A fine sense of honour there. When it comes to their own precious royal family."

"Jesus, Anne," said the doctoral candidate in eighteenth-century English history, "show a little perspective. That was forty years ago. They don't let Charles off the hook, do they? Lots of speculation about this Prince of Wales."

"This Jubilee business is getting under my skin," said the wife of the American. "It's *medieval.*"

"Interesting word, medieval," said Mark. "That dismisses it all neatly. The Queen of England is worth millions upon millions of tourist dollars a year. The republicans come from all over the world to yearn."

"You wouldn't think it was so goddamn funny," she said, "if you came with me on my rounds." She was a volunteer social worker. "West Indian families I visit have spent milk money to buy commemorative teacups and saucers. Ghastly bloody things with the Queen's face painted on them. Those black kids meanwhile don't know anything about *their* heritage, do they? I mean what the hell does the Queen of England mean to them? The Great White Mother?"

A fellow with dirty blond hair said, laughing: "The House of Windsor is the opiate of the working class."

"Even back home," said the young man standing beside him. "My mother will actually cry if you say anything against the Queen. I don't know what the hell it is. A different generation, I guess."

"Ah, bullshit," said a tall, thin man who had been introduced to Joe as Daniel. Joe thought he had been told Daniel came from Trois Rivières but decided he must have got it wrong. His English was unaccented and perfectly idiomatic. "All Anglo-Saxons are monarchists. You just have to scratch deep enough." He laughed to show it was all a joke. That he was only being charmingly provocative.

He's French all right, thought Joe. He's got one of those goddamn aristocratic noses that looks like it could slice butter. The kind that makes mine look like a peasant's potato.

"Well, they're trying to do their best to turn the niggers in Deptford into honest liegemen," said the American sourly.

"What the hell do you want?" said Joe, suddenly angry. "Those niggers in Deptford are English, aren't they? They were born in this country, weren't they? It's their damn queen, isn't it?"

The American girl looked at him steadily. She took a sip out of her glass and casually tucked her hair behind her ears. "They're black," she said calmly. "There is a difference. I can see the same thing happening here that happened back home. They'll grow up without a base, without their *own* values and traditions."

"They're Englishmen," said Joe stubbornly. He knew that in a way that wasn't quite right, but he knew it wasn't quite wrong either. And he felt better for saying it.

The room was quiet. No one agreed with him but they weren't about to contradict him. He realized that they thought arguing with him would be a waste of time. That he was too out of touch with things. Well, he supposed he was.

"I understand that a little better than some people," said the American girl. "My family came to Maine from Quebec ninety years ago. We were wiped out. I can't speak French. I don't know where I'm from. It's like we never were."

Jesus Christ, thought Joe. What he said was, "That guy who wrote that book *Roots* ought to be held personally responsible for filling people's heads with this bullshit."

"It may be bullshit to you," said the girl. "But it hurts, you know?" She pressed the heel of her hand under her ribcage. Joe realized that she was very drunk, even though her speech didn't show a trace of slurring. "Hey, Daniel," she said. "You'll teach me to speak French, won't you?"

He smiled and nodded. "Sure."

"Daniel," said the girl earnestly, "knows who the hell he is. Nobody else here does. But Daniel does. He's a Québécois."

"Daniel, our *péquiste*," said Mark affectionately. "But I shouldn't say that around Dad or he'll have a bone to pick with you."

"I don't have a bone to pick with anyone," said Joe.

"Vive Québec libre," said the bearded boy from Chatham drunkenly.

Daniel smiled. Joe saw that he was embarrassed for the rest of them. But they couldn't see it. They continued.

"To what do you owe your success?" said the Chathamite. "Why are you, as Rose suggests, so together? So Québécois?"

It isn't funny, Joe thought. They think it is, but it isn't. He is serious. It seemed to Joe that Daniel was speaking directly to him.

"What is the secret of our success?" said Daniel. "We're like the Irish, or the Jews, or the South of the Confederacy. We don't forget. Anything. The good or the bad." He laughed. "You can see it in our faces." He pointed to Joe. "We all have mouths like that."

"And that's the secret?"

"Yeah," said Daniel, suddenly becoming irritable with the game, "that's it. *Je me souviens.* It's the motto of Québec. I remember. *Je me souviens.*"

"Well, that seems simple enough," said the bearded boy. "That's easy."

No it isn't, thought Joe. He felt a little panicky. It isn't easy at all. He finished his drink, picked up his coat and spoke to Mark.

"I think I'll be going now," he said. He felt he had to get out of there.

Mark was alarmed. "Jesus, Dad," he said, "is there something the matter? Are you feeling okay?"

"Fine," said Joe. "I feel fine. I'm just tired. I'm too old for this party." He smiled. "Everybody here is too quick for me. I'm out of step."

"No you're not," said Mark, holding on to his coat sleeve. "Don't go."

"I'd better."

He left Mark at the doorway. In the hall Joe pushed the timed light switch that would illuminate the stairwell for a minute so that he could get down to street level. As he moved downward through the thick smells of curry and cabbage, something caught his eye. On the wall of the stairwell, scribbled in felt pen, was written, "Punk Rule OK!"

What a long way I came for this, Joe thought.

He took a pen out of his breast pocket and, directly beneath the slogan, wrote in his neat, schoolmasterish script Blake's line: "Albion's coast is sick, silent; the American meadows faint!"

The light in the stairwell clicked off and he was left in darkness. The penalty for tardiness and vandalism. But at last, hidden in the dusty, narrow tomb of the hallway, hidden in utter night, he found himself whispering it. I remember. I remember. Now I do.

She was a long time dying. Two years. But neither of them had admitted the possibility. That was foolish. In the early days after she had been diagnosed they would load the car and drive down to the ferry to fish for goldeye. They would drive their rods into the soft sand strewn with flood refuse and sit huddled together watching the bright floats riding the oily dark water. That might have been the time to say something. But the sun polished the heavy water, sluggish with silt, and the breeze tugged at their pant-legs and they were full of expectation, certain of a strike, eager to mark a plunging float. The magpies dragged their tail feathers along the beach and the earliest geese rode far out in the river along the flank of a sandbar. Nothing could touch them, and they pressed their shoulders together hard as they leaned into a sharp breeze that came off the face of the water.

At the end, of course, it was different. He spent every night in the armchair in her hospital room. Instead of watching a bright float, he stared at the intravenous bottle slowly drain, and when it emptied he called the little blonde nurse who wore too much make-up.

By then Marie was out of her head, wingy as hell. The things she said, accused him of. Poisoning her food, stealing her slippers, lying to her, sleeping with her friends now that she was sick – even of sleeping with her sister. The doctor explained it by saying that the cancer had spread to her brain. That was true. But why did she think of him in that way? Had she drawn on some silent, subterranean stream of ill will he had never sensed for those crazy notions? How had she really seen him all those years they had spent together? Had she read in his smoothly shaved face some malignancy?

And that of course was his difficulty. Who was he? Everything had changed since her death. His son didn't recognize him. He hardly recognized himself. Had he been lost for thirty years, in expatriate wandering? Had all those hot classrooms been exile? Was he a harder man than anyone had imagined? And had his wife known that? Was he a breaker of jaws? A drunkard who kicked at strangers in the streets, a man who punished his son by giving him pictures of his dead mother?

Or was he the man who had dreamed of water, who had sat quietly on a stretch of ashy-grey sand and watched a gently tugging line, huddled with his wife?

He began to cry in that dark passage, his first tears. He felt his way down the walls with shaking hands. Why had the light been so brief? And why was the trick so hard, the trick every expatriate and every conquered people had to learn to survive.

Je me souviens, he said. Je me souviens.

Dancing Bear

THE OLD MAN lay sleeping on the taut red rubber sheet as if he were some specimen mounted and pinned there to dry. His housekeeper, the widowed Mrs. Hax, paused in the doorway and then walked heavily to the bedside window, where she abruptly freed the blind and sent it up, whirring and clattering.

She studied the sky. Far away, to the east, and high above the bursting green of the elms that lined the street, greasy black clouds rolled languidly, their swollen underbellies lit by the occasional shudder of lightning that popped in the distance. After each flash she counted aloud to herself until she heard the faint, muttering accompaniment of thunder. Finally satisfied, she turned away from the window to find Dieter Bethge awake and watching her cautiously from his bed.

"It's going to rain," she said, moving about the room and grunting softly as she stooped to gather up his clothes and pile them on a chair.

"Oh?" he answered, feigning some kind of interest. He picked a flake of dried skin from his leg and lifted it tenderly to the light like a jeweller, intently examining its whorled grain and yellow translucence.

Sighing, Mrs. Hax smoothed the creases of his carelessly discarded trousers with a soft, fat palm and draped them over the back of a chair. The old bugger made more work than a whole tribe of kids.

She glanced over her shoulder and saw him fingering the bit of skin between thumb and forefinger. "Leave that be," she said curtly. "It's time we were up. Quit dawdling."

He looked up, his pale blue eyes surprised. "What?"

"Time to get up."

"No," he said. "Not yet."

"It's reveille. No malingering. Won't have it," she said, fixing an unconvincing smile on her broad face. "Come on now, up and at 'em. We've slept long enough."

"That rubber thing kept me awake last night," he said plaintively. "Every time I move it squeaks and pulls at my skin. There's no give to it."

"Complainers' noses fall off," Mrs. Hax said absent-mindedly as she held a shirt up to her own wrinkled nose. She sniffed. It wasn't exactly fresh but she decided it would do, and tossed it back on the chair.

The old man felt his face burn with humiliation, as it did whenever he was thwarted or ignored. "I want that damn thing off my bed!" he yelled. "This is my bed! This is my house! Get it off!"

Mrs. Hax truculently folded her arms across her large, loose breasts and stared down at him. For a moment he met her gaze defiantly, but then he averted his eyes and his trembling jaw confirmed his confusion.

"I am not moved by childish tempers," she announced. "You haven't learned that yet?" Mrs. Hax paused. "It's about time you did. One thing about Mrs. Hax," she declared in a piping falsetto that betrayed her anger, "is that when someone pushes her, she pushes back twice as hard. I am ruthless." She assumed a stance that she imagined to be an illustration of ruthlessness, her flaccid arms akimbo. A burlesque of violence. "So let me make this perfectly, crystal clear. That rubber sheet is staying on that bed until you forget your lazy, dirty habits and stop them accidents. A grown man," she said disparagingly, shaking her head. "I just got sick and tired of hauling one mattress off the bed to dry and hauling another one on. Just remember I'm not getting any younger either. I'm not up to heavy work like that. So if you want that rubber thing off, you try and remember not to pee the bed."

The old man turned on his side and hid his face.

"No sulking allowed," she said sternly. "Breakfast is ready and I have plenty to do today. I can't keep it waiting forever."

Dieter turned on to his back and fixed his eyes on the ceiling. Mrs. Hax shook her head in exasperation. It was going to be one of those days. What went on in the old bastard's head, if anything? What made him so peculiar, so difficult at times like these?

She walked over to the bed and took him firmly by the wrist. "Upsy-daisy!" she cried brightly, planting her feet solidly apart and jerking him upright. She skidded him to the edge of the bed, the rubber sheet whining a muffled complaint, and his hands, in startled protest and ineffectual rebellion, pawing at the front of her dress. Mrs. Hax propped him upright while his head wobbled feebly from side to side and his tongue flickered angrily, darting and questing like a snake's.

"There," she said, patting his hand, "that's better. Now let's let bygones be bygones. A fresh start. I'll say, 'Good morning, Mr. Bethge!' and you answer, 'Good morning, Mrs. Hax!'"

He gave no sign of agreement. Mrs. Hax hopefully cocked her head to one side and, like some huge, querulous bird, chirped, "Good morning, Mr. Bethge!" The old man stubbornly disregarded her, smiling sweetly and vacantly into space.

"Well," she said, patting her dress down around her wide hips and heavy haunches, "it's no skin off my teeth, mister."

She stumped to the door, stopped, and looked back. The old man sat perched precariously on the edge of the bed, his white hair ruffled, tufted and crested like some angry heron. A pale shadow fell across the lower half of his face and threw his eyes into relief, so that they shone with the dull, glazed intensity of the most devout of worshippers.

Mrs. Hax often saw him like this, mute and still, lost in reverie; and she liked to suppose that, somehow, he was moved by a dim apprehension of mortality and loss. Perhaps he was even overcome with memories of his wife, and felt the same vast yearning she felt for her own dead Albert.

She mustered a smile and offered it. "Five minutes, dear," she said, and then closed the door softly behind her.

Bethge made no response. He was thinking – trying to pry those memories out of the soft beds into which they had so comfortably settled, sinking deeper and deeper under the weight of all the years, growing more somnolent and lazy, less easily stirred from sleep. He could no longer make his head crackle with the sudden, decisive leap of quick thought hurtling from synapse to synapse. Instead, memories had now to be pricked and prodded, and sometimes, if he was lucky, they came in revelatory flashes. Yet it was only old, old thoughts and things that came to him. Only they had any real clarity – and the sharpness to wound.

And now it was something about a bear. What?

Bethge, with a jerky, tremulous movement, swiped at the spittle on his chin with the back of his hand. In his agitation he crossed and recrossed his thin legs, the marbly, polished legs of a very old man.

Bear? He rubbed the bridge of his nose; somehow, it was important. He began to rock himself gently, his long, curving nose slicing like a scythe, back and forth, reaping the dim air of his stale little room. And as he swayed, it all began to come to him, and he began to run, swiftly, surely, silently back into time.

In the dark barn that smells of brittle straw, and sharply of horse dung, the knife is making little greedy, tearing noises. It is not sharp enough. Then he hears the hoarse, dragging whisper of steel on whetstone. Although he is afraid that the bear his father is skinning may suddenly rear to life, he climbs over the wall of the box stall and steps into the manger and crouches down. He is only five, so the manger is a nice, tight, comforting fit.

What a bear! A killer, a marauder who had left two sows tangled in their guts with single blows from his needle-sharp claws.

The smell of the bear makes him think of gun metal – oily, smoky. Each hair bristles like polished black wire, and when the sun catches the pelt it shines vividly, electrically blue.

The curved blade of the knife, now sharpened, slices through the bear's fat like butter, relentlessly peeling back the coat and exposing long, flat, pink muscles. As his father's busy, bloody hands work, Dieter feels a growing uneasiness. The strong hands tug and tear, wrestling with the heavy, inert body as if they are frantically searching for something. Like clay under a sculptor's hand, the bear begins to change. Each stroke of the knife renders him less bear-like and more like something else. Dieter senses this and crouches lower in the manger in anticipation.

His father begins to raise the skin off the back, his forearms hidden as the knife molds upward toward the neck. At last he grunts and stands. Reaches for the axe. In two sharp, snapping blows the head is severed from the trunk and the grinning mask flung into a corner. He gathers up the skin and carries it out to salt it and peg it down in the yard. Dieter hears the chickens clamouring to pick it clean.

He stares down into the pit of the shadowy stall. This is no bear. Stripped of its rich, glossy fur, naked, it is no bear. Two arms, two legs, a raw pink skin. A man. Under all that lank, black hair a man was hiding, lurking in disguise.

He feels the spiralling terror of an unwilling accomplice to murder. He begins to cry and call for his father, who suddenly appears in the doorway covered in grease and blood, a murderer.

From far away, he heard someone call him. "Mr. Bethge!

Mr. Bethge!" The last syllable of his name was drawn out and held like a note, so that it quivered in the air and urged him on with its stridency.

He realized he had been crying, that his eyes were filled with those unexpected tears that came so suddenly they constantly surprised and embarrassed him.

For a bear? But this wasn't all of it. There had been another bear; he was sure of it. A bear who had lived in shame and impotence.

He edged himself off the bed and painfully on to his knobbed, arthritic feet. Breakfast.

At breakfast they quarrel in the dreary, passionless manner of master and charge. He wants what she has, bacon and eggs. He tells her he hates porridge.

"Look," Mrs. Hax said, "I can't give you bacon and eggs. Doctor's orders."

"What doctor?"

"The doctor we saw last month. You remember."

"No." It was true. He couldn't remember any doctor.

"Yes you do. Come on now. We took a ride downtown in a cab. Remember now?"

"No."

"And we stopped by Woolworth's and bought a big bag of that sticky candy you like so much. Remember?"

"No."

"That's fine," she said irritably. "You don't want to remember, there's nothing I can do. It doesn't matter, because you're not getting bacon and eggs."

"I don't want porridge," he said tiredly.

"Eat it."

"Give me some corn flakes."

"Look at my plate," she said, pointing with her knife. "I'm getting cold grease scum all over everything. Fight. fight. When do I get a moment's peace to eat?"

"I want corn flakes," he said with a little self-satisfied tuck to the corners of his mouth.

"You can't have corn flakes," she said. "Corn flakes bung you up. That's why you eat hot cereal – to keep you regular. Just like stewed prunes. Now, which do you want," she asked slyly, "Sunny Boy or stewed prunes?"

"I want corn flakes." He smiled up happily at the ceiling.

"Like a stuck record." She folded her hands on the table and leaned conspiratorially toward him. "You don't even care if you eat or not, do you? You're just trying to get under my skin, aren't you?"

"I want corn flakes," he said definitely and happily.

"I could kill that man," she told her plate. "Just kill him." Then, abruptly, she asked, "Where's your glasses? No, not there, in the other pocket. Okay, put them on. Now take a good long look at that porridge."

The old man peered down intently into his bowl.

"That's fine. Take it easy, it's not a goddamn wishing-well. You see them little brown specks?"

He nodded.

"That's what this whole fight's about? Something as tiny as that? You know what this is. It's flax. And flax keeps you regular. So eat it."

"I'm not eating it. What do I want with flax?" he asked quizzically.

"Sure you're crazy," she said. "Crazy like a fox."

"I want some coffee."

Mrs. Hax slammed down her fork and knife, snatched up his cup, and marched to the kitchen counter. While she poured the coffee, Bethge's hand crept across the table and stole several strips of bacon from her plate. He crammed these clumsily into his mouth, leaving a grease shine on his chin.

Mrs. Hax set his cup down in front of him. "Be careful," she said. "Don't spill."

Bethge giggled. In a glance, Mrs. Hax took in his grease-daubed chin and her plate. "Well, well, look at the cat who swallowed the canary. Grinning from ear-lobe to ear-lobe with a pound of feathers bristling from his trap."

"So?" he said defiantly.

"You think I enjoy the idea of you pawing through my food?" Mrs. Hax carried her plate to the garbage and scraped it with a flourish. "Given all your dirty little habits, who's to know where your hands have been?" she asked, smiling wickedly. "But go ahead and laugh. Because he who laughs last, laughs best. Chew this around for a bit and see how she tastes. You're not getting one single, solitary cigarette today, my friend."

Startled, he demanded his cigarettes.

"We're singing a different tune now, aren't we?" She paused, "N-O spells no. Put that in your pipe and smoke it."

"You give them. They're mine."

"Not since you set the chesterfield on fire. Not since then. Your son told me I was to give them out one at a time so's I could watch you and avoid 'regrettable accidents.' Thank God, there's some sense in the family. How he came by it I'm sure I don't know."

The old man hoisted himself out of his chair. "Don't you dare talk to me like that, I want my cigarettes – and I want them now."

Mrs. Hax crossed her arms and set her jaw. "No."

"You're fired!" he shouted, "Get out!" He flapped his arms awkwardly in an attempt to startle her into motion.

"Oho!" she said, rubbing her large red hands together in delight, "fired am I? On whose say-so? Them that hires is them that fires. He who pays the piper calls the tune. And you don't do neither. Not a bit. Your son hired me, and your son pays me. I don't budge a step unless I get the word straight from the horse's mouth."

"Get out!"

"Save your breath."

He is beaten and he knows it. This large, stubborn woman cannot, will not, be moved.

"I want to talk to my son."

"If you got information you feel your son should have, write him a letter."

He knows this would never do. He would forget, she would steal the letter, conveniently forget to mail it. Justice demands immediate action. The iron is hot and fit for striking. He feels the ground beneath his feet is treacherous; he cannot become confused, or be led astray. One thing at a time. He must talk to his son.

"Get him on the telephone."

"Your son, if you remember," Mrs. Hax says, "got a little upset about all those long-distance phone calls – collect. And his words to me were, 'Mrs. Hax, I think it best if my father phone only on important matters, at your discretion.' At my discretion, mind you. And my discretion informs me that this isn't one of those times. I've got a responsibility to my employer."

"I'll phone him myself."

"That I've got to see."

"I will."

"Yes, like the last time. Half the time you can't remember the city John lives in, let alone his street. The last time you tried to phone him you got the operator so balled up you would have been talking to a Chinaman in Shanghai if I hadn't stepped in and saved your bacon."

"I'll phone. I can do it."

"Sure you will. Where does John live?"

"I know."

"Uh-huh, then tell me. Where does he live?"

"I know."

"Jesus, he could be living in the basement and you wouldn't realize it."

This makes him cry. He realizes she is right. But minutes ago he had known where his son lived. How could he have forgotten? In the sudden twistings and turnings of the conversation he has lost his way, and now he hears himself making a wretched, disgusting noise; but he cannot stop.

Mrs. Hax feels she has gone too far. She goes over to him and puts an arm around his shoulders. "Now see what's happened. You went and got yourself all upset over a silly old bowl of porridge. Doctor says you have to watch that with your blood pressure. It's no laughing matter." She boosts him out of his chair. "I think you better lie down on the chesterfield for a bit."

Mrs. Hax led him into the living-room and made him comfortable on the chesterfield. She wondered how an old bugger like him could make so much water: if he wasn't peeing, he was crying.

"You want a Kleenex?" she asked.

He shook his head and, ashamed, covered his face with his forearm.

"No harm in crying," she said bleakly. "We all do some time."

"Leave me be."

"I suppose it's best," she sighed. "I'll be in the kitchen clearing up if you need me."

Dieter lay on the chesterfield trying to stifle his tears. It was not an easy job because even the sound of Mrs. Hax unconcernedly clacking the breakfast dishes reminded him of her monstrous carelessness with everything. His plates, his feelings. He filled with anger at the notion that he would never be nimble enough to evade her commands, or even her wishes. That he cannot outwit her or even flee her.

The living-room gradually darkens as the low, scudding rain clouds blot out the sun. He wishes it were a fine sunny day. The kind of day which tricks you into believing you are young and carefree as you once were. Like in Rumania before his family emigrated. Market days almost always felt that way. People bathed in sun and noise, their wits honed to a fine edge for trading and bartering. Every kind of people. The Jews with their curling side-locks, the timid Italian tenant farmers, the Rumanians, and people like himself, German colonists. Even a gypsy or two. Then you had a sense of life, of living. Every good thing the earth offers or man's hand fashions could be found there. Gaily painted wagons, piles of potatoes with the wet clay still clinging to them; chickens, ducks and geese; tethered pigs tugging their back legs and squealing; horses with hooves as black and shining as basalt, and eyes as large and liquid-purple as plums.

Nothing but a sheet of sky above and good smells below: pickled herring and leather, paprika and the faint scent of little, hard, sweet apples.

Innocence. Innocence. But then again, on the other hand – yes, well, sometimes cruelty too. Right in the market.

A stranger arrived with a dancing bear once. Yes, the other bear, the one he had forgotten. He led him by a ring through the nose. When a crowd gathered, the man unsnapped the chain from the bear's nose and began to play a violin. It was a sad, languorous tune. For a moment, the bear tossed his head from side to side and snuffled in the dirt. This, for him, was a kind of freedom.

But the man spoke to him sharply. The bear lifted his head and then mournfully raised himself up on to his hind legs. His arms opened in a wide, charitable manner, as if he were offering an embrace. His mouth grinned, exposing black-speckled gums and sharp teeth. He danced, slowly, ponderously, tiredly.

The music changed tempo. It became gay and lively. The bear began to prance unsteadily; the hot sun beat down on him. A long, glittering thread of saliva fell from his panting mouth on to the cinnamon-coloured fur of his chest.

Dieter, fascinated, tugged and pushed himself through the

crowd. The bear hopped heavily from leg to leg. It was pathetic and comic. The pink tip of his penis jiggled up and down in the long hair of his loins. There was a wave of confused sniggering.

The trainer played faster and faster. The bear pirouetted wildly. He whirled and whirled, raising a small cloud of dust. The crowd began to clap. The bear spun and spun, his head lolling from side to side, his body tense with the effort of maintaining his human posture. And then he lost his balance and fell, blindly, with a bone-wrenching thump, onto his back.

The scraping of the violin bow stopped. The bear turned lazily on to his feet and bit savagely at his fleas.

"Up, Bruno!"

The bear whined and sat down. People began to laugh; some hooted and insulted the bear's master. He flourished the bear's nose lead and shouted, but the bear refused to budge. In the end, however, he could do nothing except attempt to save face; he bowed deeply, signifying an end to the performance. A few coins, a very few, bounced and bounded at his feet. He scooped them up quickly, as if he were afraid they might be reclaimed.

The audience began to disperse. Some hurried away to protect their wares. But Dieter had nothing to protect and nowhere to go, and so he stayed.

The sight of so many fleeing backs seemed to pique the bear. He got to his feet and began, once again, to dance. He mocked them. Or so it seemed. Of course, there was no music, but the bear danced much more daintily and elegantly than before, to a tune only he could perceive. And he grinned hugely, sardonically.

But the trainer reached up, caught his nose ring and yanked him down on all fours. He swore and cursed, and the bear breathed high, squeaking protests, feigning innocence.

This was unacceptable. This was rebellion. This was treason to the man who fed him, cared for him, taught him.

"Hairy bastard. Play the fool, will you," the stranger muttered, wrenching and twisting the nose ring while the bear squealed with pain. The man punched his head, kicked him in the belly, shook him by the ears. "Traitor. Ingrate."

Dieter held his breath. His mind's eye had seen the bear suddenly strike, revenge himself. Yet nothing happened. Nothing; except the bear was beaten and battered, humiliated, even spat upon.

What shame he felt witnessing such an indignity, such complete indifference to the rightful pride of the bear. Such flaunting of the respect owed him for his size and his power. Couldn't the man realize what he did? Dieter wanted to shout out the secret. To warn him that appearances deceive. That a bear is a man in masquerade. Perhaps even a judge, but at the very least a brother.

But he couldn't. He ran away instead.

The house is still. He hears her footsteps, knows that she is watching him from the doorway. As always, she is judging him, calculating her words and responses, planning. Her plots deny him even the illusion of freedom. He decides he will not turn to look at her. But perhaps she knows this will be his reaction? Petulant, childish.

"I want to be left in peace." He surprises himself. This giving voice to thought without weighing the consequences is dangerous.

But she doesn't catch it. "What?"

"I don't chew my words twice," he says.

She comes to the side of the chesterfield. "Feeling better now?"

"Yes."

"Truth?"

He nods.

"Now mind, you got to be sure. I'm going down to the store. You need the bathroom?"

"No."

"All right then. I'll just be a few minutes. That's all. You'll be okay?"

He is trying to think. All this talk, these interruptions, annoy him. He burns with impatience. "Fine. That's fine. Good." Suddenly, he feels happy. He can steal a little peace. He'll do it.

"I must be careful," he tells himself aloud. How do these things slip out?

But Mrs. Hax doesn't understand. "With your blood pressure, I should say so."

His luck, his good fortune, make him feel strong and cunning. Following her to the front door, he almost pities this fat woman. He watches her start down the street. It is lined with old and substantial homes, most of them painted modestly white, and their yards flourish tall, rough-barked elms. On this street, Mrs. Hax, in her fluorescent orange rain slicker, appears ridiculous and inappropriate. Like a bird of paradise in an English garden. He waits until he loses sight of her at the first turning of the street.

He hurries to his business. His hands fumble with the chain on the front door; at last it is fastened. His excitement leaves him breathless, but he shuffles to the back door and draws the bolt. Safe. Mrs. Hax is banished, exiled.

At first he thinks the noise is caused by the blood pulsing in his temples. But it fades to an insistent, whispering rush. Dieter goes to the window to look out. The rain is falling in a gleaming, thick curtain that obscures the outlines of the nearest house; striking the roadway, it throws up fine silvery plumes of spray. He decides to wait for Mrs. Hax at the front door. He stands there and smells the coco matting, the dust and rubber boots. Somehow, he has forgotten they smell this way, a scent that can be peculiarly comforting when you are dry and warm, with a cold rain slashing against the windows.

And here is Mrs. Hax trotting stiff-legged up the street with a shredding brown-paper bag huddled to her body. She flees up the walk, past the beaten and dripping caraganas, and around back to the kitchen door. He hears her bumping and rattling it.

Here she comes again, scurrying along, head bent purposefully, rain glancing off her plastic cap. But as she begins to climb the front steps he withdraws and hides himself in the coat closet. Her key rasps in the chamber, the spring lock snaps free. The door opens several inches but then meets the resistance of the chain, and sticks. She grumbles and curses; some fat, disembodied fingers curl through the gap and pluck at the chain. For a moment he is tempted to slam the door shut on those fingers, but he resists the impulse. The fingers are replaced by a slice of face, an eye and a mouth.

"Mr. Bethge! Mr. Bethge! Open up!"

Bethge stumbles out of the closet and lays his face along the door jamb, eye to eye with Mrs. Hax. They stare at each other. At last she breaks the spell.

"Well, open this door," she says irritably. "I feel like a drowned cat."

"Go away. You're not wanted here."

"What!"

"Go away."

Her one eye winks suspiciously. "You do know who I am? This is Mrs. Hax, your housekeeper. Open up."

"I know who you are. I don't want any part of you. So go away."

She shows him the soggy paper bag. "I brought you a Jersey Milk."

"Pass it through."

Her one eye opens wide in blue disbelief. "You open this door."

"No."

"It's the cigarettes, I suppose? All right, I give up. You can have your damn cigarettes."

"Go away."

"I'm losing my patience," she says, lowering her voice; "now open this door, you senile old fart."

"Old fart yourself. Old fat fart."

"You wait until I get in there. There'll be hell to pay."

He realizes his legs are tired from standing. There is a nagging pain in the small of his back. "I've got to go now," he says. "Goodbye," and he closes the door in her face.

He is suddenly very light-headed and tired, but nevertheless exultant. He decides he will have a nap. But the woman has begun to hammer at the door.

"Stop it," he shouts. He makes his way to his bedroom on unsteady legs; in fact, one is trailing and he must support himself by leaning against the wall. What is this?

The bedroom lies in half-light, but he can see the red rubber sheet. It must go. He tugs at it and it resists him like some living thing, like a limpet clinging to a rock. His leg crumples, his mouth falls open in surprise as he falls. He lands loosely like a bundle of sticks, his legs and arms splayed wide, but feels nothing but a prickling sensation in his bladder. No pain, nothing. There are shadows everywhere in the room, they seem to float, and hover, and quiver. He realizes the front of his pants is wet. He tries to get up, but the strength ebbs out of his limbs and is replaced by a sensation of dizzying heaviness. He decides he will rest a minute and then get up.

But he doesn't. He sleeps.

Mrs. Hax waited under the eaves for the rain to abate. It fell for an hour with sodden fury, and then began to slacken into a dispirited drizzle. When it did, she picked her way carefully through the puddles in the garden to where the hoe lay. With it, she broke a basement window and methodically trimmed the glass out of the frame. Then she settled herself onto her haunches and, gasping, wriggled into the opening. She closed her eyes, committed her injuries in advance to Bethge's head, and then let herself drop. She landed on one leg, which buckled, and sent her headlong against the gas furnace, which set every heat vent and duct in the building vibrating with a deep, atonal ringing. Uninjured, she picked herself up from the floor. Her dignity bruised, her authority wounded, she began to edge her way through the basement clutter toward the stairs.

Dieter Bethge woke with a start. Some noise had broken into his dream. It had been a good and happy dream. The dancing bear had been performing for him under no compulsion, a gift freely given. It had been a perfect, graceful dance, performed without a hint of the foppishness or studied concentration that mars the dance of humans. As the bear had danced he had seemed to grow, as if fed by the pure, clear notes of the music. He had grown larger and larger, but Dieter had watched this with a feeling of great peace rather than alarm.

The sun glinted on his cinnamon fur and burnished his coat with red, winking light. And when the music stopped, the bear had opened his arms very wide in a gesture of friendship and welcome. His mouth had opened as if he were about to speak. And that was exactly what Dieter had expected all along. That the bear would confide in him the truth, and prove that under the shagginess that belied it, there was something that only Dieter had recognized.

But then something had broken the spell of the dream.

He was confused. Where was he? His hand reached out and touched something smooth and hard and resisting. He gave a startled grunt. This was wrong. His mind slipped backward and forward, easily and smoothly, from dream to the sharp, troubling present.

He tried to get up. He rose, trembling, swayed, felt the floor shift, and fell, striking his head on a chest of drawers. His mouth filled with something warm and salty. He could hear something moving in the house, and then the sound was lost in the tumult of the blood singing in his veins. His pulse beat dimly in his eyelids, his ears, his neck and fingertips.

He managed to struggle to his feet and beat his way into the roar of the shadows which slipped by like surf, and out into the hallway.

And then he saw a form in the muted light, patiently waiting. It was the bear.

"Bear?" he asked, shuffling forward, trailing his leg.

The bear said something he did not understand. He was waiting.

Dieter lifted his arms for the expected embrace, the embrace that would fold him into the fragrant, brilliant fur; but, curiously, one arm would not rise. It dangled limply like a rag. Dieter felt something strike the side of his face – a numbing blow. His left eyelid fell like a shutter. He tried to speak but his tongue felt swollen and could only batter noiselessly against his teeth. He felt himself fall but the bear reached out and caught him in the warm embrace he desired above all.

And so, Dieter Bethge, dead of a stroke, fell gently, gently, like a leaf, into the waiting arms of Mrs. Hax.

Man Descending

I T IS six-thirty; my wife returns home from work. I am
shaving when I hear her key scratching at the lock. I keep
the door of our apartment locked at all times. The building
has been burgled twice since we moved in and I don't like surprises. My caution annoys my wife; she sees it as proof of a
reluctance to approach life with the open-armed camaraderie
she expected in a spouse. I can tell that this bit of faithless-
ness on my part has made her unhappy. Her heels click down
our uncarpeted hallway with a lively resonance. So I lock the
door of the bathroom to forestall her.

I do this because the state of the bathroom (and my state)
will only make her unhappier. I note that my dead cigarette
butt has left a liverish stain of nicotine on the edge of the
sink and that it has deposited droppings of ash in the basin.
The glass of Scotch standing on the toilet tank is not empty.
I have been oiling myself all afternoon in expectation of the
New Year's party that I would rather not attend. Since Scotch
is regarded as a fine social lubricant, I have attempted, to
the best of my ability, to get lubricated. Somehow I feel it
hasn't worked.

My wife is rattling the door now. "Ed, are you in there?"

"None other," I reply, furiously slicing great swaths in the
lather on my cheeks.

"Goddamn it, Ed," Victoria says angrily. "I asked you. I asked you *please* to be done in there before I get home. I have to get ready for the party. I told Helen we'd be there by eight."

"I didn't realize it was so late," I explain lamely. I can imagine the stance she has assumed on the other side of the door. My wife is a social worker and has to deal with people like me every day. Irresponsible people. By now she has crossed her arms across her breasts and inclined her head with its shining helmet of dark hair ever so slightly to one side. Her mouth has puckered like a drawstring purse, and she has planted her legs defiantly and solidly apart, signifying that she will not be moved.

"Ed, how long are you going to be in there?"

I know that tone of voice. Words can never mask its meaning. It is always interrogative, and it always implies that my grievous faults of character could be remedied. *So why don't I make the effort?*

"Five minutes," I call cheerfully.

Victoria goes away. Her heels are brisk on the hardwood.

My thoughts turn to the party and then naturally to civil servants, since almost all of Victoria's friends are people with whom she works. Civil servants inevitably lead me to think of mandarins, and then Asiatics in general. I settle on Mongols and begin to carefully carve the lather off my face, intent on leaving myself with a shaving-cream Fu Manchu. I do quite a handsome job. I slit my eyes.

"Mirror, mirror on the wall," I whisper. "Who's the fiercest of them all?"

From the back of my throat I produce a sepulchral tone of reply. "You Genghis Ed, Terror of the World! You who raise cenotaphs of skulls! You who banquet off the backs of your enemies!" I imagine myself sweeping out of Central Asia on a shaggy pony, hard-bitten from years in the saddle, turning almond eyes to fabulous cities that lie pliant under my pitiless gaze.

Victoria is back at the bathroom door. "Ed!"

"Yes, dear?" I answer meekly.

"Ed, explain something to me," she demands.

"Anything, lollipop," I reply. This assures her that I have been alerted to danger. It is now a fair fight and she does not have to labour under the feeling that she has sprung upon her quarry from ambush.

"Don't get sarcastic. It's not called for."

I drain my glass of Scotch, rinse it under the tap, and stick a toothbrush in it, rendering it innocuous. The butt is flicked into the toilet, and the nicotine stain scrubbed out with my thumb. "I apologize," I say, hunting madly in the medicine cabinet for mouthwash to disguise my alcoholic breath.

"Ed, you have nothing to do all day. Absolutely nothing. Why couldn't you be done in there before I got home?"

I rinse my mouth. Then I spot my full, white Fu Manchu and begin scraping. "Well, dear, it's like this," I say. "You know how I sweat. And I do get nervous about these little affairs. So I cut the time a little fine. I admit that. But one doesn't want to appear at these affairs too damp. I like to think that my deodorant's power is peaking at my entrance. I'm sure you see –"

"Shut up and get out of there," Victoria says tiredly.

A last cursory inspection of the bathroom and I spring open the door and present my wife with my best I'm-a-harmless-idiot-don't-hit-me smile. Since I've been unemployed I practise my smiles in the mirror whenever time hangs heavy on my hands. I have one for every occasion. This particular one is a faithful reproduction, Art imitating Life. The other day, while out taking a walk, I saw a large black Labrador taking a crap on somebody's doorstep. We established instant rapport. He grinned hugely at me while his body trembled with exertion. His smile was a perfect blend of physical relief, mischievousness, and apology for his indiscretion. A perfectly suitable smile for my present situation.

"Squeaky, pretty-pink clean," I announce to my wife.

"Being married to an adolescent is a bore," Victoria says, pushing past me into the bathroom. "Make me a drink. I need it."

I hurry to comply and return in time to see my wife lowering her delightful bottom into a tub of scalding hot, soapy water and ascending wreaths of steam. She lies back and her breasts flatten; she toys with the tap with delicate ivory toes.

"Christ," she murmurs, stunned by the heat.

I sit down on the toilet seat and fondle my drink, rotating the transparent cylinder and its amber contents in my hand. Then I abruptly hand Victoria her glass and as an opening gambit ask, "How's Howard?"

My wife does not flinch, but only sighs luxuriantly, steeping herself in the rich heat. I interpret this as hardness of heart. I read in her face the lineaments of a practised and practising adulteress. For some time now I've suspected that Howard, a grave and unctuously dignified psychologist who works for the provincial Department of Social Services, is her lover. My wife has taken to working late and several times when I have phoned her office, disguising my voice and playing the irate beneficiary of the government's largesse, Howard has answered. When we meet socially, Howard treats me with the barely concealed contempt that is due an unsuspecting cuckold.

"Howard? Oh, he's fine," Victoria answers blandly, sipping at her drink. Her body seems to elongate under the water, and for a moment I feel justified in describing her as statuesque.

"I like Howard," I say. "We should have him over for dinner some evening."

My wife laughs. "Howard doesn't like you," she says.

"Oh?" I feign surprise. "Why?"

"You know why. Because you're always pestering him to diagnose you. He's not stupid, you know. He knows you're laughing up your sleeve at him. You're transparent, Ed. When you don't like someone you belittle their work. I've seen you do it a thousand times."

"I refuse," I say, "to respond to innuendo."

This conversation troubles my wife. She begins to splash around in the tub. She cannot go too far in her defence of Howard.

"He's not a bad sort," she says. "A little stuffy, I grant you, but sometimes stuffiness is preferable to complete irresponsibility. You, on the other hand, seem to have the greatest contempt for anyone whose behaviour even remotely approaches sanity."

I know my wife is now angling the conversation toward the question of employment. There are two avenues open for examination. She may concentrate on the past, studded as it is with a series of unmitigated disasters, or on the future. On the whole I feel the past is safer ground, at least from my point of view. She knows that I lied about why I was fired from my last job, and six months later still hasn't got the truth out of me.

Actually, I was shown the door because of "habitual unco-operativeness." I was employed in an adult extension program. For the life of me I couldn't master the terminology, and this created a rather unfavourable impression. All that talk about "terminal learners," "life skills," etc., completely unnerved me. Whenever I was sure I understood what a word meant, someone decided it had become charged with nasty connotations and invented a new "value-free term." The place was a goddamn madhouse and I acted accordingly.

I have to admit, though, that there was one thing I liked about the job. That was answering the phone whenever the office was deserted, which it frequently was since everyone was always running out into the community "identifying needs." I greeted every caller with a breezy "College of Knowledge, Mr. Know-It-All here!" Rather juvenile, I admit, but very satisfying. And I was rather sorry I got the boot before I got to meet a real, live, flesh-and-blood terminal learner. Evidently there were thousands of them out in the community and they were a bad thing. At one meeting in which we were trying to decide what should be done about them, I suggested, using a bit of Pentagon jargon I had picked up on the late-night news, that if we ever laid hands on any of them or their ilk, we should have them "terminated with extreme prejudice."

"By the way," my wife asks nonchalantly, "were you out looking today?"

"Harry Wells called," I lie. "He thinks he might have something for me in a couple of months."

My wife stirs uneasily in the tub and creates little swells that radiate from her body like a disquieting aura.

"That's funny," she says tartly. "I called Harry today about finding work for you. He didn't foresee anything in the future."

"He must have meant the immediate future."

"He didn't mention talking to you."

"That's funny."

Victoria suddenly stands up. Venus rising from the bath. Captive water sluices between her breasts, slides down her thighs.

"Damn it, Ed! When are you going to begin to tell the truth? I'm sick of all this." She fumbles blindly for a towel as her eyes pin me. "Just remember," she adds, "behave yourself tonight. Lay off my friends."

I am rendered speechless by her fiery beauty, by this many-times-thwarted love that twists and turns in search of a worthy object. Meekly, I promise.

I drive to the party, my headlights rending the veil of thickly falling, shimmering snow. The city crews have not yet removed the Christmas decorations; strings of lights garland the street lamps, and rosy Santa Clauses salute with good cheer our wintry silence. My wife's stubborn profile makes her disappointment in me palpable. She does not understand that I am a man descending. I can't blame her because it took me years to realize that fact myself.

Revelation comes in so many guises. A couple of years ago I was paging through one of those gossipy newspapers that fill the news racks at supermarkets. They are designed to shock and titillate, but occasionally they run a factual space-filler. One of these was certainly designed to assure mothers that precocious children were no blessing, and since most women are the mothers of very ordinary children, it was a bit of comfort among gloomy predictions about San Francisco toppling into the sea or Martians making off with tots from parked baby carriages.

It seems that in eighteenth-century Germany there was an infant prodigy. At nine months he was constructing intelligible sentences; at a year and a half he was reading the Bible; at three he was teaching himself Greek and Latin. At four he was dead, likely crushed to death by expectations that he was destined to bear headier and more manifold fruits in the future.

This little news item terrified me. I admit it. It was not because this child's brief passage was in any way extraordinary. On the contrary, it was because it followed such a familiar pattern, a pattern I hadn't until then realized existed. Well, that's not entirely true. I had sensed the pattern. I knew it was there, but I hadn't really *felt* it.

His life, like every other life, could be graphed: an ascent that rises to a peak, pauses at a particular node, and then descends. Only the gradient changes in any particular case: this child's was steeper than most, his descent swifter. We all ripen. We are all bound by the same ineluctable law, the same mathematical certainty.

I was twenty-five then; I could put this out of my mind. I am thirty now, still young I admit, but I sense my feet are on the down slope. I know now that I have begun the inevitable descent, the leisurely glissade which will finally topple me at the bottom of my own graph. A man descending is propelled by inertia; the only initiative left him is whether or not he decides to enjoy the passing scene.

Now, my wife is a hopeful woman. She looks forward to the future, but the same impulse that makes me lock our apartment door keeps me in fear of it. So we proceed in tandem, her shoulders tugging expectantly forward, my heels digging in, resisting. Victoria thinks I have ability; she expects me, like some arid desert plant that shows no promise, to suddenly blossom before her wondering eyes. She believes I can choose to be what she expects. I am intent only on maintaining my balance.

Helen and Everett's house is a blaze of light, their windows sturdy squares of brightness. I park the car. My wife evidently decides we shall make our entry as a couple, atoms resolutely linked. She takes my arm. Our host and hostess greet us at the door. Helen and Victoria kiss, and Everett, who distrusts me, clasps my hand manfully and forgivingly, in a holiday mood. We are led into the living-room. I'm surprised that it is already full. There are people everywhere, sitting and drinking, even a few reclining on the carpet. I know almost no one. The unfamiliar faces swim unsteadily for a moment, and I begin to realize that I am quite drunk. Most of the people are young, and, like my wife, public servants.

I spot Howard in a corner, propped against the wall. He sports a thick, rich beard. Physically he is totally unlike me, tall and thin. For this reason I cannot imagine Victoria in his arms. My powers of invention are stretched to the breaking-point by the attempt to believe that she might be unfaithful to my body type. I think of myself as bearish and cuddly. Sex with Howard, I surmise, would be athletic and vigorous.

Someone, I don't know who, proffers a glass and I take it. This is a mistake. It is Everett's party punch, a hot cider pungent with cloves. However, I dutifully drink it. Victoria leaves my side and I am free to hunt for some more acceptable libation. I find a bottle of Scotch in the kitchen and pour myself a stiff shot, which I sample. Appreciating its honest taste (it is obviously liquor; I hate intoxicants that disguise their purpose with palatability), I carry it back to the living-room.

A very pretty, matronly young woman sidles up to me. She is one of those kind people who move through parties like wraiths, intent on making late arrivals comfortable. We talk desultorily about the party, agreeing it is wonderful and expressing admiration for our host and hostess. The young woman, who is called Ann, admits to being a lawyer. I admit to being a naval architect. She asks me what I am doing on the prairies if I am a naval architect. This is a difficult question. I know nothing about naval architects and cannot even guess what they might be doing on the prairies.

"Perspectives," I say darkly.

She looks at me curiously and then dips away, heading for an errant husband. Several minutes later I am sure they are talking about me, so I duck back to the kitchen and pour myself another Scotch.

Helen finds me in her kitchen. She is hunting for olives.

"Ed," she asks, "have you seen a jar of olives?" She shows me how big with her hands. Someone has turned on the stereo and I sense a slight vibration in the floor, which means people are dancing in the living-room.

"No," I reply. "I can't see anything. I'm loaded," I confess.

Helen looks at me doubtfully. Helen and Everett don't really approve of drinking – that's why they discourage consumption by serving hot cider at parties. She smiles weakly and gives up olives in favour of employment. "How's the job search?" she asks politely while she rummages in the fridge.

"Nothing yet."

"Everett and I have our ears cocked," she says. "If we hear of anything you'll be the first to know." Then she hurries out of the kitchen carrying a jar of gherkins.

"Hey, you silly bitch," I yell, "those aren't olives, those are *gherkins!*"

I wander unsteadily back to the living-room. Someone has put a waltz on the stereo and my wife and Howard are revolving slowly and serenely in the limited available space. I notice that he has insinuated his leg between my wife's thighs. I take a good belt and appraise them. They make a handsome couple. I salute them with my glass but they do not see, and so my world-weary and cavalier gesture is lost on them.

A man and a woman at my left shoulder are talking about Chile and Chilean refugees. It seems that she is in charge of some and is having problems with them. They're divided by old political enmities; they won't learn English; one of them insists on driving without a valid operator's licence. Their voices, earnest and shrill, blend and separate, separate and blend. I watch my wife, skilfully led, glide and turn, turn and glide. Howard's face floats above her head, an impassive mask of content.

The wall clock above the sofa tells me it is only ten o'clock. One year is separated from the next by two hours. However, they pass quickly because I have the great good fortune to get involved in a political argument. I know nothing about politics, but then neither do any of the people I am arguing with. I've always found that a really lively argument depends on the ignorance of the combatants. The more ignorant the disputants, the more heated the debate. This one warms nicely. In no time several people have denounced me as a neo-fascist. Their lack of objectivity pleases me no end. I stand beaming and swaying on my feet. Occasionally I retreat to the kitchen to fill my glass and they follow, hurling statistics and analogies at my back.

It is only at twelve o'clock that I realize the extent of the animosity I have created by this performance. One woman genuinely hates me. She refuses a friendly New Year's buss. I plead that politics should not stand in the way of fraternity.

"You must have learned all this stupid, egotistical indi-vidualism from Ayn Rand," she blurts out.

"Who?"

"The writer, Ayn Rand."

"I thought you were referring to the corporation," I say.

She calls me an ass-hole and marches away. Even in my drunken stupor I perceive that her unfriendly judgement is shared by all people within hearing distance. I find myself talking loudly and violently, attempting to justify myself. Helen is wending her way across the living-room toward me. She takes me by the elbow.

"Ed," she says, "you look a little the worse for wear. I have some coffee in the kitchen."

Obediently I allow myself to be led away. Helen pours me a cup of coffee and sits me down in the breakfast nook. I am genuinely contrite and embarrassed.

"Look, Helen," I say. "I apologize. I had too much to drink. I'd better go. Will you tell Victoria I'm ready to leave?"

"Victoria went out to get some ice," she says uneasily.

"How the hell can she get ice? She doesn't drive."

"She went with Howard."

"Oh . . . okay. I'll wait."

Helen leaves me alone to ponder my sins. But I don't dwell on my sins; I dwell on Victoria's and Howard's. I feel my head, searching for the nascent bumps of cuckoldry. It is an unpleasant joke. Finally I get up, fortify myself with another drink, find my coat and boots, and go outside to wait for the young lovers. Snow is still falling in an unsettling blur. The New Year greets us with a storm.

I do not have long to wait. A car creeps cautiously up the street, its headlights gleaming. It stops at the far curb. I hear car doors slamming and then laughter. Howard and Victoria run lightly across the road. He seems to be chasing her, at least that is the impression I receive from her high-pitched squeals of delight. They start up the walk before they notice me. I stand, or imagine I stand, perfectly immobile and menacing.

"Hi, Howie," I say. "How's tricks?"

"Ed," Howard says, pausing. He sends me a curt nod.

"We went for ice," Victoria explains. She holds up the bag for proof.

"Is that right, Howie?" I ask, turning my attention to the home-breaker. I am uncertain whether I am creating this scene merely to discomfort Howard, whom I don't like, or because I am jealous. Perhaps a bit of both.

"The name is Howard, Ed."

"The name is Edward, Howard."

Howard coughs and shuffles his feet. He is smiling faintly. "Well, Ed," he says, "what's the problem?"

"The problem, Howie, is my wife. The problem is cuckoldry. Likewise the incredible amount of hostility I feel toward you this minute. Now, you're the psychologist, Howie, what's the answer to my hostility?"

Howard shrugs. The smile which appears frozen on his face is wrenched askew with anger.

"No answer? Well, here's my prescription. I'm sure I'd feel much better if I bopped your beanie, Bozo," I say. Then I begin to do something very stupid. In this kind of weather I'm taking off my coat.

"Stop this," Victoria says. "Ed, stop it right now!"

Under this threat of violence Howard puffs himself up. He seems to expand in the night; he becomes protective and paternal. Even his voice deepens; it plumbs the lower registers. "I'll take care of this, Victoria," he says gruffly.

"Quit acting like children," she storms. "Stop it!"

Poor Victoria. Two wilful men, rutting stags in the stilly night.

Somehow my right arm seems to have got tangled in my coat sleeve. Since I'm drunk, my attempt to extricate myself occupies all my attention. Suddenly the left side of my face goes numb and I find myself flat on my back. Howie towers over me.

"You son of a bitch," I mumble, "*that* is not cricket." I try to kick him in the family jewels from where I lie. I am unsuccessful.

Howard is suddenly the perfect gentleman. He graciously allows me to get to my feet. Then he ungraciously knocks me down again. This time the force of his blow spins me around and I make a one-point landing on my nose. Howie is proving more than I bargained for. At this point I find myself wishing I had a pipe wrench in my pocket.

"Had enough?" Howie asks. The rooster crowing on the dunghill.

I hear Victoria. "Of course he's had enough. What's the matter with you? He's drunk. Do you want to kill him?"

"The thought had entered my mind."

"Just you let me get my arm loose, you son of a bitch," I say. "We'll see who kills who." I *have* had enough, but of course I can't admit it.

"Be my guest."

Somehow I tear off my coat. Howard is standing waiting, bouncing up on his toes, weaving his head. I feel slightly dizzy trying to focus on his frenetic motion. "Come on," Howard urges me. "Come on."

I lower my head and charge at his midriff. A punch on the back of the neck pops my tongue out of my mouth like a released spring. I pitch head first into the snow. A knee digs into my back, pinning me, and punches begin to rain down on the back of my head. The best I can hope for in a moment of lucidity is that Howard will break a hand on my skull.

My wife saves me. I hear her screaming and, resourceful girl that she is, she hauls Howie off my back by the hair. He curses her; she shouts; they argue. I lie on the snow and pant.

I hear the front door open, and I see my host silhouetted in the door-frame.

"Jesus Christ," Everett yells, "what's going on out here?"

I roll on my back in time to see Howard beating a retreat to his car. My tigress has put him on the run. He is definitely piqued. The car roars into life and swerves into the street. I get to my feet and yell insults at his tail-lights.

"Victoria, is that you?" Everett asks uncertainly.

She sobs a yes.

"Come on in. You're upset."

She shakes her head no.

"Do you want to talk to Helen?"

"No."

Everett goes back into the house nonplussed. It strikes me what a remarkable couple we are.

"Thank you," I say, trying to shake the snow off my sweater. "In five years of marriage you've never done anything nicer. I appreciate it."

"Shut up."

"Have you seen my coat?" I begin to stumble around searching for my traitorous garment.

"Here." She helps me into it. I check my pockets. "I suspect I've lost the car keys," I say.

"I'm not surprised." Victoria has calmed down and is drying her eyes on her coat sleeves. "A good thing too, you're too drunk to drive. We'll walk to Albert Street. They run buses late on New Year's Eve for drunks like you."

I fall into step with her. I'm shivering with cold but I know better than to complain. I light a cigarette and wince when the smoke sears a cut on the inside of my mouth. I gingerly test a loosened tooth with my tongue.

"You were very brave," I say. I am so touched by her act of loyalty, I take her hand. She does not refuse it.

"It doesn't mean anything."

"It seems to me you made some kind of decision back there."

"A perfect stranger might have done the same."

I allow that this is true.

"I don't regret anything," Victoria says. "I don't regret what happened between Howard and me; I don't regret helping you."

"Tibetan women often have two husbands," I say.

"What is that supposed to mean?" she asks, stopping under a street-light.

"I won't interfere any more."

"I don't think you understand," she says, resuming walking. We enter a deserted street, silent and white. No cars have passed here in hours, the snow is untracked.

"It's New Year's Eve," I say hopefully, "a night for resolutions."

"You can't change, Ed." Her loss of faith in me shocks me.

I recover my balance. "I could," I maintain. "I feel ready now. I think I've learned something. Honestly."

"Ed," she says, shaking her head.

"I resolve," I say solemnly, "to find a job."

"Ed, no."

"I resolve to tell the truth."

Victoria actually reaches up and attempts to stifle my words with her mittened hands. I struggle. I realize that, unaccountably, I am crying. "I resolve to treat you differently," I manage to say. But as I say it, I know that I am not capable of any of this. I am a man descending and I should not make promises that I cannot keep, not to her – of all people.

"Ed," she says firmly, "I think that's enough. There's no point any more."

She is right. We walk on silently. Injuries so old could likely not be healed. Not by me. The snow seems to fall faster and faster.

Sam, Soren, and Ed

A PUBLIC park on a weekday is a sobering place. From Monday to Friday, before they are lost in an anonymous surge of weekend pleasure-seekers, the truly representative figures of Western decadence are revealed. On the placid green expanses of lawn these humans jut up, sinister as icebergs, indicators (I am moved to think) of the mass of gluttony, lechery, sloth and violence which lurks below the surface of society.

I don't, of course, presume to except myself from that company. I've been a regular here throughout this muggy summer. Most afternoons I can be found planted on one of the bright-blue benches whose inconveniently spaced slats pinch my fat ass. Unemployed for longer than I care to remember, I come here to spend the day in as pleasant a manner as possible. That means eyeing the nymphets who scoot by, jiggling provocatively in the pursuit of frisbees.

And eating. At the moment I am gnawing a chicken leg embalmed in the Colonel's twenty-seven secret herbs and spices, and swigging a Coke. When that's finished I'll top off with two Oh Henrys which have dissolved in their wrappers from the heat.

I'm not the only degenerate dotting the landscape either, although the park almost always empties by four-thirty. Fifty yards away a teen-age couple – he no more than fifteen, she barely having crossed into puberty – lie in a spot of shade rubbing their fevered groins together, lost in the sensations of an open-mouthed, tongue-entangled, gullet-probing kiss. Even at this considerable distance I can hear the rasp of stiff denim on stiff denim and their zippers metallically zinging in unison. In a way I wish them good luck in their striving. It is hard to accept that such effort and persistence could go unrewarded.

The guy by the drinking-fountain is, however, another story and not an object for benevolent glances. On him I've kept a wary eye. For the past hour, shirtless and barefooted, he has practised some arcane martial art. He has slashed, punched, stabbed and kicked the air, crushing imaginary windpipes, rupturing imaginary spleens, squashing imaginary testicles, and deviating imaginary septums. An extra-Y-chromosome type if I ever saw one, and tattooed for good measure. A powder keg capable of exploding at anything an overweight, sparsely bearded man with weak eyesight like me might say or do, however amiable and unprovoking.

If that character had the courtesy to get lost I might be able to completely relax and enjoy my afternoon. Behind me I sense the silken movement of the river as I smell its effluvium, a piquant mix of algae and industrial waste. Its counterpart in movement is the traffic on Spadina Crescent which winds in front of me. Fragmented by shrubs and elms it is a pattern of hot light, flickering chrome and flashing glass. Paradoxically peaceful, I find. My preferences run to urban jungles.

I check the time. It is a quarter to five and the runners from the YWCA are late. I never miss them if I can help it.

Now please don't get me wrong. My interest in these ladies is not lascivious. How could it be? The women are deadly serious about this business of running and make no concessions to spectators. They make their appearance attired in baggy grey pants stained with unsightly blotches of sweat, or in unflattering cotton shorts and shoes pounded shapeless and grimy from many hard miles on the asphalt. Unlike the sweet young things that wiggle voluptuously down the via dolorosa to health and beauty in satiny track suits that cling erotically to their nubile frames, these women clip along with a choppy, economical stride that efficiently devours distance. They are training for the city's annual twelve-and-a-half-mile run along the river bank.

I recognize the strength of the dedication and the determination that propels them mile after boring mile. Good God, I admire it. With a chicken leg in one hand and a Coke in the other, I salute them even in their absence. Hail to thee Marys full of grace.

And right on cue they appear. Suddenly, through the screen of trees I spot the leader of the pack, the she-wolf herself. As always, it is the tough little breastless redhead with stringy thighs who labours first up the grade from under the Broadway Bridge. Another runner appears and then another. As they top the rise their faces go momentarily slack with relief, thankful that this terrible straining against gravity has at last subsided. Seeing their faces dissolve with the release of tension makes me associate all this sweaty effort with sex. But that is not really accurate or correct. Perhaps it is merely bewildered and lost they look, like dazed survivors of some catastrophic wreck. It is, however, only a matter of seconds before my heroines recover their composure and stride, and press formidably on.

The solitary front runners and high achievers fly past and the field is claimed by knots of women who shuffle along huddled together in groups of five or six for mutual encouragement and support. They straggle by, gaping mouths a mute plea for oxygen, wisps of hair plastered to flushed cheeks, arms shining with a patina of honest sweat. Brave girls!

And last of all come the stragglers, the beginners, the fatties, the pigeon-toed camp followers of that other regiment of women. These are the ones I really wait for, to see safely on their way. I *do* worry about these women. I sometimes imagine them reeling, lurching from sunstroke, and finally crashing to the pavement without anyone to spring to their aid. The old girls with blue rinses, knobby knees and a visible circuitry of veins in relief on their calves; the stenographers with secretary's spread; the overweight teen-age girls blooming with acne who run to fashion their bodies into objects worthy of the witless adoration of future Prince Charmings – these are the sheep which comprise my fold and I am their shepherd. If not as good-looking or athletic as one of those young blond studs who man ski patrols, I am, I believe, as dedicated.

My eyes study these tail-enders, alert for signs of danger or imminent collapse, and in doing so come to rest on one woman. About her there is something troublingly familiar, although this shouldn't be, because I am convinced she is a novice runner, a new addition to the daily procession. In any case, I don't recognize the running garb – white tennis shorts and a cheerful yellow T-shirt.

This woman gives every indication of being in rough shape. Having just finished the climb from under the bridge, she is trying to walk the tightness out of her calves. As she limps along, one hand on her hip, one working on her rib cage trying to squeeze out a stitch, her head hangs down so that a fall of hair obscures her face. But there is something about her – the strong body, the generous, ungirlish proportions – that strikes a resonance of familiarity in me.

She throws her head back and begins to run again, her arms pumping awkwardly at her sides, her legs moving jerkily. It is Victoria. My wife. Or rather, more correctly, my estranged wife. The woman whom I haven't set eyes on in four months. The woman who hangs up when I call. The woman who wants a divorce *right now and no more funny business*.

And does she look awful! Her face has curdled to an alarming hue, the grape-purple of strangulation victims – except where she has gone ashy white about the eyes and mouth. In this thirty-degree-plus heat, my wife's brains must be frying in her obstinate head. My duty is clear. I slip off the bench, drumstick in hand, and hustle out to intercept her before she does herself irreparable damage.

Victoria obviously doesn't recognize her hubby. The man whom she once kept so spruce and neat is clad in wrinkles and food stains. I've laid on a few more pounds of lard and grown a scruffy fringe of hair on my hoggish jowls since last we acrimoniously parted. When Victoria finally realizes that this stranger is bearing down on her with obvious intent, she veers away sharply to avoid attack or an obscene proposition. Consequently, I'm forced to break into a ridiculous trot to pursue her.

"Victoria," I call cheerfully, identifying myself as a friendly, "it's me. It's Ed, dear."

Victoria is so exhausted her face is incapable of registering surprise, or even dismay at my condition. Apparently even the usages of common civility are beyond her wasted powers. This from a woman with whom I shared bed and board for six years: "Ed? Get the hell away from me. What the hell are you doing following me, spying on me? Get lost."

"Victoria," I cajole her, refusing to answer her preposterous accusations. "Darling. If you could only see yourself. Stop this nonsense. You're risking heat stroke."

How the hell does she do it in these temperatures? Twenty yards and already my pores are leaking buckets of water and quantities of vital salts and minerals.

"Don't be ridiculous. Go away," she gasps, plodding puritanically along. Rule the flesh.

"I'm not being ridiculous. Every year there's a rash of high-school football players dropping dead all over Dixie from heat stroke. It's a fact."

"Benny," she says, her breath catching raggedly, "told me not to talk to you. So I'm not."

"The body has to be trained for this," I explain. "You have to build your tolerance for this stuff." Tangentially I add, "And tell that shyster Benny to jam a statute book up his ass the next time you see him."

"Only a mile further," she grunts to herself, studiously ignoring me. She lowers her head bullishly and ploughs forward.

"All right," I say sternly, all bristly authority. "If you won't stop this, I'll have to stop you for your own good."

A desperate, harrowed look crosses her face. "I'm finishing," she announces through clenched teeth. "Unlike some people I know, I don't quit on things."

"I suppose that remark is supposed to reduce me to jelly?" I comment acidly. An unfortunate choice of words. I note that I *do* tend to quiver when in full, precipitous flight as I am now.

"Take that remark however you wish. I'm not in charge of your limited conscience any longer. Thank God."

Lulled by her righteousness, Victoria seems to slow slightly. I speed up and make a grab for her arm. But she is an elusive girl; she weaves trickily, steps on the gas and spunkily spurts a few steps out of my reach.

"Touch me," she warns hoarsely, "and I'll scream. I'll yell rape, you son of a bitch."

So that's it. Marital brinkmanship. As so often with us, this has become a test of wills. But she doesn't frighten me off. Victoria was never one (unlike me) who wished to call attention to herself. She could never, in all our long married life, tolerate public scenes. Still, she is a worthy opponent, a tough cookie. Centuries of flinty Scottish feistiness are distilled in her being. She is industrious, self-reliant and persevering. A proper helpmate on the stony road of life.

This escapade is taking its toll. I puff as I pursue her. She squeaks a barely audible, definitely feeble "Rape!" that is not meant to be heard by anyone. It is merely to serve me as a warning.

Throwing all caution to the winds I lunge and catch hold of her wrist.

"Help!" she fairly bellows. So much for theory and past experience. This is not the Victoria I knew. She struggles and tugs ferociously on the end of my arm. I find myself forced to shuffle along with an apologetic, schoolboyish grin pasted on my mug, striving to achieve the right effect – the quintessence of harmlessness.

"Help me! Help somebody!"

"Shut up, for Christ's sake. *Jesus.*" I nod encouragingly to a passing motorist whose face darkens suspiciously behind the windshield. "What the hell are you doing? Do you want to be arrested for public mischief?" I mutter to my wife.

Then she does it. "Rape!"

I am seriously considering letting the silly bitch go when I sense his presence. It is as if he dropped out of the sky, although he must have watched the entire farce from the wings, only awaiting his cue. I manage a half-turn to face him, and then Mr. Kung Fu from the park hits the arm to which Victoria is attached with one of those tricky Oriental chops. Just the kind of snappy blow that makes the arm go dead and lodges a locus of electric pain in the neck.

Victoria is released. She sprints away without a backward glance, leaving me to face the belligerent music. This is *not* like the woman I recall. Surely she has an obligation to explain?

Meanwhile my attacker has squared off and assumed an appropriately menacing stance from which to launch a devastating offensive. His hands revolve slowly in front of his body.

How do you handle a character like this? A man who has spent interminable hours in some seedy, smelly gymnasium devoting his time to preparing for just such a moment as this, when, without fear of judicial reprisal, and in good conscience, he can cripple another human being for life.

"This isn't what it looks like," I say lamely.

He doesn't answer me.

"You better not hit me again," I tactfully warn him, "unless you want to get slapped with a lawsuit that'll bleed you white." This sort of approach sometimes works with the cretinous types.

He takes a step towards me. I find myself thinking very hard. The inevitable question arises. What would Sam Waters do in such a situation? I have a good idea what Sam would do, but I know equally well that I am incapable of imitation.

My one arm is still relatively useless, although the numbness is being replaced with pins and needles of breathtaking pain. I extend my good arm to fend off my assailant, only to discover that I am pointing my forgotten drumstick, daggerlike, at his black heart.

"What the fuck's the matter with you, jerk-off artist?" he demands. "How come you were bothering the lady?"

Perhaps it is an indication of the incorrigibility of human nature. Even in such disastrous circumstances ol' Adam rears his cynical, ugly head. The unregenerate, childish Ed cannot help himself. "That was no lady, mister," I blurt out. "*That was my wife!*" Old dogs cannot be taught new tricks, and old jokes, I find, are still the best.

I brace my porcine pan for a two-knuckle punch when . . . lo and behold, a police cruiser creeps to the curb to investigate this contretemps. At the sight of the long arm of the law manifestly before him, my friend grows suddenly pacific. It appears that they are on a first-name basis. Evidently he will do no snitching; this gorilla wants nothing whatsoever to do with the boys in blue. When *I* am asked whether he is bothering *me*, I give him a long, hard look, long and hard enough to make him squirm, before I sarcastically pronounce him "one of nature's noblemen."

So our business concludes, though not quite satisfactorily. I cannot help thinking that Sam Waters would have handled it in a more efficient, more *masculine* manner.

It is only when I am safely at home knocking together my supper (peanut butter, banana and corn syrup sandwiches) on a kitchen counter frustratingly littered with dirty dishes that Benny's treachery really begins to eat away at me. *How dare he counsel my wife not to talk to me!*

Benny and I go some way back. As university students we shared quarters in a derelict old house on 14th Street. Now, however, we are barely on speaking terms. This is because the disloyal bastard agreed to represent my disloyal wife in divorce proceedings.

That is not to suggest that Benjamin and I saw eye to eye on everything even back then. But I can say I liked him a hell of a lot better in 1968 than I do today. *Tempus fugit.*

During the late sixties and early seventies Benny was a priapic, hairy activist who kept the bedsprings squealing and squeaking upstairs and the kitchen table circled by people full of dope arguing how to remodel the world so that there would be a chicken in every pot and a stereo in every living-room.

In those days Benny was a great nay-sayer and boycotter. When he bought groceries Benny packed two lists. One enumerated necessities. The other listed brands or articles that were *verboten*: Kraft products; grapes and lettuce picked by non-unionized workers; Angolan coffee, lifeblood of Portuguese imperialism; South African wine – all were comestibles which never passed his lips.

Benny walked around with a millennial light in his eyes. He intended to dedicate his life to eternal servitude in a legal-aid clinic. For my uncommitted ways he had nothing but contempt. My flesh was weak. I remember his discovering my contraband peanut butter, a proscribed brand, and righteously dashing it to the floor in a Calvinistic fury. God, I loved him for it. He was a kind of moral standard.

But that evangelistic Benny is no more. He's dead. Affluence did him in. The hirsute, wild-eyed Benny is transmogrified. He is razor-cut and linen-suited. His ass cupped lovingly in the contoured leather seats of his BMW, he tools around town on the prowl for extra-marital snarf. You see,

Benny knocked up money and then, in a rare interlude of common sense, married it.

The longer I think about Benny, the more I am bugged. He ought to be treated to a piece of my mind. It's only a quarter to six; I may still catch him at the office if I phone now. In any case, I need to get Victoria's new address from him. I've been after him for two weeks to reveal all, but he hasn't budged. He's not telling.

I phone. His secretary informs me it is impossible to speak with Mr. Kramer. He is with a client.

"Please tell him it's his father-in-law," I say, "and inform him it's important." I know this will beat him out of the bushes. Benny's Daddy Warbucks bought him his partnership in this firm of shysters. The old man, I am convinced, still has his proprietary talons sunk deep in old Benny's carcass. Benny will talk to Papa.

There is a fussy delay, lots of hum on the line and background thumps.

"Daddy? Benny here. What's up?"

Daddy? Daddy?

"It's Captain Ed calling Corporal Benny. Captain Ed calling Corporal Benny. Come in, Corporal Benny."

There is a moment of hesitation at the other end of the line. Then Benny speaks to me in a tone usually reserved for converse with dolls and children.

"Now that you've finished with the collegiate humour, Ed, what can I do for you? I happen to be very busy right now. I think my secretary *may* have just mentioned that to you." You'd think I'd just piddled on the carpet or something.

I ignore him. Squirm, you bastard. "I want to talk about this divorce, Benny. I don't like what's been happening. It is turning into a dirty, nasty business."

"Only because you insist on regarding it as *personal*," Benjamin replies smugly. That piece of idiocy is the just measure of the legal mind.

"You know," I say, attempting to adopt a fey and whimsical tone, "if there were any real justice in God's universe, he would have provided a cosmic hammer, preferably silver like Maxwell's, to bang people on the head when they make idiotic statements. 'I'm not getting any younger.' *Bong!* 'There is no such word as can't.' *Bong!* 'Don't take this personally.' *Bong!* You'd be a foot shorter right this minute, Benny. The point is, it *is* my divorce! Victoria *is* my wife! Jesus Christ, of course I take it *personally*, you ass-hole."

"Same old Ed," he says uncertainly, jollying the madman.

"No," I say, "it's not the same old Ed. Ed doesn't sleep too well any more. He's getting fat and cranky and he's verging on vicious, Benny. This is a new Ed and he's not going to be fucked over any more. Personal, *shit.*"

"You know what I mean by personal. We've gone over this again and again," Benny says impatiently. "I mean that you should get yourself a lawyer, a professional. You need someone to conduct your affairs in a civilized, businesslike way. We could put an end to this rancour and bad feeling if you'd just get a lawyer."

"I don't need a goddamn lawyer to tell you and my wife that I don't *want* a divorce. No divorce. That's it. As they say in your business, Benny, that's the bottom line. No divorce."

"What you want and what Victoria wants are two different things, Ed."

There is an awkward pause. I jump in with both feet. "I get the feeling Victoria is being told what she *ought* to want by somebody else."

"What is that supposed to mean?" Benny is beginning to sound irascible, dear boy.

"Excuse me if I say his name begins with a B and I wink in your direction."

"Oh Christ. Now I've heard everything."

"Then quit acting like a goddamn harem eunuch guarding the sultan's favourite honey-pot. Give me Victoria's address."

"No."

"I ran into her today. She told me that you told her not to talk to me. Is that right?"

"Not quite."

"Where the hell do you get off telling her not to talk to me? I thought a divorce lawyer had the responsibility to aid in a reconciliation. How the hell can we be reconciled if you keep standing in our way? It's your duty to give me her address, for chrissake."

"My duty is to my client. To protect Victoria and her interests. Right now that means keeping her away from you. You have this talent for making people feel guilty. How, I can't imagine." This seems to genuinely bewilder him. Victoria's sympathy for me seems as bizarre to him as mourning a dead rat.

"Victoria has a conscience, what can I say?" My heart leaps at the news of her . . . regrets? "I wish the same could be said of you."

"I can't afford one. I work for a living. I don't live your sanctified existence."

"Benny, you have cut me to the quick." I pause ominously. "I am a man in love, Benny. I can't afford the luxury of a conscience either."

I sense Benny's ears prick up at that. "Ed?"

"Yes." I try to sound as dangerous as ever I can.

"What does that mean?"

"Give me Victoria's address. I'm finished being a nice guy."

"Are you threatening me, Ed? You better not be threatening me."

"We lived together for a long time, Benny. You know old Ed. Hell hath no fury like a roomie scorned."

"Out with it. Just what the hell are you trying to say?"

"I have a lot of free time on my hands, Benny. I could learn to be a real nuisance. You know how I get when I'm *thwarted*." The word sounded positively hell-like on my tongue. "How would you like me trailing you around town, keeping tab on your extra-curricular activities? Rumour has it you're still a ladies' man. I could keep track on who you're shagging, Benny. Just like a big-league scout. With reports to the manager, Mrs. Benny, and perhaps even your owner, the father-in-law."

"You son of a bitch."

"It's a possibility, Benny. Don't push me too far, I'm near the end of my tether. God knows what might pop into my head next. You always claimed I was erratic, remember?"

None of this makes me feel as rotten as I should. But all is fair in love and war and this is a bit of both. Sometimes I feel entirely disassociated from what I do. It's a malady of the modern age. Since Victoria left me there has been entirely too much drift in my life. Sam Waters is the only firm point, but he can't replace a wife.

"I suppose I have no choice, do I?"

"None."

"Victoria has moved to 719 Tenth Street East. She's in Apartment 23." Benny clears his throat. "Ed," he says sinisterly, "let me tell you how much I'm looking forward to seeing you in court."

"Benny, Benny, nothing personal."

"Fuck you."

"One other thing, Benny. Is there anything else I should know?"

"Like what?"

"Oh, for instance," I inquire with feigned merriment, "does Victoria have anything large, jealous and dangerous lounging around the house? Something sporting two hairy balls? A live-in friend?"

"You're a goddamn degenerate. You make me sick."

"We all grow up in our own surprising ways, Benny. Look at you, a BMW socialist. We make our way in the world however we can, don't we?"

"Victoria has told me stuff about you, Ed, that I didn't believe until now. And I'm going to make you admit to every humiliating detail in court. Every one of your pathetic tricks. Dressing up in a suit and tie every morning, walking out of the door and pretending to go to work for two months after you'd been fired. A moral coward," he says disgustedly.

"Okay!" I shout. "You try it! Get me on the stand! If I can't handle a two-bit shyster lawyer whose term papers I used to *write*, then I resign from the human race!"

"*Proofread!*" he yells. "Proofread!" That got to him. Benny is very touchy about his intellectual abilities because deep down he suspects, quite correctly, that they are extremely limited. "It isn't as easy as you think, smart-ass. You'll find out."

When I get Benny going I can drive him absolutely berserk. Get it in and really twist it, Ed. "Oh yeah," I say. "That really tough lawyer stuff. Habeas corpus, juris dictionae fundandae causa, caveat emptor, annus mirabilis, hocus pocus."

"I'm hanging up now," says Benny. "But before I do, I have one question for you."

"What?"

"When might we expect your novel?"

Click.

I'm not sure any more that I want to face Benny in court. He appears to have mapped my soft underbelly and knows just where to slip the thin blade into my cuts.

The novel. Driving through the dusty haze of a soft summer evening to Victoria's apartment building I reflect on my metamorphosis into an author.

I still regard the idea of the book as a master stroke. Not, mind you, the idea *for* the book, but the idea *of* the book. After being unemployed for a full twelve months I had to invent a plausible occupation. People were always asking me what I *did*. I didn't *do* anything. I was simply unemployed, which doesn't qualify as an activity but is, rather more accurately, a state of being. In the animal kingdom it has its metaphorical equivalent in the hibernation of the bear or the woodchuck, or in the pupal stage of various insects. Or so most people seem to think. Particularly employers who never want to hire anyone who isn't already working for someone else.

So one day, in answer to the inevitable question as to what I did, I replied that I was a writer. It just popped into my head. I noted a cessation of embarrassing questions. The news circulated among Victoria's friends and my acquaintances. Nobody questioned my sincerity. It appears they regarded this profession as socially unproductive enough to appeal to me.

The strangest thing was that this public confession got me writing. Sort of. I admit I have spent more time thinking about writing than actually writing, and even more time talking about writing than actually writing. But still, if one announces one's membership in that illustrious company of joyous spirits, living and dead, who have judged the pen mightier than the sword, one had better evince loyalty to the side and scribble.

However, from experience I can testify that authorship is a trying, taxing business. It is particularly so in my case because I can't seem to get interested in writing about what I ought to be writing about. I mean, after all, I was once a seriously considered candidate for a Canada Council grant, a genuine, copper-bottomed A-student with a double major in English Literature and Philosophy. I was going to ship out for England and write a dissertation.

Consequently, I am capable of bandying around the names of some pretty thoughtful people: Blaise Pascal, Soloviev, Ellul and even Simone Weil. I was even forced to read some of their books. In fact, at one time I had a very strong affection for Soren Kierkegaard, who, at least in the flesh, seemed to have much the same effect on people that I have. Like me, the gnarled little Dane didn't mix well at parties, was inclined to goad people into a frenzy, and made too much of a love affair.

Because of my exposure to great thoughts I feel a vague obligation not to reflect too badly on my education. I feel I ought to at least take a shot at a Big Book. Somehow I can't seem to manage it.

My first Big Book was to be about my generation, a revealing tale about what it was like being a Canadian university student during the Vietnam war. Let me tell you it wasn't easy having to vicariously share the guilt and agony of *their* war like some poor cousin.

There was, of course, the question of Canadian complicity. But we lacked the necessary stage properties to put on a really top-notch performance. We had no draft cards to burn and there was the lingering suspicion that if we desecrated the new flag we might be taken as friends of the Canadian Legion. Back then, twelve or thirteen years ago, we didn't even have our own black problem, though we did have plenty of relatively unmilitant and unfashionable Indians. So we imported Black Panthers from Detroit to address rallies and harangue us as motherfuckers. Somehow the home-grown product, cats like Lincoln Alexander, didn't seem capable of that.

This novel about the groves of Academe came along quite briskly for some four or five pages and then I started to worry about a title. What was I going to call this masterwork? My first choice (because it has a nice hollow sound) was *The Lost Generation*. But that was Gertrude Stein's line, and the bunch from the twenties, Ernest, Scotty, etc., had earned their right to it by a lot of self-destructive behaviour. It just wasn't fair of me to pinch it.

But mulling over the word "lost" got me reminiscing about my grade one teacher, Mrs. Edwards, who wouldn't countenance the word. Unless any object, be it eraser, jumbo pencil, or crayon, was indisputably proved to have been irrevocably blasted into a time-space warp, in Mrs. Edwards' mind that object held out hope of being recovered. Hence, it was not lost but *misplaced*. All Mrs. Edwards' charges were firmly taught to blithely chirp, "Teacher, my pencil is *misplaced*."

So I began to wonder, if my generation couldn't be lost, might it be misplaced? *The Misplaced Generation.* And somehow, having once thought that, I couldn't return to my novel with the same serious, sober heartiness I had shown before, and so I abandoned it.

I then began my second Big Book, the story of the seduction of a Washington-based Canadian diplomat by an American anchorwoman, a little tale that was to be a parable of Canadian innocence pitted against American worldliness and savvy. But the longer I sat at my kitchen table with the chipped Arborite top, the soles of my stockinged feet being concussed by my downstairs neighbour's stereo, the more utterly at sea I found myself. No matter how hard I tried to skilfully manoeuvre my characters, they just wouldn't steer. Nothing my diplomat insisted on saying sounded diplomatic or persuasive, and my anchorwoman kept wanting to unhook her bra and cast off her panties at the drop of a hat, which didn't jibe with my attempt to portray a metaphorical view of the relations of our two nations. That is, unless I could work in a scene of enforced coitus interruptus. That Big Book died too.

I note with some dissatisfaction and envy that Victoria's apartment building is obviously newer and better-maintained than my own. From where I sit in my parked car I am also able to see that it has a security door and one of those buzzer panels that force you to ring the occupant to get the door sprung. That might cause me some problems.

I get out of the car and begin to nonchalantly cruise the sidewalk in front of the building with my hands stuffed carelessly in my pockets, and an eye cocked on the entrance. When I finally spot a couple standing in the vestibule waiting for a taxi, I go up to the door and hopelessly fumble in my pockets as if looking for my keys. No one knows anyone else in these buildings and after twenty seconds of watching me rummage in my pants the man obligingly opens the door. I smile and shake my head ruefully and jangle a set of keys at him.

"You always find 'em after somebody takes the trouble," I say in a fair imitation of bemusement at the world's wondrous workings.

He nods and smiles in agreement.

I locate Victoria's apartment on the second floor. I know she is in because I hear the stereo playing Cleo Laine. My heart melts a little. My wife is nuts about Cleo Laine. I knock on the door.

Victoria doesn't take the chain off the door when she answers it. This is untypical. Perhaps living alone has made her more cautious. At one time, to my worry, she was too trustful, a petter of stray dogs, distempered cats and their human counterparts.

I let her see clearly who it is.

"What do you want?" she inquires sourly.

"Please let me in."

"No."

I dart my hand through the gap and grab the chain. This is a desperate measure. It isn't going to get me in, but it prevents her closing the door in my face. Of course, she could break my wrist by banging the door on it, but I'm willing to risk agony for love.

Victoria doesn't slam the door but she does bite my thumb. Right on the nail, hard. I almost faint, the way I did when I was a boy being vaccinated at school. There is something about me and pain. But I grimly hang on, issue an exquisitely pitiful moan and think of Sam Waters and all he suffered. Speaking comparatively, this is nothing.

The pain suddenly subsides and Victoria is gone. She comes back and shows me a claw hammer. An Iroquois squaw displaying the instrument of torture to Père Brébeuf.

"You let go of this chain, Ed, or you'll be sorry."

"Tear my heart out and feed it to the dogs," I declare dramatically. "Here I stand, I can do no other."

"I'll smack you, Ed," she says, beginning to cry.

"Please. Please let me talk to you."

"Damn it," she says, quietly snuffling, apparently resigned to my entry, "let go of the chain so I can unhook it."

"No tricks? Promise?" I say doubtfully.

"Let go of the damn chain!" she shouts in frustration.

I do and she opens up. I go immediately to the kitchen sink and begin to run cold water on my thumb.

I am a little disappointed to see that the skin isn't broken or the nail discoloured. I won't be able to play this for much.

"They say a human bite is far more dangerous than a dog's," I comment matter-of-factly. "The bacteria in the saliva are more dangerous. Maybe it has to do with the carbohydrates in our diet. Maybe they provide a richer culture."

No answer.

I poke my head around the corner and peer cautiously into the living-room. Victoria has flung herself in a resentful attitude across the chesterfield.

"You have a very nice apartment," I say. "You should see the place I'm in. The tile's lifting off the kitchen floor and the walls are so thin I can hear my neighbour's bum squeaking and rubbing on the bottom of his bathtub."

"So move."

I take a deep, contrite breath. "I know I had no business butting in today," I say. "But I was worried about you. You looked so goddamn awful."

"Check out a mirror. Worry about yourself. How long have you been sleeping in those clothes?"

She's right. I should have, at the very least, changed my clothes and showered before coming by. To be perfectly frank, a trip to a barber might have been in order too.

"Excuse my appearance," I say. "It's just that I've been so busy –"

"Ha!" An explosion of bitter disbelief and contempt. "Busy doing what? Just what in hell has occupied so much of your time you can't wash your clothes or comb your hair? Tell me, Ed. That's one I want to hear."

"The novel," I say uneasily, beginning to shift my weight from foot to foot nervously like a small boy called up on the carpet, "I've been working hard on the novel."

"Excuse my scepticism," she says tartly as she gets up and flicks on the television.

"Turn that off!" I shout. I'm angry now. I *am* working on a novel. I have nearly seventy pages written and I can hardly sleep some nights for the notions that pop into my head.

Victoria ignores my request and fixes her pretty, long-lashed peepers on the TV. Two pitiful clowns on the screen are gambolling around a grey, wrinkled elephant in artificial gaiety, trying to make an audience of children laugh. Cleo is still belting it out on the stereo. I can hardly hear myself think in this bedlam.

"I repeat, *I am working on a novel*."

"Misdirected, wasted effort," she says.

"Take that back!" I shout.

"Misdirected, wasted effort," she repeats calmly, enunciating each syllable slowly and distinctly.

"This coming from a person who considers running around in thirty-degree weather an activity worthy of a rational being. Talk about misdirected, wasted effort," I say acidly.

"You just aren't capable of understanding, are you, Ed?" Victoria coolly asks. She begins to lecture in her professional voice. Victoria is a social worker and doesn't often forget it. "You won't allow yourself to understand because you intuitively sense that what's behind it all is self-discipline. And self-discipline is something you don't have and never will have."

"Judge not lest you be judged."

"To hell with you, Ed. *You* wrecked our marriage. I kept giving and giving –"

"To anyone who asked," I interrupt.

"No, to you. And you kept taking and taking. Well, I'm through giving, and I'm through holding my breath watching you drift, hoping something will happen and that you'll take your life in hand." She pauses and says somewhat sadly, "You're just like one of those goddamn jellyfish, Ed. You just drift along with the tide and when anyone gets within range of your tentacles you sting them. All you know how to do is float and sting."

"Old Ed and the great Muhammad Ali," I say sarcastically, miffed by this unflattering comparison, "float like a butterfly, sting like a bee."

"I rest my case."

I walk to the window and look out at the patchwork of roofs. I am near the end of my tether but I won't let go. "I don't like the way I'm living now," I manage to say in a voice that is all counterfeit normalcy. "I want us to live together again. I don't sleep very well. I've gained twenty-three pounds."

"Ed," says Victoria, not unkindly, "I'm sorry. But I *do* sleep well. I've *lost* five pounds. I can make friends without worrying about what you will eventually do or say to them. I haven't gone to pieces and I won't go to pieces. You look after yourself now. I'm through begging you to watch your weight and be nice to people. You can eat fudgy-wudgies until you can't get through the door. You can insult nuns on the street for all I care. Do what you wish. But I'm not going to be there typing your résumés or pressing your suits so that you appear presentable at interviews for jobs you don't make the slightest effort to land. You're a big boy, Ed. Sink or swim. I always believed you could make something of yourself. I'm not so sure any more. I don't think you have the guts it takes."

Her tone is not really callous but I am alarmed. Things have come to a dreadful pass. How my wife has changed! And

I am in part responsible for what she has become. I feel a great sadness. How I have disappointed her. I remember how, when first married, we lay in one another's arms and talked about what the rest of our life would be. Sun, shellfish and wine in Spain. The click-clack of my typewriter as I wrote the Big Novel. The click of her camera shutter as she photographed the sober, dignified peasant faces of Spain.

My throat hurts terribly. Something, maybe my heart, is swelling ominously in my chest.

"Where's the bathroom?" I ask abruptly, afraid that I might shame myself by beginning to sob in her bright, modern and airy living-room.

Victoria directs me.

I discover she has turned the bathroom into a hothouse, surrendering to the female impulse to demurely disguise its basic function. The place is a veritable hanging garden of Babylon. Potted plants suspended from the ceiling, potted plants on the toilet tank, potted plants on the vanity. All are signs that the *ancien régime* is eclipsed. I would never have tolerated any of this had I been resident.

My hairy face stares palely and uneasily back at me from the mirror. This tropical atmosphere, this humidity, this rank foliage, awaken in me some primal jungle fear. I am overcome with stark anxiety; I feel watched and hunted. It is all I can do to prevent myself from casting about in search of two yellow cat-eyes blazing behind a fern frond, or prevent myself from surveying the floor for sign of fresh leopard scat.

I run some cold water into the basin and splash my face. Momentarily and profusely I give way to tears. In a moment it is finished. Perhaps I am more aggrieved than sad. Certainly I am troubled and uneasy. My wife is no longer the woman I had remembered. Or perhaps more correctly, living in isolation from me has made her more of what she was. Independent, collected, realistic.

A person could give way to paranoia. The two people with

whom I once lived, Benny and Victoria, are in league against me. I feel betrayed by the fact that they have changed while I remain faithful to the past and old loyalties. Benny is not the person I once knew, and neither, apparently, is Victoria. They have entered the long, dark tunnel of personal histories from which I am excluded. I feel left behind. A man standing on a tarmac watching my holiday plane lifting off for a brighter, sunnier, more welcoming place.

And because these people change, because they are in a state of flux, they seem unreal to me. Sam Waters is much more real. I put my faith in him. I think of his example before I go to sleep and when I wake.

Sam Waters made his appearance in that sad time after the failure of the second Big Book, and like Pallas Athene springing fully armed from the forehead of Zeus, he arrived on the scene unaccompanied by the normal pangs of artistic birth. Perhaps it was automatic handwriting. Or, put more poetically, the Muse in her beneficence gave me a sentence. In any case, I don't know where it came from. There I was, sitting at my kitchen table on a bleak, lonely Sunday afternoon, doodling dispiritedly – mostly hanged men – when I heard this sentence. Actually *heard* it.

"Sam Waters had been a plainsman, a buffalo-hunter, a wind-drinker, a free man before he became the sheriff of Constitution."

I wrote that down and looked at it very hard. There it was. Yes, I said, nodding to myself, sure he had. And?

"And because of the long vistas he had looked steadily into and the clean rain he had tasted, he didn't care much for towns. Sam Waters was too big a man to feel easy in towns. They made him feel pinched and cramped and restless. And worst thing about them was that their smells made it difficult for him to breathe, and no town smelled worse than Constitution, because Constitution stank with the worst smell of all – hypocrisy."

I edged forward in my chair and began to scribble in a white heat of composition. No more Flaubertian search for the *bon mot*. It flew fast and furiously. I was tapping some strange vein in my psyche, and pressing on for the mother lode.

"The good, honest citizens of Constitution had wanted Sam Waters as sheriff because of his hard fists and big heart and quick draw. They wanted a man tough enough to have undergone the Blackfoot manhood trial, twirling crazily around a lodge pole suspended on bones skewering the muscles of his chest, arms and legs. They wanted a man wily and cunning enough to have stolen ponies from the best horse thieves of all the Plains Indian tribes, the Pawnee. And they wanted a man cool enough to have faced down Doc Holliday in Abilene, relying only on a poker face and a Colt Peacemaker with six empty chambers to make a coldblooded killer who was wasting away with consumption and so didn't have much to lose anyway, quail when he looked into a certain pair of cold, blue eyes.

"Such a man, the good, honest citizens of Constitution felt, would be a match for the whiskey-crazed Texan drovers who tore apart Constitution each year when they reached the railhead with their herds and tried to forget all the hard miles with rotgut, Madame Louise's fancy ladies and general, unbuttoned hell-raising.

"But at the moment the people of Constitution looked on their sheriff as a liability and a danger. Men stepped aside and looked at the toes of their boots when they met him making his rounds, and women pursed their lips in disapproval when he touched the brim of his Stetson to them. They didn't want anything to do with him ever since that fateful day when he had eliminated three perils to public safety and content in the space of six short hours.

"They had applauded the first. On a hot August afternoon, while everyone watched from the safety of their homes and stores, Sam Waters had stepped into the dust of mainstreet toting his Sharps breechloader and drilled a slavering, rabid dog who had lurched toward him, jaws snapping. That had made him a hero. The Mayor had insisted on having his picture taken shaking Sam's hand beside the carcass of the poor dead brute.

"But later that evening Sam had been foolish enough to do away with two other mad dogs, far more dangerous than the first. Their names were Rafe and Lucas McMurchy, and Sam, in trying to arrest them, had met with resistance. When the two brothers had hauled iron on him in Madame Louise's knocking shop, Sam had been forced to cut them down.

"The problem was that the boys had gotten a bit too frisky with one of the upstairs girls. She had crashed naked out of a third-storey window and fell screaming into the street below. She had died several hours later, and nobody was about to thank Sam Waters for avenging a common whore. And certainly not when she had met her fate at the hands of Rafe and Lucas McMurchy, sons of Chas McMurchy, a man who owned five thousand head of cattle and every soul in Constitution. Every soul save one, and that soul Chas McMurchy had sworn he'd see in hell if he had to take apart Constitution brick by brick and board by board to do it."

And that's where I stopped, although my pen was primed and I knew, as sure as ever I knew anything, that there was plenty more where that came from. And I wasn't wrong either. In the last month, in odd moments, I've written, without effort or reflection, sixty more pages of Sam Waters' story. Not that I've admitted this to anyone else. My goodness no. If the news got around that old Ed was writing a Western, what rejoicing there would be in the camps of the Moabites! How Benny would snigger. Victoria might even brave a comment about the essential banality of my mind. And I must admit, my infatuation with leathery old Sam says something unflattering about his admirer.

You see, Sam has assumed an awesome substantiality in my mind. He has become a yardstick against which I measure my conduct. Good old Sam. Unchanging and solid as the proverbial rock of Gibraltar. Always there when I need him, as I need him now. His figure looms up before me, rangy and slackjointed. His hands are *brown*, of course, and also *sure*, *strong*, and above all, *capable*. His eyes are blue, a *faded* blue, *washed clean* by wind and sun. Sam's speech is *slow* and *deliberate* and his voice never cracks or falters in a tight situation, just as his bowels never loosen nor his hands sweat. The thing about Sam is that he generally knows what the hell is going on. He has no phobias, doesn't suffer from anxiety attacks, doesn't suspect he is hypoglycemic, or entertain suspicions of his latent homosexuality.

Victoria taps softly on the bathroom door. "Ed, are you all right?"

I don't want her in here just now so I lock the door. It seems that I have spent a good deal of my time hiding from Victoria behind locked doors.

She hears the sharp click of the lock turning. She questions me uneasily. "What are you doing in there, Ed?"

"Thinking."

"Ed, don't do anything crazy. Come out of the bathroom." Because of some stupid answers I gave to a silly test Dr. Brandt gave me once, Victoria thinks I am capable of doing myself in when depressed. Little chance of that. An exhibitionist, the only way I could go out would be like Yukio Mishima, slicing through my guts with a Samurai sword. But I don't have that kind of jam or pizzazz.

"Go away."

"Ed, please come out."

I ask myself at this juncture in our dialogue, what would Sam Waters do in a situation like this? Why, it is as plain as the nose on your face. He would open the door and, cloaked in the dignity of one of nature's noblemen, walk away from the woman who could no longer love him. But Ed, well, he presses whatever advantage he has.

"I want to make a deal," I say.

"What deal? What are you talking about?"

"I'll come out of here on one condition."

"What condition?"

"The condition that you give me a chance to prove to you that I can change. That I can reform myself."

"You're not moving in here, Ed. That's final. I'm not taking you back."

"Did I say anything about moving in?" I ask indignantly.

"No."

"Well then, just listen. Just listen to me for a minute." I continue, growing grandiloquent, carried away by my idea. "Like a knight giving proof of his valour to his lady love, I want to face the scaly green dragon of Sloth and the basilisk of Irresponsibility, and, armed only with trusty Self-Discipline, massacre the sons of bitches."

"Ed, come out of there."

"Listen, Victoria," I say more earnestly, dropping my oratorical tone, "I'm only asking that if I prove to you that I can carry through with something really difficult – if I prove I can stick to something – that you'll take me back for a trial period . . . say six weeks. No strings attached. But if I fall on my face you can have your divorce – uncontested."

"Your mind is positively medieval. That's the most preposterous thing I've ever heard. Come out of the bathroom."

"What have you got to lose?" I wheedle.

"My toe-hold on sanity, that's what."

"A test. Any test. You set it, darling."

"Fine. Jump off my balcony. That ought to do it."

"Victoria," I say, "I am serious."

"This is stupid and childish, Ed. I don't want any part of it. It is just another one of your games. It doesn't mean anything."

"Victoria, don't you see," I say seductively, "this is your way out? The easy way to get me out of your life?"

"Not to mention my bathroom."

"I can change, Victoria. I can."

"You want a test, do you?" she asks, and there is a touch of both malice and glee in her voice.

"Yes."

"You had your laugh for the past six years, Ed. But he who laughs last laughs best. Okay. I want you to finish the River Run, Ed. All twelve and a half miles."

"Good God, Victoria, you don't want to test me. You want to kill me. What does that have to do with love and fidelity and things like that?"

"Take it or leave it."

I have no choice. Faint hope stirs in my chivalric breast. An ordeal. I fling open the door and attempt to embrace her. I am repulsed.

"You goddamn madman," she says, turning on her heel. "I need a drink."

"Don't bother pouring me one," I call after her. "From this moment henceforward I am in training."

Two days later and at last I am determined to sally forth on my adventure. I debated this for a long time. On Tuesday I thought I was coming down with one of those horrible summer colds. Wednesday I devoted to mental preparation. But this morning a zealous Ed awoke.

I energetically yank on a pair of cutoffs, lace up my dirty sneakers and amble out to be greeted by birdsong from the fine old elm on the boulevard. I begin to run. For two blocks I plod along feeling heavy, ponderous, doughy. I stop and walk for a bit to recover my wind. In a short time I realize that I'm not going to begin to run again. It is a stupid way to prove a point. Twelve and a half miles? She has misunderstood me. That wasn't what I was talking about. It was love I was speaking of, and in a moment of poetic rhapsody she bound me with mundane specificities. Love is never having to run twelve and a half miles. Love is offering to. But only a piker accepts.

I sit down on the curb and watch the traffic flow by for half an hour. Victoria's unfairness angers me. I brood. It feels like it may rain, so I go back to the apartment.

The minute I step inside the door it hits me. There are dirty dishes crusted with old goop littering the table and kitchen counter. The bedroom smells stale and the bed looks like a rat's nest. There are long hairs in the bathroom sink and a ring in the tub so substantial that honesty compels me to describe it as a ledge.

This is my mess. The visible excreta of the life I have led in the last few months. The door to the medicine cabinet hangs carelessly open on its hinges, the way I had left it the night before. I punch it, shatter the mirror and cut my knuckles. Trailing droplets of blood, I go back to the kitchen.

"Fuck it," I say. "Fuck this life. Fuck these plates." Three of which I smash in the sink, shards dancing up to patter on the wall and floor.

I sit down on a kitchen chair and feel my hand throb and stiffen. It can't be escaped any more. For months I have held Victoria responsible for the way I live. I have held her responsible because it didn't take me long to discover that I didn't manage well on my own.

But there is no avoiding it. It may seem an obvious point – but those dirty dishes are mine. It is my filth in the bathroom. And I am living this crazy goddamn life stuck in neutral. All this is *my* mess, not Victoria's.

And I admit to myself that I am scared because I realized I must sink or swim. I am afraid because Victoria isn't here to prod and cajole me over the rough spots any longer. This is my rough spot.

And suddenly, for whatever reason, I think at this minute of my old humpbacked cigar-puffing Dane. Perhaps because my first memories of him are associated with feelings of aggrievement and persecution. My introduction to him was by way of a philosophy professor who was a demanding, half-crazed German who belonged in nineteenth-century Heidelberg rather than a North American university of the sixties. Whenever we malingered or bitched about the work load, he would repeat to us one of Kierkegaard's entries from his journal.

"There is nothing everyone is so afraid of as being told how vastly much he is capable of. You are capable of – do you want to know? – you are capable of living in poverty; you are capable of standing almost any kind of maltreatment, abuse, etc. But you do not wish to know about it, isn't that so? You would be furious with him who told you so, and only call that person your friend who bolsters you in saying: 'No, this I cannot bear, this is beyond my strength, etc.'"

He would announce this sternly to us and then add with Teutonic glumness, "I refuze to be a valze vriend. I will stretch you."

I have one of my rare charitable thoughts. Perhaps Victoria has done me the favour of telling me I can stand alone. Perhaps she has done me the favour of making me bear the stink of my own loneliness.

And so I get to my feet and go back down into the street. I think of Soren taunted and jeered at in the streets of Copenhagen. I take heart from his observation that "one is tempted to ask whether there is a single man left ready, for once, to commit an outrageous folly." And Sam too. I don't forget Sam and what he suffered and how he overcame the odds.

I begin to shuffle down the street, muttering through my teeth, telling myself the story.

"After they struck him with coup sticks and quirts they stripped off every bit of his clothing and took away his boots. The old scars on his body, the puckered, ridged hole on his shoulder from a bullet he had caught at Antietam, the sabre scar on his belly, turned blue in the cold April wind.

"Looking Glass indicated he could begin to walk. The young bucks expectantly fingered their lances and edged forward, impatient at the restraints imposed by their chief. But Looking Glass had set the trial and conditions. They dared not defy him. Sam Waters would be unarmed and naked, but he would be given a hundred-yard head start before the braves were loosed in pursuit.

"Twenty yards out Sam spat grimly. What the hell? he thought. He paused and waggled his bare ass derisively at his captors. There was a howl of rage. 'Huh sutkis weepa hupka, kaksakis nuhka!' he taunted them in their own tongue. Let's play dog. You sniff my ass and I'll growl.

"On he walked, hardly aware of the bedlam he had created. He didn't feel the cold. He was preoccupied only with making the river three long miles away. He marshalled his strength. In a moment, he would be running for his life. Running bare-footed across sharp rocks that would slash his feet, and cacti that would lodge their wicked needles in his flesh. He would have to disregard the pain and press on. And when he reached the icy river, running fast with snow melt and whirling with ice cakes, he would have to plunge in and allow the current to sweep his exhausted body downriver either to his death or to salvation."

I scrape along past the neighbourhood Texaco station where I buy my gas. Ernie the pump jockey waves to me.

"When Sam heard the whoops behind him he sped away. He didn't look behind. He didn't need to. Sam knew the lithe, ochre-streaked bodies were hot on his heels, closing fast, trying to get into range for a spear cast that would bring down the great Bull Head, the white warrior."

Past the shopping mall. A young matron pauses from loading her grocery bags in the trunk to watch me go by. Does she imagine that I am pursued by Brass Pot, Trader Bell and Wakshee, and does she know they are gaining on me? I pick up the pace.

"A spent lance skittered off the rocks by his legs. Sam's energy was flagging. His lungs burned, his chest heaved, sweat coursed down his brow into his eyes. He glanced down at his feet. A bloody pulp.

"A coulee. He staggered down one slope, branches whipping his face, ploughed through a spring drift spraying the snow with specks of blood, scrabbled up the opposite bank, fingers tearing at the earth."

Easy does it! Make Cameron Crescent, swing back on 14th Street and coast home.

"Sam could see the cold grey river flecked with ice floes as it snaked along. But the cries of the braves behind him were more distinct and had a triumphant note. One final effort. He began to sprint. A lance whistled past his head. He began to zigzag, darting and twisting to elude his pursuers."

A car horn blasts sharply behind me and a guy in a grey Buick forces me up on the sidewalk. I hadn't realized it, but in sympathy with Sam I had been weaving from side to side down the road, dodging Shoshone missiles.

I press on for home, a public spectacle. A couple of kids even go so far as to follow me on their bicycles, giggling and chanting, "Go man, go!" like onlookers urging on a ledge jumper. Maybe it is their intent to rifle my pockets for change when I collapse. But I disappoint them. In fact, at the very moment Sam is clawing his way out of the river shivering, retching and coughing, miles upstream and safe from his howling captors, I am fitting my key in my lock; coughing and retching. I have gone a considerable way my first time out. Perhaps as far as a mile.

I showed up at the River Run. But only to watch Victoria run. She did a lovely job, and I was proud of her although I didn't tell her so. There was a man waiting for her at the finish with a thermos and a sponge.

I am not trying to fool myself or anyone else when I say that

I could have completed the run if I had chosen to enter. By September 14 I was running six miles a day and had dropped seventeen pounds through hard work and fervent fasting. I am quite sincere and honest in saying that I could have – no, *would* have – finished it if I had ever toed the starting-line. It was that knowledge which gave me the strength to refrain from making a point that would have meant nothing.

I've changed in some ways. They are difficult to describe fairly and accurately. For instance, my domestic habits haven't improved much. My dishes are seldom done punctually. I don't barge in on Victoria or even phone her any more. But I still sometimes sit outside her apartment in my car, plotting extravagant schemes to regain her love. Even though I don't believe in their efficacy any more.

But then again I've found myself a job. They can't keep a good man down forever. I'm a salesman in the chinaware department in Eaton's. I'd be lying if I claimed I liked my work, but I can bear it. It sure the hell beats working in a community college as I did before.

In a month and a half I've learned all the patterns, never been late for work, or obviously insulted a customer. Mrs. McCuish, my supervisor, is quite taken with the way I handle the old biddies. I have discovered a latent and surprising talent for the jollification and pacification of the blue-haired hags who stalk our aisles searching out that special piece for that "set" which has been growing like a cancer in their china cabinets since their marriages forty-five years ago. As Kierkegaard suggested, I find myself constantly amazed by my capacity to absorb abuse.

Speaking of Kierkegaard, he is slowly supplanting Sam Waters as my guide through life's pitfalls. I've discovered that his approach is much more relevant to life in a department store than Sam's. Sam is dying a slow death as I continue to transfer his story to paper. He has lost some of the importance he had when he resided principally in my imagination.

No, it's Soren whom I contemplate as I fondle a piece of Doulton and make ecstatic faces across the counter at some dame who is starting a daughter-in-law off as a collector. Continuing the family tradition.

It is Soren I think of when I ask myself why I gave up Victoria. As he forsook Regine, did I forsake Victoria? No. I merely understood that I would only embitter her by surprising her at this late date. She needed to be done with me. And my completing the River Run would only anger her by confusing the picture of me that she had built up over our years together.

That's not to say that I intend to leave it at that. I am going to show her I can finish something. The something is my Western, my story of Sam and his tribulations. Victoria will get a xerox copy of the manuscript in the mail. If she shows it to her friends or even Benny I won't care. They'll laugh, of course, and perhaps even doubt my sanity, or ponder the pass I've come to – selling plates and writing dusters.

I've already chosen an epigraph to my book, from Kierkegaard's *Journals*. It's my apology to Victoria and my admission that she was right all along. A kind of absolution that may surprise her, and, I hope, touch her. You see, she always expected more of me.

Soren wrote: "What ability there is in an individual may be measured by the yardstick of how far there is between his *understanding* and his *will*. What a person can *understand* he must also be able to force himself to *will*. Between understanding and willing is where excuses and evasions have their being."

Afterword

BY LEO MCKAY JR.

A very good book is a mystery and should remain a mystery no matter how many times we read it. This mysteriousness is part of the ineffability of all art and what makes it possible to re-approach freshly a familiar painting or a piece of music. That we never fully solve the mystery of a work of art enables that work to yield new insights and perspectives even after multiple revisits.

I've read *Man Descending* many times, and each time I've noticed some new detail, some previously overlooked gem of description. The full impact of the following sentence, for example, taken from "The Watcher," escaped me until the most recent reading: "So I luxuriated in this steamy equatorial climate, tended by a doting mother as if I were a rare tropical orchid." Aside from its succinct beauty in describing the character's sickly childhood, the mix of hard and soft consonants makes the sentence itself patter and squish with moisture.

The tautly controlled poetry of the prose stands out to me now as never before. Notice the rhythm of the following paragraph, taken from later in the same story:

> A thunderstorm was brewing. The sky was a stew
> of dark, swollen cloud and a strange apple-green
> light. The temperature stood in the mid-nineties,

not a breath of breeze stirred, my skin crawled and my head pounded above my eyes and through the bridge of my nose. There wasn't a thing to do except sit on the bottom step of the porch, keep from picking up a sliver in your ass, and scratch the dirt with a stick. My grandmother had put her hat on and driven into town on some unexplained business. Thompson and my aunt were upstairs in their bedroom, sunk in a stuporous, sweaty afternoon's sleep.

There are many such paragraphs in this book, short sections that could stand on their own as poems, so electrifying are the images, so powerful the language.

Guy Vanderhaeghe notices startling details and renders them on the page so that they in turn startle the reader. "Poplar bluffs in the distance shook in the watery heat haze with a crazy light, crows whirled lazily in the sky like flakes of black ash rising from a fire" ("Reunion").

These stories reveal Vanderhaeghe's remarkable social eye. He takes note of how people interact, how they treat each other, how they view each other. In the following sentence, the protagonist of "The Expatriates' Party" is visiting England and commenting on how he regards his hosts. "He was sorry to see the English look like the landlords of boarding-houses, possessors of a testy dignity, forced by straitened circumstances into a touchy hospitality."

Interior realities are masterfully evinced here, too. Vanderhaeghe shines a white light into the souls of his characters, making them reveal their luminous selves when presented on the page. "Dieter lay on the chesterfield trying to stifle his tears. It was not an easy job because even the sound of Mrs. Hax unconcernedly clacking the breakfast dishes reminded him of her monstrous carelessness with everything. His plates, his feelings" ("Dancing Bear"). I challenge anyone to find a briefer, more elegant, more revealing description of any character in any book by any writer. There is writing as good as this, but none better.

Moments of great emotional and physical intensity are realized in *Man Descending* with a truth that rarely transfers so clearly and powerfully onto the printed page. Again and again and again in these stories, characters' heads swim with realization or fear or disgust. People turn infirm or ill. Someone scrapes a knuckle, goes bodily numb, peels off and examines a piece of his or her own skin. And in these places, where lesser writers seldom bother to prod or when they do either blur the moment with inexact language or use it merely as a pivot point for plot, the visceral poetry of Vanderhaeghe's prose transforms the banal into the sublime.

Ogle, in "A Taste for Perfection," is slowly losing sensation in his extremities. In an attempt to revivify himself, he makes his way to the hospital's physical therapy room, where he finds a basketball. As Ogle holds the ball, Vanderhaeghe tells us that "he relished the pebbly grain with his fingertips." A brief moment of somatic contact described so aptly that in a single sentence we can feel that ball in our own hands, and in doing so enter into Ogle's experience just long enough to understand the fullness of his desperation.

At the end of "Dancing Bear," as Dieter is making his last grab at a measure of autonomy, Vanderhaeghe's description is so perfect and complete that I always find myself struggling for air as I read the following passage, as though Dieter's consciousness were closing in around me.

> He tried to get up. He rose, trembling, swayed, felt the floor shift, and fell, striking his head on a chest of drawers. His mouth filled with something warm and salty. He could hear something moving in the house, and then the sound was lost in the tumult of the blood singing in his

veins. His pulse beat dimly in his eyelids, his ears, his neck and fingertips.

He managed to struggle to his feet and beat his way into the roar of the shadows which slipped by like surf, and out into the hallway.

And then he saw a form in the muted light, patiently waiting. It was the bear.

"Bear?" he asked, shuffling forward, trailing his leg.

Vanderhaeghe's vision in *Man Descending* is rich and encompassing. He shows us relationships between men and women, men and men, parents and children. He takes us where power meets vulnerability, where violence meets despair. All the gravity of the book is cheered by the half-light of humour. All the humour is tinged with sorrow. *Man Descending* gives us a lush, generous, fecund view of a complex, difficult, knuckle-barking, beautiful universe.

I began by saying that a very good book was a mystery. I'll conclude by saying that great books, aside from being mysteries, reveal a mystery to us. A great book can transform the reader, transform the reader's perception, transform the world. This is what reading *Man Descending* does for us. While our eyes are on the pages, we admire the book itself, its breadth, its insight, the mastery of its art. When we lift our eyes from the page, we see the planet as though for the first time. The sparkling particulars of creation are brought into shaper focus. We are given to wonder at the private cosmos of each person we see. We realize anew the endless possibilities of the world.

BY GUY VANDERHAEGHE

New Canadian Library
The Best of Canadian Writing

M&S

Short Fiction Collections in the New Canadian Library